A Gay Dirt Passage

POO
P D
ECK

Also by Joseph Brennan

Crab Bait
Loose Lips▲

▲*Loose Lips Odyssey series*

2

POOP DECK

Joseph Brennan

HARD CROSSING

Coral Sea

FIRST EDITION

PUBLISHED BY HARD CROSSING PRESS 2024

THIS NOVEL IS ENTIRELY A WORK OF FICTION. ANY REFERENCES TO HISTORICAL EVENTS, REAL PEOPLE, OR REAL PLACES ARE USED FICTITIOUSLY. OTHER NAMES, CHARACTERS, PLACES AND EVENTS ARE PRODUCTS OF THE AUTHOR'S IMAGINATION, AND ANY RESEMBLANCE TO ACTUAL EVENTS, PLACES OR PERSONS, LIVING OR DEAD, IS ENTIRELY COINCIDENTAL.

ISBN: 978-0-6455553-9-4

Softback ISBN: 978-1-7636235-0-7

eISBN: 978-1-7636235-1-4

COVER IMAGE NH 82680 USS OKLAHOMA (BB-37), ARCHIVES BRANCH, NAVAL HISTORY AND HERITAGE COMMAND, WASHINGTON, DC

AUTHOR PHOTOGRAPH BY KIM NGUYEN-VAN ZOEN

THIS NOVEL IS THE THIRD OF MANY STORIES JOSEPH BRENNAN HAS PLANNED.

DISCOVER MORE AT **JOSEPHBRENNAN.COM**

For Dickie,

captain, my captain

SUN DECK

UPPER PROMENADE DECK

MAIN PROMENADE DECK

A DECK

B DECK

C DECK

D DECK

E DECK

B R

Dirt;

. . . this curious dirt factory, the body, must despite its own uncleanliness shun as dirty anything in the outside world which resembles or represents the body's own 'dirt' . . .

—The Fantasy of Dirt,
Lawrence S. Kubie, 1937

She waited for him in the Hudson, her bow bulbous and black and her funnels yellow. A hard man's vision of an ocean liner, more an overdone destroyer by design than having any of the cruiser elegance of a prim transatlantic Queen. She came from a great city of ancient German industry, of seafarers and shipbuilders and slutboy slammers. Whereas he was from the countryside of the Reich's easternmost region. A place of men-hauled nets and handlines and wholesome grass-kneed wrestling among the reeds, away enough from the Baltic to not have seen it as a boy. But to know water, growing up among the sunken lakes. Naked swimming between harvests was church, before being pulled one summer from a rope swing near Lötzen, many years ago, when "Nazi" was far from a poor villager's every day. Stolen in one of the Reich's secret cult crusades. *The great find* in the East Prussian manhunt for the Aryan Prometheus. Taken from his Mutter und Vater as some kind of one-thousand-year model of the Germanic man.

Crew List

Gün Bauer . . *One-thousand-year model of the Germanic man*
Robert Bell . . . . *Senior First Officer, Cunard*
Mr White . . . . *Chief Steward, Cunard*
Mr Wolf . . . . *Signalman, North German Lloyd (NGL)*
Fosco Indelicato . . . . *Capo, New York Mafia*
Frankie Fischer . . . . *Brownshirt, NGL*
Curt Winter . . . . *Engineman I, NGL*
Aurik Braun . . . . *Bodyguard, Waffen-SS*
Łukasz Weber . . . . *Wireless Operator, NGL*
Mr Winkler . . . . *Baker, NGL*
Mr Weiss . . . . *Engineman II, NGL*
Kenneth Arnold . . . . *Steward I, NGL*
Carl . . . . *Engineman III, NGL*
Werner Weiner . . . . *Photographer's Assistant, NGL*
Dick Horn . . . . *Chief Officer, NGL*
Piggy . . . . *Steward II, NGL*

29 August

HUDSON
Pier 99
Pier 98
Pier 97
Pier 96
S.S. QUEEN OF BERMUDA
Pier 95
Pier 92
S.S. ROMA
R.M.S. AQUITANIA
Pier 90
S.S. NORMANDIE
Pier 88
Pier 86
S.S. BREMEN
Pier 84
Pier 83
Pier 81
Pier 80
Lincoln Tunnel
Pier 77
Pier 76
Pier 75
W. 60th
W. 59th
W. 58th
W. 57th
W. 56th
W. 55th
W. 54th
W. 53d
W. 52d
W. 51st
W. 50th
W. 49th
W. 48th
W. 47th
W. 46th
W. 45th
W. 44th
W. 43d
W. 42d
W. 41st
W. 40th
W. 37th
W. 36th
W. 35th
Roosevelt Hosp
DeWitt Clinton Park
St. Clare's
12th Ave.
11th Ave.
West
N.Y. CENTRAL

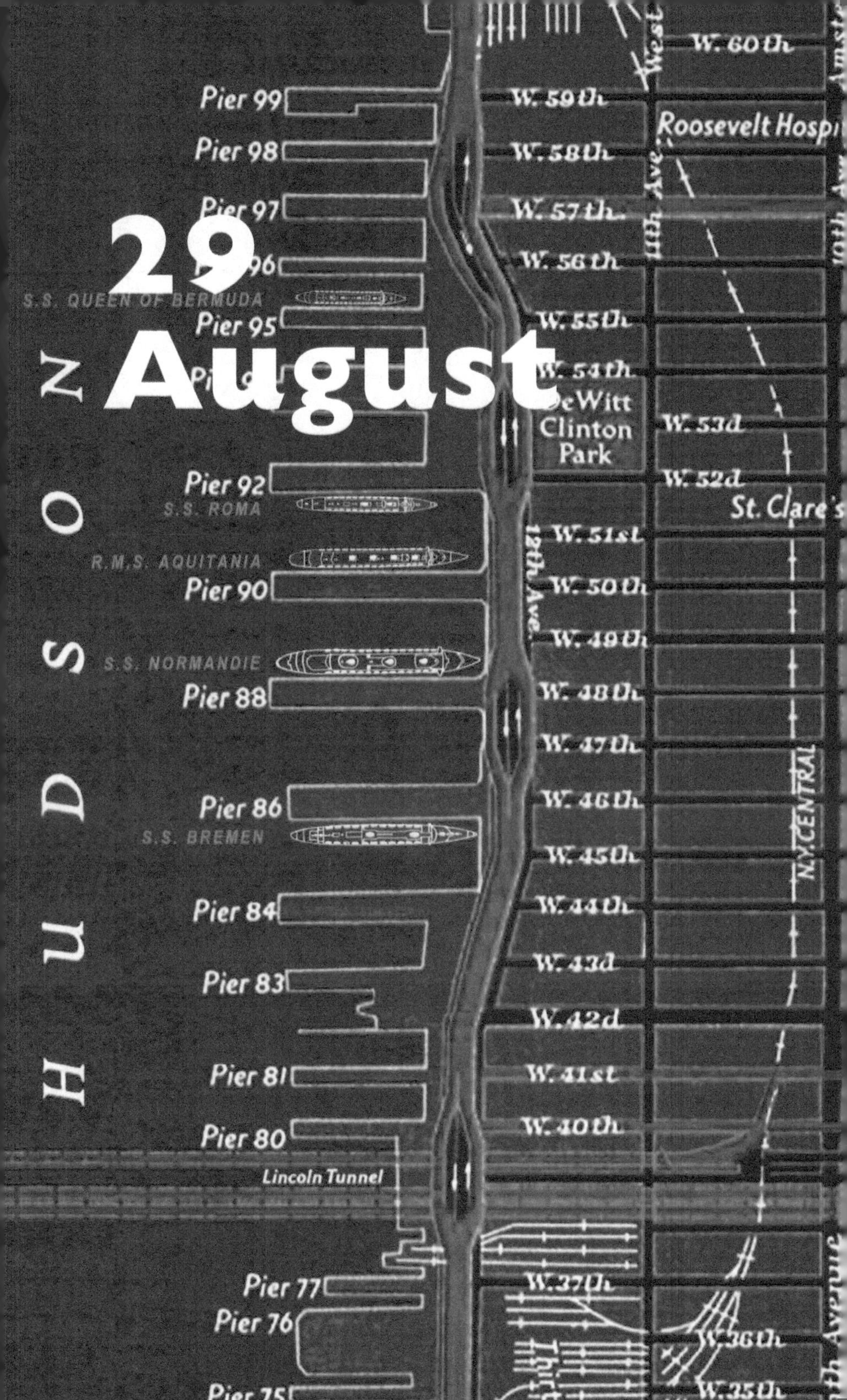

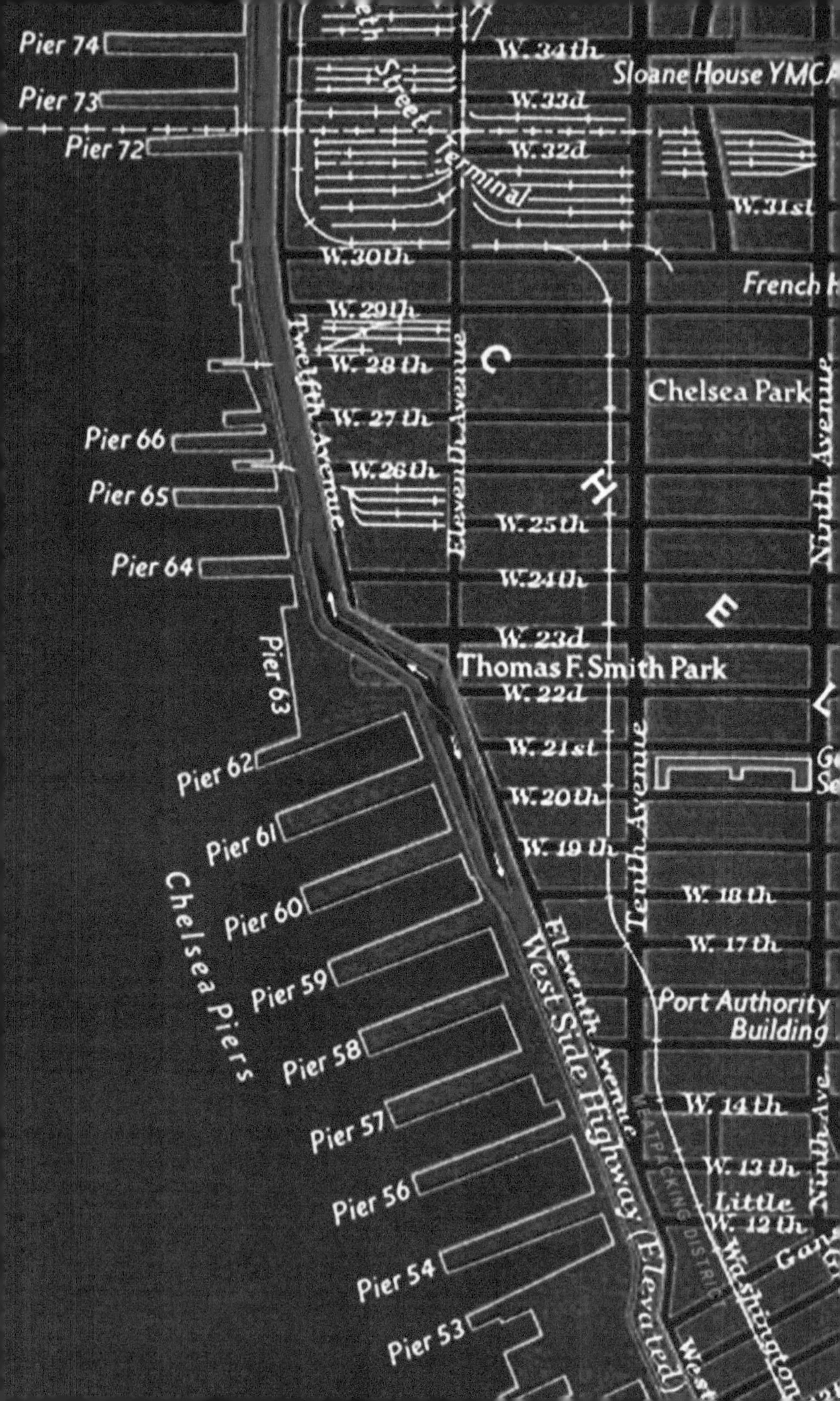

Pier 74
Pier 73
Pier 72
Street Terminal
W. 34th
Sloane House YMCA
W. 33d
W. 32d
W. 31st
W. 30th
French
W. 29th
W. 28th
W. 27th
W. 26th
W. 25th
W. 24th
W. 23d
W. 22d
W. 21st
W. 20th
W. 19th
W. 18th
W. 17th
W. 14th
W. 13th
W. 12th
Little
Twelfth Avenue
Eleventh Avenue
Tenth Avenue
Ninth Avenue
Ninth Ave.
C
H
E
Chelsea Park
Thomas F. Smith Park
Port Authority
Building
Pier 66
Pier 65
Pier 64
Pier 63
Pier 62
Pier 61
Pier 60
Pier 59
Pier 58
Pier 57
Pier 56
Pier 54
Pier 53
Chelsea Piers
Eleventh Avenue
West Side Highway (Elevated)
Meatpacking District
Washington

He paced before the Nazi flagship *Bremen*, arrived the day before; he and her models of German pride in North German Lloyd's New York *Pier 86*. It was a balmy Tuesday summer's morning and the gathering storm of war was felt by all New Yorkers. Could be seen out to sea, too, tasted as smog spit on the tongue. The clouds black as his uniform. For some, all that the darkness approaching the Verazzano Narrows stood for was a promise of relief to a week of sacks stuck sweaty to an inside leg of sailor whites. Not for German sailors. For whom black clouds were felt more as a foreboding of a conflict to come. *Ja*, Germans dreaded what was to come more than the Americans. And him more than his own countrymen again, having travelled in on the *St Louis*, to jump ship to *Bremen*, to prove his mettle. The ship was to the brim with brownshirts but he would go it alone just with a guard of ten black *SS* at his beckoning. A test of his destiny. A marker of his manhood—to steer the fate of the ship and prove himself, all in absolute secret.

Since *the swing*, his life had been a town-to-town touring of secrets. There had been a roundup all over the Reich, not only of undesirables, of so-called polluters of the master race, but of the best of the best of the best. And he was the best found so far. Little more than a flesh museum piece until last night, he jumped at the chance for action, prompted by the failure of some one hundred and fifty *SA* shakers.

Those are the brownshirts . . . blended into the *Bremen* crew and swelled to that number on this one ship since '35. A year when these undercover party cadres had become fully immersed in all German ocean liners, and all foreign crewmembers had been purged. The brownshirts had failed to persuade the ship's present captain on the importance of following Kriegsmarine High Command orders. Despite the clearest instructions two days out from New York: To camouflage and head to a German port immediately. *Intend to continue*, the captain had sent back in reply to the order from Berlin, *to disembark passengers in New York then head to Havana*. That order from Berlin came some seven hundred nautical miles out from the finger piers that gripped *Bremen* and that he now paced along.

Bremen had a sister, *Europa*. Her captain had not had the same consideration for the passengers on board. *Bremen*'s sister's brownshirts having performed better there, bending that captain to the cause of a turn back;

granted, only one day out of home. *Bremen*'s captain's decision to continue to New York and spew the near eighteen hundred from the ship's bowels did not lead to a dismissal, mind. There was no such luxury to pick and replace for the ship's race to safety ahead that would be, bet on it, a highly perilous one.

In the last war, many of Germany's liners had found themselves stranded in foreign ports to be claimed by the enemy, to then run the Atlantic highway after the war under foreign shipping lines. And the present captain had proved a certain loyalty to the Nazis, certainly more than the man's predecessor, who'd bowed out in '36. The current man's experience was needed if *Bremen* stood any chance of getting home. But he would also help ensure it. O yes, *Bremen*'s voyage back would be observed most carefully, not just by the German High Command, not just by the press of world, but by his own secret Order. That was the group who'd snatched him. Plucked him from an East Prussian lake swing all those years ago. Now, he would be the man behind the scenes of *Bremen*'s dash home.

This would be his first great test. No wonder he paced *Pier 86* so much. The scale of the task ahead of him felt as heavy as the ship he was yet to board. The one that when built had the seal of the city from which the ship took its name in relief atop the prow, showing this boat as some great ambassador for a proud

German port. A grand symbol of the Fatherland. When *Bremen* had arrived in New York at 1800 hours the night before, some of the *SA* heavyweights on board were dressed down from a high authority in the Reich. It was then he received *the letter*, as part of an *SS* takeover that had been happening all across the Reich. On arrival yesterday, the New York Port Authority promptly showed itself to be in no rush to let the liner back on its way. *Bremen* was quickly pinned to the pier by in-port paperwork, like some misunderstood giant in a children's yarn.

He took no action during the night. As again the *SA* men showed failure, this time in port, unable to break the back of Port Authority clerks hitting the liner with a litany of safety checks and searches and lifeboat raises and fallings that promised to keep *Bremen* there for days to come. Even the fuel barge and food trucks had not come through the night, as the New Yorkers would normally get right to. For the mission, he wouldn't be introduced to the captain. O no, not formally. Maybe they would not even cross paths. His taking up office on board was to be kept clandestine. His time on *Bremen* would not take up a single line in any ship log. No future report on the dash either, should it be a success.

To make room for him and his elite personal guard of ten, men were simply swapped out, names assumed from the official crew register. Switched out. The older of the brownshirts, mostly, the ones still tied to the old *SA* ways. To Ernst Röhm who, infamously, couldn't keep bent passions out of Nazi business. These old guards were simply tossed out like heavily soiled bathwater, to sink into the mud of the Hudson. Right in and underneath the pylons of the German shipping transatlantic lines, never to be unearthed.

It was the only way, given the scrutiny. *A stickling for protocol*, as one guard had put it. That was the Port Authority pen pushers' best means of keeping *Bremen* prisoner. All under the guise of U.S. neutrality—rumour had it, acting on the direct instructions of President Roosevelt, the man with the long memory. A memory stretching back now more than ever to the armed German merchant ship antics of the Great War. He didn't know the specifics, just the broad strokes. But he'd be hungry to learn. It was all important to the chess match, especially for the fates of the flagships. The Queens on the board of the waters' war.

When *Bremen* had pulled in the day before, to give an example of moves already made in the game, it was to a welcome party of some thirty men on the pier, rucksacks over shoulder, hoping to hitch a passage back to the Reich. Those that had been stuck cock-stump deep in a New York poof, maybe, when their ships slipped their moorings and sped home without warning, perhaps. Such as his own *St Louis*; she left without passengers on the twenty-eighth, just two hours after *Bremen*'s arrival. The hopes of those left behind would be dashed. O yes. Sorry, Klaus, you'll have to seek out the hospitality of an American port hole a while longer. A long, long while more. Maybe it was time to take up more lasting roots in West Village?

The New York docks had long double-storey fingers, but the stacks of the largest liners in the world reached well above these. Maybe this was why *Bremen*'s had been earlier lengthened. To bring it up with the newer ships whose fierce building *Bremen* had brought about. Up with the *Rex*'s and the *Normandie*'s and the *Queen Mary*'s. His pacing led him to wander beyond *Bremen* and out of sight of a handful of his private guard. Next finger down his feet took him, three berths over, pacing now in front of France's pride in the French Line pier, in front of *Normandie*, tied up at *Pier 88*. The same bulbous bow as on *Bremen* but a hundred feet longer, thereabouts, thirty thousand tonnes heavier, thereabouts as well.

On the voyage over, *Bremen* and *Normandie* had come into sight of each other. Usually this would be a cause for great excitement on board the liners, rising even the most silver-spoon reared of guests to common cheers and salutes across the waves. Not this time, though. Tension of war kept spirits low like a drip feed of poison to morale, and the *Bremen* veered away, to stop the two symbols of Germany and France from running parallel to New York.

But we beside now, he thought. *Brüder.*

Silly to think of great iron marvels as female, he always thought. He longed to have the two brothers share a finger. A friendly fingering of brothers to break the tension. It made sense—they shared a border after all. Admittedly one that was made sharp with the jagged wriggling of the men of the Maginot Line.

Surely there way round this unpleasantness.

As he paced, *Normandie* crawled, with Frenchmen that spat from their decks in the direction of his own high up, home-port insignias, the *SS* on his lapel. It was so stinking a summer morning that the bulges and arse cracks of the Frenchmen were wet, cocks like a damp baguette. The smell of that place between their thighs hitting him like a barge of bulls in heat. He defied the spitting French sailors by standing his ground, nose in the air. They must have thought he was making some teasing-of-their-culture gesture. Truth was he was just deepening the whiff of them. A hard respect for their stench. He drew deep the smell of French junk like a trawler gunning for flounder.

'What you stareng at, boy?' came close.

Before he could answer, darkness dragged him under. *Vive la France!* the dark called as he fell.

He came to bare chested and bum up in the cabin of an English officer. He could tell this right away from the assortment of English books; a mix of Admiralty manuals and literary titles like *Treasure Island* and *Robinson Crusoe*. There were also especially English artefacts, such as rusty relics of railway expansion. The cabin had uniforms pressed and hung, one displayed for that day's work—black with shiny brass buttons against dark wood panelling that held a pleasurable smell of wood oil, cigars and rum. There was a desk, too, and only one bed, which he was on. Windows were open and looked out onto two red and green funnels of a liner alongside. A much smaller ship. The colours of Italy on her pipes. With a three-funnel liner beyond that, in black and red, smaller again and faded in the smog. It was like the pages of *Chums* in this place, all save for the part of the whole scene that made him most sure he had come to in the cabin of an English officer—that was on account of the man riding his rump like a polo player.

'Welcome back,' his rider said in a pomp English tone. 'Lie still, son. This might sting.'

The smell of alcohol had been what had brought him to, while off the pants of the officer riding him, he also smelt an Englishman. The crotch, warm and squishy like a clotted cream scone. His rider's man parts smelt sweet; of jam and a bit like a mince pie, in the swelter of the New York summer on the Hudson. More refined than the wet baguettes of a shipload of Frenchmen. He preferred cream tea to coffee and cigarettes. He loathed cigarettes.

Englishmen smell different to Germans, *ja*, are creamier, he thought pinned to the bed. His back sweated under the officer's perineum—that soft channel between a man's jewels and staff, adding to the English scent of the cabin. Gaining clarity of vision now he picked out, too, a photograph of a handsome man in the same uniform that hung in the cabin. His English officer, *must be, yes*, was stood next to a small boy in the photograph.

'Vater?'

His head was still like some shipping channel off the Irish coast. Foggy.

'A father,' he repeated, his English very good but not often with the opportunity to practise.

'You speak English,' the man said in a rich,

Adam's-apple plunge sort of fashion. 'That helps matters. Yes, that's my son. I don't get to see him much, I'm afraid.'

A sharp pain made itself known in the dull throbbing at the base of his head. He took quick intakes of breath like a sailor thrown into an ice tub. Trying to move . . . he could not. His English rider kept him put.

'Sorry, son. I must stitch you up. *Those brutes!* they gave you a nasty gash. You may bite down on my pillow, if it helps.'

He focused in on the photograph of his Englishman. The man had a large sharp nose with a bump on its bridge. Cheekbones were defined by a pointed chin and soft concave cheeks, like the gentle beds of English sand pools at the feet of chalk cliffs. Handsome, in a British way, but awkward standing beside the boy in the photograph.

'I thought it better to patch you up myself, rather than take you to the hospital. There's some narrowminded men in this city now. Some frightened men. *Bremen*'s poor stewards have been getting quite the pounding in the back alleys these last few years.'

Pounding. He pictured these young stewards with their wimp chests pressed to bill posters at the back of butchers. With their pants bunched at the knees. Angry American and French and British cocks, cut and uncut, straight and hooked, taking turns at a good ol' buggering. Not that he would have experience of any such group fucking . . . it was just . . . he had the perverted mind, you see. He sometimes feared that these persistent thoughts of buggery would be seen some day. That he would blurt out what he was thinking. Or worse still, act on it. That all restraint would be taken from him. That was the stuff of Nazi boy nightmares.

'All the worse these poundings have become since that flag incident of '35. You heard of it, son? When demonstrators yanked down that Nazi flag from *Bremen*. Brave of you to wear that uniform . . . you look a very smart boy in it, but not all will appreciate that. I'll give you one of my uniforms to wear while you are here. They won't bother you in it.'

'Why you help me?'

His English rider took a break from skin needlepoint to rub knuckles along his cheek. The man's hands were large—a father's hands. The skin dry from years in the salt air. And the fingernails, short and neat. They tickled his lips.

'We're all just pawns in this, son. I know that. You do what you need to do in our position. And that's not always what you want to do. I have a special place inside me for boys like you.'

The words didn't quite match the action, were dirty but also a prudish clean. He wondered whether English as his second language kept him from understanding their full meaning. Or if it was just his bent brain again. Cloudy in the fog of a French bonking.

'And you are all done,' his rider said after a few more pricks to his nape followed by a pushing up.

'Stay,' he asked, his hand on English thigh. 'Stay on me.'

'As you wish,' the man said. 'You are a most beautiful boy. Are you tired, son?'

'Mm-hmm,' he murmured.

Truth was he wasn't. He'd slept the day away. It was now teatime, and he was sure to be up all night. Yet still, he repeated, 'mm-hmm,' wriggling sweaty between English legs, 'uh-huh.'

His rider eased down on top of him, all the way until their faces met on the pillow. The man from the photograph came into coloured life to rub the rest of his senses. Lips pink and hair rich brown peppered with tiny specs of silver around the temples. Eyes bluish grey, like sea splash on the bow of a battleship. And breath of cream and jam and English Breakfast tea, made his mouth water. The sound of himself sharing an Englishman's pillow, the intimate rubbing of feathers under linen, the sounds of men tending to duty in other parts of this foreign ship around them. The smog and stink of the city through the window, of ship oil and rotting fish, dirtying them. But between their lips, just sweet smells and the noises of a man father-aged and he, young enough to be the man's son.

'My name is Robert,' his rider said, little specks of spittle coating his lips.

He licked these up.

'I am your Günther,' he said, biting his lip where he could still taste a bit of Vater Robert spit. 'Being on me. Is good, ja?'

'Very good, yes. Very good indeed. May I sleep with you, my Günther?'

This time he delayed his response. More confusion on what the man meant. His delay gave Robert ample air to recline onto him completely, pulling a young father's squishy dad bits from his lower back and between the damp recess of his bum cheeks under the lubricant of a New York summer.

Robert had unbuttoned his pants while he was unconscious, but not pulled them off, just bunched them down some few inches so his bum parting was on show. The pants having been perhaps a bit too tight for the fashion; him also possessing a rump that was larger and plumper than most men. Proportionally as bulbous as *Bremen*'s pear-shaped bow, especially in contrast with a slight, boyish waist . . . the effect was that the fat cheeks of his bottom spilled over the top of his folded-down pants, and heaved against the band, like the rise and fall of an ample bosom in a pulled-tight corset in a moving-image drama set long ago.

He pulled the band down himself, freeing his bum to bob and Robert's bulge, fat and rising, to slide right between his hills. He clamped Robert there. Cuddled using his bum, the sweaty wet man bits of an English dad.

'Yes, Vater,' he said. 'You sleep in me, ja?'

Robert's face rashed red as an English rose. 'I *am* tired,' pushing up. 'But perhaps it would be best if I didn't sl——'

He stopped Robert's retreat using the same hand on English thigh, slipped a little higher up now, to cup an English peach. With the other hand he spread his sweety bum cheeks so that the extreme recess of his crack, the moistest part of him, was a wet dock for the fattening part of his rider's fatherhood.

'We discussed about this already, no? Sleep, Vater.'

And Robert sunk in, like his arse was the muddy bed of the Hudson, out of which neither of them may ever emerge again.

'*So!*' screeched a womanly man, candlestick in hand. Dressed in a robe at the threshold of Robert's cabin and the rest of the British liner. 'You're the *Na——zi boy!*'

He was new to sea life, and North German Lloyd had done its bit under Nazi rule to strip Jews and slutboy servers from its crew lists; but still, as was the way with the sea, and as *Bremen*'s previous captain had shown through a resignation protest, the power of "that party" at sea could only govern the natures of seamen so far. That was to say . . . he recognised the screech immediately as of a lily steward, a chief one at that.

The screech ripped him from slumber under the stubbled chin of his English rider, bringing a red burn to his face like little blood berries scattered onto snow. Robert didn't wake, dad bits still firmly wet docked. Though he had not thought himself at all tired, he had managed to sleep with an English father after all. He squeezed his eyes closed again, hoping he might be second-time lucky. Wishing the womanly man away.

'Don't worry, Günther,' the man said strolling in. 'Robert will not be roused by me. It's his sleepy time now. He was *that* worried about you, bless. Even though we have *St Clare's Hospital* on West Fifty-first Street, an easy drag, just one street up of here. Then *Roosevelt* above that. But *no!* he was insistent on playing doctor with you. *All day!* compressing that nasty slice of yours, just to let you sleep before he stitched you up. You godly *gorg* boys get all the personal touches.'

The lily man came in closer and put on a white glove, just to light a cigarette that was made obscenely long with a white holder.

He avoided the man's gaze and the puffing. He hated cigarettes . . . turning head away from the entrance and to the window and the red and green stacks of the liner beside.

'How do you fancy an Italian?' the lily said.

He shrugged.

Lily giggled. 'You'll soon change your tune, I expect. That's S.S. *Roma*. No *Rex*, mind.'

His eyes looked a little further. To the ship with three funnels in red and black stripe. Out of focus, like a magic lantern slide. Out the corner of his eye he could see the smoking man tracking, like a sub a convoy.

'Yes, you prefer the British, don't you, boy,' the man said. 'Beyond *Roma,* that's S.S. *Queen of Bermuda*, of the Furness Bermuda Line. Not of the prestige of the transatlantic route, of course. Running between New York and the overseas territories. But, like our *Roma*, with a connection to the *Rex*. And a bit of a key piece in the chess of things, you know. On 12 June last year, the *Queen* was intercepted by the U.S. Air Force's new toy, the Boeing *B-17 Flying Fortress*.

'More famously, these *B-17*'s had intercepted *Rex* one month earlier. The photograph of the interception, *B-17* at funnel height, was splashed over all the papers of the world. The U.S. Navy was furious, called fowl. Tried to stop any more of such things. But the Air Force is a bit of a new bitch on the block, something to prove. And, you know, maybe we'll help them with that. They want their own branch, bless. Imagine that. Army, Navy *and* Air Force? What an age we live in.'

He recalled the *Rex* image, Italian affairs often being in German papers.

'But back to *Bermuda*, best I use that shorthand, I think. What day is it? O yes, the twenty-ninth, isn't it? Well, to-day she'll receive the news that she's been requisitioned by the Admiralty for conversion into an armed merchant cruiser. O yes, Britain isn't waiting for any formal declaration. Word is she'll lose a funnel. As a decoy or to improve her range of fire—that's yet to be seen. Important, *Bermuda*, even if not one of the two *Queens* on the board.'

He hated the womanly man's riddles, smoke stinging the eyes. He pinched them shut again.

'I see you met Taureau,' the man said right into his ear, blowing smoke between him and Robert. 'Lucky Robert found you before the bull of the French Line dragged you back to *Normandie*, as he is wont to do. Yes, our poor Robert has been guarding you, bless. But now you can slip away. I've taken some precautions, you see. To ensure my best friend here gets the rest that's good for him. Slipping a little,' the womanly man gestured in the manner of sipping a dessert wine, '*something-something* in his morning English Breakfast tea.'

'How you know me?'

'"How *do*," dear boy. And my answer: little birdie on *Bremen* told me. Your new role, it's eagerly awaited by the powers that be. You've made quite the impression on your . . . what do we call them . . . *patrons*, in the Reich, and now that I see you, with my Robert, no less—*have you no shame, slut!* Sorry, well, now that I see you . . . I can understand why. Remind me of myself at your age. Using what mummy gave you.'

'You know Herr Himm——'

'No names, please,' the steward said, eyes sweeping in the sockets like the heads of gossiping wives at high tea. 'But know that I know. I speak in riddles because I must. We must. Men like you and me.'

I being nothing like you, he thought.

'But know that I know and that I am here to help you with your task. To help you slip *Bremen* away and back to Nazi Germany. But you'll have to work fast. You'll have to use, as you clearly can, slut charms from the great ma-ma. But on a rougher sort than Robert.'

'Why you will help me?' he said.

'My dear boy. There's no question here of *will*. I *am* helping. I *have helped* already. Dear Robert here has a wife, understand. Women always get in the way.' The soft man muttered that last bit under breath. 'But a powerful woman, she is. She has a hand in something large. Something that will shape this coming war and the world after, plotted in bed with Robert's father, an Admiralty major player. *Spoilers!* Right, yes, I know. They are sympathetic to the plans of the Reich. But Robert. Sweet Robert. He is not privy to any of it, won't hear of it, so can't help you. And before you ask me why, I say it's because I won't let Robert be involved. I say it's because I love him. *Hands off, bitch!* I say it because he is not built for this. I say it because *he's mine!*'

He stared dumbfounded at the lily stranger laying out an illegal love before him. He might have just fallen asleep under the chin of the man in question while that man's dad bits were in his boy crack, but none of that was as dangerous as this limp tongue. The one licking cigarette stick was as women are, with no fit with his experience of men.

'You are not one to trust on,' he said.

'I can prove it. I know things, things that have happened to you that only those in your intimate company know of, as well as events you know are coming but that have not yet come to pass. I will list a few of these for you . . . Before your little tap-tap on the head, you came in on the *St Louis*, now you are tasked with controlling the crew of *Bremen*, using soft power to ensure safe passage home. You will not come under the captain directly. That is a man who has been, how shall we say, *inconsistent* in party matters. But let's give specifics, for the purposes of showing you that *I know*.

'*Bremen* has before played host to secret missions under the nose of the current captain and the American amateurs. There was that Germen doctor spy case that came to a head last year. He was living in Yorkville near Eighty-sixth Street and Third Avenue on the Upper East Side. Haven't heard of it? Come boy, it's the German district. Best wurst in the New World—*I would know!* Any who, the F.B.I. were onto this doctor, determined to bring him down.

'The good doctor built up quite the network of informers, one which got nubbed right *there*,' pointing in the direction of what he assumed was *Pier 86*, *Bremen*'s pier, 'with a violin case stuffed with secrets.' Pause, 'alright, *since it's you!* There were stolen plans and photographs from an aircraft plant in there. The Yankee navy's *Vought* scout bomber and, you guessed it, the army's *B-17*.

'The doctor knew the ball twirling was over and fled without passport or ticket in May last year on *Bremen*. The F.B.I. demanded the current captain let a plane board in the sea. The cap said it was too rough. The cap also refused to give up the doc in Cherbourg, returning the doc to the bosom of the Reich. The cap did good then, probably the reason why he's being let continue now, after letting loose his load here, instead of taking the bastards back to Germany. But disobedience is not ignored. Good then, in '38,' hand rising in the manner of a scale, 'naughty boy now in '39,' other hand falling. 'When it counts more. It's such flip-flop foolishness that won't be tolerated by our German clients in the coming war.'

Maybe it was his command of English. Not as clear as a native speaker. But the term "client" felt wrong. He didn't understand it.

'As for those events that have not yet come,' the

chatty steward went on, 'that only those at the very top know about . . . *that's right!* I know all about little plots from both sides. About the British plan to trick your mob into sinking the S.S. *Athenia*, a wet U-boat captain made to think the liner was a military target, to kick unrestricted warfare at sea into gear—*maybe I shouldn't have mentioned that!* O *dear*. O well. Back to your side and plots you know of, too. I know about those involving Poland and shall I say poor bastards of Dachau and a radio station. Sounds like a nursery rhyme, doesn't it? O yes, that's got your little bum-roll all dry, hasn't it? Operation let's-just-say-name-starting-with "H." Guess we can say it, Himm——'

'*Stopping this!*' he cried, feeling his eyes sweep himself now, including up and down the contours of his English rider, imagining the man slotted into his sweatiest fold as one enormous earhole poised to expose him. A handsome, treacherous reef of father parts that could sink him.

The lily steward had proved knowledge from the highest level. Operation Himmler, that was the false flag radio station hijacking to start a war.

'I keep from him and accept your help, ja.'

'O *yeah*, I thought you might. My pretty little bum-bum friend. Welcome to my fold. Meet your new bestie. Meet, Mr White.'

30 August

Up

SUN-
DECK

Buffet

Restaurant

Dancing
Floor

Up

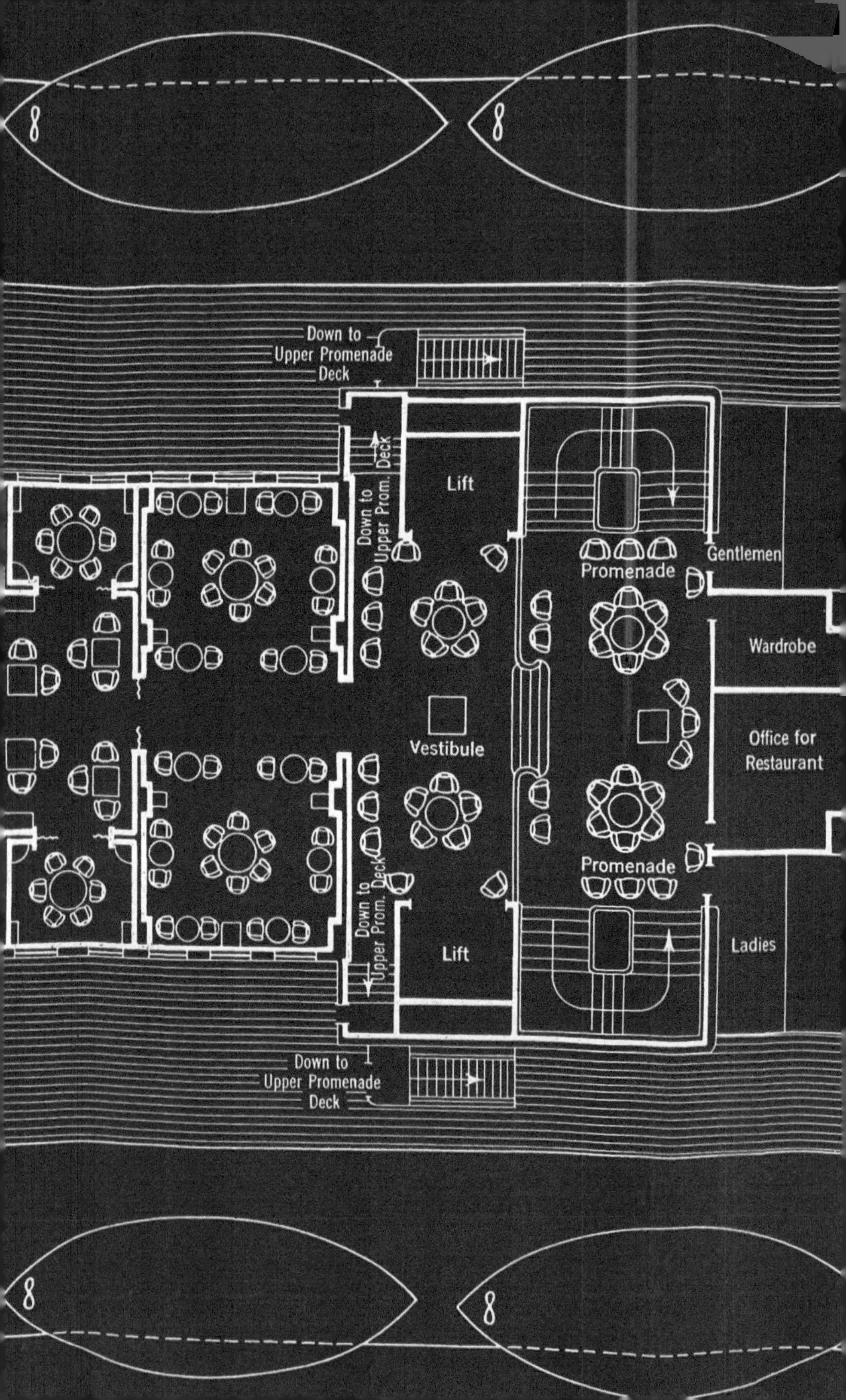

Down to
Upper Promenade
Deck
Down to
Upper Prom. Deck
Lift
Gentlemen
Promenade
Wardrobe
Vestibule
Office for
Restaurant
Promenade
Down to
Upper Prom. Deck
Lift
Ladies
Down to
Upper Promenade
Deck

He felt like the village vicar's vice of a slut son. Walking *West Side Highway* in a black outfit that *he knew* an English father did not approve. All while that man lay drugged—warm so recently between his crack. Coming out of the Cunard Line's *Pier 90* brought him in front of West Fiftieth Street. He backtracked along the way Robert had carried him, but only a little while, to then elevate onto *West Side* to avoid the finger-piers pavement. Not wishing to tempt another bonk on the head. But courting trouble, too. Like some fundamental affront to red-blood Christian men. He peacocked his black Nazi uniform down the raised highway all the way from West Fiftieth to West Thirteenth. Getting honks and bottles thrown and, ja, more spit of men as he went the forty minutes it took him to strut there. Taking up one of the offers to 'get in, boy' from men in bowler hats would have got him there in seven, but he wasn't that much of a slut for trouble. It was why also he avoided the drifters underneath the highway.

He'd slipped away while Robert was sleeping, and as White was out of the way, too—to fetch them an olive cocktail, the lily had said. He slipped from Robert's cabin, aft, on *Boat Deck*. Passed the dome of first class, down a flight of stairs and onto *A Deck* and the first of R.M.S. *Aquitania*'s enclosed promenades, this one the *Garden Lounge*. Such enclosure of the walking decks that had much of R.M.S. *Titanic* about them. He fancied himself a second there. Rubbed his crack, imagining the times that he might've been able to slip out of Robert's cabin late at night if the man smuggled him on board. They'd walk together then, and maybe Robert would take him into the *Entrance* for first class just off it, too.

With its parlour palms, ornate wrought-iron banister and lifts, grand glass dome, Corinthian columns and Louis XVI decoration, the first-class *Vestibule* had nothing of the Spartan Germanic restraint of the *St Louis* he'd sailed in on. The Hamburg America Line ship that had brought him there that was sometimes charted for cruises by the Reich's Strength Through Joy organisation. When juxtaposed, the grand hotel feel of *Aquitania* was everything his homeland's rulers detested. *St Louis* had lines that were clean, sometimes curved, but never ornately scrolled.

Despite the French influence, or maybe *because* it was so clearly copied from an everyman's image of a chateau, *Aquitania* was O. So. English. Like a country manor house in the Continental style. A palatial hotel on the English Riviera. Everything about his Englishman he wanted to discover, over tea and toast and hand under a linen men's night dress. But still, he left it. It was an adventure of a different time. It was of a different era. The last of the Edwardian liner style, last of the four funnels, so old-fashioned beside the three funnels of the stolen *Vaterland* and *Imperator*, allowing for more spacious interiors, and certainly very old next to the just-two-stack, deco chicness of *Bremen*.

Bremen stewards with knowledge of slut things about a city as open to crime as New York were his source of intelligence once he'd cleared Cunard and was back among North German Lloyd stock. Little inroads were being made with the crew, though so far it was really only lily-whitest types who were willing to open to him. They were easy to please, really, these sluts. Letting these men stay a short while in bed offerings in *Sloane House*, one of the two newly constructed Y.M.C.A. dorms, did the trick. These *Y dorms* were colossal monuments to young transient men, with almost as many rooms each as there were normally passengers on *Bremen*.

Already, a reputation for endless lines of dropping soap in the showers were legendary at *Sloane House*, the largest dorm in the New World and in convenient reach of easy sailors. Well, legendary among those in the know. Founded in '30 as cheap lodgings for men of the armed services, one of the slutboy stewards called it *a colony of likeminded men*, with a wink. The boys who took his cash to this new colony—located between West Thirty-fourth and Thirty-third Streets—thumbed rides there down *West Side Highway*. More willing to take the risk with handsome motorists.

Some of these men would not make it to *the Y*. Failing to score a ride from a passing motorist, like a honey to ants a riverside park would get them sticky instead. *DeWitt Clinton Park* between *Pier 92* and *94* had enough trees and shrubs for a soft German-liner boy to get bent over and buggered in. Pissed on and beaten, too, depending on the traders that evening. As welcome a showering for these sluts as any offered at the *Sloane*. How fast his command had folded him in with the clandestine customs of seamen. Not that he would know what slutboy winks and soap drops and piss-ups meant, of course. He had not yet found his sea legs, so to speak. But his brain wondered. And he made the leave to stay happen for these men. Such was the power he had. Or, at least, the cash to pass out.

Very grateful steward sluts much less choosy than he gave some suggestions on where he should drink. Sluts pleased with slips into showers where soaps were impossible to keep hold of suggested *Webster Hall* or *Rockland Palace* when pressed on where in the city *men like yourself might drink.* Two places known for their faggots' balls. A possibility, he thought at the time. Certainly, places where his body might get him a sympathetic hearing from a powerful Manhattan mogul or two. But on longer thought, that was all a bit too obvious for his style. More of a younger Mr White manoeuvre, he figured. And at East Eleventh and West One Hundred and Fifty-fifth Streets, would definitely mean needing to take a man's riding to see through. He could pay drivers himself, of course. But where was the adventure in that? No, life experience told him that he shouldn't need work that hard or splash any cash himself to find men willing to lend a hand to an Aryan as angelic as he. All it should call for is a bit of boot leather grind down.

A member of the *Bremen* officer ranks was the one to suggest a closer option, not far back from the shipping lane. He met this man at the cabin gangway for *Bremen*, with its black picket fence and covered tunnels onto the ship, it resembled more the queuing point of some great ice creamery than a ship in port. The man to suggest the spot, a Mr Wolf, was a signalman on the ship and didn't look much like the lily stewards. Had drifted into his conversation in a trench coat and hat, a long and skinny man with a slight hunch that would only get worse. A spinal deformity, certainly. An odd bedfellow for the steward sluts with their prim appearances, he thought, those men who he had sent skipping with news of a stay at *the Y*. Hmm, left him with a misfit impression, this Mr Wolf, that made him unsure that slippery soap nights were this man's particular trade. Still, Wolf's venue suited him much more than any of the others proposed. He could walk there. Yes, it was the word of a Wolf what led him the forty minutes from one Cunard finger to another. From *Pier 90* to *54*.

Cunard and White Star Lines had shared *Pier 54* to play host to that century's greatest triumphs and greatest bow dives to the seabed. In '12 the White Star Line's *Titanic* never reached it, its passengers' rescuer *Carpathia*, a Cunarder, calling in instead to unload those who'd survived the terrible sound of iron scraping alongside Atlantic ice. Then in '15, Cunard's *Lusitania* left this pier for its German *U-20* rendezvous, never to be back again. *Lusitania*'s sister, *Mauretania*, who snatched the Blue Riband from her—the contest for the fastest transatlantic crossing—called *Pier 54* home, too, and retained the Riband for twenty years, the longest period on record. From '09 until *Bremen*'s '29 coup. And with it, *Bremen* brought something new.

The era of national pride in a liner and the birth of the "monsters," as they became known.

Around the time of *Bremen*'s challenge to the old liners, new piers were being built between Forty-fourth and Fifty-fourth Streets. The direct access to *West Side Highway* he enjoyed from *Bremen* for his peacock down to where the big boats used to be, was all part of the plan Manhattan and the Hudson had to make way for the new monster ships of state that all started with *Bremen* herself. It wasn't easy for Germany to slide on in, though. *Bremen* had completed her Riband-snatching maiden voyage with the indignity of a Brooklyn-side pier. Despite the official line that there was nothing suitable for North German Lloyd to lease in Manhattan, the linger of ill will after war toward the Germans was difficult to ignore. A ship like *Bremen* could not be ignored for long, however. And North German Lloyd got its first Manhattan pier.

In '32, *Pier 54* caught fire. Or so Mr Wolf had happened to mention in a sketch of some of the sights he'd encounter on his saunter to where he could bend men with power in port. A deep blow, this fire, but soon forgotten as *Luxury Liner Row*—as the new piers where all the monsters were tied came to be called—stole the show. *Bremen* being, really, the first in this esteemed lineup. *Normandie* took victory for France in '35, docking at the French Line's side of *Pier 88* on her maiden voyage—when she also snatched the Riband from the Italian Line's *Rex*, who had herself taken it from *Bremen* in '33. Britain to Germany to Italy to France . . . it played an anachronistic anthem when learned now.

'34 saw Cunard merge with White Star, the only way to bring the Riband back to the British. It was what finished the *Queen Mary*, pulling men back to her to scrap off the rust of a once proud line's financial hardship. Finally, Britain had its great challenger to French dominance. And it worked. *Mary* did it in '36, then again in '38, to still hold the record to-day. Yes, the second European war had come long before now, waging along finger piers of New York's Hudson, and *Bremen* started it all. Why should his first great mission be to bring the ship of state back to the Fatherland? Well, what better test? Honour was at stake.

He'd known really nothing of this history, *Bremen*'s Mr Wolf having filled him in on a walk to the stepping-on point of the highway, making sure he headed that way . . . Expanding the brain was not part of a flesh sculpture's day. But he was learning now. Something of *Bremen*'s stake in the quest for dominance of speed across the seas. And just maybe, of why such feats might matter in times of conflict as well as peace.

The air was fetid around the forgotten old fingers that had touched the biggest liners of yesteryear. And got only thicker as he moved towards the warehouses and factories of the alleyways off the main grid in this part of the city. Any luxury, had there ever been any here, had long moved mooring, like all the best big boats. The smell of French meat baguettes and English cream dad bits long been drowned out by the stink of New York's pit of the roughest labourers, of the slums of a failed immigrant dream. Of the Irish and the Italians. It was so thick in the air he was not entirely sure that the smog of the whole city—in a desperate state of rapid building of itself out of a great depression—had not had its source in these very streets. Like here was New York's one fat smokestack. Sure, the decade had given the New York visitor the *Chrysler Building*, the *Empire State Building*, the *General Electric*, mighty monuments that seemed to mimic *Bremen* herself as a late '20s floating Art Deco masterpiece. But there were sinister notes here.

The '20s were spent building, breaking the roughnecks who worked without harnesses with hot rivets on the high beams. This continued in the '30s, when now New York had its skyline. Its cloud scratches that screamed progress to all, every man who couldn't help but look, also at the iron monsters steaming in. That was America, in his eyes. A great show city, some permanent grand exhibition. Some winter garden built of concrete. Drawing men in. First the immigrants then the visitors, especially after the quotas of '24. Brought in to witness the brave new world, while from the old, from Europe, great cities afloat were what men travelled in. How insular America was. It seemed like it would never have a liner of its own.

The closest the United States Lines had come was its *Leviathan*, the largest ship in service from '14 to '22. But that did not count. That ship was stolen from Germany as war reparations. Formerly the *Vaterland*, one of Hamburg America Line's trio of biggest liners the world had ever known, caught in New York when its captain had been too timid to attempt a dash back home at the outbreak of the Great War. Yes, his mission again. *Do not let history repeat itself*, as was a line from his orders. Britain got Germany's other two great ships. The title of the biggest in the world was held by these German sisters from '13 until *Normandie* in '35. It was the last time Germany would attempt such a thing. Such a great blow to his homeland's pride these loots were, he needed no ship's signalman to point them out to him.

He knew what it was to be stolen.

He was a provincial boy at heart, a farm boy. Albeit, yes, a bit naughty. Show me a man who's grown up as royalty among men. As better than the rest based on a bloodline philosophy and skull and skin measurements of a science dedicated to defining genetic superiority who is not a bit cocky. But he was a rogue, too. Certainly, no man to bend to the suggestions of limp wrist old servicemen. No. He had no time for White or what the man was plating up for him. He would make inroads among the immigrant powerful of New York City to keep *Bremen* from being just another of America's great heists.

It took no time at all for the lanes off the streets that backed onto the finger piers of the city to fester into hangouts for the destitute. Long after midnight, forty fathoms from *Luxury Liner Row*. For his personal guard—all of whom he was yet to properly meet, but most that had been eagerly awaiting him back at the mooring ties of *Bremen*—he had arranged beds in the *Seamen's Church Institute*, a recommendation of one of North German Lloyd's New York representatives. These lodgings were the churchmen's answer for young seamen preyed upon by those interested in sailors that loitered around the docks between ship outs. His mind was bent enough to imagine what such interests might encompass.

Better they be tucked away in clergy-run beds than in the crew cabins of *Bremen*, which continued to be searched by the city authorities, and who might discover with a little probing that they are not the men they had been switched in with. 'Look here, see,' he imagined one of the Port Authority inspectors saying in a coat to the ankles and hardboiled kind of way, pulling his ten guards out of bed one by one by the dick, holding the lads up in lineup to photographs of men now in the mud of the Hudson. 'Not a match, see.' He could nil afford that.

That his bodyguards would be safely sleeping, even away from the hands of other seamen just wishing for a fondle of some German stock, showed his leadership style. He'd protect their arses. Hell, had not even told them where he was heading, nor any of his plans, nor met with them in person to advise their alternate lodgings. Just left instructions in their cabins. He did not know the men, but his harvest days had planted deep an instinct to protect those innocent—in this case guards to the ways of seamen. It was on his mind even as he pushed his own body into flesh advantage. The legs of his trousers now stained with the shit and blood of animals, running out from nearby warehouses.

Declining to take the uniform Robert had offered him was not only a sonly defiance. His pants still too tight and fragrant with the sweat of his bum and Robert's dad bits . . . recent exertions getting ridden that had plumped up his behind even further. No, he got no pleasure out of disobeying the wishes of a cream-tea father. There was strategy in wearing his *SS* uniform. However much danger it courted. It was a risk that was needed if he was to get *Bremen* out before war was declared. It was a magnetic mine for the bodies of American naval personnel and, his real target, those with clout over the Port Authority—whose headquarters was conveniently located nearby.

The winks of handsome roughnecks dragging on cigarettes told him he'd reached the right rundown entrance. Great big wooden doors of a warehouse with a row of windows on top, smashed if not completely covered in the grim of animal fat. He was let in right away into an orgy of sweat and jazz and mixing skin shades. It was like a deranged mind's fantasy of the bars on *Bremen* and her sister *Europa* in the years '29 to '33. During prohibition, when these ships became havens for Americans racing to a drink. Booze cruises of debauched expression.

Now that alcohol flowed freely here . . . down the bumps of man chests to be licked up by the lisping tongues of other men . . . now that prohibition was behind this city, places like this seemed to cater to a persistent love for the underground—through provision of other kinds of banned indulgences. Fleshy ones. The service of legal spirits to men as loose wristed and long haired as these kept the underground alive. A criminal den in a shutdown slaughterhouse within a wind's sniff of the smelly docklands trade of the transatlantic shipping routes.

It was with a feeling of getting bogged down in mud that he spotted the chief of the British lily stewards near immediately. Like a rusted blockship in a sunny harbour. Mr White had an olive pinched between petite fingers and shared a drink of cloudy spirit with a circle of other men equally old and revolting. Slurping from the ab cuts of a Black man. Yes, segregation was still in force in the New World, but there were no rules in this slaughterhouse located a breath held from the burned old Cunard pier.

Nein! he shouted inside himself. *Nein, nein, nein.*

It wasn't the Black man that put him off. That man was big and muscled and glistened with all the world's strength and rowing resolve to change things, all the will of a slave-ship revolt. It was the lily White he despised. That tongue with boils that seemed to darken the Black man's skin, to burn a proud ebony. His dirt mind thought a moment on the pretty contrast of a Black cock of fabled oversize disappearing between his pure chalks. How pretty a spectacle. How epic a breaking in of a tiny, no-colour arsehole. How tribal. How savage a sacrificed-virgin arse fucking.

O yes, he was more resolved now that he'd got there in his own shoes—he would find his own solution. Use his wits, his body, his instinct, to locate himself the man in this place he needed to bend, or that he would bend for, to get *Bremen* out. The secret big men of the Reich believed in him enough to give him this task. He never thought he'd get such freedom. Meat statues normally don't get given jobs to do. O yes, he'd take it on himself. With *the vigour*. That White was here was a good sign, he reasoned.

This being the place!

He stuck to the walls of the slaughterhouse. Walls splashed with blood that he traced a path along like braille. Bullets wedged and gelatinous residues in the outlines of men. Death was routine here still, even if the trading in animal carcass had come to an end. He let the blood of rubbed-out men stain him, all to avoid a spotting. It was a *dive! dive! dive!* out of sight of the shifty English Q-ship that was White . . . listing so queerly, so false flag, sucking the spirits from the tribal scene of a Negro man spread.

On his way away from White he came into contact with the outlines of living men. Groans and gyrations of man bits up against and into *not meant to be an* "*in*" parts of each other, slapping his ears in a lurid soundtrack, grabbing for him, too, in a living dead kind of fever dream. He'd had his formative years in the dorms of the prime-most cuts of men. Yes, he'd been paraded around the Nazi boy camps and schools and colleges. He'd seen those bits pulled and rubbed up against each other in the release of healthy Germanic thick and white pee-pee.

But nothing like this . . . and the triumph of his will to stay schtum. To stay on the blood-spray walls. To keep from being dragged under by those who reached for him. It rubbed up with his need to avoid being seen by White, or any other of the warehouse whores. He sweated further into his crotch seam, in the dark. Like he'd fallen waist deep into a lake at night, after the snap of that rope swing, and now waded further out even though he could not swim. Though his feet were planted now, it felt like there was nothing to ground him. Like now was his last chance to make it back to shore.

But then he caught sight of a man out of place at the side of the bar, like a pontoon he could land on. Could this be, just maybe, the New York shaker he had snuck away from Robert for? Pushing through the fucking bodies, repulsion feeling them, like slimy seaweed wrapping the feet, he made it to the bar side, where he was at last alone in the dark.

'*Oohh!*' the man said, voice deep with the flag colours of red and white, hand flying by the ear. 'Back up yous cocksucking fanook. Me's ain't no stump yous wanna try 'n' hump.'

He begged to differ.

Wearing a white singlet tucked in tight with a belt buckled about where the cord was cut from Mutter, the man chewed gum and watched, not watching, the scenes of Sodom in the bar. Brilliant-white singlet, like it'd never been worn. But wet under the armpits and around the chest sweep of it, both places where thick black hair laced with musky droplets spilled out like curly wigs stuffed in there. A delicate gold chain about the neck with a crucifix caught off kilter in the black curls, like a cutter on the rocks.

He'd found himself a gen-u-ine New York wiseguy.

His wiseguy had chest hair darker than any hair-prone part of himself could ever be. Even those hairy parts of him where the sun had, in his experience, never shone, would never reach those blacks. And the face was full of the same black hair, but in a sawed-off, sharp-razor shadow that . . . not that his sheltered life in rural Germany then as a travelling flesh art piece would give him any knowledge of such things . . . would cut his white skin open in a rash of billions of specs of Italian red, should he give a hump a red-hot go.

'Off yous fuck, fanook,' the wiseguy said with a

shove that pushed him at such an angle he stumbled into the low light.

A mirror behind the bar caught for him what the wiseguy would have seen. Freshly fired porcelain on any objective scale of ancient Aryan bloodline. Eyes so coral-sea blue they glowed. Sliced at the top of the spine by a mob of fretting Frenchmen. But that last bit wasn't in the mirror . . . flashes of purple and green and hot pink from the vice entertainment in the warehouse flavoured his features like a lightshow on a cathedral. All carved by the hands of craftsmen with knowledge of how to sculpt the perfect man. Nose a little Roman, with a bit of a bump that gave distinction, cheekbones high and chin and jaw sharp, like he was constantly clenching his teeth.

He had modelled for Arno Breker for Germany's public works. To inspire the world on the ideal male physique. Statues in marble to his exact likeness that would stand for one thousand years in a capital of the world. It was why he had been taken and guarded.

The wiseguy stopped chewing. He had the man's full focus, to be grabbed by his uniform front and pulled in close to the bar. The man's stench of rub-on alcohol and underarm was the only smell he'd take willingly back to Germany.

'Oohh,' no hand gestures this time. More quiet. Chewing come back. The wiseguy grabbed his chin and cheek in a clammy palm with hairy knuckles and turned his head side to side. 'Yous are a pretty fanook, thoughs.' The wiseguy then peeled apart his lips to see his teeth, to then grab his shoulders and look him up and down like all men do. 'Fosco Indelicato, charmed. I'm a capo. You want a job, kid? I'll give you a job.'

'I am born in Germany, ja. I do not needing job here.'

'Too bad. Yous found it.'

'I am soldier, ja. See my outfit.'

'Look around you, kid. Plenty of my whores playing dress up. Show some respect, huh? Take the job.'

Fosco was right. There were others in the warehouse wearing uniforms. Even a few dressed similar to him. Counterfeit garments, he suspected. The men in them New York boys playing out a fantasy or working for Fosco in the prostitution business.

'I am soldier,' he said.

'Oohh, one of my crew then. Maybe.'

'I can't stay. But you helping me . . . You in the power place, ja? I am on *Bremen*, need to getting her out. You will helping me, ja?'

Fosco pulled him more into the light and came in close, like a Jew checking clarity in the *Diamond District*.

'Come, fanook. Come with Fosco. Yous have mama's spaghetti and meatballs.'

Fosco led him through an office at the back of the bar and up a narrow, creaking wooden staircase to a cramped flat in the eaves. Smudged animal fat on the window, adding smog to an already dirty view of brick buildings soiled with soot. The sound of warehouse whores could still be heard in the attic of this building, a constant burden for this Italian mob captain, no doubt. Fosco's trousers were abandoned in a lump just inside the door, leaving the Italian immigrant with only cotton shorts with tomato stains and a white singlet tucked in.

The stains drew his eye.

'*Oohh!* none of that,' Fosco said with a slap across his face. Not a friendly one, hard as everything about the man. 'Yous eyes up here,' an "up yours" gesture pointing the way.

He nodded as the slapped side of his face ripened to the colour of the tomatoes diced on a board in the flat. It took balls to take force to a face like his.

'Good. Now yous strip for Fosco Indelicato.'

Confused, his face stinging, he contemplated a flee from the flat. This wiseguy was clearly mad.

Nein, he thought. He would do what it took. He stripped down to a similar state of undress, only it was tight briefs instead of cotton shorts. White underwear, as pristine as every part of him.

Fosco seemed satisfied with that.

His cock was the kind that the Ancient Greeks would not deem aesthetic. But in the flesh instead of marble, most pleasing. Ample. The bulge in his briefs promising a phallus worth men's worship.

'Good. Yous ain't heavy. I'm glad. Don't have to put the kid in cement shoes. I don't need the paperwork,' each sentence said with hands in the manner of a street-band conductor. 'Come, we eat.'

He didn't get all the lingo. At first, he thought "heavy" referred to weight. But any man could see from the lean cut of his uniform that he was taut all over. A weapon, perhaps? Being in a state of only tight briefs did confirm he had no weapon on him. None of metal, anyway.

A large pot on the stove stood cooling, bulging with big balls of mince in what he guessed to be a Sicilian red sauce.

'Mama's own recipe, brought here by ship and turned to American tongues. *Mwah!*' two fingers and thumb in a thrown kiss from the wiseguy's month.

'We discuss about my own ship now, ja. About this, you will——'

Fosco slapped him again, across the other cheek using the backside of the same hand. Here was a man used to slapping boys about.

'*Oohh!* show some respect. First we's eat. Don't you disrespect mama's recipe.'

He nodded, red spreading across his whole face like Sangiovese spilled over a crisp white tablecloth.

'Now yous strip more.'

Palm to his reddened face, he eyed up the door.

'*Mamma mia!*' both hands in the air like the Virgin Mary in prayer. 'Fosco ain't no cocksucker. We not use mama's plates.'

Before he had time to contemplate how they would eat meatballs on spaghetti without plates, Fosco had him spun round and his briefs ripped from his rump. His bum jiggled as it had done bum to bum with his English rider. Though now with a line of red from the aggression of a New York capo, a treatment of his perfect white buns his Englishman would never have dished out.

Suddenly, the bulging biceps of an Italian immigrant who worked out in the New York gyms showed themselves like the girths of the mooring ties that kept

Bremen in port. And with the swiftness of a revolving door—offering all the pressure relief in a skyscraper, a Berliner's invention—he was flipped over and onto the crown of his head, the jelly of his bum cheeks falling apart to the pull of gravity like a yanked away gelatine mould.

There was a mirror on the ceiling. *For why?* It showed him what his wiseguy could see.

His rump was ample. Meaty. The only fatty part of him. It splayed in two juicy cheeks like the jowls of some mammoth bovine. The capo was creative. Had created with the turn upside down of him a bowl out of which no liquid could escape. His hole. His opening. His hidden passage between his lower cheeks, shown to him for the first time in the ceiling mirror, like a clown bent over to peer between bangy pants in front of a dresser. And it was pretty in pink. Not white as he imagined. The most delicate, complex knot of skin, pinched and pulled into him.

Fosco slapped his gelatine. His bottom normally, but now that his arse was spread and looking up to the ceiling. Now, this was his bum bowl.

'This'll do for mama's meatballs,' Fosco said, ladling out the mince in tomato sauce into the bowl that was his arse.

It soon filled up.

Like a yodelling young mountain man in high socks and suspended knee-length shorts, full up on good local beer. It was hot. Burnt his hole a little. But not too much to take. Like he might lower himself, bum first, into a fresh-poured bath. Maybe a little too hot for his bullocks, but he'd soon be in and stewing. The spaghetti came after. Twisted in from a height as a twirled mound at the spilling point of his bum bowl. It soon sunk to tickle his taint and hole, to bring welcome yeast to his entrance point.

Until this moment, Fosco had been in a state of gym flip. Muscles holding his thighs to allow the splay of an arse bowl able to take mama's meatballs. But now that the plate was set, Fosco pulled over a wooden stool and a fork and spoon as a place setting on each thigh. And then released. To let his neck . . . freshly stitched by his English rider . . . take the load. It burnt at both ends. Hot in different ways. Steaming meatballs stacked on his hole, his efforts to keep the bowl level pulling on the stitches of his neck. Fosco seemed content with his role as plate. Ready to eat. Twisting the four pins of a fork around his knot, using the spoon for the final gather up and into the mouth.

'Al dente,' Fosco said, eyes rolling back with the bite into pasta. 'As only mama can make.'

It must have been a comical scene. But with the grime and stench of animal fat and the splinters of rotting wood in his tearing wound, he missed the joke. He looked around with just his eyeballs in the sockets, searching for mama, who must have only recently cooked the pasta to that perfect bite. But as always in his life, in this world that he moved, no woman was present. He did, however, catch glimpse of a poster above the bed in the one stove, one table, one sleeping arrangement flat. It was of *Bremen*.

Of course. Fosco, like many Italians, had come to New York in her. He had only need mention the name of his ship in ropes to have the clearance needed to get back to sea. Fosco would put on the pressure of any officials to make it happen. The *Port Authority Building* was just a few Straße turns away. And Fosco was the sort to pressure the necks of any pencil and clipboard boys as a sport—their bosses, too. But why dinner then? he wondered. Was there something more? Something of use the capo saw in him?

Mama's meatballs misbehaved in his bowl as he struggled to keep his arse level. They rolled in the fresh-young cheeks guarding his hole like weather balloons in a gale. Dodging the fork. But Fosco got most in the end, regular top-ups from the pot.

'You serve good food,' Fosco said. 'Stick with me, kid, and you'll do alright.'

'I am born German. Why you being help to me?'

Fosco had a nose broken in more than one part,

crooked as a turnip tail, and bonfired-toffee eyes, like the lightest tones in the Negro-body cocktails that were getting slurped from downstairs.

'You're breaking my balls here. What're you breaking my balls for?' Fosco said, denying him eye contact. 'Maybe Fosco just wants to help out a pretty fanook. We're not all out to whack, you know.'

'Too much paperwork, ja?' he said, smiling, though it pained him.

He was learning. While a wiseguy ate from his arse, he figured out it was best to flirt and pander to the man's ego a little. Caught as he was, upside down between a mob captain's hairy thighs. He didn't know what a fanook was, but Fosco probably was one, too.

'You not need telling me,' he said, licking his lips. 'I don't wanting you get in trouble.'

'I like you, kid,' Fosco locked eyes again. Those deep browns, they were the kindest part of the man. 'Fuck it, what the hell, you'll be off to-day anyways,' Fosco stretched hands overhead, cracking the knuckles like a card sharp about to bluff. 'And I don't want to hear you talk about me getting into trouble no more. You don't know shit. I can take care of myself.'

'You are boss,' he said. 'Whatever you wanting.'

Fosco lent through his spread and pinched his face. 'You're a good kid. Learn quick. You ever hear of Lucky Luciano?'

'No, boss,' he said.

'Oohh,' rocked back, a finger in to scoop out some stray spaghetti from his knot, lingering to tickle his boy-cave opening a little. Then a lick of the finger that'd done it. 'What the fuck they teaching kids nowadays? The man is a legend, a hero to mine and yours peoples. A fucking Robin Hood. No, now I have to educate you. Hang tight, kid,' Fosco said, ladling out more meatballs. These dropped like mines to his hole, which quivered with the feeling that what was about to come would be something really good. 'Get yourself comfortable. Boy, have I got one hell of a history lesson for you.'

Charles "Lucky" Luciano came onto the scene around the time of *Bremen*, the man setting an example that differed from other mafia bosses by being up to working with non-Italians—at a time when some were so elitist as to only work with Sicilians. Good business was good business, as Lucky Luciano saw it, and the man's vision of a national crime syndicate, a kind of co-operation between mobs—Irish and Jewish included. An operation that even had figures like Joseph Kennedy Sr., current U.S. ambassador to Britain, on its books. Well, this had its origins in '29.

Fosco gave him his lesson as meatballs made their way from mama's pot to his bowl to the jabbering mouth of a not so wiseguy. Lucky ended up in the slammer in '36, doing thirty to fifty years. 'Here's the good bit, kid,' Fosco said, arse-bowl meat coming at him in chunks. 'Lucky Luciano's still in charge from the inside. Even after the pigs moved him in '38.'

Mama's pot without meatballs now, Fosco turned to a much smaller pot on the stove. Out of which the wiseguy scooped out more meatballs to drop from a height into his bowl, one by one that splashed in, as the history lesson concluded.

'We're in the waste management business, that's what we call it, kid, but what will get you wet in your panties is that we have the longshoremen on our books. There ain't no ship loaded or unloaded on the entire Manhattan waterfront that Lucky ain't got control over. So yeah, when I say your boat is good as home free, you better believe it.'

All meatballs left in the flat were in his bowl now, ten in total. Piled up. Out of the sauce like cannonballs in a shallow pond . . . the meat sat weighty. Ten balls of mama's, two more of his own in his sack hanging low, low, low below his bowl.

'Give your boss a drink, kid,' Fosco said, an eye on this sack dangling toward his head. 'You owe him one after that story.'

Not waiting for a response, Fosco pulled his dick up and over, dipping it into the sauce of what remained in his bowl and then leaning over the bowl to take his dick in the mouth.

'I ain't asking,' Fosco said out the side of the mouth, his dick clamped under Italian tongue.

It was not nothing, to piss in the mouth of a wiseguy when upside down with remnants of mama's spaghetti and meatballs in your rump. Not really sure how to go about it, actually. But knowing that he'd come this far and, really, was a little further anything to stop him? He pushed.

It bubbled mama's meatballs first. For a good while, in fact. Unfolding all the tightness of a young Aryan hole and inviting the rich tomato and some spaghetti strands *into him*. Like the wet army of a new southern ally into a stronghold of the Reich. He panicked at first, his German boy hole sphincter chumping down on the pasta like a hungry little bottom feeder. Bringing mama's recipe inside him. Fosco showed first evidence of patience, lips clamped on his dick as his Aryan anus gobbled up some American-tinkered-with ancient recipe. Bubbles of his anal grab recooking the food left until his eventual stream came.

Fosco drank deep and appreciative and demanding of his relinquishing to the last drop, occasioned by an intensity of gobble up and fart bubble of the dish at his own end. He knew his piss would be refreshing. He drank mostly water in the swelter of that New York summer. Gallons and gallons of the stuff. At one point Fosco pinched, backed up then released his cock to allow the piss to be seen, spraying into the wiseguy's mouth like a mountain cyclist pouring water down the throat from a height. His piss was like liquid quartz, crystalline, like from an alps spring with shimmering-silver mineral deposits. Highly filtered. Fosco seemed pleased.

His piss was *clean.*

The ten meatballs Fosco had piled in his bowl rolled like logs down Canadian river rapids as he pushed and pushed to get out and into Fosco the last of the only drink he had to offer a mob captain. It was a relief for him to empty out. And all this pushing had made his knot looser than it ever had been that meal, choking on sauce and chewed bits of spaghetti and the odd chuck of mince small enough to tumble into him. This wiseguy was turning his arsehole into a gobbler in the extreme. Fosco then took advantage of his hole's opening to the tastes of Italy. Took the chance to feed him. Push into the wide eating of his arsehole each of the golf-ball-sized meatballs from the second pot, one by one. To then lick his bowl clean.

'Yeah, kid, I'll have your harbour clearance to-day. Whatever you want,' Fosco said. 'But save mama's meatballs for me, you hear. I mean it.'

He sat between *Bremen*'s stacks on a table set up on the roof of *Sun Deck Restaurant,* a dining alternative for first class. He'd carried the meat packed into him all day, from the wee hours spent as a serving bowl for an Italian wiseguy until now. The restaurant under his feet gave peacetime diners a panoramic view of the seas when steaming at speed. But his private table was better this evening. The cigars of this save-face German liner puffing above him, he more privileged than any who'd come before, anyone moneyed enough to enjoy a meal under him. Not that this stopped him shifting uncomfortably, having ten of mama's meatballs stuffed inside. Ten inches of Italian meat stretching him out. He didn't know much of the arseholes of men, but surely this Italian meat reached right into his gut. He'd avoided eating all day in fear of disrupting the lunch packed into him by a New York mafia capo. Ready to return them unmarked, like they were ten G's, should Fosco run true on the threat to come calling. Had any man been this aware of his own arsehole before?

Food ever obsessed him. In his rope swing years he'd nip into a hotel in the sunken lakes, into the kitchens to pinch some portions of goulash, ladled into a sheep-stomach flask, or a schnitzel stuffed hot in his briefs, his father too poor to put anything on the table other than him bent over for a belting. He'd needed more than a father's leather to fuel his activities around the lakes. Workers at the hotel would spot him some, give chase with a wooden spoon on occasion; though really, he was sublime enough to get away with anything. That hotel would become a favourite among the Nazi party powerful. There were even whispers of them setting up a settlement among the East Prussian lakes. The perfect place to hide some Nazi secrets.

Fosco's balls *up* him, as the ship pushed back from the pier he felt that naughty boy again, as this time the meat in sauce had been ladled by another man, his own arse sock his sheep stomach. He felt the balls roll within him as he watched the smoke from the stacks getting sucked into the lungs of the city. Plumes went well above his head. These stacks used to be squat but were lengthened after first-class passengers who had the run of *Bremen*'s topside promenade decks made complaints. He thought he wouldn't much mind a smokescreen now. To swallow him. Plus, he didn't mind pipes squat either, he liked a good pipe girthy, wide like the hard palms of a father.

He sighed.

He'd left no note for the Vater from *Aquitania*, the English officer who had stitched him up, who had been the first to ride him. On his side plate appeared a bread roll. It must have been placed there while his eyes were on the smoke. He looked about him but there was no sign of its server. Who had set up this table for him? He did not know.

After the swing, selection of what food went into his meals were the jobs of others. Men in white dresses, of a different kind to the hotel, with precise measurements in portions prepared in a food laboratory rather than any chef's kitchen. He was the model German, so food was something administered, like drug feed for a prize stallion. He had no say otherwise, taste had no bearing. This was extreme nutrition. The Nazis had special diet kitchens for their soldiers, you know. Catering to any stomach disorders. All in service to the super soldier. He being the most super of them all.

He bit into it. It had a tangy taste. Perhaps it was stale. That didn't stop him from eating it all. He'd fasted long enough. Complex carbohydrates were rarely on the menu. Now that the fear of Fosco calling started to subside with the slide by of the Manhattan docks, he could at last eat again, whole-grain food like breath after a wreck freedive, the place of Fosco in his thoughts coming to be replaced by his Englishman.

Fear became a kitchen table inside him that he dreamed Robert would give him eggs and yeasty yumminess on. Now that his rump was stretched with the mince of a secret family recipe. It only made him want for a Father more. *Bremen* backing out was like the men in his life. Away from the pier and a place of peace. One long pull followed by three short ones of the ship's whistle marked the 1800 hours New York pull away. Almost a full day had passed since meeting Robert. This time was not the ship's usual departure. There were no well-wishers on the pier, just clusters of New York Police Department officers.

It was not without send-off, though. French sailors lined the stern of *Normandie*, waving at those on *Bremen* in North German Lloyd dress—not at him, though, straight-backed between the stacks. Not at an *SS* uniform. Waving at fellow sailors. Some of the *Bremen* stewards waved back, teary eyed. Seamen have a different code, he was starting to see, a transnational bond. Fewer boundaries.

On the last visit to New York, *Bremen*'s crew had bettered *Normandie*'s in a Y.M.C.A. soccer match. They should have been steaming out now with the trophy from that win on display in the passageway on *A Deck*. *Should*, 'cause New York's Y.M.C.A. saw it as too risky to send it on her. Yes, it was clear, for many of the teary men waving across the Hudson between the two ships, there was a wondering whether they would ever meet again. Were their days of ballgame fun behind them?

It was Wednesday.

'I would have helped you, you know,' Robert said sad and distant a while later in what little smoke did sink to their level, *Bremen* puffing along, the city skyline sinking in her wake. 'If you had let me.'

He had gone distant. Lost time in his thoughts. Maybe it was the hunger playing tricks, but his first food after the fast made him feel worse. Emotional. Open to things. More starving. They were well away from the finger piers now, the great buildings rubbed out by the smog. The young Vater was lit from behind by the steamy New York summer, the backdrop out of focus, as they steamed toward the black of a storm. A storm that had been brewing since he first laid eyes on *Bremen*.

'You did help. I not forgetting it.'

'I wanted to do more. I wanted to be part of your story.'

'You can, ja,' he said, Robert shaded red by the setting sun. 'Sit. Eating me.'

Robert smiled. 'Eat *with* you.'

He knew what he meant. He wanted to offer Robert the meatballs within him. He was desperate now to. To take the intimacy they already shared a step further. With *Bremen*'s engines getting well and truly warmed now and Fosco Indelicato's influence in the Port Authority already flexed, he knew the timing was not right. Still. He went hot. He felt reckless. Something was coming over him.

The fog was back like after the French bonking. Like some terrible reparation. He imagined himself tipping the table over and backing onto Robert's face to reveal meatball after meatball from his bottom, like a magician an endless succession of boiled eggs from the mouth. Imagined it . . . but also had to dig fingernails into his thigh to stop himself from jumping up and doing it. What is wrong with me? he thought.

'You being tease,' he said at last, a shake of the head to snap the compulsion away, and a hand wave to the seat opposite.

'Your English is very good.'

'I have no one to practising with me.'

'That is a shame.'

'You coming with me, yes,' he said.

'I want to.'

Robert. Sweet, Vaterly Robert. The creamy Englishman wanted to be told to come. To abandon a son and an English future, to return with him to the Fatherland. He sensed it. Why couldn't he bring himself to *tell* Robert to do it. To demand a reckless abandon. To order the man at the table. To plant a seed of treachery in a perfect Englishman. Because he cared for the man? Because he couldn't guarantee a win in the war to come? Because he foresaw only defeat on his own path? Because while the idea of having the young Father eat meatballs from his bum might sound like fun, in principle. In practice, well, it might get messy fast? All of it.

Robert was a bit out of breath, he now noticed. Could this father, for all the years the man had on him, be as nervous as he was? Robert also carried a kit bag. A brownshirt came upon them.

'Sorry, I got lost in this great ship,' Robert said, a wave of the man away. 'Please tell your captain I will share a drink with him another time, and the pilot that I will be there in time to return to harbour.'

The brownshirt was out of breath, too. What was all this, he wondered. Sweating. Feeling unwell himself. That damned fog. But still with it enough to give the guard a curt wave himself to leave them. The time he had with Robert was limited. The father had made intentions to leave clear. He wasn't prepared to share anything of their time with one of the brownshirts.

'Share the sunset place with me, ja?' he said after they were alone again, trying hard to sound older than Robert made him feel deep, down there.

'What happened yesterday? Where did you stay last night?' Robert said, still standing. Resisting. Broad-footed like the father might take up stance at a urinal in an officer's ship restroom.

Which of the two was the easier to answer?

Would he give his Englishman the truth? Afterall, it was almost exactly to the minute only twenty-four hours since he had met the man. Of course, he shouldn't. He must lie. And yet, with a simple asking, he couldn't. Robert had some power over him that he couldn't understand.

'I discussing about the topic with an Italian friend, he speeding things on the docks. Pressing Port Authority persons. The "yes, we leaving" came through on this morning.' What compelled him to reveal that?

Robert sunk into the seat opposite at their lonely dining place between *Bremen*'s stacks—and sighed.

'Seems you didn't need me. I'm not sure I could have got that clearance for you. Certain I couldn't as quickly as your Italian friend—it came through at four-thirty this afternoon, I understand. Flying colours. No violations. Was he an officer from *Roma*?'

He knew of course of the Italian Line ship. He didn't answer. His head was a muddle, but he was not so reckless as to let slip a mafia connection . . . not yet.

'What did this Italian ask of you in return?' Robert then asked.

He tried to stop himself from answering. But was powerless.

'I doing dinner with him,' he said.

Robert nodded. 'You are of that age where men will do things for you. The mafia run much of New York. That was a smart move, to seek out this man. Just dinner?'

'Ja,' he said. Not lying, but not a whole truth, either. He had to draw blood from his thigh to resist detail spilling out, like that he became—was currently—*Bowl of Fosco*. What power Robert had . . . he was glad Robert was the one to say mafia, because he was close to blurting that out, too. Made nervous by the obvious association between Italian friend and wiseguy.

'And do you know why the elected authorities were so keen to keep *Bremen* here?'

He thought this was obvious too. War was a certainty now. But that couldn't have been what Robert had meant. 'Teach me,' he said.

'Ah, you'll like this,' Robert said with a smile that let the first raindrops of the storm run over the father's teeth. 'Because of Kaiser Wilhelm.'

He did not expect that. He turned his head to one side. 'I do not understand. You learning me, ja.'

'Let this be my first lesson then, son. And maybe the most important one for years to come. The reason I can't come with you, in part, is because of my son. In part because of my men. But also, and this hurts the most, because of my country. Because of my ship, *Aquitania*, and all the others, which are satellites of

Britain and the struggles at sea. The clashes of these symbols, the great rivalries in merchant shipping between Britain, France, Italy and your own Germany. The relentless quest for pride.

'These symbols will—I feel it, *truly, I do*—these ships will come to mean everything. To you and me, and maybe, just maybe, the outcome of the entire war we all know comes. And it all started with the S.S. *Kaiser Wilhelm der Grosse*—like *Bremen*, of the North German Lloyd shipping company. The biggest, the fasted. Dreamed up by the Kaiser after seeing the White Star Line's R.M.S. *Teutonic*, launched at the very end of the last century. Setting the standard for this one. *Teutonic* showed the potential of armed merchant cruisers. *Kaiser Wilhelm* did too, in the Great War, turned so deathly effective. Word is around the docks that you might have munitions under your swimming pool?'

He did not answer. He did not know. Terrified by the knowledge that he would have told Robert if he did. What had come over him?

'I will stay with you for the pilot, the man is a good friend of mine,' Robert said as plates of food were set before them by a team of servers that had not been there before Robert arrived. 'Until I know you are safe. Out of the harbour. Then I'll go.'

Robert's dejectedness stayed for a dinner of sausage and sauerkraut, washed down with schnapps and followed by a warm apple strudel. Dinner all served on first-class china, white with the North German Lloyd crest in blue. It was very, very naughty of him to feast like this. And not what the Englishman sought, an indulgent sunset meal. Here was a man longing for a firm hand to hold into a cause, however ruinous. He wanted that too. But did nothing. Curious, he thought. Distracted by plotting routes to market for the meal in the bum. *Who to feed it to?* What was wrong with him?

The last meatball to be pressed into him crowned at his opening. He had to press down the urge, pull the meat back in. Resist the want, this time imagined as a grab hold of Robert by the hand to lead a path into one of the *Grand Suites de Luxe* to deliver a meatball dinner direct into Robert's mouth—how perfect, an American immigrant dream of a dish. How his Englishman would relish the meat in his rump. Or maybe, he thought, he could pull Robert into *Palm Court* on *Main Promenade Deck*, for a less anal romance, to show Robert that he had complete run of the ship. He thought on how Robert might marvel at *Bremen*'s split-funnel design that gave ample space to salon and entertaining spaces. After *Aquitania*, a game change certainly.

Now was the time. The *Statue of Liberty*, the gift from France, the "fuck you" to the tyranny of the British. It had drawn the men onto the decks open to the sky, they climbed her rigging to wave the symbol bye-bye. They could laugh at that, he thought, from their ship garden. Robert could self-loath in that rare way that only a good father can. They could make a go of it. Run into ruin together.

But. He. Let the moments pass. Let the fog confuse him, and instead of plotting a stow away they ate separate meals on cold plates as somewhere else on the deck the sounds of Nazis singing *Horst Wessel* while performing the Heil Hitler salute at the passing of the lady of liberty sounded. That only made their own silence sting more. Wedging them apart like a determined tugboat. Not until even the *Empire State Building* was a total blur—shimmering in the hot rain of the New York distance—did Robert at last speak again. Leaning across the table, Robert wiped some powder from his cheek, come off the bread roll he'd eaten when alone.

He leaned in, too. They were close now, in the manner of two spies at a dignitary dinner.

'Why are you so special?' Robert whispered. 'Tell me, I need to know. You must tell me before I go.'

He pulled back a little, but Robert's hand caught his to show it was not meant with malice. He hadn't taken it as such. He knew what his English rider meant. Why was it he had all this power? All this influence. The whole *Sun Deck Restaurant* to themselves. It sounded so unreal as the answer to Robert's question rose inside him. Like something out of that boys' adventure book where he had pictured this officer's cabin after his bonk. The tale of the lad from East Prussia who finds himself in secret command of the whole of Germany's most famous liner. Racing home against all manner of threat. Pure fantasy.

He leaned back in his chair, the rain spits now turned to windblown licks of an Atlantic storm, and the rumble of thunder coming just in time for his mouth to open. He'd make something up, of course. Though a look at him might make them guess, he'd never told his story. How he came to enjoy the protection he did. Why he moved around in castles with his own guard. Not another soul in the Reich outside of the circle. Certainly, he wasn't about to start with some Englishman with loyalties declared elsewhere, about to leave him on the eve of certain war.

Ja, he'd lie. He told himself that right up to the end. Was sure he would lie. Until, like the splay of his arse cheeks to the flip of a wiseguy, he felt compelled beyond all means of stopping it to open his most intimate folds so that another man might see the origin of the truth inside him. So that a father might know him, the son of a people:

'Because I being the one-thousand-year model of the Germanic man.'

He was the meat puppet of the Reich, a mythically medical thing. The truth of his plucking from an East Prussian swing so as to stand muscle taut and in wrestle poses as the perfect Aryan specimen came out of him and across the table with all the scourge of a tummy bug. As much as he tried, he couldn't hold it in. Robert didn't dismiss his story outright, like the Father normally would a son's tall tales. It wouldn't have hit like a bum whipping had the man. He knew it were fantastic, yes. But then, so was the Nazis' fucked-up, superior-race worldview, all based on selective truths rooted more in myth than testable fact. In illusion powered by pseudoscience. Well . . . even the pseudosciences had their field days. Whole expeditions plotted across the globe, led by young German explorers eager for some dirt on their knees, grappling-hook grabbing through ancient caves, rolling about in safari adventures rooted in a hunt for the origins of their master race. This was the ancestral heritage *SS* research organisation, *Das Ahnenerbe*, founded by Himmler.

These men's travels through Scandinavia, wider Europe and the Far East were already legendary, chronicled in *Time* and *National Geographic*. But the hunt for the origins of the Aryan race obsessed itself at home, too. More secretly. Laboratories and human experimentation without ethics tore the limits of accepted principles in cutting into bodies of finely formed young men, mixing archaeology and genetics in highly fatal transfusions between exemplars of the Nordic look. Specimens from dusty tombs and looted relics of the world's earliest civilisations stitched and switched into bodies of the most beautiful men of the Reich.

Long before Hitler, before the mutinies of the Imperial Navy broke the heart of the last Prussian king, before even the Great War, in an age of Kaisers not yet toppled. Before all of this, secret societies of men met to plot a return to romanticised opuses of the past. *Germanenorden* or Germanic Order was just one, founded in Berlin in 1912. With a swastika as part of its symbolism and an interest in reviving the Teutonic Order, it would play a part in bringing a certain party to power. Yes, that's the one. Now that the swastika was the national flag, following Hitler's outrage at it being torn from *Bremen*'s deck during an earlier visit to New York. Now that it flew at the stern of this ship, with the great skyline of New York City as its canvas. Now that has happened, ideas once confined to secret Berlin gatherings were being taught in schools. All those stages were set. Steps towards a final solution that would cleanse the Germanic bloodline for all time were underway.

Imagine. To be able to *point to* . . . to give a lay man, spectacled, pasty, with no aesthetic merits and even less scientific background, to say to that man and a club-footed illusionist, *look! here he is, we found him*, here is not only proof of a tie to the Teutons, to Germans as the original Nordic Aryans. Not only that, but too, using "science." To say to that man, here is the Holy Grail that previous crusades failed to find. Here *he* is, here is "the One," and it is from him that, like Adam, all pure men shall come. All proper Germans. And he was plucked as a boy from a lakeside of the land of Kings. Of course, it had to be East Prussia.

Was it such a stretch? For Himmler to hunt for such a thing as the modern origin of the species. This was the man who'd selected a Büren castle as the cult site for the *SS* and future centre of the whole world, based on occultist advice. Who'd showed a lovingness for the total tumble into fringe science and ultimate trust in eugenics. Surely not all that far-fetched when a mere corporal of the Great War is now the accepted saviour of the German peoples. The last King of

Prussia, Wilhelm II, abdicated following revolution in '18 and lives in exile. The last in a three-century Prussian bloodline. But what is three in the grand scheme of a thousand-year Reich? And where better to ensconce the new *symbol* of a Teutonic King than in the mythical realm of East Prussian castles? Where he had bounced between since being plucked as a young boy.

Robert stayed schtum as his command of English was tested. Schtum during and in the afters of his scattered setting out of his ceremonial role in the New World Order. Unblinking, even, as heavy rain filled their empty plates, Robert's face frozen with all the surprise of a birdie when water was poured into a dried out old bird bath. Although in his head it was all perfectly clear. Perfectly rational. A glint in a father's eye told him language was failing him. Though in his head, just his head, he could draw on any number of cases-in-point to demonstrate that him being snatched as a boy from the fields of Europe's bread bowl to be groomed as the totem of his people was one of the less bizarre missions to come out of Berlin.

What about the Spear of Destiny? The very instrument with which Roman legionary Gaius Cassius Longinus is said to have pierced the side of Christ at the Crucifixion. How it so obsessed Hitler that in the days after *Anschluss*, the annexation of Austria in March '38, the Führer journeyed personally to *Hofburg Museum* in Vienna to claim it, entombing the spear beneath *Nuremberg Fortress* along with relics of the Holy Roman Empire, whose reign was close to one thousand years. Himmler had had a replica of the spear in the man's private quarters since '35. He'd seen it. O yes, occultism and the hunt for holy relics were the lifeblood of Nazism and the German future. And he had been deemed the Reich's greatest breathing talisman.

And now he had his first mission, was not only a symbolic thing. What he wished for—*a real purpose*—had come. He was to get *Bremen* home, just he. Only he. Probably because men would fall to their knees and follow him who was so pure-looking. He was one of the many public works, in the flesh. Fosco had succumbed already. Why should that not continue, ja?

All this was clear in his head, but to try and convey it in whispers over the whistle of a steamship, the singing of a crew, the waking of the turbines and in English he rarely got the chance to practise . . . he couldn't. And was feeling fevered. Paranoid. Saying things he shouldn't. Not able to control himself. What was in those meatballs? Robert looked concerned. But at least did not laugh, letting him stumble through. The eyes, sad and caring, said the Father would not stay now, even if he begged.

'You not believing in me,' he said. 'You not thinking I can be success for my people. Das ist mir Wurst.'

Robert turned head to one side.

'This is sausage to me,' he translated. 'We Germans saying this to mean we don't care.' But he cared much for sausage. 'You cannot telling. Not anyone,' he added at last, giving up on any more in the way of explaining himself, feeling the time when Robert would join the harbour pilot for a flee back to the finger piers approaching like the ticks of a clock to the time of a hanging. Feeling that Robert would feel only relief to have him in the wake of a harbour pilot. Robert would be glad now, he thought, that no commitment was made to stay. That soon Robert the Father would be taken away from the madness of a Nazi quest to put him on museum thrones of castles sieged and breached centuries ago.

How ridiculous it was. How silly. How pointless. How childish. To think that he could actually be anything other than a pretty thing. That he could lead men. Robert would surely, first thing on return to England, destroy all of the man's own son's children's books, in fear of similar delusions taking hold. Why had he felt compelled to tell Robert the truth?

'I fear for you,' Robert said, standing, coming round the table to cup his face and kneel between his legs. 'Make men respect you, son. Give them no choice but to follow you.'

Their final meal was done. They braced into the rain. Robert then looked at a brownshirt standing guard at one of the stairways. Normally the brown uniforms of these thugs were not permitted on *Bremen*, but all was different now the ship carried no passengers. Robert eyed the man up with distain.

'From respect comes love. And you'll need love if you're going to survive. Men turn on those they do not love. In war, sometimes even those they do.'

With Robert by his side. With a Vater's experienced hand, he felt he could make men love him. Not so sure how he'd fare without a Father's love.

He felt dizzy now. Food had not helped. His tongue too heavy to speak.

'Listen now,' Robert said, lips rubbing his earhole. 'You are a treasure. But because of my life, my son, my wife. That's why I'm letting you go. I'm an island right now, son. Maybe this will not always be the case.'

'Do not be leaving me, ja,' he said suddenly, panicky, forcing his tongue, a tear escaping to compel a father to see his distress. Wanting for Robert to grab hold and kiss him. He'd never kissed a man. Had his bum eaten out by a brash Italian wiseguy. But never pressed his lips onto another man's. Tasting Robert's spittle post stitch-up was the closest he'd come.

Robert looked at him with warm, wide eyes.

He waited again too long.

'I can't,' Robert said, wiping his tear away with the mature pad of a thumb. Something in the father's eyes. Fear, was it? A glance to the brownshirt. 'I have to leave. Now. But hear me,' thumb with his tear now rubbing his lips, he tasted himself there. 'You have to make men want to serve you. They need to hunger for you. Come to see you as their provider of food. That's an order, son. I've known bakers to make friends with powerful engineers with the sharing of bread from ship bakeries. You can learn from this. You must make inroads where you can. Make men see you as their source of protection, their next good feed. Their reason for being. Only then will they follow you. '

Like the sage sayings of any good father, Robert's decree felt like it was being burned into his brain. Nailed. Like by a king's henchman to castle gates. They were out at sea now, out of the harbour, the waves picking up roughness as that storm once in the distance spun all around them. The harbour pilot would be leaving soon. And Robert, clearly, was anxious to not be left behind.

'Bye, Vater,' he said. 'Be protecting your son, ja.'

He sobbed.

What a silly boy he was.

And then Robert was gone.

He sat alone in the rain probably around as many minutes as he had years in this world, the storm hiding his tears. That was how long it took for the pilot boat to appear in *Bremen*'s wake back in the direction of New York. He did not hate Robert for not staying with him. All he had was regret for not making a move. Not grabbing hold of Robert's warm Vater bits and pulling the man by his side, ordering the Englishman to stay. He did not know, how could he, but he felt that Robert was lost to him forever. That even should he survive for years ahead, letters to "Robert Bell, Senior First Officer, *Aquitania*," would come back to him untouched, not even by prying tracks of the censors. As if someone near the man would know he would regret letting him slip away, know he might ask for a reunion—and block it. Block his words with all the wicked spite of women. Send any requests to try again back unseen. Any letters he might pen lost across the no man's land of the Atlantic battlefield.

Regret, slipperiness and a fogginess were his sorry companions for the stormy nighttime descent to *Sun Deck* to join the rest of *Bremen*'s crew. His impaired vision was in part from the rain over his eyes. He did not even blink the wet away. The sting of a salty storm coated his soles, too. But the fogginess was something else. Something like a sickness. That feeling, when you know, something is not right. Something pushing him on, like a drunkard's desperate search for the bottle.

In the aftermath of his telling Robert of his secret mission, as a symbol of Germany, trusted to get another symbol home, he had no concern for being loose of the lips with the father. The man was kind and honourable and, he felt, would be a vault to the end. He also had a feeling that their meeting might spur the man to jump feet first into love with a boy next time one came along that was strong enough not to let the man give in to anxiety. To bring an island to land.

Robert would be alright, he reasoned with what reason was left to him in the fog. But when it concerned himself, he was not so sure. What choice did he have other than to heel to fatherly advice now that he was alone? And as per the impulses around the meatballs inside him, impulses he had to draw blood with a fingernailed pinch just to keep at bay . . . well, they were feeling now beyond any control. *You have to make men want to serve you. They need to hunger for you. Come to see you as their provider of food. That's an order, son.*

In his missing the man, he took the order maybe not in the manner that Robert might have intended it. He took it as an order in a literal way. Bent the suggestion over and into his own, like that bottle-hunting drunkard might misunderstand a polite smile as an incitement of sex. Laced it in a Nazi macabre way of thinking about soldiers and his own purity. Of Christ and the loaves and the fishes. Licking the last of the powder of a bread roll from the tight fold of his mouth. Mulled the order over in the crazed sort of vacuum Robert's departure had left. Reached into his tight whities to pop out then in again the last in the crowning mama's meatballs, staining his underpants and getting an idea. Vater gone, he'd feed the men to make them love him.

It was just after eight o'clock in the evening.

Men of the *SS* military branch, Waffen-*SS* warriors, got more on their messroom plates than their Wehrmacht brothers. But much less meat. This was to bring them closer to their Führer, who called those consuming meat "corpse eaters." Himmler was on board with this, praising such values. It meant he, as the model man under the *SS* arm, received only supplements and no meat. Maybe that was why he was so obsessed now to have real meat inside again, from both ends. And as his first act in his secret mission, he'd birthed a plan; and it seemed to him in the fog as logical as any icebreaker. Any trust exercise between a young commander and his unit. For he did not agree with his Führer. Men needed meat inside. He already had the loyalty of his *SS* guard, but they were all who knew him. So, one by one he would give the brownshirts a nibble of some arse-held meat, show them where their food was coming from. Get them to love him, without knowing him. That was the length of it, he said in his head. But he'd inch up to it. Take his time.

The men whose love he courted were in the *Ball Room* getting an address by the captain. For all the Americans knew, *Bremen* was on course for a voyage south to tropic waters, having actually changed course north. In New York, the captain had cleverly set up the ruse by requesting navigational charts for the Bahamas, Caribbean and the coasts of western Africa and South America. Suntan oil in the dam loads had been packed for the cover. Full topside passenger lighting on for the pilot, now even navigational lights were extinguished with the new course set. Of course, not even the Americans were that naive, but it was worth the shot. And now, the captain was telling the entire crew of nine hundred and fifty the ship's true intentions. He would tell select men his own next.

It was a time of high anxiety on board. There were twenty-sex lookouts on deck with all odds stacked against *Bremen*'s successful slip into the storm. For the pilot out she'd had a New York police patrol launch close astern and a U.S. Coast Guard ship about three-quarters of a mile behind that. The last would not be easy to mislead. After Robert had gone and the lights had gone out, he couldn't locate all of his personal guard, just nine out of the ten. But with this almost full unit, he gave the order for all the brownshirts, some one hundred and fifty of them, to be herded into him one by one.

His guards made it easy, seeming equally as drunk as he on the idea. On the suggestion of one of his guards, in fact, he had the kitchen give the men some bread on the way to his marshalling point. To give them something in their tummies while they awaited a nibble. He saw no harm in it. He was taking suggestions. That was the kind of leader he'd be. Look at him, he was good at this. Bread would go well with mama's meatballs. And besides, his feed was not intended as a feed, exactly. It was a symbolic feeding. Like the wafers a priest might administer. Not meant to sate but to fill in a spiritual way. So, having the men fed a little first was fine, in his eyes. He set up his little tuckshop in the *Bowling Alley* on *Upper Promenade Deck*. Fitting, he thought in his fog with a giggle. A place of balls rolling into hungry gutters. What better place for some second-hand meatballs?

Effecting a mass assembly of some one hundred and fifty Nazi paramilitary men stationed on a fleeing ocean liner was no Sunday brewhouse piss-up, mind you. But at least they were all together. A good number of them, in the *Ball Room*. Were it not for the captain making it easy for him, he would have searched the ship for some communal showering. For in his current frame of mind, men all showered together, right? *Bremen* was no troopship refit, had no provision installed for the group washing of soldiering men.

That was no matter to the stormtroopers of the Reich in his mind. Though now far diminished in the black shadow of the *SS*, the *SA* still had long enough knives and memories of how to wash each other, en masse, between missions, he reckoned. And that would have helped in the herding, had he not had the benefit of the *Ball Room*.

The *Bowling Alley* was as Spartan as the schools he'd stood nude in after his snatch from the lakes, for the gazing upon by young men. All smart sharp lines with no decoration. When the men started coming to him, they appeared groggy, too. He thought this with pressed face to the greasy wood of a bowling ball's spin. Perhaps the captain had loosened up rum rules as a celebration for the *Bremen*'s successful release, he thought. The fog stayed. Soaking up his head, like bread into a thick red sauce. The only clarity: Robert's instruction to feed the men, to make them love him. And he needed love now, more than anything.

Thankfully, the men had been adequately briefed by his nine out of ten guard in how the feeding would proceed. Crawling in an orderly line up to his bum bowl. He rubbed his face in the messy oil of the alley as the first mouth, gingerly, locked lips. Sliding about in *Bremen*'s changing course, like an ill-fitted refuel amid rough seas. He felt the quiver of *SA* volunteering tongue on the blonde downy jowl between puckered arse lips and the sweep of his buttocks. And he pushed.

The last meatball Fosco'd tucked into him shot into the first to his bowl with all the force of a gobstopper cannoned into a mouth-breather. The poor dumb fucker choked on it a little. After some seconds of tapping grease alley in desperate search of an abdominal thrust that might send the meaty obstruction back from whence it came, the first in line managed to get it down. What Fosco'd put in him must have developed suitable mucous during its bake. The baking away in his arse that had made the mince more tender. Under the writhes of choking, the whole meatball squished up and slid down the man's throat with dis-ease. Though enough updraft that the arse candy had imparted on the receiver what it was.

'Leberknödel,' the man said catching breath, slippery crawling so to whisper it into his ear.

'Name, soldier,' he asked in Fatherland's tongue.

'Fischer,' the man panted, eyes wet. 'Frankie Fischer, *master*.'

Fischer was a muscled man with a soft voice, evergreen eyes now bloodshot with the deep throat. Puffy cheeks. Tongue out like a dog overheated. An athlete and—would be—one of the biggest builds in any future troopship's showers. But now on all fours, flushed and dribbling down the chin. A glutton for the getting packed meat forced down the gullet. Fischer had named a popular German take on the meatball, made often of liver and sometimes of pork. With rich flavours that the lining of his own German arse sock may have added to the Italian recipe. A Germanised meat made of steamy summer marination. He'd *done it!* taken an Italian-American staple and turned it in the mouth of a handsome German into a taste of home.

'Is good, ja,' he replied in mixed English. 'An Italian mama's meatball, was from a Deutsch.' He patted a dribbling Fischer on the head, it seemed the appropriate action. 'Good, Junge. But greedy. You must share, ja.'

He gave Fischer a pass for the arse mince greed. Chose not to punish. It was partly his fault, after all. His lack of control of the meatball that'd sent it as a projectile into this servant of the Reich. This thug in the Straßes but now with the pussy boy lips planted to his arse. His delivery needed refinement. A laboratory diet ensured his production of nicely formed and textured and mouth stretchingly large logs each day before *Bremen*. With all the reliability of the Cape Town Noon Gun. Firing out was easy, second nature, clockwork. An emptying relief. But never had he thought the need would be there to work the reverse. To pull back into the chamber rather than to push out.

It was unnatural.

Real men push into the world. Like how the *Bremen* gets her speed, by that bulbous bow pushing into the waves, displacing them. Real men expel onto others. Conquer and occupy other men. And the shape of the meatball . . . a real cannonball . . . it was unnatural to him, too. Something of the hands of hairy-chest Fosco, of Italy to America migration, instead of a giant German sausage of his own making.

'Little nibbles, yes,' he shouted back in native tongue, faceplant again on the grease ally. He would speak in German from here on.

As much as he gave pussy-boy Frankie a pass, he remained angry at the loss of a whole meatball when he had such little reserves and so many mouths to feed. He felt the upset of a breadwinner with too little food for the table. He gave an order to Frankie, even now dribbling on all fours, struggling still with the ball's movement through manly pipes. He ordered Frankie to hold back the others while he practised.

'*Yes, master*,' Frankie said with mince spittle in the manner of R.M. Renfield from Stoker's bloodsucker.

He pushed as soft as he could. But it was no good. He was a demigod of the Reich. Hardness had been bred into him through the special exercises they'd put him through since being plucked from an East Prussian swing all those years ago, bounced from special trainer to special trainer so he could pose before boys from all corners of the Reich—a coming of age story for another time. So, instead of coming out slow and controlled, a second shot was fired instead, a Fosco ball into the already red eye of his dribbling Frankie.

'Scheiße!' the Frankie shouted . . . a little late. Cursing not the arse-marinaded ball to the centre of the eye, *nein*, this did not cause any upset. Instead, Frankie cursed for the one bounce then greasy slide toward the endgame of the alley of his precious meat.

Still on all fours, Frankie was now slip sliding on the oiled isle. He was quicker, however. More agile than the dribbling pussy boy thug. Elbowing muscled Frankie, greedy for his arse-marinated mince. His elbow sent Frankie, his first feeding, all-foured sliding, making the opposite eye red.

'*Nein——nein——nein!*' he shouted in run-on succussion. '*Bad, Frankie!*' asserting his dominance in front of the more than one hundred men in there. They were all awaiting a feed.

Bremen was an oiled machine. Tidy. But her service life was long and along this alley, oil and oil and oil had been laid again and again without any stripping back. Brushed on without the kind of careful maintenance that was required. The result was an alley with the finish of the inner rings of a wetlands tree, sticky out bits of year on year, layer on layer fallout of blonde hair and hand sweat of roll-by-roll frequenter of the novelty of a bowling alley on a transatlantic liner. An alley that had been tended to by a boy better bent to the demands of an all-powerful *mein Führer!* rather than the requirements of proper wood treatment. It should have been stripped back then oiled.

He snatched up the Italian prize, picking off the odd blonde hair that'd stuck to it and wiping these into the dribble of Frankie, who held both eyes now. Like a monkey seeing no evil. Then he repacked it. And tried again. Taking no risks this time. One hand slippery gripped to the ball runway, the other cupped over his swollen arse lips. Fingers spread out like the prongs of a pasta spoon, to catch his repacked meatball each time it shot out with force.

He shook like a shitting German Shepherd during his meaty ball practice, as the hundred and more on all fours in a line down the alley and out the door grew impatient, their backs rising and falling like hungry big cats, getting ready to pounce. Exercising their deep-throat tubes in anticipation of a stuffing. They had a cult-like pull, mama's meatballs.

For his part as their feeder he tried to ignore the stretching of men's spines. His focus, what was left in the fog, was on the craft of dishing out. Getting one of Fosco's balls to crown ever so gently, to hold at the tipping point of roundness. Then—the real skill in it all—to pull it back in. It was pure. Real male. Muscle flow. Not only calling on muscles he'd not ever used. But ones he did not know a man possessed. Like the prostate further in, that pulsed with the roll in and out of the line of Fosco's balls inside him. Like wet ball bearings in a marvellous machine.

Then, with all the impossibility of the black ball popping back out of a pool socket after a pocketing, his muscles around his arse lips rolled a ball out, held it, then drew it back in. Again and again until he'd attained all the ease of a bored sailor on leave, doing knots and with nothing else to do other than blow a wad of Dubble Bubble. At last. His tight muscles mustered, he gave Frankie the nod to man the procession and fed more than one hundred men out of his bum. Like Jesus feeding the masses between hill mounds. The smallest provisions, received gratefully by tiny scratches of the meat each, like leatherjackets under a Hudson pier. And done with a headcount. And name ticking off a list. For he had an allegiance to form.

On his orders, those men not in attendance were then to be rounded up from *Bremen*'s deepest folds and imprisoned in the *Automobile Room* on *G Deck*. Left to bob at the waterline during the ship's defensive zigzag, like upside-down pufferfish, to wait court martial back in the Vaterland.

His role as leader of men in the coming war had begun, or so he believed.

31 August

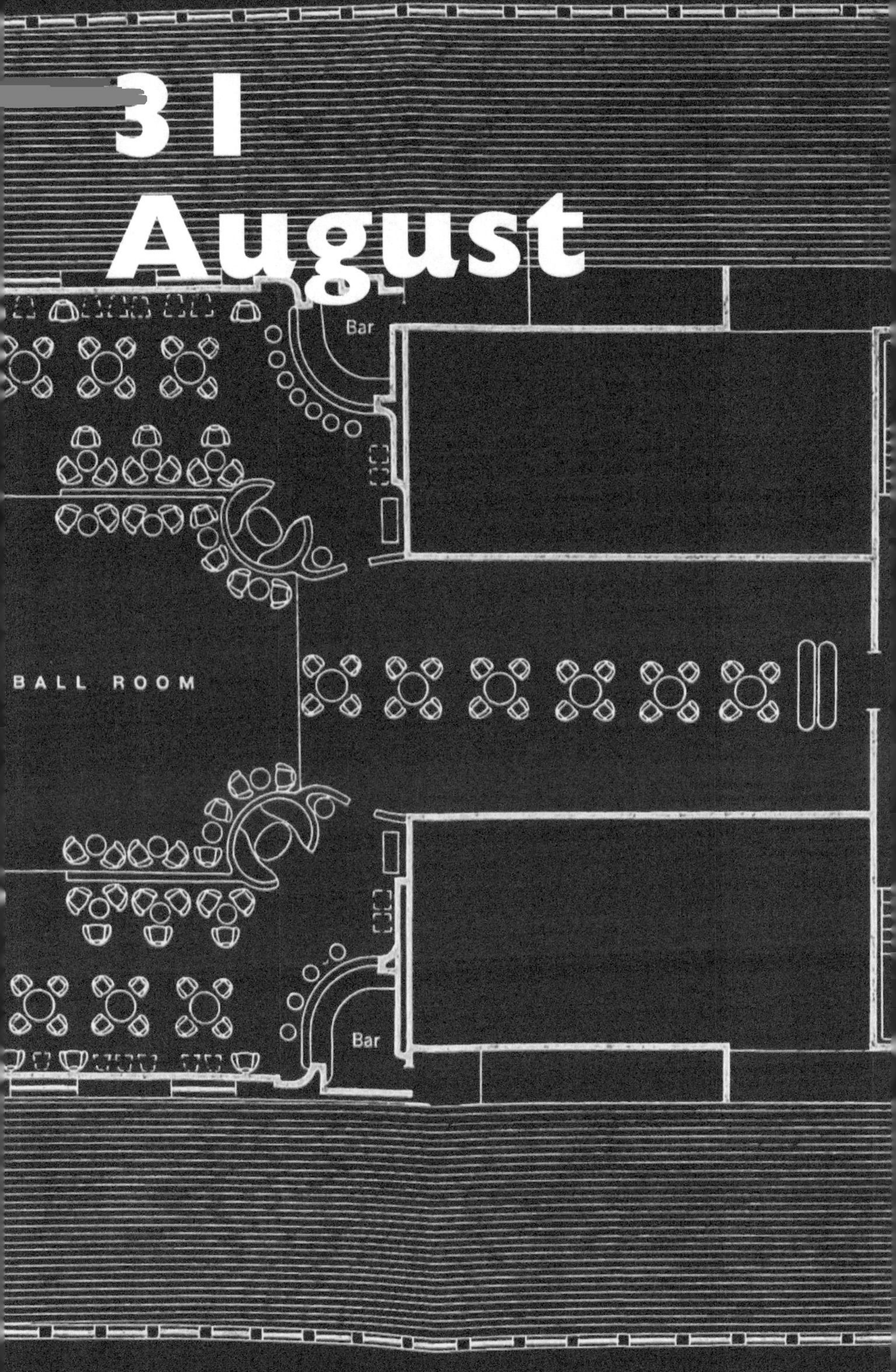

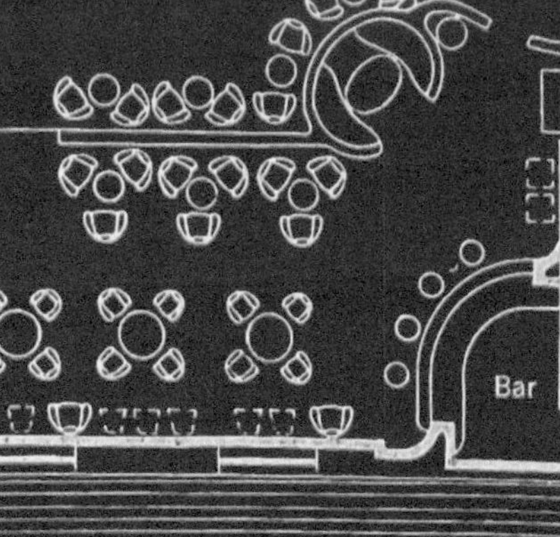

MAIN PROMENADE DECK

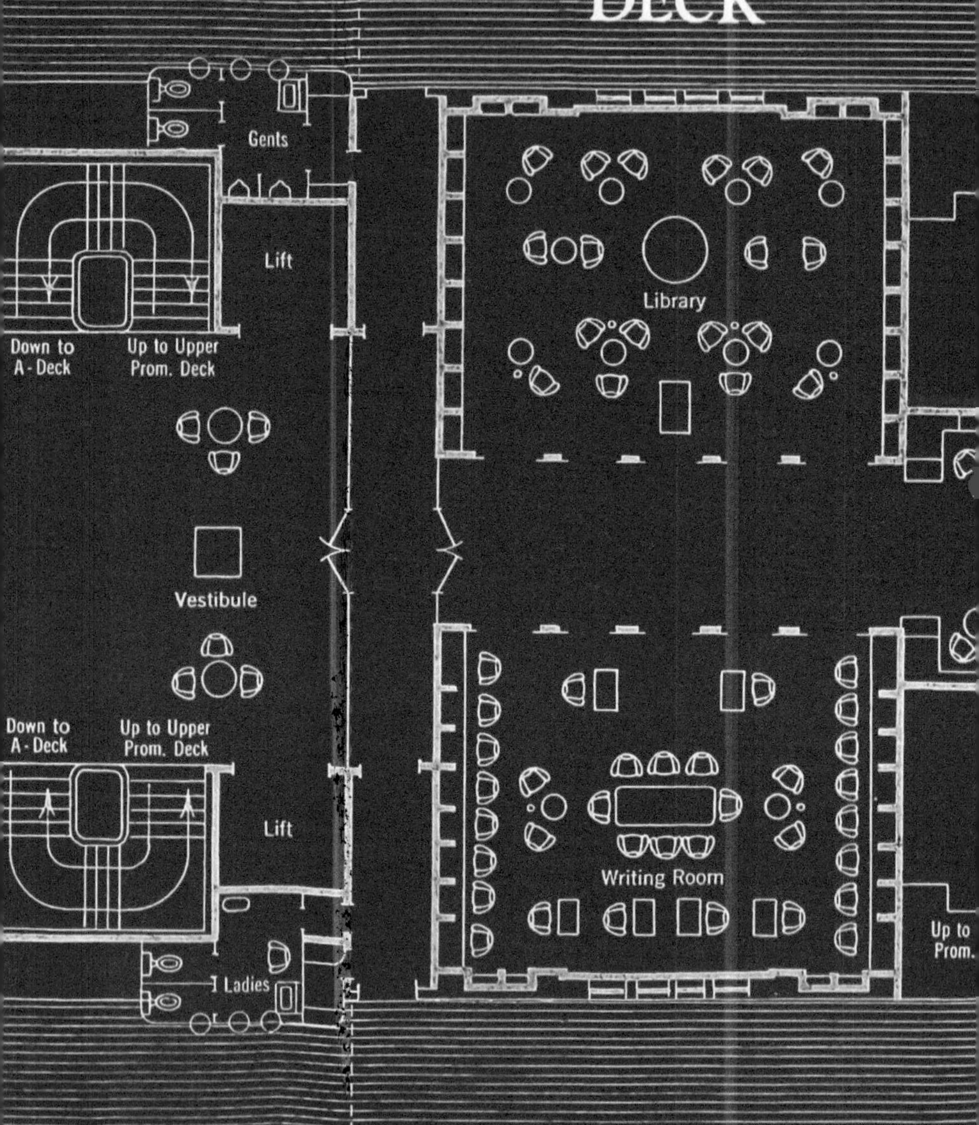

Empty and Fosco meatball upon meatball stretched, he was thrown against one of the open outer windows of *Main Promenade Deck* like a ragdoll over the rim of a toy chest. He'd headed down the stairs next to the *Bowling Alley* entrance, slipped into German Labour Front gear he'd had the foresight to snatch when he saw it piled in a third-class bunk room during the day, to burst through the doors to the first-class *Promenade*. All its windows open. Not long after midnight and alone again, having fed more than one hundred paramilitary men from his bum hole. The deck log for the night just passed recorded three entries of crew members placed on restriction. An electrician for being drunk and shining a torch in a reckless fashion between the *Ball Room* and *Writing Room*. A florist, of all things, for shining a light on *Main Deck*. And a dishwasher from the kitchens, for smoking on deck while the ship was darkened. Yes, already crew were moving about doing what they shouldn't be. His *Bowling Alley* game having come in a room with windows. *Could I have been seen?*

The storm had picked up. It lashed his cheeks in shards as he grasped his buttocks in the loose slacks of a poor boy, to keep them from clapping in the gale. The shards' origin had swallowed the stars and moon and with them any light, *Bremen* completely blacked out and on a jagged trajectory that threw his tight body about like a shiny ball in a pinball machine. It was liberating, a once rural boy on the high seas, a ship to himself. It brought him back to his young boy days, mucking about in rags.

It was dangerous. He slipped a couple times, feeling top-heavy after having dumped his ballast. Like the Hamburg America Line's S.S. *Imperator* before her bottom was filled with cement. He was pleased not to have to see the *SA* eaters anymore, many who he imagined still licking his meatball remnants out of the ball oil of the alley. It was a heavy responsibility, having that many mouths to feed. He did like, however, the feeling of knowing that he would remain inside that many men for so many hours, long into a new day. Like his will was now inside them. His wishes impregnated.

There is something in that, he thought. Was the fog clearing? When he fell next, he stayed on the iron a little. Legs spread and flat at right angles. Gymnastics training after being snatched from a swing rope for a higher Reich role had made him a flexible little fuck. The wet of the rich passengers' walk soaking through the thin cotton of his slacks to wet his arse cheeks like a splash of water on the face before a shave.

It was then he saw it. Through the rain on the deck. A tiny glow of red like the navigation light of a little fishing trawler capsized to starboard. The light moved to him. Dropped down between his spread legs. It was from a cigarette, the body of its dragger crouched so that the knees of a stranger rubbed his little nipples.

'Hello, pretty boy,' the stranger said in his own tongue, in coveralls, smelling of engines. 'Want to see a dead body?'

It was like a scene right out of a deckhand's first dreadnought in a boy's adventure story. Perhaps minus the "pretty."

'Well?' the stranger pressed.

'Hell, yes,' he said, bolting upright. Realising his disguise had worked.

He was just one of the pretty scallywags again.

When in Munich, he thought. *Drink with men, yes.*

'Come.'

The engineman pulled him up by the small of his back, like a rescued slut pulled into the hero for a danke pash. The engineman's hands were scrubbed clean but there was no getting rid of recent oil from under the nails nor in the sharp calluses of the hand. Here was a grease monkey of around thirty, in stained and sweaty-dark overalls. Thick sideburns and black stubble, filthy grey necker about the throat, tied and tucked in. Ripe in the back of his mouth.

'Take a peep in there.'

The engineman had taken him back to the doors he'd come out of from the stairway down from the *Bowling Alley*. Just forward of which were large sash windows that would be more at home at a Bavarian manor house than on a transatlantic liner. He hadn't noticed them on account of the full blackout order and the starless night. Having to press his nose into the salt spray on the glass to see in. And even when pressed up, only after his eyes adjusted some did the body come into shape.

How had the oil man spotted this one? he thought.

The oily-fingernailed hand that'd tugged him to his feet and then the sash ventured to his rump now, hardened fingers wandering like a crab's legs dancing in sea foam. The engineman joining his nose on the glass.

'Want to touch a dead body, pretty boy?'

Freed by the possibilities of his rural farm boy disguise, he nodded with the same upright excitement as before.

Would we poke him with a stick, like kids might a dead vagrant under a bridge, he wondered in a hot rush. *Or could rub our hands over him, yes.*

'Naughty boy,' the engineman said with a squeeze and release, one hand on the glass of the window.

Could my thoughts be heard?

'We better be quick,' the engineman said, pushing up with the hand on the glass.

It opened with the ease of a greased piston. How did the engineman know they could get in?

Inside the compartment smelt of pipe smoke and port. Bookshelves ran three storeys round all four sides of the space, with armchairs with leaf motifs and round side tables in a moderne oriental style. Lamps reached high between the armchairs—they would feed ample light for study to the chairs—and had broad, squat shades, like how *Bremen*'s stacks used to be.

It was a body in a library!

His engineman untied curtains at the corners of the sash windows, pulling them to complete blackout. There was not much discernible light coming through the rain clouds, but there had been some. Now he was plunged into a darkness so complete his eyes panicked the brain, straining without any shape to find. The noise of the engines and the crash of the bow through seas at high speed filled him with the dread of passengers on a crashing airship.

He reached for his engineman. Tripping on the body instead. As he knocked over one of the lamps with a great crash, light came on from the corner.

'Quiet time, pretty boy,' his engineman purred.

He clambered to his feet to take in the scene.

No struggle exempting the evidence from his own tumble, the body lay chest down, knees bent, legs crossed, naked as mama made the guy. Like a desperate to pee-pee Turk at a bathhouse, laid out on the side. He thought Turk on account of the dead man's hair. Here was no natural German, *though body lain on a Nazi flag!* Ah, but torn and mud grubby, *in no Nüremberg rally would the Führer allow this flag appear.*

Starting at the ankles, he made a survey . . . Skin looked unstressed and still a sun-kissed olive. No sign of struggle of the muscles, save for this most strange pose. He lingered on the arse in profile. The hairiest part of the corpse. Hairs long and black that came out of the crack thick as the bristles of a factory floor brush and ended in swirls on each cheek, like the most darling whirlpools. A slender waist that broadened to the shoulders and neck, where hung a thin gold chain. By which point he knew without seeing the face.

It is Fosco!

He dropped his eyes back to the arse. Hairy and plump and pushed out by the queer crisscross pose. Took it in. Got a little watery-mouthed doing so.

He won't like that, he thought.

Like a schoolboy giggling instead of crying when hit with shocking news, a tiny grin pursed his lips.

Slap

He cupped his face, having forgotten himself and

his engineman. Wide-eyed.

'Show some respect,' the engineman said, checking the doors.

There were a few. All locked.

'Now,' the engineman said—he still held his reddened check—then grabbed Fosco's ankles, pulled the wiseguy straight and flipped the wog flat on the stomach, 'want to touch him?'

He dropped to his knees like the opportunity might be snatched away as quickly as the slap. Rising his right hand, giving a wink to his engineman then bringing it down with the force of a strongman playing the game hammer. He landed flat against the left cheek of Fosco's rump—and kept his hand there.

His strike rung through the *Library* like a dinner gong.

But instead of hushing him as a cardiganed librarian might, his engineman chuckled. 'Naughty pretty boy. Be quick now with whatever you want to do. Now's your chance.'

Fosco's rump was cold. Firm of muscle, but still with skin soft. It told him Fosco hadn't been a corpse for long. Such little respect he was showing now to the man who'd fed his bum and from which he then fed more than one hundred. And he wasn't done with the disrespect . . . it was then the sleight of his other hand up the wiseguy's shit crack, while the slapping hand stayed put on the rump. It was damp on his sleight of hand. And warm. Like the arse part of a towel in a hammam.

'What's it like in there?' his engineman asked.

'Sticky,' he said.

His engineman dropped beside him and slapped Fosco's other cheek in a similar fashion, sliding in the other hand, too, to join him like they were a single man in backwards prayer.

'Spread 'em, see,' his engineman said, in English, like a copper in a detective picture.

He really *won't like that*, he thought, in all seriousness now. But he did it anyway.

Arse cheeks opened like a freshly baked loaf, the inside of them doughy and wet and creamy white. Starchy. But covered in hairs.

The engineman lowered into the bowl of Fosco's arsehole spread, like a chef smelling a soup.

'He was fucked. Recently. A dirty fuck.'

The engineman gave the dirty hole a lick.

He noticed specs of tissue caught in the thick hairs around Fosco's shit hole. Like ticks on a bear. Here was not a man looking to get some batter up the bum. Or at the least, not prepared to—some of these specks that carried onto the engineman's tongue. Fosco had been force fed some man cream. And was not the kind of wog to take that lying down. The hole was all blown out. Like the inside of an automobile hit by a bullet. Or one of the folds in the crust of a strudel. If he were a betting man, he'd wager that Fosco had been fucked after death. Nothing about the ruined gape before him showed any sign of a working muscle during a fuck. Also, each side of the crumble pie were little black lines, indented in the cheeks each side of where Fosco had been creamed. Like the arse cheeks had been drawn open by clamps that had on them hairs with wet paint that left a mark. The crossing of the legs, like a lady at tea, screamed to him a degrading, after-death bum breach, where the legs were lifted and folded all pretty, like the hem of a lady's frock.

He'd seen enough.

He whipped round the *Library* in search of clues to distract from the messy bowl of Fosco. All rather standard. Doors were locked, there were five of them. No keys told him, from the outside. The window they'd come through was unlocked, of course, had one of those simple latches, and easily opened from both sides. Curtains told him there were three other windows, probably fastened. No clothes. No signs of struggle. Books all seemed in order, but the volume of books on the shelves didn't make it easy to tell whether any were missing. Only one of the shelves was fully stocked, books pressed in tight like between two heavy mantelpiece bookends. The rest of the room's shelves were fairly even, all with a slight slant to them that said they could take another book or two.

'Still with me, pretty boy?' his engineman asked. 'Men fuck men too sometimes, pretty boy.'

He turned back to face the stranger. What did it say about him that this engineman seemed to think his stomach was tuned sour by the sight of another man's seed in Fosco? More shocking to him was seeing that, likely, this here was a case of Fosco as a corpse, then seeded. His mind raced through the fog. How much longer would they stay there? he thought. It was so risky. Those curtains could only hold out so much light. And, he knew, the captain was serious about the "no light" order. How soon would one of the regular sweeps of the deck to ensure the order was being enforced bring an officer by their window? It was reckless alright, but still he swept for clues. Dropping his eyes back to Fosco's mucky arse bowl to avoid his engineman's probe. He still had the cheeks spread, why? Did it suggest that actually he was fine with the sight of a dead man's cream fuck pie.

Oil stains on the rug.

His engineman may have scrubbed the skin good and clean at the end of the last shift, but the oil was thick on the coveralls, especially in the bends of the joints. The knees of the engineman had marked the carpet, like a place setting in front of Fosco's fucked spread.

Were these marks there when he first dropped to the floor to slap arse? Surely not. But then, the carpet was heavily patterned. Would it have been easy to spot? He looked over Fosco for any other oil stains. No. Nothing. Save for the little lines by the hole, the rest of Fosco was clean as the stem of a wooden spoon, where only the scoop had been in the sauce.

His engineman got to standing to put boot to Fosco this time, rolling the wiseguy onto the back.

He managed to pull his hands away just in time.

'Maybe you're more for the front of a fucker.'

He probably was. But seeing the face . . . the little gold crucifix caught in black curls of the chest like ribbons in an Irish fairy tree . . . he wanted to look away more . . . *is that a prick of blood on the neck?* As he continued his scan of the *Library* for other clues, his engineman went in for a smell of Fosco sausage and sack. It drew his eye back. That part was as gooey as the Italian's arsehole bowl.

'Vaseline,' the man said. If any would know the scent of petroleum jelly, a common agent in the greasing of grinding machinery, a dirty ship engine room worker would. 'Smells of arse, too. Pretty boy arse.'

He got a look from the engineman like the scene was about to take a turn. *Bremen* shifted course beneath them doing some kind of evasive manoeuvre, then he got another slap across the cheek. More in the manner of shipmates at the end of a ballgame this time.

'Just yanking you, pretty boy. I know it wasn't your gut this wog was fucking.'

Vaseline. Partly from the German *Wasser*, for water, and other part from the Mediterranean, the Greek for oil. A product that retains water. It coated Fosco's dick, of the Med', oiled and up the arse of one of the Germans on board. Of the killer? Or maybe someone who came before. He took Fosco's dick in now. Had to. It was the biggest clue in the library. It was a sight to behold. Vaseline had kept it fresh and engorged. Fat and floppy; it had fallen up beside Fosco's hairy belly button. The cock foreskin was the only white part on the Italian whose two fat, low-hanging balls were in a glistening pink sack. So low hanging they rested on the rug like two plums sat in a gunnysack, bringing more oil stains to the *Library* floor, to its *sole*.

He had to look, he told himself. Owed Fosco that much. To look long and hard at the wiseguy's wang. Even if when living the man would never have allowed it. Pinched him a little, that. Now that he came to think of it. Now that there was proof Fosco had courted more than the use of pretty boy bums as bowls. The man pumped Italian cream into pretty boy funnels too, it seemed.

He would conduct a little experiment.

Add another sensory dimension to his clue gathering. Licking the middle finger of his dominant hand, he slid underneath the worn band of his slacks and up his own little bum hole. It was still nice and loose down there on account of the meatballs more than a hundred men had coaxed out of him with a lick and a nibble. Then he gave the sample finger a deep sniff and bent down to smell what lubricated Fosco's member. It wasn't an exact match. He knew, of course, it wouldn't be. His own arsehole still smelt mostly of tomatoey meatballs. But above the faint smell of gasoline off the ointment, there was a distinct note of earthiness to the cock. It was of the same genome as his own earthy pipe. *How scientific!* Yes, Fosco's cock had been up the arse of a pretty boy. A seasoned one at taking such tools of men, for the smell of bum was subtle and without mess. Better than he could offer, he bet.

Squish

Suddenly he had another sense engaged. Still warm man meat sliding up his lips, nose and through his hair, as his engineman pressed his face in . . . got to rubbing his nose in it, up and down between cock and sack of a slain Italian.

'Yeah, get in there, pretty boy,' engineman said in a dirty, to-a-slutboy kind of way.

He didn't fight it, let it happen. The *Haferlschuh* fit.

And when the grinding stopped, the fingers gripping his hair released . . . he allowed his head to continue its slide. His lips to go loose, to peel back and his tongue to fall free as he slid down and under the hairy join of Fosco thigh stuck with scrotum, mouth wide by arrival, with one of Fosco's plums to come in to gag him. For old times' sake.

'Alright, that's enough of that,' the engineman said. 'Time to go. Let's give the poor fuck a Roman send-off.'

'What?' he asked, face hovering above Fosco's oiled meaty bits, one half of his hair slicked back with the jelly off a wog's cock and pretty boy's fuck sock.

'Like that did you? Taste nice, them balls?'

He nodded. 'Is nice, yes.'

'Well, they won't for long. The poor bastard will stiffen and stink up soon enough. Do him a favour. Send him for a swim with the fishes. Let him meet his maker.'

He didn't resist. Didn't disagree. Knew it was what Fosco would have preferred. Finally, a chance to do something the man that'd fed from his bum bowl would have wanted. To avoid any disgrace on mama. Nothing in his fog made him think that it would be better to in some way preserve the scene.

The engineman bundled Fosco up with flag and carried the wiseguy out the window. Under the flag was a torn page from a book and a photograph. *How's these for clues?* he thought, snatching them up to study later. The slacks he was wearing had no pockets, so he slid the clues between the cheeks of his arse. If his engineman had seen them, this was not let on. He then tidied the room back to how they're found it, save for some carpet staining. Curtains tied back, he shimmied the sash window closed again and joined the engineman at the nearest gap to the sea. Confirming, *yes*, all other windows in the *Library* were latched.

Rain lashing and the swell so big that sea spit reached all the way to their place on *Main Promenade Deck*, 'any parting words?' the engineman whispered in his ear. He drew a blank. What could he possibly say to the man who had made everything that was now happening, happen. This very dash across oceans to safety, possibly. Certainly nothing could be said in front of this rough stranger from the engine room.

'How about thanks for letting me suck on your nut,' the engineman said as his mouth quivered, waiting instruction, 'you ungrateful little fuck.'

And then Fosco was gone. Hurled through the gap with one great swing. But not quite fair enough to clear the hull. Banging somewhere between *E Deck* and *F*, with a thud that rung out. Like the bang of a starting gun. The engineman pulled him back into the ship and through a turbine hatch next to the stairs he'd come down from the *Bowling Alley*. Just as footsteps in pursuit kept his heart racing.

Through service quarters and deep into the *Boiler Room* passageways. Then up some decks again. To cabin nine hundred and fifty-two on *D Deck*, where he could hear heavy metal. Was it the anchor? And where he was stripped and put to bed by the engineman, the sounds of what could be chains bashing iron shaking through him. Just managing to relocate the torn page and photograph in his pile of clothes before being pressed into the single bed.

What was it that made him go along willingly towards what was certain to be a brutal first-time fuck? Like a wooden sailing boat direct for the rocks. He could have blamed in on the fog. Something inside him that made him feel powerless to perverse impulse. That Nazi nightmare he'd always feared. But there was a more empirical explanation. Something written into the prongs of his grooming as a flesh sculpture for every German man.

St Louis brought him to New York, but what had led him onto the *St Louis*? This was probably the first evacuation ship of his side, bringing German dignitaries back to the Reich. He'd heard of the plans for the war on the way over. Yes, his knowledge of things to come came not from being a trusted party, but from being present at meetings where men spoke of sensitive matters. Often nude, posed as an object of inspiration. These men were of course welcome to touch and feel the flesh object of the Reich. On other ships, such as purpose-built party ship M.V. *Robert Ley* he had posed, too. But for the workers of the Reich, men never allowed to touch. He remedied such unfairness now.

The engineman was kind at first.

I'll be gentle, the man even said.

That was until those calloused fingers with black grease in the cracks reached his arsehole, still slicked with the oils of Fosco's meatballs, but which in the stench of engine-room sweat and darkness of a lightless crew room deep in the hull of a speeding ship in blackout, must have just translated as the preparedness of a slutboy.

'Ay, what do we have here then,' his engineman said, three fingers thrust in, like a dirty boy scout salute. 'So then, that's how it is.'

The holding him tenderly was ditched for a choke and fuck of his hole fierce. As fast and ungallant as Fosco's final swim. He bit down on the cheap foam mattress and breathed through the nose as he was throttled and angry fucked from behind. Whimpering for Daddy Robert. Distracting himself with the grunts of men's engines and chains and thoughts of the case . . . so to not focus on an engine room worker whipping up a first creaming of his tomatoed-paste pipe. Not how any boy wants his first up-the-bum basting.

How had this fucker of his minced knot seen Fosco in the dark? How could this engineman possibly know they could get into the *Library* via the window? Or that it was unlatched? Why did the man raping his bum sock want to dump the body? Why was it taking his rapist so long to dump a load up his shit pipe now? *That seals it, yes,* he thought as the engineman finally shuddered a load up his gut, snoring promptly as a sweaty mess, clung to him straight after, his own seal loose as the poor slacks he'd happened upon in that turbine hatch.

Yes, yes, he decided as he shat out the dick then seed of his snoring engineman, all over the mattress, and as he fled up to his deluxe quarters on *A Deck*. Through his porthole he spotted a light on the horizon. It was the *Nantucket Lightship*, which they passed under the cover of wet weather at a distance of seven miles. *Bremen*'s silent slip to safety was going to plan, despite some misdemeanours of the crew. The most serious of which would never be entered in any deck log. *Yes,* he resolved as the lightship was taken by the rain, he would take on the case of the New York wiseguy buggered and dead in *Bremen*'s *Library*. He and this ship owed Fosco that much.

‘Well, that is that, yes,’ he said to the quiet comfort of his *Grand Suite de Luxe* cabin come daybreak. Close to the bow. Away from much of the rest on board. The lowly crew quarters and *Dining Hall* all the way under him. Down, down on *F Deck*. Low rank and file had been moved aft on captain’s orders, sending them even further away. He did not bend to such dictates of the North German Lloyd company. ‘That’s what fucking in the arse feels like. Messy and no meaning, yes.’ It didn’t bother him particularly, the meaninglessness of getting fucked in the bum for the first time. Or at least he didn’t think so. ‘Some little bit sore, yes,’ he added. ‘Some dirty.’ He’d showered before climbing into bed in his cabin on *A Deck*. The dirty feeling now was of a different kind, his bum was rather clean after his shat and shower. The dirt was under his skin, like out-of-reach blackness under the fingernails. He felt like others would be able to take one look at him and see that dirt. See the seed of another man in his gut, clinging there, entering his bloodstream, even after the shat out. That's the kind of dirty he felt. Head hurt too.

The ship's stabilisers were fighting to keep *Bremen* upright. They worked on the principle of flooding great chambers on each side to counteract roll. An even keel was out of the question at such a speed in these conditions, and a heady sickness of the constant banking against the peaks and troughs of the sea felt like his only companion. What he'd come to call *brain fog* that had started on that place between stacks above *Sun Deck*. Twenty-seven point five knots they steamed through the foulest weather. With no navigational lights. Beating a passage blind through swells that crashed against the ship's hull with such force that the screws in the mounted fine furnishings torn their threads. It was the stuff of sending a man mad. Who knew seasickness could be this bad.

Scratching at the door

'Come, yes,' he called.

That was a mistake. Like cats hankering for milk, in crawled the more than one hundred *SA* men from last night. Looking for a feed. How had they found him? They marked their passage into him with white oil, like the wool fat on a frigid-water swimmer, the stuff men would rub on their bodies before braving the winter Baltic. Though this white was from the bottles and bottles of suntan oil taken on board as a decoy for the supposed cruise to a sunbake port. Used by the men to soothe the chafe of knees and palms that had grinded on a bowling alley, lathered on the lips and corners of the mouth, too. Cracked from all the nibbling like piranha lips. Nip, nip, nipping on the pulsing of Fosco's meat from his butthole. They pulled back his blanket and carried him to a place by the porthole. A man under the bend of each limb while others up front of the queue lapped at his angry arsehole like it were a saucer of delicious diary, tongues reaching into him to clean out what remained of meatball sauce and cream of engineman.

'*Fuck yous!* Enough,' he said firm when he was sure there was nothing left of another man's insert to get at. 'Come by the *Bowling Alley* in two hours, yes.'

It worked to clear them out. Feeling the need to provide, like a bird to a nest of greedy chicks, he pulled into service his nine personal guard again, none of whom had the hunger of the *SA* men, all who seemed a bit done with him, actually . . . but who did what they were told. *Where was the tenth?* To the kitchens he sent a few to bring down a feed for him, and fifty-fold of that for his bum.

'Good German sausage,' he instructed. 'Make them big ones, yes.'

He drank black coffee that in his young body he hoped would be a reverse colonic. Cleansing and making room for fat sausages to be stuffed in. Around four at a time, with a big pile for refills, he envisioned. He'd pulled the two clues from the *Library* to study these materials while he waited on sausages to stuff in. The page had a list of Blue Riband record holders. The fastest across the Atlantic, starting with *Royal William* in 1838 and ending with *Queen Mary* in 1936, an average speed of twenty-four knots between them.

Bremen was in there, of course. Three times, no less. Tied with the great *Mauretania* as the most times to snatch the Riband. *Rex* was there too. He fingered the Italian liner on the list most of all. She had been the one to oust *Bremen* in '33. Just on the Westward Passage, mind. It took *Normandie* to wrestle away *Bremen*'s Eastward record, in '35. His fingers on the *Rex* moved from damp page to the sticky gloss of the photograph.

He recognised it. Planes at funnel height with a racing *Rex*. The image of a Yankee air force desperate to prove itself to the world. What lengths would those air boys go to prove their worth? What role did an Italian liner and now wiseguy have in the bigger scheme of war things? A symbolic one like himself, surely . . . he thought as the fingering went into-bodied. What better way to pass the time on a long sea voyage?

I
September

The *Bowling Alley* had gone much the same on second rollout, and when he woke again into another day it was with an expectation of more scratch, scratch, scratching at his cabin door. All morning he waited in his cabin, fresh piles of sausages at the ready, brought down by his guard the night before. But scratching never came. He had told them to come to his cabin, hadn't he? He even went topside to the *Bowling Alley*, but that was empty as well. After takedowns of some pins along the alley as he waited some hungry mouths to feed, again without any takers, a meander through the ship inevitably brought him past a good few dozen *SA* men. He recognised them, vaguely, like faces second night in a jazz bar. Once so doting, but all who now avoided his stare. Some of the burlier ones dared even mutter some obscenity at him as he passed, even spitting a wad of hatred in his wake. It was as if they had all been poisoned against him. Those from the *Automobile Room* had been set free, he overheard. It was all rather odd, he thought.

Laughable, really, given these were the men who had eaten so eagerly out of his shit hole on more than one occasion. For them now to resent him for it. Treat him like some kind of lily trickster that had made them do it. Very odd indeed. When he'd done so much to comfort them. The day before, for instance, he'd timed his feeding of the brownshirts with the noon lunch in the crew's *Dining Hall* on *F Deck*. Word spread quick and his arsehole was soon a more popular canteen for the men, fresh to him with still the flour of bread-roll starters. They'd been hungry enough then. This feeding coincided with a scare on the *Bridge*, when a ship was sighted, causing a great acceleration and sharp turns.

But he'd steadied the men eating from him. Made it into a sort of below-deck game, them slip sliding on the bowl oil as sausages came out of him like some kind of balloon-twisting entertainment at a children's party. Keeping the men's mind off the perils, that's what he'd done. Gripping the heads of feeders to ease the sausages in and down the throat as *Bremen* turned hard to port. Taking the anxiety from the men. The kind of leader he was.

The ship sighted, a freighter likely, had been caught in time by the lookouts in the *Crow's Nest* on the ship's foremast, before they could be spotted and the sighted ship could radio their position. It was not easy to feed while all this was going on, his personal guard whispering updates in the ear.

Fucking ungrateful swine, he thought now, sending the sausages back to the kitchens and resigning himself to not try to feed them anymore. It had clearly not brought him love.

He resolved to throw himself into his work. Problem was, there wasn't a whole hell of a lot for him to do. He may have commanded great lust among the ranks of the powerful *SS* at home. But at sea, under the great secrecy of his role in a clandestine Nazi world order, there was little that he *could* do. The captain did not know he was there, so he was not party to any of the *Bridge* discussions. He got his daily updates from his personal guard, of course, who got their information from *SA* men, the spies among the crew. All rather informative, but not with anything for him to actually *do*. He hadn't needed give any orders other than instructing men to eat, and even that was no longer holding. Even if he was in a position to steer the ship, instructions came from the German Naval High Command and had been clear. They were making for Murmansk, that great Russian port that was ice free year-round. And the ship must be ready to scuttle at a second's notice.

On top of his new unpopularity, it was another day of punishing rain and seas. Welcome as a cloak for their dash to safe waters; but still, grim to endure. He spent it hiding from the brownshirts, feeling their hatred of him growing with the swell. Expecting them to come bashing instead of scratching now. *How am I meant to lead when they all hate the sight of me?* he thought, rocking in the corner of his cabin.

He tossed between corner rocking and under-covers cradling like a ceaselessly stalemate game of *Schleuderball*—of northwest German origin, it's a game that involves two teams, a leather ball with strap and the objective of getting the ball in the opponent's end zone. He played both sides in his mind in his cabin, put in the position of the brownshirts then his own, to try and figure it all out. But in the cheese holes that was his mind at sea, he couldn't find fault in how he had behaved. All was in an attempt to make the men love him. Was there, he wondered, somewhere in that, the fault itself? It was on the bedside of his losing toss and turning under the steam of the ship through a storm, like a toy tug in a splashing bath, that a different purpose came to him. *Idiot! The murder. That's your job to do, yes. Solve it!* Just why it had taken his mind so long to think this way, he could not say. The wobble was still with him—two nights now. The fog of the brain. His one-mindedness on Robert's instruction to feed. It lingered, like mist on a fjord that refused to lift.

His eyelids snapped open with the idea of sleuthing. Just for a moment. A mad glimmer of something to do. Every distraction for a seasick sailor. Like every poor labourer in a sleepless night. Every wheat fields worker of the Reich. An activity grander than the dreary daily toil, the toll that being useless on a ship in constant peril took on a man. The idea coming to him as all groggy visions do. Confidence in his abilities ebbing away as inevitable as the tide as soon as the eyes were open, all gone by the rub of sleep from them.

How silly a little boy I am.

He wouldn't know where to start solving a murder.

He bounced from the bed and to the porthole. Hand on the glass. Icy and rumbling under the pound of waves so big they reached as high up as his bed on *A Deck*. He then made his way on uneven footing to his bedside to check his wristwatch. It was the early hours. When fishermen left their wives to head out trawling. Not having the confidence to net anything of any great market worth, he should have crawled back under the covers to pinch the eyelids tight and wish for sleep in place of silly notions of murder solving.

But he was too wired. A scuttling was likely. As soon as another ship had spotted them, fabric piles on the promenade decks would be turned drunkards by flammable liquid and set ablaze. And it would be into the lifeboats for those who were quick enough, as the sea cogs let in all of the Atlantic. Just fifteen minutes it would take to send her to the seabed. The survival rates of a flee into such seas, they couldn't be good. *No*, he thought. There will be plenty of time to sleep later. Under crashing waves after a scuttling.

He burst from the room naked and into the corridor of the *de Luxe* cabins passageway.

Crash

Into the chest of a man in black, into his missing personal guard. *Where've you bloody been?*

He hadn't got to know their names. Never did. They changed that frequently and had always been there, well, since his teen years, anyway, whenever out in the world fishing or swimming or camping in the downtime of being a model of the one-thousand-year Reich. Never had he paid them any notice. Probably because never before had he needed to. He did now, though. He believed himself good at faces and knew straight up that here was a face he hadn't before seen on this passage. He'd have remembered this one. This was a face worth stealing from a rope swing.

'Which one are you?' he asked in the chest of his newfound bodyguard. Warm and musky like a pile of cut grass in the sun.

'Aurik.'

'Aurik what?'

'Aurik Braun.'

'Aurik Braun what?'

'Aurik Braun, sir.'

'That's better, yes.'

Aurik Braun was very tall and broad shouldered and exceptionally handsome in a roughhousing soldier kind of way. Sharp. Nose like the business end of a bayonet, jaw and cheekbones like tank teeth, cheeks like shallow foxholes. Eyes like the trunk of a spruce. If he was marble and pretty and a symbol of the master race, here was the man to cut through him. Here was a warrior. Here was the man he'd follow into battle. Here was the photonegative of himself, hair dark as the uniform Hitler's soldiers pledged allegiance to.

'Don't normally run into one of you lot. You listening at my door, Aurik Braun?'

'Yes, I was, sir.'

He had asked the question with a sly mouth, to unsteady the guard, certainly not expecting an honest answer. Aurik felt fresh. Aurik shook him back to his senses some.

Sea life, it'd taken a toll on him. He'd come to see the world differently, right down to the parts of the ship. Here was a whole new world. Where rooms were like ships in a fleet. The "library" the "bowling alley" the "sun deck" the whole of the "A deck" promenades, with their different classes, fenced off and guarded and tier ticketed from each other. In his mind, not places but ships within flagship. Some rude, some kind, some simple, some complex, some with murder in them. *Library*, *Bowling Alley*, *Sun Deck*, whole of *A Deck*, sly sea dogs, sneaky Q-ships toying with him. Pulling him inside them, getting him doing things he normally wouldn't. Certain-as-fuck things he shouldn't. Yet that seemed so natural in the moment. What *was* wrong with feeding hundreds of men from his arsehole? And a little of it had started before *Bremen*, with New York's *Pier 88*. It started with freedom.

Aurik cleared throat, another ship on this ship pulling him in. *Yes*, there was no doubt. He would have remembered this one, even if he could not describe all of the other nine. Probably mostly because he and Aurik were around the same age. That was a new sensation, one that showed him clearly that he had *come* of age. That the time had come when he was not only being guarded by men his senior. Why was this mission of his such a surprise? Of course he should have a fate grander than a fleshy sculptural thing. Of course he should have a fighting use to the Fatherland.

Aurik's manner surprised him. Holding his eyes. Not shying away from staring him down. Not straying down for a peek below his waist, either. Stern. Ballsy. Like this man had seen it all before. Memorised him, inch by inch, and now sized him up in the eyes only.

Waffen-*SS* men received not only different rations from their Wehrmacht-foxhole mates, but an ideological diet different, too. By way of the *SS-Leitheft* periodical, that entertained with stories of Aryan adventure while also indoctrinating. Think of it as an officer's *Boys' Own*. He was the centrefold each issue, in whatever theme that issue had. Loin cloth, Teuton cloak, nude lake swing like his own home. He imagined Aurik Braun fapping, spewing seed all over his bod——

Aurik cleared throat

'Listening, yes. Why then, Aurik Braun?'

'Because I was worried about you.'

'In you come, yes,' he said, pulling Aurik into the cabin and shutting the door with a slam.

Having given up on the hope of having men feed in his cabin, he felt a rush of embarrassed at the state of dishevelment he'd got the *de Luxe* accommodations in. Suppose that came with staying secretly on a liner speeding for safe harbour. No steward cleaning or doing a turndown service. No slutboys to mother him.

He pushed Aurik onto the bed, sheets and blankets in bunches like the sands of a tidal estuary at dead low. Then he had his arse cheeks pulled apart, backed his hole into the soldier until he felt the young man's nose poke in, letting go of his cheeks to clamp Aurik into him, the muscles in his arse drawing the soldier to his centre. He was finally acting on his first foggy imagining, from dinner with Robert.

This is good, yes, he thought.

Aurik didn't fight it, but neither did the man nose-fuck him, as perhaps he had planned. The soldier sat straight-backed and stoic, nose deep in him, mouth breathing through a narrow channel between his arse cheeks and dick sack. Like a soldier in a flooded tren-ch. No chance this one was giving away any position.

He looked back, Aurik held his stare like out in the corridor.

'Well,' he said after some minutes of no movement later. 'What do you make of this?'

His taint tickled as Aurik mumbled some reply, still without any movement otherwise.

'O, for God's sake,' he said, arching his back just enough that Aurik lips had no obstruction but so that a good length of the soldier's nose was still inside him. The tickle of breathing and stubble teasing his arse lips now as well. 'Well? out with it.'

'I think you should see a doctor about this arse-hole.'

He pulled out and backed up onto the mirror. 'What you mean, soldier?' he said, inspecting it.

The lips looked a bit pouty. The hole wide and well-diluted. All very open. Like the mouth of a puffer fish filling up. Big, cavernous, eager to take manly lengths. But not unhealthy. Pretty and bulbous pink. No sores. No lacerations. He was young enough, elastic enough, to take some bum-hole abuse.

Aurik sat still. Didn't look uncomfortable, nor embarrassed, even. With residue sausage oil slicked up the length of the nose that was just inside him. Concerned, perhaps. A little crimple of the brow suggested. He never wanted to smooth out crimples so much. Like that feeling when just one thing in a sacred space is out of place. He had to fix it.

'That arsehole of yours. It's bringing a world of strife your way.'

He went lightheaded. Like the poison inside the puffer fish had been sucked into that sausage cavern of his. Like being made to watch a convention of specialists confirming him the hypochondriac's every fear; he could not keep from being overwhelmed. Stumbling toward the bed and knowing he would not make it. Feeling something in that moment that only those who have been really sick would know. Being powerless in the face of oblivion. Aurik sprung to action, catching him just as darkness took him under. He was right back where he started, was his last thought, back with the French along *Pier 88*.

2 September

A - DECK

134 132 128 126 124 120

118 116 114 112

Gentlemen Ladies

113 111 117 115

Grand Suites de Luxe

Suites de Luxe

✠ Upper Pullman Berth

✻ Removable Upper Pullman Berth

129 133 131 127 125 123 119

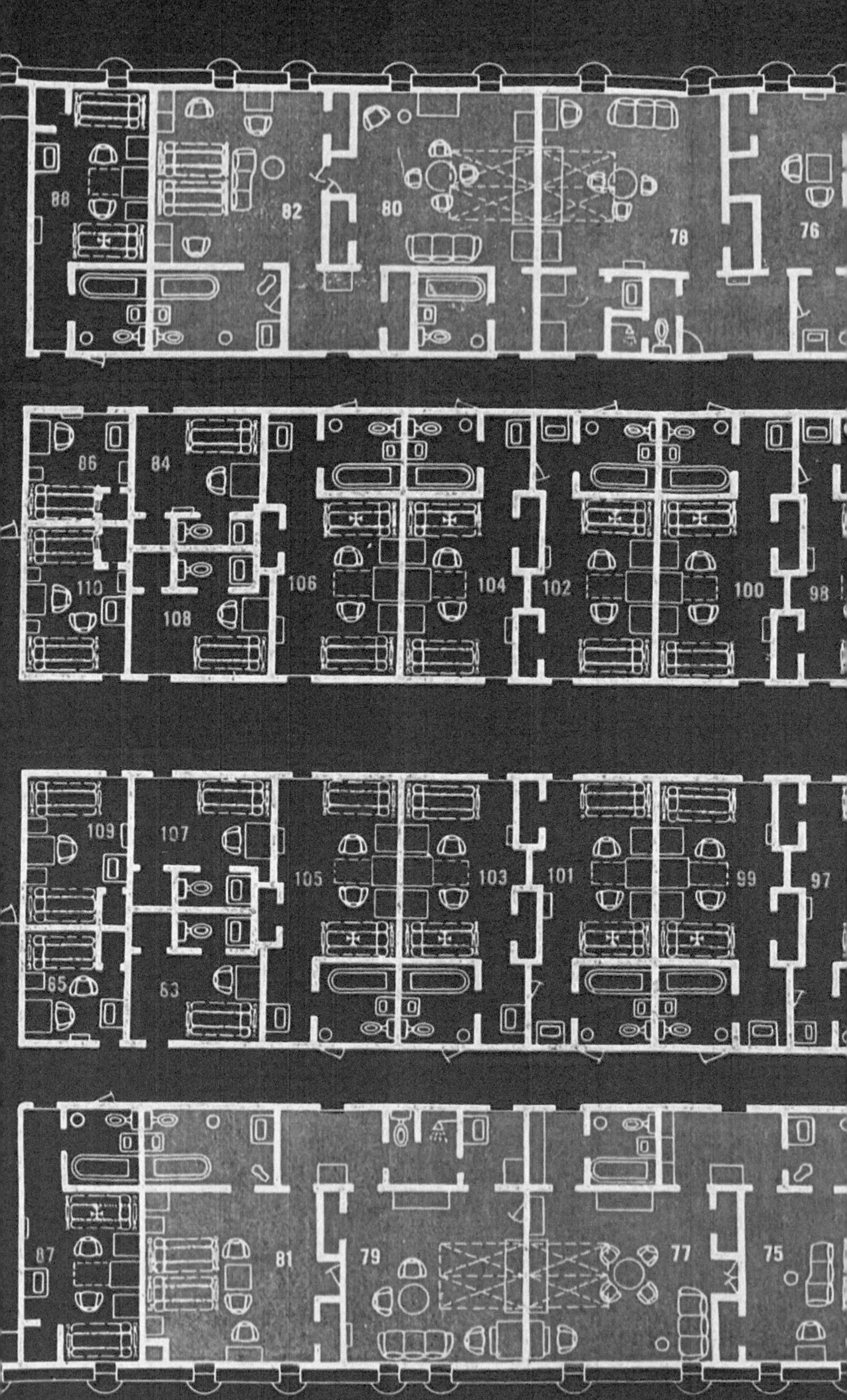
88
82
80
78
76
86
84
110
108
106
104
102
100
98
109
107
105
103
101
99
97
65
63
87
81
79
77
75

Aurik was there when he woke.

'When are we?' he asked.

'It's the second of September,' Aurik said. 'It's a Saturday.'

He had passed a whole day stumbling only as far as his cabin confines and its threshold. He was happy to see Aurik. Felt rested for a change. Until the sausage grease in his arsehole reminded him, drew back to his memory the feeding of all those men, made the brain muddy again. Made him aware of his hole, taking all the good feeling away like an inside-out, energy-sucking serpent. He narrowly avoided giving his grease hole a three-fingered rub, as were the characteristics of his muck head now. It had gotten him into so much trouble. Would he ever be rid of that sausage slick?

'What have I done?' he said to his soldier in an instant sweat. Fear and heat rising in him. The dread of regret having come over him like a storm on a no-shore-in-sight swim. The realisation that it had *not* all been one big bad dream.

'You're made a mess, mate,' Aurik said to him straight, the familiar salutation apparently foreign to the soldier in the bed with him. Maybe Aurik felt "mate" was needed, he thought, under the circumstances. The soldier trying the word on like a fatherless man attempting to comfort a skinned-knee boy. 'You forced one hundred odd brownshirts to feed on drugged mince from your arsehole. None of them are happy about it.'

Drugged?

He looked about the cabin.

'You've got a mutiny in the ranks,' Aurik went on. 'Those men don't much appreciate being made to hunger for another man's arse food.'

It was different here to where he had last woken. Smaller, more functional.

'Where we are?'

'On the *Upper Promenade*, in one of the wireless officer cabins. The stunt you pulled hasn't yet drawn the attention of the captain. I managed to persuade this fellow to get us in here.'

'How'd you do that then?'

'Well, not by sucking arse, that's sure.'

'Uncalled for,' he said, head bowed.

Aurik showed a glimmer of a smile. Perhaps there was hope for light-heartedness between them.

'The browns won't bother us here. Plus, I've made this contact, who can keep us informed on what's happening.'

'You've been busy, yes.'

Aurik beamed at that. What had he done to deserve such loyalty?

'And what is happening? Where are we?'

As he said it, *Bremen* took a sharp swerve to starboard and stayed there. They were onto a new course. It rolled him over and into Aurik's lap. A completely innocent sea roll that had his face, still showing signs of sleep, land on something warm and soft and meaty between the handsome soldier's legs.

Swiftly pushed off.

'It was an accident,' he said, no attempt to hide the hurt in his voice.

'Sorry. Just don't want you to get the wrong idea, is all.'

'Why are you even helping me then?' he said, retrieving his wristwatch from a new bed's side.

It was noon.

Aurik ignored him.

A rap at the door had Aurik throw the blanket over him like a constable hiding a corpse from a courtier. He sulked under the cover but kept quiet as Aurik got a whispered update at the door. He let the men talk while he listened from beneath thick fabric, like a jealous wife behind the drapes of her husband's office after dark. Queer analogy, he thought. The image of a jealous wife shook from his head—*for why?*—he turned to more important thinking; such as, how fortuitous it was he had managed to run naked into the chest of the one man on the whole ship willing to help him. And just when the rest of his guard had seemingly fucked off.

When he heard the door close, he threw the blanket back. He was naked still but kept himself covered for the comfort of his soldier.

'We're in the vicinity of Nova Scotia, and the gig's looking like it could be just about up.'

As Aurik spoke the ship shuddered and a roar rose through the iron like *Bremen* was running aground.

'We've changed course to avoid a U.S. Coast Guard cutter, but our real danger is from two British cruisers. They're looking for us. We've increased speed to twenty-nine knots. Well above the ship's service speed. Our only hope now is that we can cut through them without being seen. Foul weather has saved us so far. That's for sure. The two cruisers, *Berwick* and *York*, have *Walrus* floatplanes and catapults aft. They know that good chance we are in the area. Poor weather has kept these planes out of the air. The weather continues to be poor, which means we just might have a shot.' Aurik sat breathless on the bed, the vibration of a ship pushing its limits punctuating the situation's seriousness. 'O yes,' Aurik added, 'and our troops have marched into Poland. We are officially at war.'

They sat not speaking for a good while after that, as the news filled the borrowed officer's cabin like sand in an hourglass. He felt like his time was running out.

'What happened, mate?' Aurik asked, less stiff this time. Better able to tend to his pain.

He knew what the soldier meant. He'd been under *SS* guard for pretty much all his formative years and had never set a foot wrong. Never rubbed men the wrong way. Any of his personal guard who'd been with him for any length would know this.

'I met an Italian wiseguy,' he said.

He sighed, and set out the whole story, starting with a French bonk on the head and ending with Aurik's nose up his greased-with-sausage shit pipe. What had he to lose?

Aurik smacked of Robert on the roof of *Sun Deck* as he told his story. Sat silent and concerned on the bed for the whole sordid tale. From French spit and fist, to an English daddy sat stitching on top of him, to a lily steward licking spirits out of the ab cuts of a Black man spread, to an Italian New Yorker with influence eating meatballs out of his bum bowl then stuffing some in him, to his last supper with the Daddy that wouldn't stay, to an insatiable need to have men eat the Italian meatballs inside him, to the finding of Fosco dead with hole stuffed in the *Library*—O yes, nothing was left out—to all the clues he'd gathered and the footsteps in pursuit, to the engineman seeding him deep in the hull, to yes *finally* and with great embarrassment, 'then backing my man pipe on and off your nose. Sorry yes, soldier.' *What was I thinking?* Through the whole account, Aurik gave nothing away, save for a little cripple of the brow that said the soldier was thinking something through with deep concern. Night had come, his telling being that detailed.

'Say something,' he said, Aurik avoiding his eyes for the first time.

Aurik looked at him again.

'Right,' the soldier said, grabbing his hand and pulling him from the bed, the cabin and along the promenade.

'But I'm naked,' he called, a little too loud.

'Quiet,' Aurik said short and pulling them through an opening, pushing up against him inside a hatch into a chamber for the fore funnel. 'You've said enough. No more talking.'

Had he given them away? he thought as the footsteps of someone on promenade patrol came closer. They let out a conjoined sigh of relief when the steps had passed. But they stayed pressed up.

'You're going to have to trust me,' Aurik said, breath smelling stale and bitter, of a spit he had an urge to taste.

'I do.'

'Right,' Aurik said.

And they were running again. The iron and wood of the promenade decks were like chilled oil on his bare feet, making him slip a few times on the around-corners moves and the down stairwells, to then getting shoved into small compartments to avoid being seen by those crew conducting sweeps. But he never bloodied his knees or even had a knee or elbow near enough to a step or other hard surface to leave a mark. Aurik kept him tightly enough in tow that when a slip did occur, he was swiftly lifted back onto his feet and into a running position, like a Vater lifting his Sohn in the waves.

Aurik was getting quick handle of him, he thought with pride. He went deeper into *Bremen* with Aurik than he had with any other man, including the engineman. Right into the round bottom of the ship and a vast chamber, possibly one of the automobile holds. Confusion hit him with all the strength of a wave against a seawall when Aurik at last brought their run to an end. It was dark. It was flooded. A wave actually hit him, sending him off his feet without Aurik to catch him this time. He landed hard on a floor that felt like stone. Like the edge of a dock. Were they sinking? Was a scuttling underway? Was this water from the opening of the sea cogs?

He looked around for Aurik but couldn't make out any shape in the darkness.

'You trust me, right,' Aurik said in his ear.

He still couldn't see the soldier.

And before he could answer, got a man's kiss on the chin—a fist. He could not win. Again, it was back to the start to the spit and fists of Frenchmen.

3 September

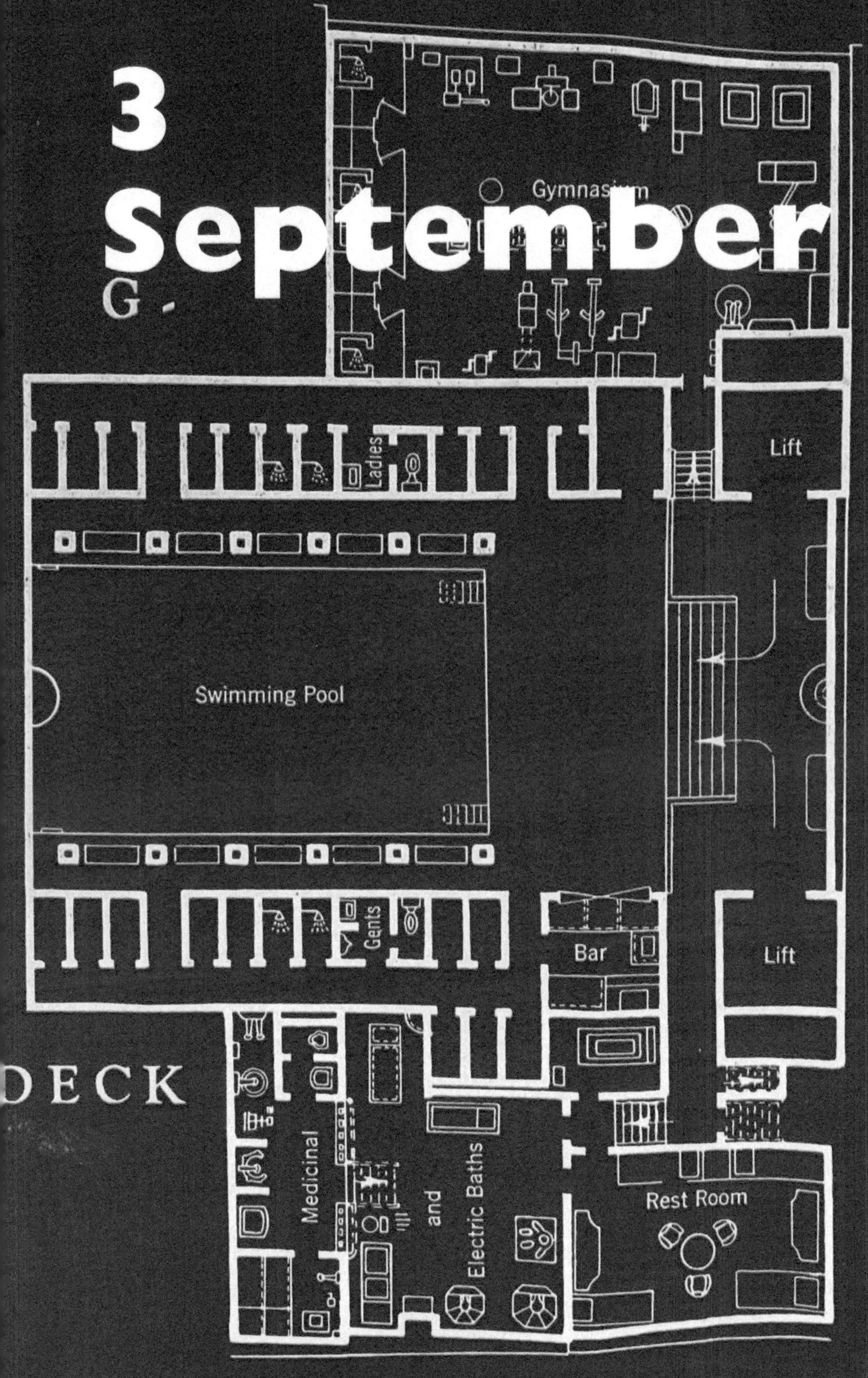

G

DECK

Gymnasium

Lift

Ladies

Swimming Pool

Gents

Bar

Lift

Medicinal and Electric Baths

Rest Room

A - DECK

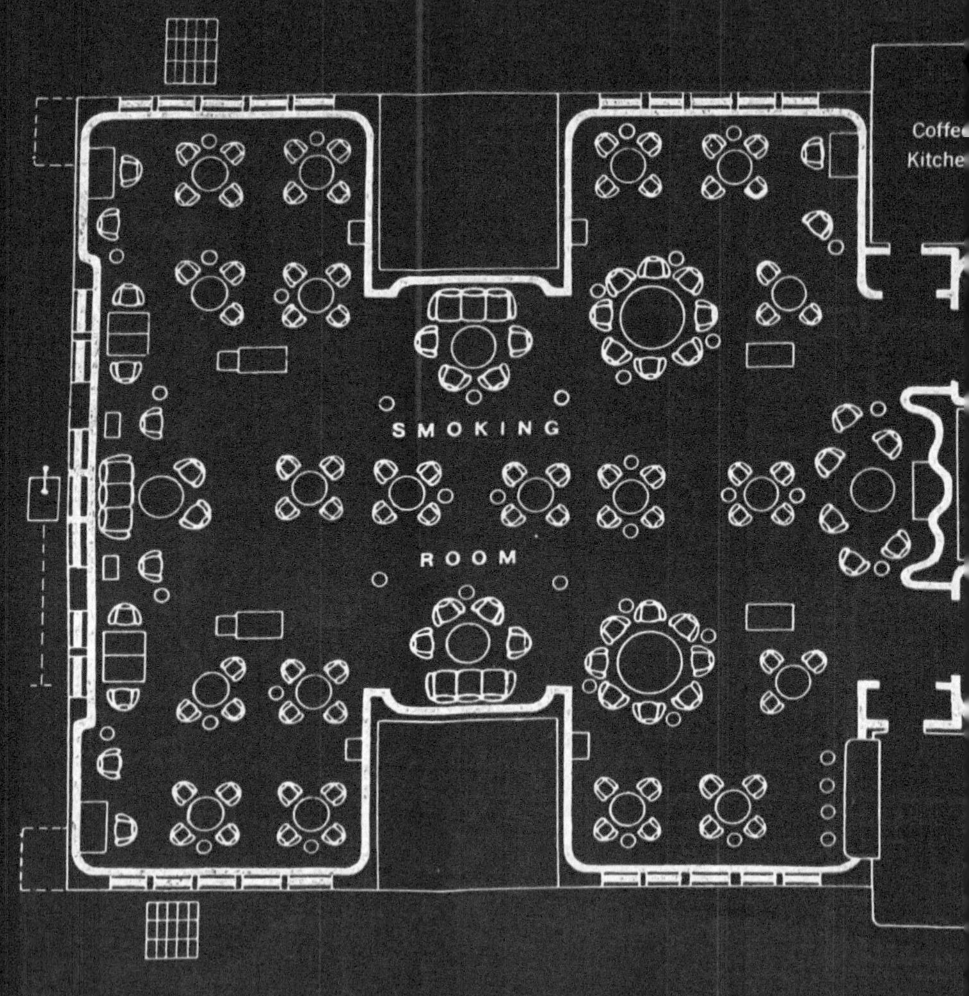

He came to in a chamber of light after another spell. Without any conception of time, but based on his present peril and all the accoutrement that had been assembled to tie it all together, a good many hours must have passed. Like a lighthouse beacon in the eye of a storm, he hovered above the sea. Its waves crashing beneath him, but not in any way nature intended. He was above the ship's swimming pool. Normally it would be closed in such rough weather and dangerously high seas, its contents leaping from its basin to lick the walls of the room. The entire ceiling above him was lit through large tiles made of frosted glass, and the wave pool illuminated by porthole lamps, fresh air being pressured through the saltwater pool showing itself in bubble streams. The overall effect, with the portholes of light under the water, was somewhat of a ship on its side slipping below the waves. Engineers giving their final breaths so that their ship may go down proudly, its lights still on.

Aurik—leaned arms crossed against one of the great columns of granite—sprung forward and into the pool beneath him. Like an orderly into a water birth. *It's time,* the jump in said. He was harnessed at the shallow end of the pool, low enough that his nipples skimmed the oscillating surface of the water like smooth stones being skipped out to sea. They were the lowest part of him, his ankles the highest, bound and strung up at the same main anchor point; his arms bound, too, behind his back. Not too girt that he couldn't swing. A boy again, back at the lakes.

Aurik was only wearing underwear in the water. Through porthole lights he looked fondly on the dick of Aurik, rising with the bubbles and visible through evanescence of thin underpants. His longing to taste the man's spit turned to a wish for something more solid. The briefs clinging to Aurik's cock like shrink-wrap around cured meat. He saw how close they were in age now. Their bodies could be brothers. Aurik's chest that little bit bigger, little bit harder, little bit more disproportionately defined, from tougher work than he. With the sway of the ship, he swung too. Like the Devil's pendulum. Entirely at Aurik's will.

Aurik put two hands on his waist to steady him. His bum cheeks pressed up behind him to touch Aurik's fingers, on account of having been strung up the way he was. Like a shark caught in a trawler's net, nipples grazing, ankles high. Strung up on the public pier for all to see, to rot and stink in the sun for the pinched-nose fascination of non-fishing folk. For boys to poke with sticks and throw stones at.

Why?

'Father was an addict,' Aurik said, as if his thought had been spoken. 'Morphine was his game. We were very poor. And he had got very hurt in the war, at Masurian Lakes in 1914. To-morrow is the anniversary of that. They thought he'd die and they gave him the drug to handle the pain. It ended up handling him.'

'I don't understand,' he said. Masurian Lakes was where he'd been plucked from as a kid. 'You let me down now, yes? You're scaring me, Aurik.'

Aurik gave his nipple a little pinch. 'It's good to be scared sometimes,' Aurik said with the pulling up of one corner of the man's mouth, like it'd been pulled by string. 'Being a bit frightened might have kept you from trouble.'

He'd been fucked rough by an engineman, but that little pinch was more intimate than any deep-hulled dump. Like his nipple was a live switch for a wire.

'Trust me,' Aurik said.

He nodded, his teeth clicking like a male Irish dancer's toes. 'I'm cold.'

Aurik pulled from the pool a hose that was running. The pressure was that strong the stream leapt out of the pool and across the frosted panels of the ceiling. 'The water's nice and warm. Close your eyes for this next bit.'

He did as he was told.

In an instant he was not cold anymore.

The pool was heated seawater. Done so using a novel idea, directly above the keel, snuggling its basin between the ship's boilers. Saltwater bathing was still fashionable as a tonic. Eyes closed as he was told to, he thought in the dark that he had been plunged into the pool.

But then he realised that he was still dry . . . on the outside.

While inside he was flooding.

He opened his eyes to try and understand. He felt himself getting heavier with a rushing, filling sensation. He could no longer swing.

He looked between his nipples to see that, yes, Aurik had thrust the hose inside him. He felt his service corridor go rigid inside him under the pressure of the gushing-in sea. It had all the cornice aspirations of a fireman's hose. Would his mouth open in a moment and water gush forth? Turning him into one tube, a kind of nozzle on top of the hose's own nozzle.

No, he thought, spotting a tub of Vaseline on the pool edge, the same lubricant that had eased Fosco's death fuck . . . *I'll burst my insides first.*

Like he was some nature boy riding a whale, with the misfortune to have found himself sat square on its blowhole, his burst point was approaching.

'Please,' he said, his belly bulging grotesquely. 'I'm scared.'

'And . . . release,' Aurik said.

As suddenly as it had rushed in, the sea was now leaving him with the same force. A great arch of salt and debris from his chamber shooting from the centre of the pool to strike the room's far end.

Aurik gave him another playful pinch, to the opposite nipple this time. 'Eyes on me, chief,' Aurik said. 'You don't want to see the flush out.'

He had a sense of the chunks leaving him. Should probably have felt embarrassed by it, he supposed. Those pesky bodily functions, unsightly and foul on the nose. Nothing romantic in them, right?

But he didn't feel embarrassed with Aurik. He felt more like a ship now, undergoing a deep clean. No. Rather. A burning hulk at its moorings after an arson. An unskilled fire brigade might flood with water from the dockside, sealing the liner's fate with a capsize. But not Aurik. Aurik was too skilled for that.

He was *Bremen*'s sister in '29, *Europa* burning in the fitting out. To be saved. She was meant to sail with *Bremen* as a double maiden voyage, you know. Not meant to be. But still able to be a running mate from '30.

'I'm not scared anymore,' he said, pulling his chest back and holding. To then swing forward like he might have done as a boy from a rope climbed onto from the water of one of the Masurian lakes. Giving Aurik a split-second kiss on the lips. His own trusted running mate. Like the nipple pinch, it was more intimate, more tingly, more of the first-time shivers than any stinky engineman's gut nutting.

Aurik let him. Kindly, even pursed lips in return.

'That's the man I want to follow,' Aurik said. 'Try to hold it a little this time.'

He nodded. A bit nervous now. Like a paratrooper about to be flung from a plane for the first time, realising at the sliding door that he actually needed to do something other than just go numb and let it happen.

A lather of the brass hose head with more Vaseline. 'Here we go again,' Aurik said with a swift thrust.

The sea rushed back.

It was still a shock to the system a second time. A completely foreign sensation, your gut blowing up with the ocean. Another manning your cogs. That one man alone able to prevent you bursting from the inside like an overinflated balloon.

'Get ready to hold,' Aurik said as again his belly bulged. 'Now!'

He sucked his arse in with everything he had. His *Bowling Alley* muscle practise came in handy at last. And succeeded a little at first, sea spraying from his clenched anus like a leak from a failed bulkhead bolt, deep in the hull. But the pressure was too much.

'*Ah!*' he exhaled as his hole burst wide.

Aurik was on hand to help. Thrusting a fist into his gushing gape. 'Try now,' Aurik shouted back.

As elastic as he was, with age on his side, he felt a little shock at the sight over his shoulder of a hand plunged in. But Aurik knew best. It was easier to hold having a hand up there, and he was able to create a seal around Aurik's wrist. In plugging his pipe, Aurik had stayed nose-to-nose with him. He felt *in it together* because of this.

Aurik kissed him this time.

'You're doing so well,' Aurik said.

And he felt Aurik's fist unclench inside him. Such experiences as this brought new anxieties at each erotic turn, such were the nature of a test of limits. The worry at this point was whether Aurik's unclenching would undo the seal they had made together. But the look in his plugger's eyes said *you've got this*. And sure enough, with a flexing of the muscles between his arse cheeks, he tightened to hold the sea in. Aurik's fingers giving his belly a mini massage from the inside. It made him hard. Aurik had found a place of pleasure inside that no pumping engineman could.

Then, with one hand up his pipe and the other under his chin, to choke him a little, Aurik shook him up like a bottle of beer. He swung freely from his anchorage. The massaging continued. The seawater swish, swish, swishing inside him. Dislodging any stubborn debris like champagne poured then shook in a pasta sauce bottle, ensuring the inside was truly sparkling.

'Now,' Aurik said after a good part of an hour of this, as Aurik brought him steady again, his whole body a fizzy tingle, 'start pushing.'

He didn't want to push out Aurik's hand. He'd happily shat out the cock and nut butter of the engineman, but this one up in him now . . . here was one he only wanted to retain. He wanted to hold this man's hand forever, chafe of rope and a belly full of sea being no reason to ever make him want to let go.

But he trusted Aurik. Did what he was told. Pushed out the hand inside him. Crowning with regret the prize, like an egg from the House of Fabergé. He wished he could hoard it for himself.

With his push behind it, the gushing reached higher this time, marking the wall like a flood-depth indicator.

'*Fucks ah!* is good, yes,' he cried. It was the ultimate release.

Again, he didn't look at what was expelled. He trusted Aurik that it was better not to. Imagined instead of shit and poisoned seed and chewed bits of sausage and maybe meatballs that it was seaweed and fish and silt flowing from a raised shipwreck. Aurik's fist an oyster knife scrapping off shell and barnacle. Shucking him without any damage to the living flesh. Keeping the tasty bits delicate and flavoursome.

Aurik didn't look either, keeping his eye, giving little kisses to top and bottom lips of his wide-face gape as he shouted out in decompressing pleasure.

Ja, there was pleasure in it. And when empty, deflated like a weather balloon with all the air sucked out, Aurik left him without the sea for only a few desperate breaths before repeating the process. His cock nodding encouragingly to Aurik each time the Vaseline tub was called upon to grease the cogs.

They went on and on in this fashion until there was no seaweed left in him. No barnacle that had not been scrapped off. And only then, after the last drip of clean saltwater from his exhausted, inside-out pipe had dripped to the pool. After this, with the deftness of a seasoned sailor on ship ropes, Aurik pulled one of the threads in his harness that was his undoing. Twisting him over as the rope unbound, to land in Aurik's arms.

Aurik then carried him from the pool.

He knew he would not have the strength yet to walk. But he felt well otherwise. Clear in the head. Scrubbed clean from the inside. Aurik knew how to cure that what ailed him, wrapping them both in a blanket that was folded and kept dry in the passage-way outside of the pool. And he buried his head into salty nape, safe and clean and clear at last in another man's arms.

Few men will know the sensation of a deep flush out. Of *getting clean*. Utterly. Not just after but that feeling during—when full. The preparation; hours for a thorough flushing. The abstaining from eating. The holding of the water. The shaking up of the body to dislodge any unpleasantry—headstand then upright like an egg timer. Then the gushing release. And repeat. And repeat. And repeat. Until all waters run clear. The thoughts during an entirely up the arse bodily experience, reaching deeper than any unwelcome engineman's cock or batter ever could. The thinking on what would come after. The thinking of who would enjoy his fresh hull, what that man might do. No limit to it. No fear to the one presenting. Dick to mouth to dick to mouth. To a sucking or an elbow in.

Almost none will luck upon a man to do it for him.

Aurik's blanketed hold of him was comfier than any first class four-poster. Aurik's nape, a muscled pillow. They had emerged onto spitting but got only the last drops. The rain that had started over dinner with a British officer on the roof of *Sun Deck*. To run down Robert's teeth and to stay with him since then, as a fog all over. That was gone now. Dawn was coming, and though overcast—a good thing, keeping planes from seeing them—there was a bit of warmth to the air. Romance, even. They were on the lowest topside deck, right at the stern. The part of the ship where you lean over the railing to contemplate a liner's wake. The great mixing pot of navy and white. To the side of that view of the turning point of the turbines, Aurik set him down. Mattresses had been stacked right in the middle, on this landing on *A Deck* at the back of the ship. Why he was unsure.

Using a rag, Aurik dried a spot right at the ship's back shelf for them. Then pulled out some dry mattresses from the inside of the pile like a cunning traveller might towels from a poolside rack and stacked the mattresses on the bit the man had dried, with a space for them left just before the railing. Aurik carried him over and sat there with him on the dry spot. There, backs on something soft, the rest of the ship was out of mind. They couldn't be seen here. Strict orders to stay off the open decks and the dawn hour kept any disturbers away. An army blanket made Aurik's hold warmer.

Aurik's legs dangled over the edge, daring the sea to try and reach them, while he curled up into Aurik's side. The rain had passed, but the swells were those of a great storm. Rising each side of *Bremen*'s wake like a parted sea. It would have frightened him, if Aurik wasn't there. He kissed Aurik's neck, tasting the sea there, holding the man's waist like a shipwreck survivor a bit of ornate panelling ripped from a lost vessel. It was everywhere, that taste. Like that feeling you get on your skin after a spirited day spent in the sea. Pleasant. Tasty. But a bit dried out. Not only on his lips and skin and the neck of Aurik. He felt that taste inside him, too.

The salt of the cure.

He was a man with the sea in his blood and his bum. A true sailor now.

'Did you cure your father, too?' he asked.

Aurik pulled him tight but did not answer. More salt of the man's own running down the cheek. He kissed Aurik's salt away and climbed on top. He wanted no grease this time. He didn't want to ease the pumping or oil the grain in the wood. He wanted to keep it natural. Salted skin rubbing on salted skin.

'I'm sorry for asking,' he said, Aurik hard and pushing through wet undies in the centre of his blown-apart hole. 'You spit on me, yes.'

Aurik did, square in the eye.

It stung some.

He liked that it did and could see that it made Aurik feel better. To know that he was sorry. That there were no ranks between them. That he would submit to abuse from the man. Will it.

He scooped up the wet of Aurik from his cheek and eyelashes, adding the spit to the salty gape of his arsehole, and released Aurik's dick from the briefs. Aurik was small but felt perfectly formed in his hand, and went straight in.

Aurik must not have anticipated him being so deft with such things. With ease, Aurik lifted him up and off the cock. High up so his belly button was level with Aurik's nipples.

'*No!*' Aurik scolded, spitting on his chest, banging

his back against the rungs of the railing at the end of the ship with such force it surely bruised the spine. 'We can't, we can't, we can't,' each can't in time with a spine bruise. To then pull him back near the chest.

He dangled there in Aurik's hands, rocking in a sulking kind of way, like he had in the cabin before they'd met.

A simple tilt would have sent him over and into the churn. He cared not that the soldier had hurt him. Physical traces left across his back made him only want for a physical trace of Aurik inside him now as well. Like the flogging cravings of a lonesome monastery monk, he had the total faith.

'Then chuck me in, yes,' he said, 'because if I cannot have you inside me, then I do not want to live.'

Aurik sighed. 'I failed then. You are not cured.'

'I am clear in the head. The fog is lifted. My want for your seed is real.'

What did that mean? he wondered in the pivot of his soldier's firm hands. Had he discovered something sacred in the fog?

'I want to.'

He started to bounce, testing Aurik's muscles.

'Onto your prick or into the sea, yes. Your choice, but only one of those two for me.'

Rocking now. Tempting a tumble in.

Reluctantly, Aurik lowered him back on. His warrior unable to hide an exhale of pleasure as the sensitive outside skin of dick rubbed up with the freshly shucked lining of his cock sock. His hole, as thoroughly exorcised as a young priest recently possessed, fully attended to by soldiers of the Vatican, his cunt like the petals of an iron flower. Like the hull of a ship with explosive cargo getting set off. Hole wide with jagged shards all round. Beyond repair, sure to sink, a disbeliever would claim.

As he bounced in Aurik's lap, like a jockey on the trot, the spit of Aurik he'd scooped from his eye worked itself up into a lather, like the foam that forms on the crest of a wave, or the shaving cream of a Vater he couldn't remember. Like the wake that marked a zigzag path behind them from *Bremen*'s desperate steaming, Aurik's white left a trail inside him. He was getting the best kind of hurting physical trace. Like the glorious bubbles beyond a running true torpedo.

It was nothing of an engineman's greasy pole. How thankful he was that Aurik had cleaned him out thoroughly so he might have his second chance. Something every man deserved. This is what a man's first fuck was meant to be, he thought as he bit into the mattress behind Aurik's head, of a higher quality than the bedding on *F Deck*. The scene, he thought as the sun started to rise over the rough horizon, that happens in story time. The happy introduction to the learning that life is not always alone.

It meant something, he thought, bouncing in Aurik's lap like a giddy, good, getting-so-big-now boy on Daddy's knee on Christmas morning. It meant messy could be meaningful.

It meant love.

Aurik's petite prink and his wholly prolapsed hole meant he could bounce in his lover's lap for hours.

They could make love forever, maybe. He fancied, the sun now having cleared the horizon, larger than he'd ever seen it.

The sun was bigger at sea, he realised. Everything was when he had a warrior of the Reich growing inside him. Maybe they could do this until it disappeared below the waves again.

But no. Like what his virgin fuck was really like. Life. His life. Was not that story.

They didn't have all the time in the world, so he did what Aurik had told him in the pool. He held it in, used what muscles had not completely failed to clamp down on cock. To ensure he got what his cunt needed.

He threw off the blanket. The wind caught it, carrying it into the ship's wake. It was little in comparison to the liner, so little that it was like a handkerchief that'd slipped the fingers of a waving sailor saying goodbye to all the cocks in port.

Aurik's head went back.

He covered Aurik's mouth as the man inside shuddered and cried approaching release. It was enough to bring him to the end, too, tumbling into each other as they sped through the sea. He didn't finish with the engineman, but Aurik would finish him now.

Just then voices and footsteps came from behind the mattresses.

I do not care about this, he thought as they fell into each other.

Catch me, if you must, as they came together.

This Aurik is a good seed.

Hands were upon them even as he was still gobbling last ribbons of seed, holding it up inside, sucking like Aurik had taught him. Aurik might have been small, but the man's roots ran deep, depositing a heavy load that despite best suction efforts spilled from his bomb-blast bum to coat his fuck cheeks, like the cream from a cake greedily eaten. He continued to bounce even as the hands on him started to hurt, the sound of his seeded hole something like a cream pie onto a face, over and over and over again. That clinched it. From first sight of his hole in Indelicato's ceiling mirror to the wide spreading of Aurik's icing. He had become a clown for such things.

'*Stop that!*' came a cry in his ear—a panicked, shaky cry.

He had cried out too when he came. It was quite the commotion. His own seed having shot as vigorously as Aurik's, striking so high as to coat the lips of the man inside him. No engineman could make him come like this.

‘Enough now,’ Aurik said, top lip coming down over the bottom one like a pinsetter, scooping his seed in and to the back of the throat.

He did as he was told.

Stood over them were two men in officer dress. He recognised one as the signalman he’d met in New York, Mr Wolf, the one who’d set him on a path that brought him to Fosco. The other man was new to him. Short and bespectacled and bookish, buggy eyes though broad shouldered, like a boxer’s bookkeep. It was this latter one who’d had the panicked speech.

‘Fetch us some disguise,’ Aurik said. ‘Both of you.’

The men did as they were told. Aurik was that kind of man. Once the deck was clear, he was head down again in Aurik’s lap.

‘I said enough,’ Aurik said, firm but not unkind.

‘I know,’ he said, muffled, smiling with Aurik’s deflating cock in his mouth. ‘Just tidying up, yes.’

Aurik’s cock descended in jolts, like a casement stay catching in notches. Its compactness meant he could take it all, plus sack and two cherries, held in his mouth like the balls were marshmallows, Aurik’s softening cock a cocktail Frankfurt—gagged in his throat at first, receding into itself to then slip into the chamber of his mouth, resting snuggled between clouds of nutted Aurik nuts. There, one final long ribbon of seed planted itself on his tongue, like a soft sweet left on a lover's pillow. *You should savour this*, the ribbon said.

'I *am* cured,' he said in defence to the concern in Aurik's eyes. 'I just care for you, that's all.'

Aurik smiled and ran a thumb over his lips. He let them fall apart, to nibble on Aurik a little.

'I can live with that,' Aurik said.

Though the peasant in him said there was something more to it.

'Tell me,' Aurik added, 'how did this mission of yours come about?'

'I got a letter with my orders. Just before *St Louis* left, yes. Said I'd have ten guards ready at the pier. This letter told me to jump ship. So I did.'

Aurik nodded.

Resolved to prove he was cured, he curled off Aurik's cock and sat with air between them to wait for their play clothes. It made him wonder about cures himself, feeling the desire for Aurik like an addict's lust for the next hit. It was as frigid as a ship caught in ice at *Bremen*'s stern without their blanket. Aurik pulled him in under the arm.

'I believe you,' Aurik said, seeing into him. Like the seed inside was some special elixir that now meant his mind's every worry was now Aurik's, too.

And Aurik kissed his head, watching together the red of the first clear day of the voyage.

Spring and **grunt**. Spring and grunt. The sounds of a man exerting himself into a mattress, so recently familiar in the quarters of an engineman. It tore the privacy from their sunrise like a sheet from a secret painting, forcing a retreat to a corner of the second-class *Smoking Room*. Getting there called for a hoist up decks open to the sky as he and Aurik traversed class. They stayed naked, Mr Wolf and the other man with the buggy disposition leading their walk to second class. Once dressed in the clothes provided, they took up thigh-to-thigh positions on a striped sofa, like two cruisers on Newfoundland patrol. They sat underneath an oil of a quaint seaside scene—a harbour pathway marked by a straight row of mature trees, with ramblers strolling and sailing ships with sails under wind. There were two others already waiting at their nook, sat opposite in winged chairs, then there were two further simple-backed chairs to be taken by Wolf and buggy, completing a circuit of a round table of dark hardwood with a chess match in the throes.

'Name,' he said to Wolf's companion, he couldn't keep thinking of the man only as a bug.

'Wireless Operator Mr Weber,' the man replied as if over radio to the enemy.

Bremen continued steaming at a speed unsafe for the conditions. She made the knights on the chessboard rattle under the groan of her engines. Yet, he felt less on edge. Had the ship slowed a little? Or maybe it just felt like this given, for now, she ceased her sharp turns, risking a beeline. The clearing weather was letting all guards down, it seemed. The men in the winged chairs stopped playing when they arrived. The "castling move" had just been played—the king tucked away by a rook, guarded from a pursuing queen. These men were dressed different.

A signalman, a wireless operator—then based on how the others were dressed—an engineman and a baker enter the second-class *Smoking Room* of Germany's premier liner . . . it was like the opening of some brewhouse joke. But the faces of the men who joined them were dead serious, huddled round the table like conspirators before a gold-train heist. He and Aurik were disguised as officers.

Do you like the English legends? Aurik had asked so only he could hear on the naked walk to their smoke room.

I don't know, he had replied, an odd question for a warrior type who'd just creamed inside to ask.

Aurik nodded as their dicks bobbed along and they slipped a little on the wet deck of the *Bremen*. What to make of the nod, he wasn't sure. Judgement there, maybe. Should he have known the English mythic canon?

I do. The Robin Hood ballads were my favourite. Father read them to me as a child. While the King fought in the Crusades, Robin Hood made trouble for the corrupt rulers back home. While you were sick, I was making trouble. I've been assembling a rag-tag of rebels sympathetic to our cause. Ready to kick up a ruckus for us. Think of them as your merry men. I picked them for you. One from each of the ranks. Do you like that I did this for you?

He had had his own back with a nod on their slippery dick bob. Not sure of whether he liked that Aurik had done that. Not sure that he liked acting out a legend that was unfamiliar. Aurik had an intensity that was hard to read, he thought now, in the *Smoking Room* as the merry men gave their updates. *Robin Hood*, what man had he heard mention that name before?

'Been nothing said about no body,' the engineman said, middle-aged and body-sweat smelly. Unshaven, not the sort to normally see any of the topside decks. Worlds away from second class. How he hated enginemen. 'And about *your* engineman——'

He bolted upright, how had Aurik time to fill the merry men in? Had Aurik told of his bum oiling?

'——his name by all best guess is Mr Winter, the only one of us men of the engines getting talked about. Weird things. Acting strange, you know. Other than that, no news of him or any dead body from——'

'Nor among the bakers, about a body,' the man in cleaner whites cut in, smelly too, but of a sweat that was mixed with sweater notes, from the kitchen, unmistakable in toque. Dried custard and baking flour on the sleeves. On the older side too, a real fatty. Like all the sweets of this fine ship had been tasted in halves by this one greedy fellow.

Aurik wasn't kidding on the rag-tag tone. These men were not main men, that was evident. Not ones ever to come near the captain's *Chartroom* or even the chiefs of the galleys or turbine rooms. These were the men easy to turn to espionage because theirs were lives that never came into contact with secrets that mattered. Men not really to have benefited from Germany's restored pride. Auxiliary ships. These were not attractive men. Nothing of the newsreels or even rural photographs of noble Reich labour. Very easily turned on the promise of adventure or some kind of advantage from a man as handsome as Aurik.

He was, however, keen to hear more from the engineman at the round table about that one engineman in particular, who'd rooted his hole round. But before he could ask, Aurik was speaking.

'Useless. What *do* you know?' Aurik asked the table, sending him a fleeting look that seemed to see as he did. That these were not the kind of men in any station to help their cause. Though, at least they had a name for his engineman. A Mr Winter. Sounded about right.

Weber, the wireless operator, like Wolf the signalman, was younger and mildly attractive, if rather timid. But potential there. Something akin to what Wolf had already shown him in New York, he thought. Not the same sophistication, same style, but some future about the fellow. Some flair for life at sea. Wolf, though, with a Weimar worldliness, was the real cunning of the group. The one who'd witnessed Aurik come inside him, after all, without any foul cry.

That Wolf, he thought, *will know something*.

'You talk now, yes, Mr Wolf,' he said.

Aurik shot him a suspicious glance, for all his lover knew, they had not been introduced.

'The weather has cleared some and the order been given to paint the ship,' Wolf said with disinterest, the same coat as on the Hudson. 'It will be an undertaking, that's for sure. All watchmen have already been called to prepare the bosun chairs and the lifeboats will be lowered right to the waves. The ship will don a sea grey without a point below twenty-seven point five knots. All hands on deck to-day. Plus, word is that the captain has given an order for most of the three thousand mattresses from the passenger rooms to be taken on deck as protection from possible shrapnel. You can hear the lads at it already. You will not be able to access any of the rooms topside, comrades, certainly none of the promenades, and will need to be careful in the corridors of all the decks, too.'

Aurik nodded, that same small smile and crinkle of the brow he had come to court. Aurik had delegated the merry men's roles well, with two of this group at least. Done a good job with the assembly, given the circumstances. He gave Aurik a squeeze under the table to show he approved, high up on the thigh, though the tiny timid cock of his lover was nowhere to be held. At first . . . in his pre-sea state, he may have been satisfied with just *thinking* about cock. But having seed again since his swim, his brain was getting foggy once more. He dug about in Aurik's crotch until the little cock could be caught. Like a hungry factory worker checking a Krabben pot in the river where all the muck of industry gets washed in.

'Yes,' Wireless Operator Weber chimed in, 'our captain will paint the whole sea if he has to. *Bremen* will go grey. *And at speed!* Our army's *fuck trek* through Poland has closed off the *Wireless Rooms* as a matter of great urgency. But I have a direct link to the captain, and he is listening. I can get you the latest information.'

Weber spoke slightly crass now, but in a way that seemed to make the bookish boy more uncomfortable than anyone else. Hard to read. Put on. Like any impression of the man was a message come through on a faulty wireless. Acting more brash than Wolf, a man clearly dirtier in the pants.

Wolf was the most at ease, better placed than the sweaty engineman and baker to see him pumped full of Aurik seed at daybreak. A sly character, too. He knew even less of what to make of this man, and that there was no mention nor even a nod of recognition to him, from New York . . . that caused confusion, yes.

'Good to see you again,' he said to Wolf, tiny Aurik cock in hand under cover of table. 'Thanks for the suggestion in New York. It ended up being helpful to our cause.'

He chose his words carefully and watched close the reaction of both Aurik and Mr Weber to his disclosure that he and this man had crossed paths already. Curiously, both men he watched seemed uncomfortable with his gaze on them.

'What's your names?' he said to the engineman and baker.

'Might I chime in, fellas?' cut in a new voice as baker and engineman opened mouths to reply. This speaker was something truly foreign, a steward tongue if ever he'd heard one. 'But forgive me, prey please. And do not send me away, for I *so——so——so* want to join your little club.'

They all spoke in their native tongue, though the stranger in the second-class *Smoking Room* came into their campfire huddle with the wank syntax of an Englishman.

'A steward,' Aurik said to the stranger, shadowed somewhat in the still low sun. 'I've been looking to add one of you to our fold. Come, comrade, smoke with us.'

Stewards were the sluts of the Atlantic. You needed not be a seaman to know this. They were softly spoken, and soft of skin, too. They sucked on the wealthy gent wallet, not because they needed the money, but because they wanted to. It was why he had refused the help of that certain chief steward of the Atlantic sluts. The one who had warned him to keep hands off Robert. This *Bremen* slut steward was young, but he couldn't arrive at a number. Women's paint on the face and a high voice made the man come over as a boy. Certainly, here was a slut who got by acting much younger around men; was queer, but also with some contradictions. Tall and broad shouldered, eyes bright and blue but that were muddy in the smoke of the room, like a propeller stirring up sand in a tropical lagoon. An empty bleakness to them. This slut needed no further invitation to join, skirting the knees of the seated party like a prostitute taking a middle-of-the-row seat at the opera. Not there to soak in any culture. Just after a lap to play on. Parting a place between him and Aurik on the sofa.

'I can bring some radio chatter of my own,' the steward said, not Germanic-looking, either, the rounded features of the English, 'what day is it? Yes, it's the third,' then in English, '*innit?*'

He and Aurik cocked head when the steward said the last bit, it was no word he recognised. This steward was jaunty at the slant of their necks. Like so many of the sluts, here was a fellow who loved to tease handsome men.

'Well, how's this for something to bring to the table,' picking up the black king from the checkerboard and fingering its cross. 'Two British cruisers are on the hunt. Yes, don't say it, I see by your look that you knew this,' the steward said to Weber.

He of course knew this as well. It was one of the first reports Aurik had given him. From some stranger in a hallway outside his cabin. That stranger must have been Mr Weber, he now reckoned.

'Probably knew also that these are called *York* and *Berwick*, having lurked most recently in the waters off Halifax.'

'I reported on this already,' Weber said, a snatch of the black king away from the steward to place it back on the board. 'Perhaps if you'd stick to your own station, it'll ensure we get any such account firsthand.'

The steward nodded in a knowing way, like a chess player two steps ahead, 'ah, yes, quite; I take your point. But I bet you did not know this titbit. Yesterday, around lunchtime, there was great excitement on the *Bridges* of both cruisers. The tension had been building for the commanders of the cruisers for some time, since August twenty-eighth, to be precise, when orders came from Commander of the Home Fleet to these two H.M.S. boys to go on the prowl for us and *Europa*. We were still at *Pier 86* at that time, so quite the unfair state of affairs.'

They closed the circle of smoke over the round table, like boy scouts scooting bums closer to the fire to catch all the details of a ghost story.

'The two cruisers were close, but not together when the order came through,' the steward went on. '*York* was in Halifax, Nova Scotia, that's in Canada, you know, ready to sit and wait to sail out like a crab under a rock; while *Berwick* was further south, in Bar Harbor, Maine, U.S.A. Such a pretty place, full of Yankee sailors—*O those lucky Brits!*' The steward gave a forlorn look, before continuing. 'The order came through close to teatime, while *Berwick* commander's whites were being laid out in his in-port cabin. They'd been pressed and were warm for a special soiree at the Frenchmen's Cove yacht club there—all those men in uniform for a dance at the yachty, *how lovely!* Anyway, that's just a little tease of the kind of detail I can bring you boys. We stewards get the best kind of pillow talk. And now, for my party favour to you all. To really show off. I'll take you back to yesterday.'

The steward paused to sip from a milky, fizzy fit of a drink. He hadn't noticed the tipple until now. The drink, like this man, seeming to have appeared out of thin air. Like a silk surprise from an alleyway magician's bag of tricks. Effervescent cloud in a champagne coupe.

'*Ah!*' the steward said, tracking his eyes like sex cruisers in a steam train carriage, gulping all the drink down quick. Followed by a belch and a small hiccup.

'I shouldn't do that. The instructions curated by its creator are clear. Small sips, you know. But he does also say to drink three to five of these. So, I suppose I can be forgiven for getting the first one in me quick. I'm a thirsty boy,' the steward said, eyes flicking to Aurik and then back to him.

'What is this drink?' Aurik asked.

'Why the Hemingway, of course. As in Ernest. I'm surprised you did not know, Mr Braun.'

'How do you know my name?' Aurik asked.

'It's my order to know your name.'

What a strange way of putting that it's a steward's business to know such things, he thought. Stranger still given that Aurik's name was not on any *Bremen* crew list. How did the man know it? But then, he thought, Aurik had been running round to assemble a merry men for him, and this here was a strange man, one who, by all appearances, had a gift for getting intimate information that would otherwise be confined to the cabins of powerful men. Knowledge of the commander of a foreign cruiser's whites being laid out, pressed and warm, he thought as an example.

'And your name?' Aurik asked.

'Kenneth,' the man said.

'Kenneth who?'

'O, just Kenneth.'

'Kenneth who?' he said this time.

'O, since it's *you*, Kenneth Arnold, charmed. But please, call me Ken.'

He did not answer this. He would not.

'Well, Mr Braun?' Kenneth went on, eyes bouncing between he and Aurik like a tennis ball, a to and fro in a match between foes. 'May I be you and your master's server? May I make for you a Hemingway, so you may forever know what it means?'

He looked to Aurik, who gave him a small nod.

Like the final pages of a potboiler, our interaction engrossed Kenneth. There was something in the working out about all this, he thought. Getting a measure of Aurik and him under the guise of offering a drink, like a seamstress distracting a prude with small talk while getting a detailed inside leg.

'Go on,' he said, answering for Aurik, a tug of the same man's soft dick.

Was this to assert his dominance over Aurik or to throw Kenneth off their game. He wasn't sure. It was almost 0900 hours. An odd time for such a strong drink. But they were on the sea's time now, and he hadn't had any conception of a morning-appropriate beverage since waking underneath an Englishman.

'Only if we all get one,' he added.

'Bring unopened bottles of all the ingredients and

make the drinks in front of us,' Aurik chimed in, speaking loud to cover the rubbing of dick pinched in pant front, 'so we might see how it's done and to ensure the freshest of drinks.'

Aurik spoke in such a mature way, he thought. Not at all the tongue of a poor boy, nor his own lake mouth.

Kenneth needed no further incentive.

'But of course, I would only use unopened champagne.'

'Sealed and unopened everything, steward,' Aurik said, giving him a wink, expanding in his hand.

Kenneth nodded. 'Gentlemen, I will be back momentarily,' and swept from their smoke circle and the room.

The meeting had taken on all the trimmings of a drinks-before-a-dinner-party murder mystery set in an English manor house. The sophistication of one, too. He thought of Robert and cream teas, it comforted him. Without an English daddy, he relied on the man whose aesthetic cock he held to know how to proceed with merry informers and wily lily stewards.

While waiting, he let Aurik stay in the hinterland of not-quite-hard, keeping his lover on edge, just with a gentle continuous rubbing that would serve them both in getting the most out of this meeting, he reasoned.

It took close to twenty minutes for Kenneth to return, time he and Aurik used to formulate a plan for the day. Plotted among more trusted company.

'Got to find my engineman,' he said during this planning. 'I have the cabin, nine hundred and fifty-two on *D Deck*, forward, right in the bow. The fellow's taken a berth in third class.'

Mr Weiss, their engineman at the round table, was entrusted with the cabin search, while their signalman, Mr Wolf, was cast in the role of double agent.

'Be very active in on-deck painting and mattress pulling,' he told Wolf, the one of his merry men he liked best, the rawest with him, 'impress the officers about your value, so you might tell Aurik and me at our next get together about what parts of the ship are off-limits. You track the men stripping those mattresses all day.'

Mattresses were currently being taken from all passenger accommodations not in use and stacked along the promenade decks. He had seen evidence of this already at the stern, at Aurik and his *fuck perfect* spot. Put there as protection against shrapnel and to be set alight in the event of a scuttling. He imagined the big enterprise of men laying mattresses, putting faces to feeding mouths—yes, there was still that matter to contend with. The mound of mats stained with the record of honeymooners and wayward slut stewards creating a mosaic of foreboding for events to come.

Still with some clarity of mind after Aurik's flush out of his hull, he saw now that his behaviour and that of others—the hunger of the brownshirts for his meatballs—was the result of some kind of drugging. The baker, now known to him as a Mr Winkler, he tasked with gathering information on food preparation, especially for the *SA* men, to learn more about how the poison may have been administered to him and then to these men, and to make sure that no more was coming through. Weber, meanwhile, was to, once Kenneth had returned and divulged the rest of whatever story was offered, confirm its accuracy. Either through knowledge of events the man had or through listening in on discussions at a higher level, if needed.

'You need to keep us updated on any ships around us,' he said to Weber, narrowing his eyes a little now, getting a bit stern. 'Any news on those two British cruisers is to be given to us immediately. Understood?'

Weber nodded.

Aurik gave his inner thigh an approving squeeze, adding that each man would be sought out by Aurik for updates throughout the day. All were to give his lover their cabin numbers. Aurik would call by, but none of the group would be informed of where he was staying. For security. Aurik made him feel special.

'Good,' he said after the plan was laid out. 'Thanks. Aurik and me will solve the murder.'

As it played out, the steward's drinks fetch proved just enough to set out this plan for the day ahead. How silly of Kenneth to give them such an opportunity, he thought. Feeling a move ahead in the game for once. That is, if the steward's intentions were not all honourable. How could they be on a pansy like that?

'Sorry to keep you waiting, gentlemen,' Kenneth said wheeling in a butler's cart on which were four bottles of champagne, one bottle of absinthe and seven coupes.

Aurik inspected the bottles, they were unopened. Giving a nod to Kenneth that the service of drinks could begin.

Kenneth lined up seven coupes in a circle like they were chalices for a King Arthur piss-up. 'One jigger of absinthe into each glass, a champagne glass of course. Then, holding up a bottle of Pol Roger,' with a skin of frosting all over, 'it's iced champagne poured in until the tipple attains, in the words of its inventor, "its proper opalescent milkiness."'

The drinks bubbled white like curdling, watery milk.

'Wonderful,' Kenneth said, sipping one first then passing them around. There was a clink of glasses, 'and now back to my story. It was September first—that's two nights ago—around seven in the evening. A pretty time to be on deck with the sailors. The sun would be not long down . . . usually, but not that night. Not on the first: it was spitting. Only a sailor into that kind of degradation would brave it. Anyway,' another long sip and toy of the bubbles on the surface, this time with one finger after the other, like a pianist playing Hanon. The story went on, 'just dark and spitting, *Berwick* and *York* joined company for their hunt for us.'

He brought the glass to his lips for a sip of his own, only after all in his company had done so already. He was acting a bit like King Arthur himself now, he thought, letting his men taste the wine first. As the drink went on the incline into his mouth, minuscule droplets leapt from the surface and across his lips. Spontaneous emulsification, it's called. Like a mad chemistry experiment. But this soon settled down once he'd taken some inside him, like the popping of a cork to let the champagne sit a while. It was strong and tingling on his tongue.

'They had already missed *Europa*,' Kenneth said, 'her helmsman had not been as kind as our own dear captain. Had not carried her passengers to their destination. No, it was straight back to Germany, *passengers be damned!* Not the case on *Bremen*. Now where were we? O yes, *Europa* has quick-dashed back, this only made these two British cruisers all the hungrier for us, their would-be German spoil. *Imagine!* They came close, but it was the United States Coast Guard that almost caught sight of us. Within ten miles, if you can believe that, when visibility was around two. Close enough to keep the lot of you rolling at night, I should think.'

His thoughts drifted to the fact-checking task he'd assigned poor Wireless Operator Weber. Was it possible that the *Bremen* had as intimate a knowledge of positioning of unfriendly ships as the description this steward was giving? He had a strange feeling come over him. Like he was being put under a trace by some bent witch. He rubbed Aurik rougher. Between their legs they had come up with their own means of communicating. A method known only to them, and all most *under the table*. They both downed their drinks.

'Thank you, steward,' Aurik said. 'But we should not stay here any longer. We will think on your position and get back to you if we feel you can be of use.'

Aurik was such a grown-up when speaking, he again thought, while he still had the poor boy's tongue.

'You are right to think of discretion,' Kenneth said. 'All the decks are full of men. The painting order and the clear weather has drawn them out. But our here little *indiscretions* will be quite secret. Senior stewards such as I carry the keys to the passenger pleasure spaces. And you need not to fear. On my return, I locked the door to this room from the inside and let loose the curtains. We shall not be disturbed.'

A clever action, he thought.

'But about our Brits,' Kenneth went on, drawing him back, 'by the time of their rendezvous, we had already slipped passed the cruisers. But don't weep too much for our British adversaries, my friends.'

This was all getting a bit silly now, he thought. The man's tone was so queer. Though the strength of Hemingway's creation was making itself known to him, too. He dove into the bubbles of a second glass.

'On the second of this month,' Kenneth continued, 'that's yesterday, my boys, these two cruisers thought they had us in their sights. *Spotted us!* It was about this time in the morning. That was when both ships recorded in their logbooks that a state of war had been declared between Germany and Great Britain. It made the hunt for us that hungrier. And at lunchtime, quarter past twelve—time for meaty sandwiches, mmm, yummy—a large liner was sighted by both, sounding action stations. They thought it was us.'

Not all of the party drank their Hemingways at the same speed; for dramatic effect, he assumed, Kenneth took this opportunity in the story to line up a new round. Something that hastened any stragglers to catch up on the swallowing down of addictive, alcoholic milky stuff.

'It wasn't though. Us, that is. We have been charmed on this voyage so far. But it *was* a ship of state. Three funnels to our two. Yes, you guessed it. It was the *Queen Mary*, on her way to New York . . . will she make it? We'll be the judge.'

Kenneth dipped fingertips into the glass again, deeper than the bubbles this time. Like those lily fingers were mines dangled into a channel. Then Kenneth shallowed it all down in one throat-opening tilt. That was drink number four for the man, he thought. A skill for opening the throat that meant the whole thing, bubbles and all, disappeared inside Kenneth like pebbles down a pool drain. A sucking sound coming from the steward with the gulp—a slutty sailor trick, indeed.

'"But Kenneth," I know you're thinking, "well, he might have made all this up." I'll leave you to labour on my worth to you and yours, Mr Braun,' Kenneth said, attentions back to Aurik again. Kenneth slid a ringlet-stained cocktail napkin in front of Aurik like a tapped-out gambler placing a last-ditch bet. It had the cabin number two hundred and thirty-one scrawled. That's on *B Deck*. 'Should you need it,' the man added. 'Nice and snug, sandwiched between the *Purser's Office* and the stairwell.'

'What of the war?' Aurik said to the other two. Strategically, perhaps. Either a measure to exclude or include Kenneth, he wasn't quite sure.

'Our chances of getting through without mustering for a scuttle continue to deteriorate,' Mr Weber, the wireless operator, said to the circle, smoke from cigarettes rising from the middle of their huddle like from that campfire ringed with scouts. Weber seemed to have lost the crude tongue when folded in with the company of a slut steward. 'That's why I came to find you all,' Weber said, eyes buggy and darting behind thick spectacles. 'Our situation has been perilous. I can corroborate much of what this man has said. Though I do suspect embellishment.

And believe succinctness is something that needs to be worked on, *the fruity fuck!*' and the tongue is found again. 'I reiterate the value of a man sticking with his own station.'

Kenneth took this like a bull would red satin.

'There are advantages to swimming cross stations,' Kenneth said, the man running wet fingers over three of the chess game's white back row, from the rook through to bishop. 'Especially in times of war when the situation changes so rapidly, the sides, too. And it's those little *in*'s that mean life or death.'

Swaying a little, Kenneth gave the clock on the wall a long study.

'You want *absolute proof*? Alright. Right now, at this very moment, a British ocean liner is faltering, having been torpedoed by one of our U-boats in the first act of naval warfare.'

That got the table's attention, all turning on Mr Weber.

'It's only happened this hour,' Kenneth said to the wireless operator. 'Your people may not have even heard the ship's distress calls yet. But mine have.'

Aurik brushed the tension away like it was an unwanted smoke.

'We shall see. And how is it that you've come into this information?'

'I have my sources.'

'But you have been in here with us, if it's only just now happened.'

'I spoke with them, my little informers, en route to collecting the bottles for our drinks. There's a bar located just outside this room, up one flight of stairs. I have keys, remember. But I opted to head to one of the first-class bars, right aft and up some decks. And took advantage of sympathetic lips along the way. I too can use my time wisely, gentlemen.'

He swept the paintings of the *Smoking Room* for the second class, looking for the whites of eyes spying on them. How did the man know? His hand now rubbing Aurik's trouser fly with all the force of dry sticks rolled together to start a campfire. His Hemingway gave him the idea to press tiny Aurik into and then out again. From an outie to an innie to an outie, like a bobbing fish game with rod he'd played as a child. Or, like his arsehole had become since boarding this ship.

'I had the feeling that you might require something more from me,' Kenneth continued. 'To show my value to you.'

'We shall see. Leave us now,' Aurik said, annoyed or afraid, he could not tell. Maybe his fish game had left Aurik as a kind of halfway-there eunuch.

'This ship,' he spoke up, 'you know her name?'

'S.S. *Athenia.*'

That name, why was it familiar? Then it ran true. Was that the same ship that was uttered on *Aquitania*? The prophecy of that limp of wrist man in Robert's shadow, the one that perhaps regretted mentioning it. The sinking caused by German fire but that the British, somehow, had a hand in. Had it come to pass? Had the war at sea snatched its first iron damsel?

'Leave,' he barked, 'all of you, yes.'

And then, like the magician's parting trick, the steward was gone, and with the girly man the rest of the smoke-circle comrades Aurik had assembled for him. Gone just in time for the sound of footsteps and the clinking of paint tins . . . but something held them from an own scatter, deep into the ship. Made them pause instead of scurry from the all-hands-on-deck order and the painting of *Bremen* unseen against the grey horizon.

What could it be? Perhaps that having any kind of company had become foreign.

Aurik leaned in so that lips rubbed his ear. Erotic as a cock-bouncing.

'What is your role in the Reich's plans?' Aurik asked.

'I will inspire men through film and flesh tour.'

Aurik just nodded and crimpled the brow.

He was back at the opening of his *Bremen* passage. It was late afternoon on the aftmost edge of *Sun Deck Restaurant*'s roof, near where he'd had a meal with Robert. When she launched, when stubby stacks new, this roof area was known as *Recreation Deck*, and near where he'd dined housed the catapult for a lauded idea. A mail plane anchored in lee of the forward funnel that could be called upon for use. This calling would come ahead of New York or Bremerhaven, when the catapult would turn on a swivel base, out over the ship's cutting through waves, to send the plane on its way with a belly full of letters. Getting passengers' mail to arrive hours earlier than the record holder for the fastest crossing did herself; well, it was a real novelty of the age. But with time, as with most things, this wore—faster liners came along. The catapult was removed. Now all that remained was a mass of ventilators and the noise and heat of forced-draft blowers sucking hot exhaust from the boiler rooms, keeping passenger recreation to clearer-sky decks lower down and much more aft of *Bremen*'s cigars. He'd missed the heyday and now this was just somewhere to sit with Robert then Aurik.

The sun was low on the horizon. The sky was overcast, but mercy came in the rain having stopped. It gave *Bremen* her day of painting. Aurik had tried to make him spend the day sleeping, but he was too pent-up for that. He wanted to go with Aurik on the rounds, to all the cabins of their merry men, to gain knowledge. But Aurik would not allow it. The rest of his guard had vanished, perhaps imprisoned by hordes of brownshirts. The *SA* men had settled into their hatred for him, it seemed. Had channelled a rage at a forced feeding into an active hunt for him. Aurik tried to hide from him how anxious the man felt. Like Prince John's men after Robin Hood. How desperate their situation was. He could see in Aurik's locking him away that something was very wrong.

He'd ended up in the *Swimming Pool* while Aurik did the rounds. It had become a sanctuary. A place to remember Aurik's treatment. He floated there, in its chamber of light. Thinking of himself flooded. Willingly. Like the *Vaterland* had done in open ocean, when in the same year that the Great War began, she'd let in the sea to one third of her watertight compartments. A daring sea trial designed to demonstrate that she was no *Titanic*. Her owners watched on with great concern when she'd filled up in '14. Like how Aurik watched him now, during visits through the day. Arms crossed, leaned against one of the *Swimming Pool*'s granite columns. But he knew what his hull could take. Yes, he felt like the *Vaterland*, that ship of state, later stolen. Felt similarly ready to take on an iceberg, if only Aurik would let him try. If only Aurik would flood him again. Aurik, though, refused his every request.

Even this late afternoon sitting together was only after his begging. A demand, in fact, tears part of it, for some fresh air and time for them to be together. Aurik had conceded to this, a dash up the first-class *Vestibule* and to this place at the top and on the edge, backs to the *Bridge*. On the way up, on the deepest landing of the first *Vestibule*, he'd paused at a statue. Of a knight with sword and shield with Bremen crest, tall and slender. A Teuton, obviously. How obsessed Germany had become with her Teuton past. How it had fuelled his own coming of age. How it spoke to him about what his snatch from that rope swing might actually mean. No real power, no real sway over German men. Just a pretty thing to be looked upon.

'I lived in Hasenbergl, in Munich,' Aurik said, not to him, to the trail of white stretched before their eyes. 'Father took money when men came by, to have me in *Lebensborn*. For me to live there. That's the *SS* breeding program. He pimped me out like some kind of bull to pay for the drugs he wanted. He did this when I was just a boy. Right at the start of the program, four years ago. They educated me there, gave me every opportunity. I took each one. As a boy I looked like I'd have much promise as one of the fathers of the Reich. My own father's cold heart was the making of me.'

In profile against the diving sun, Aurik's features were like a stonemason's first cuts into marble. Sharp and confident as only an experienced chisel could make, if a little raw. Having had the man's seed, craving it above all else, he could see why this man beside him. *This one*, here, yes; this would be the best stud of a nation. Not as pretty as he was, not as gentle-lined, but more handsome in his own eye. Less perfect in the best kind of way.

'They were kind to me at first. I thought it was the most wonderful thing that had ever happened to any boy. I had friends among the other boys of the *Lebensborn*. I could still visit my father. I forgave him and he was proud of me. I was happy. That was until they started bringing me the girls.'

In '36, the year Nazi Germany hosted the Olympics, sculptures in stone of nude athletes at each other's sides were erected. Like those of Karl Albiker's discus throwers and relay runners in the stadium grounds. Men of stone come together as towering monuments of virility and endurance and men going the distance. That same year, a young student put in a thesis for the award of Doctor of Medicine. The would-be doctor puts homosexualists together with fetishists, paraphiliacs, sadists, masochists, urolagnists and passion murderers. The thesis' subject and title, simply *Impotence*. When the normal wishes of man are blocked, as they are in the homosexual, the idea of sex with a woman may induce disgust, aversion or vomiting, and absolutely no ejaculation. A homosexual man is an impotent man, this thesis said.

'I practised with the other boys,' Aurik said, still only to *Bremen*'s white froth. 'Just to make sure that it all works,' rubbing the dick, 'you know,' setting the little fella free, 'down there. I was so much smaller than all the other boys. They poked fun at me for that. But I didn't mind. That got me hard, the making fun of. Not normal, right? But you like what you like. And when I shot I always gave much bigger loads than any of them could. They admired me for that. In the *Lebensborn*, that made me a legend—the stud with the best seed. It was the women making fun that I couldn't stand. Who were they to judge?'

Impotence was an attractive metaphor for the homosexual in the century before this one as well, in works of French and Brazilian novelists. Aurik as in any way impotent was absurd to him. But what would he know of matters of art and mind medicine?

'Is this the *Poop Deck* then?' Aurik said to him, adrift of any kind of logic in the flow of things, four legs and one very little pee-pee maker dangling.

He had drifted too, pushed impotence from his thoughts, to return instead to Teutons and statues of ideal men, penises always as tiny as Aurik's.

'Well?' Aurik pressed, 'tell me. It's important.'

'What is this *Poop Deck*? I don't know what that is,' he said, the cold side of his body, the half not pressed up alongside, cross with Aurik, who had refused to fill him in on what had been learned from the merry men—to fill his gut, too. *Not yet*, Aurik had said to both.

Aurik shrugged. 'Nor do I,' Aurik said. 'I mean, I have some idea. It's an elevated navigational deck above a cabin at the rear, isn't it? Think of all those Caribbean pirate ships, when the ship's captain's cabin was at the back of those wooden tall ships, and the wheel was above it. That's what you think about when you think of a poop, isn't it?'

He shrugged this time, he'd never given a poop any proper thought. 'Does it matter?'

'I'm not sure,' Aurik said, though in a way that left him unsure himself . . . was Aurik's response an answer to his question or the man's own? Aurik pulled away, like a tug leaving a liner at the heads of a harbour.

Feeling the cold between them, he took Aurik's hand and put it between his thighs. It was coarse, like the rivets in a hull. He turned it over to see scarring there. How had he not seen this before? The scarring was unmistakeable, it was from fire.

'Who did this?' he asked, tracing the bumps and bubbles of the skin.

'I did it to myself.'

'For why?'

Aurik nodded. That same nod from their dick-bob that morning.

He would not let it go this time. One hand still tracing the scar tissue, the other cupping Aurik's chin and turning the head so they looked into each other rather than at the ship's past. 'I don't understand you. You make me, yes.'

Aurik let out a long sigh. Breath hot and sour with the scent from the gut. It washed him like the vapour spices of a mulled beer. 'Okay, friend. It was in Berlin, it was 1933. I had not long been given up by father to be part of the breeding program. I was a very little boy then, but the prep was rigorous. It was . . . a political education. An ideological one. Our enemies would call it a brainwashing. There was, in truth, little reading in this education. It was mostly a physical training. There were some books, I admit. Books on eugenics, Schallmayer, Ploetz, Laughlin. Other than that it was war games. An endless summer camp of swimming and wrestling and mock fighting in teams.

'I excelled at this. I needed to if I was going to stay in the program, to prove that I would grow into a man of superior makeup and to get access to what I truly wanted, which was to learn. To read. To better myself. But an inquisitive mind is not one for conformity, and I soon realised that the kinds of ideas I craved could not be found in any Nazi textbook. This is the background. But to my scars . . . I was in Berlin at the *Kaiser Wilhelm Institute for Anthropology*, that's where they measured me, tested me against charts of the superior Germanic man. Charts that, I'm sure, are now based solely on you.

'I would be brought out on excursions with young *SS* men sometimes, all part of our indoctrination. One of these field trips was to the *Institute for Sexual Science*. The boys I was with were tasked with raiding the archives. And invited me to take a look at all the pornography on offer. It was the men in these piles that caught my eye. After a good long look and rub with these materials. Once the older boys had finished, the smut objects were taken out into the street and burned. But these boys were not ideological purists. They stuffed their favourite photographs from the pile, of men mixed in, down their briefs. Their own personal looted treasure.

'As I watched the books and papers and photographs burn, one . . . well, how do I describe . . .

it *pulled* me. I had to have it. And without thinking, I reached in and it was mine. That was my first taste of real pain. To make the treasure mine, I needed to smother it under my shirt. It was spring, but the loot burned like the underworld. The burns on my belly were little enough that I could scratch them off in time. But my hand was changed forever.'

'What is it you grabbed?'

'A book. Was called *The Boy-doll*. Don't ask me why I wanted it. What man really understands why he wants what he wants? I just knew I needed it. Without knowing anything of its inside. Fancy that. It wasn't the easiest to get at, there were better-known obscenities in easier reach. But I wanted this one. It was set in Berlin, on Friedrichstraße, after the Great War and before *all this*. Before the Nazis. It was a story of two males, one a whore, the other his master, utterly obsessed. It does not have a happy ending.'

Before he could ask more, for the story of the book stolen from a burning pile intrigued him, Aurik put mouth next to his ear, speaking faster and more urgently than he had ever heard the normally calm soldier.

'Tell me something from inside you. Something no one can see.'

He knew exactly what to say. 'I have a little brother, no one knows he's here but me.'

Aurik turned head to one side, he'd pulled Aurik.

'The Nazis taking me asked if I had any kin,' he said. 'Something in me told me to say "no." The men that took me just smiled and nodded at this. I'd made the job easier on them. Mother and father were killed in front of me. My brother was hiding under the bed.'

He'd seen Aurik as a photonegative of himself since first meeting. Hair and eyes dark and deep, him blonde and blue-eyed and surface. But in the black of the man's eyes, he saw himself deepen now, too.

'Never told no one that before. And were I had, I would've said I'd done it to protect Artur. That was his name. I called him "Art." He was littler than me. We shared a bed, so the lie to the men who wanted me was easy. He used to snuggle under my chin in the cold and were I telling anyone else this much I'd say I done what I done to protect Art. But really, I was just scared they'd want him more.'

Aurik nodded that same dick-bob sort of way. But pressed lips to his as well, telling him these nods were kind. 'Thank you,' Aurik said, returning to *Bremen*'s white agitation, drifting away again. 'It's not here. No. This is not the poop. There's no cabin under us. I don't think it's *there*, either,' pointing to the spot where they'd sat that morning, *Bremen*'s aftmost deck. 'No. That bit *there*,' pointing to the edge of the next deck below them, a first-class games deck promenade, which then led down to a smaller games deck for the second-class passenger. 'Must be that one, it has cabins underneath.'

He rested his head on Aurik's shoulder, the warm of the man spreading to his cheek like an arse towel-flicked. Feeling open as a book with broken spine.

'Okay, friend,' he said with a sigh. 'Let's say it's that one, yes.'

'*Titanic* was the last ship to have a proper poop.'

'Okay.'

'So they say. I don't think that's true though. How could it be? She had sisters come after. People are just mad to make the most famous ships the last of their kinds. To make certain pieces fit.'

He pinched Aurik's earlobe between his teeth, the man he nibbled on seemed the perfect hypocrite. Desperately trying to make pieces fit, logic be damned.

'Pay attention,' Aurik snapped. 'Stuff like this is important now. Now that I know you a little.'

'Why is it important?'

'Well, I need to protect you, don't I? We need a code, just us. Say I said to you, if anything bad happened, meet me on the *Poop Deck*. You'd not know where it is, would you? You'd probably go to the stern.'

'Pick a place we both can be sure is what it is then.'

'*Ah!* but that could be the code bit. A thing that's contested. You know, "meet me on *Poop Deck!*" I bet even the captain would need to think about that one. Poop decks are not what they used to be.'

'Okay, so *that's* what we've chosen as our *Poop Deck*, is it?' pointing to the divide between two games decks.

'Yes, I think it is. Those sheds. Remember those.'

'Good to know.'

'It is. Because you're the one steering this ship, from the rear. At least you should be. And I might not always be here to try help you work out things like where the *Poop Deck* is, or whether there even is one. You may need to make up your own poop deck in life.'

'You're a strange one.'

'Maybe, but remember our code and keep it secret. This trip, let's call it *right there*. You may need go somewhere without me. Should something happen. You may need to see something you don't want to see. Maybe you'll need to go to our *Poop Deck*.'

He felt like Aurik was slipping away from him with all the worry. Like he had turned into a burden. Something that was once a novelty that had turned sour. It reminded him of that mail plane. Sitting there made him realise that his first memory of hearing of S.S. *Bremen* was when a young pilot of the mail plane failed to return. It was a tragedy that had made him remember a name. That was his earliest memory of the *Bremen*.

Men always returned, or so he had thought before that happened. He connected the story now with his own not-returning—to his brother, who was gone when he returned after his snatch . . . that return happened about the same time as the mail plane. How was he only connecting that now? Aurik's anxiety after a day of trips between the merry men, together with the sad deck of former recreation and wonderment that they sat on, made him start to worry that, one trip, Aurik may not come back. That what they had may be just that catapult. A novelty to be removed one day.

'Have we met before?' he asked, out of nowhere. If Aurik could spend their time on silly things like poop decks and book burnings, he could speak on random topics, too.

Aurik looked at him and smiled. 'Yes, but you didn't see me then.'

'But I see you now,' is all that he said, impulses inside him becoming harder to resist again.

The guilt of his own arrogance before this mission stopped him from asking more. He knew what he had been like. That was just the kind of thing he would have done. Not seen someone like Aurik. Plus, the fog was back. And it was too long passed having those Hemingways to blame it simply on alcohol. The cure had only been temporary. He dared not tell that to Aurik, either.

'Not really a locked-room mystery, is it?' Aurik said as they climbed through the aftmost *Library* sash, as the glow of the sun on the horizon receded into black.

'Guess not,' he replied, dropping the curtains. 'That disappoints you, yes?' locking the sash.

'It does,' Aurik said. 'They're the most fun to solve.'

This was the first opportunity they had to get in the *Library* all day, and his chance to claim back something of control over the situation. To wade through the fog before it got too thick. Aurik may not want to update him on the intel of the merry men, but he still had his little mystery to solve. Aurik protested, of course, but some guilt at the man denying him an update and a seed-gutful probably helped swing activities his way.

'I wouldn't know this answer,' he said with a shrug.

'I would,' Aurik said. 'I read.'

The last bit, a bit of a mean one, he thought.

'Maybe it was meant to be, yes?' he said, trying to sound as smart as Aurik clearly was.

'What do you mean?' Aurik asked.

He felt his way to Aurik in the dark, took his lover's hand, and then felt a path to the wingback next to the window. Gently guiding Aurik to seated, spreading the man's legs wide and undoing button and fly to then open Aurik's slacks and pull the little Frankfurt he adored through the Y of white briefs.

'Not the time,' Aurik said flat, though did not make any moves to otherwise deter him. '*Really* not the place.' He thought of the stains on the carpet.

His own slacks and briefs down around his ankles, he'd learned to ignore Aurik's protests in the fucking-him arena a little. Plus, his impulses could be denied no more, nodding to himself as he slid bare arse down Aurik's front to slot into that warm place between Aurik thighs, his lover's little prick snuggled in the middle his arse cheeks like an appetiser inside a full-size burger bun.

'We need to take the time,' he said, wiggling Aurik's snail awake. 'Let your little fella have some fun, yes.'

This is what he needs, yes, he thought. *Relieve some tensions.* He reclined his head onto Aurik's shoulder and kissed the lobe. Truth was, he felt like he needed it, too. Like Aurik's seed had become the drug.

'Okay, but we need to be quick. Why was it meant to be a locked-room mystery?'

He smiled, feeling Aurik stiffen between his cheeks to prod his arsehole, like a timid turtle poking its head out into the world.

'Because they are the best kind,' he said with a smile, pretending he was as smug about smart things as the man poking the head of a tiny prick inside him. 'Maybe because, were it actually a locked-room mystery, poor Fosco would not be found.'

'Nonsense. Your engineman found it.'

'Yes, but how?' he grinned, maybe he'd tricked himself smart.

'Now *I* don't understand.'

'Just a sec. Let me get the little fella down, then we can talk murder twists and turns, yes.'

Treating the chair arms like a gymnast's parallel bars, he was spun round on his knees for a whispered tuck-in tale for an incy dick. 'There was once a dick belonging to Aurik, yes,' he whispered to the dick slit, smelling perfectly of men's room porcelain, 'this dick was littler than all the dicks, but had special powers, in big, big, big balloon balls. You mustn't be frightened now, go into the cave and pump, pump, pumpy time, until all the cream is over all the walls. There's a good boy, yes. Let the grown-ups talk now.'

Aurik didn't seem to much appreciate him talking to his lover's little dick like it was a toddler. Not to matter, he knew in time Aurik would come to see that he considered the tiny tool between Aurik's legs as the most precious tiny thing in the whole world.

He gave Auick's piss slit a little lick, just to wet it, giving a tiny prick some small help to slip on in. Then with the same parallel-bar nimbleness, he was back seated, Aurik's little member pressing hard on his knot.

'Spit on it,' Aurik said, a sharp intake of air telling him it hurt.

'He doesn't need spit,' he said back. 'We've had a story, he's got a kiss, now I'll tuck him in.'

He wiggled, Aurik's dick pushing apart the folds of his knot like a sailor forcing a knife between braids of a hawser line.

The breath deepened. Aurik gave out a little yelp, and then the fella popped in.

'You're dry. It hurt.'

He probably was still a bit salty inside from the *Swimming Pool*.

'Piss a little, yes,' he said. 'It'll help.'

'Don't be stupid. I can't piss while hard.'

'Yes, you can,' he said, kissing Aurik's neck as a vein bulged.

He felt a slight, now-familiar filling sensation. Like water seeping into the pinch point of a full balloon pulled under water.

'Stop now, yes,' he said, and started to bounce.

Aurik's worm moved freely now. The feeling of his best-fucker's piss splashing inside him like a watery message in a bottle at sea. He could go on like this for ages.

'Now the little one's sorted. Let me tell you my idea.'

The exercise was about settling Aurik, too. His lover's head on one of the wings of the chair, eyes to the slit of view showing the trade of *Main Promenade Deck* that day, men carrying buckets of paint and hauling mattresses.

Still bouncing, he reached over and switched on the lamp in the corner. Aurik remained calm, head reclined, eyes on the slit view of the deck.

'I'm counting on none of them *out there*,' a head tilt to the same view, 'noticing anything weird. Maybe our killer counted on the same thing.'

'With the curtains open,' Aurik said.

'No, I know this now. The curtains must have been closed. Kenneth confirmed that this morning. You'd do that. Make sure. Door locked, curtains closed.'

'Window locked, too,' Aurik said.

'Now you're getting it.'

'But that's impossible.'

'That's why it's a locked-room mystery.'

He felt smug with that.

'Don't beat the bush with me,' Aurik said, a little grin as some piss escaped from his seal to run into his lover's wiry shrubbery. 'Tell me, mister smart detective, sir.'

'It went something like this,' he said. 'The killer came into the *Library* to get ready the murder scene. The windows were checked and made sure they were locked. You take precautions with a murder as planned as this. Props were left with the body. The body was posed on the Nazi flag, and there was that photograph of *Rex* and page, in the cold sweat of Fosco's back. This was all planned. Really carefully, yes. Windows were checked to be locked and curtains were let down so no man would see the killing. At least one lamp would have been turned on. As we can see, even during the day the curtains make the room dark.

'Preparation is key to any successful murder,' Aurik agreed. 'Especially a locked room mystery.'

'Yes, the killer came to the *Library* to get it ready.'

'And this would have been done, likely, while we were still in New York,' Aurik added.

He nodded, to both of Aurik's contributions.

'Windows were locked when the killer left after preparing the scene, though the big mistake the killer made was to *not lock* the *Library* door between prep and kill. Probably because they did not wish to raise suspicion when Fosco was led there later. Hard enough getting a dumb wiseguy into a place of books, but if you have to unlock the room first . . .'

'And also knowing, as our steward made clear this morning,' Aurik said, nodding now too, 'that there were many others who had a key. It was important to lock alcohol away from a crew, but not to lock away books. Locking the *Library* before it *needed* to be locked would only raise suspicion among the crew.'

He nodded.

'So, the killer should have chosen another room?' Aurik asked. Suitably engaged in both his telling and pissful bouncing on his man's little member. It showed itself to be the perfect means of keeping his leading knight of an inner circle interested.

'No,' he said. 'The *Library* was good. The body was always meant to be found, but at the right time. When a library would mean something, too.'

'So, what went wrong?'

'*Someone else* used the room, someone who shouldn't have.'

'Maybe one of the crew?'

'No, we'd still have our locked room mystery in that case. It only had books, not pricey alcohol that could hurt a man's responsibilities. No, the captain would not have minded men reading. Better way of passing the time. Smarter way,' he said with a kiss to Aurik, his own smart guy. 'The one who came into the *Library* was someone who *should not* have been there.'

'Surely, then, it was a terrible place to commit a murder? If men were welcomed freely. The chances of getting caught would be high.'

'Timing was all things, yes. But it'd be locked for killing. And think, when do ship men read? Well?'

'During downtime.'

'Yes, when bored. When killing the time in New York, or maybe once we were on our way, at sea. Late at night, to read just with a candle. But not at the good bits. Like when we were leaving the pier.'

'All the men were on the decks then, waving to *Normandie* and singing.'

'Yes, what better time to kill in a library? When all eyes were at the city and the river.'

'So then, why wasn't the killer put off by the scene being changed.'

'Don't you see? The killer did not know. Had no way of knowing the locked room had been messed up. Unlocked. That's why you do that stuff early, so you can get on with the killing. Remember, too, that the curtains were down, and at least one lamp would have been on. The curtains *had* to be down. The killer could not see that the window was unlocked and would have no reason to think it was. The door had been open, and then was locked by the killer once the kill was done.'

'So . . . who opened the window?'

'Someone *who did not belong* in the *Library* of S.S. *Bremen*. Had to be, yes?'

'It was reserved for first class, so everyone.'

'Not true. Remember, the captain would not have cared.'

'It was an outsider. The pilot?'

'He would have been too busy. He would be with the captain the whole time.'

'There's no one else left,' Aurik said, shuddering toward a conclusion.

He was thinking his little idea through as he bounced on dick, wishing the conclusion to bodies found dead in a library were as easy to rub out as some seed from Aurik's tiny cock. But the bounce, he found, was a better method of deduction than any pace in front of a fireplace. More of the fruit for him.

Yes!

'There is only one man it could have been, yes,' he said as Aurik splashed seed inside him. 'The man in the *Library* was Senior First Officer Robert Bell of R.M.S. *Aquitania*.'

'No beddy-byes yet,' he said from his knees, a kiss to Aurik's piss and cummy cock. 'We's be going again in a min. Need your head in on this. You'll help me fuck this through, little man, yes?' He crawled to the keyhole of each of the five entrances to the *Library*, drip of a stud's milk trailing the way. Then it was back on the prick. It slid into his cummy bum like a candle into custard. 'Interesting that,' he said, bouncing Aurik hard again, his crawl having told him the doors to the *Library* were new, like they had been added specially for this voyage. Were the entrances to the *Library* before all open? Closed off only with long silk curtains, perhaps.

'What's interesting,' Aurik's eyes rolling back.

'Goes to show you. You got to solve these things where they happened. Before I turned on the lamp, I saw that light from outside was strong along where the window curtains meet, and around the jam of the doors. But nothing from the keyholes. My crawl has shown it: something is broken off in the locks. That tells us the window was definitely unlocked *before* the murder happened. The killer then locked the *Library* and stuffed the holes to stop anyone finding Fosco.'

'But the killer hadn't counted on the window?' Aurik asked.

'Yes, and neither did my engineman.'

'Let me guess, you have a theory on that too?'

'You bet your seed in me's I do. My new little idea goes like this . . . before leaving New York there was a meeting with all crew in the *Ball Room*. Robert was taken up with the pilot and asked to wait outside the *Ball Room* under *SA* guard, to be meeting the captain afterwards. Robert would have said he needed to piss. Would have said it in a more polite-Englishman-like way than that. But in a way that pressured the guard to see as Robert knew, that as a senior officer, Robert would be the one better trusted to go off on his own to look for a bowl to fill with brew than for the guard to follow Bell and leave the pilot unwatched. The brownshirt would have pointed in the direction of the doors leading to the *Library* and *Writing Room*, left of that was the nearest piss point. It would have been easy for him to, doors blocking any view, slip one extra set of doors further and into the *Library*, it were the same way.'

'Maybe Mr Bell was the killer.'

'No,' he said, not only because he couldn't face the idea. He bounced harder.

'It's hurting again.'

'Then piss some,' he said annoyed. 'Sorry,' another kiss on the lobe.

Aurik muttered something about him taking the fun out of fucking, but pissed as was told.

It helped his thinking. To be flooded again.

'Robert couldn't be the killer *because of the key*, yes. He did not have it. And if he did, he would have no reason to then unlock the window. No. Our scene calls for both a killer *and* a Mr Bell. As two fellas, not the one man.'

Aurik seemed a bit disappointed in not being able to pin the whole thing on his British father from before he had seen Aurik.

'But why would he want to go into the *Library* at all then?' Aurik said.

'That I don't know yet. We put that to one side for now, yes. Stay on what we do know. Robert would have been on edge, yes. He has a good seed way about him. Doesn't like risk. He didn't come when I asked—I'm not jealous . . . anyway. He would have gone in knowing that the guard was just down the corridor. This would explain why, when on hearing footsteps, he must have assumed it was the guard, unlocking the window and escaping out onto the promenade. He was breathless when he met me for dinner, and it was clear he'd been giving the guard the run round. Maybe Robert had been spotted leaving the *Library*.'

'By that greaser who took your cherry?'

Bit mean that, he thought, bouncing harder still.

'I reckon so, yes. Not all the oil boys were in the *Ball Room*; they had important work to do to get *Bremen* up and running, warmed up for the dash. Our engineman used this as an opportunity to do none of each—not work or hear what the captain had to say. He had a smoke break on his mind—this arse you using tells me the man had a selfish way about him. He took the *Turbine Hatch* to the first topside deck, which just so happened to be between the *Ball Room* and the *Library*. He saw Robert climbing out of the window. That's how he knew the window was unlocked. He hadn't the time to check it out then. But he would make time later, after the kill.'

'So, it was your engineman who opened the curtains later?'

'Makes sense.'

'But why?'

'Men's nature. Don't you see? Let's go one by one.'

He used fingers for his points while he bounced.

'One, the killer. Well, he had to close the curtains. It was the only way to kill in secret then keep it secret. To make sure the body weren't found until the right time. Yes, the killer would have turned off all lights and closed the curtains after the deed were done.'

'Agreed,' Aurik said.

'Two,' he nodded, second finger raised, riding Aurik's wave, 'my cherry picker. No way this oily fucker just stumbled on seeing the body in the *Library* with no lights and curtains drawn. And no way he would know he could get into the room by the window if he hadn't seen that it was open. And were it Robert climbing through that tipped the fucker off while having a smoke break, then Robert's role as a British officer was certainly enough of a tease to open the window later and look and see. Once he'd seen it, the body, its the boy in all of us who wants to share it. But it was night. So, my fucker opened the curtains and lay in wait for someone to show the body to. Maybe because it would be more believable that Fosco could be seen through the window. That's why the curtains were open when I was told to look in.'

'But why'd that Winter fellow choose you?'

'Two options to that. One, it was random. I just happened to be there, having come down from the *Bowling Alley* and onto the deck at the right time.'

He felt Aurik deflating a little inside him.

I don't like that option either, little man. He thought, tightening his hole around the small sausage inside him.

'And the other?' Aurik said.

'That he went after me.'

'That sounds more like it.'

'Okay. Maybe rather than retreating to his post after seeing Robert, Winter followed him.'

'To you,' Aurik said, hard again.

Was Aurik's hard state, he wondered, at the chance to have an own theory, or at the prospect of him in peril. It was dark thinking. But these were dark times, and how much did he really know about the man inside him? Though he was showing himself deft at murder theorising, the fog was making him paranoid. Whichever it was, he turned his focus to getting a further one then two then three loads out of Aurik.

The man may have a tiny prick, but with a substratum of scrotum that bulged with cream, this method of deduction was proving the most fruitful. Aurik pumped another batch of cream into him, and more on top of that, load after load like ricotta into a cannoli pastry. Something that had him thinking of Fosco and how he found the Italian . . .

'Winter fucked Fosco before fucking me,' he said a little sick, as Aurik found room for more filling in his gut, like the final squeezes of a baker's piping bag.

Those grease stains, he thought, were surely on the carpet when he came into the *Library*, and though he didn't see them before Winter had joined him on the carpet, he *had* seen those little lines of grease either side of Fosco's hole. From the cracks in Winter's thumbs, where no soap scrub could reach and that had rubbed off in the sidewards tension of an arse spread of Fosco for a seed dump from a dirty engineman. Was a man like that really going to wait for him to see the body without having a go at it first? From what he knew of the man, from the experience of getting his hole beaten in. He thought then that there was no way.

He gave Aurik the latest deduction, also the view that Winter must have been doubly intrigued when he turned up in poor clothes. He felt the relief of breaking the back of a puzzle; Aurik seemed even keener on the corpse fuck getting pinned on his cherry picker. A pinning timed with the latest pump in of some seed . . . when also the sash of the *Library* window was thrown open.

It was dark outside now, as the head of their wireless operator poked in.

'What is it, Mr Webber?' Aurik said, more perturbed than any kind of embarrassed, head still jerking with the pumping of cream inside him—now an overflow onto the armchair cushion.

'I, um. Sorry to interrupt,' eyes searching for somewhere else to look. 'But I thought you'd want to know. Thought you'd want to be *the first* to know.'

'What? Spit it out,' Aurik said, red in the face.

'A distress call has just come through. An ocean liner, in this last hour, has been torpedoed.'

'Another one,' he spoke up, his bouncing slowing, looking at the clock.

It was now almost 2100 hours.

'No . . .' Mr Weber said. 'Not *another*. It's the S.S. *Athenia*, just been struck.'

'I don't understand,' Aurik replied. 'She's been hit again? Twelve hours later.'

He leapt to standing on the chair arms and then to the floor, some of Aurik's pudding spraying across the man's face as he did so. He couldn't help himself, giggling as Aurik started retching. Turned off, it seemed, by one's own bum baste.

'*No!* don't you *see?*' he said excitedly, blown out, spinning. Load upon load of Aurik seed spraying carpet and curtains and books and poor Mr Weber with no idea of where to look. 'That steward, that Kenneth Arnold, he got the times mixed up. A.m. from p.m., easy to do when drunk as a donkey. But the point is, he *knew* the ship would be hit at around eight in the day. He must have confused eight a.m. with p.m.'

'He's our killer?' Aurik asked, mopping up seed.

'Maybe, no, not sure,' he replied, getting fingers up his hole to stem the tide of seed from his sausage gash, tasting a little, not caring any about the audience. 'But don't you *see*?' licking fingers and fishing for more. 'It's much, much, much, much more than that. He is the man who knows what's to come.'

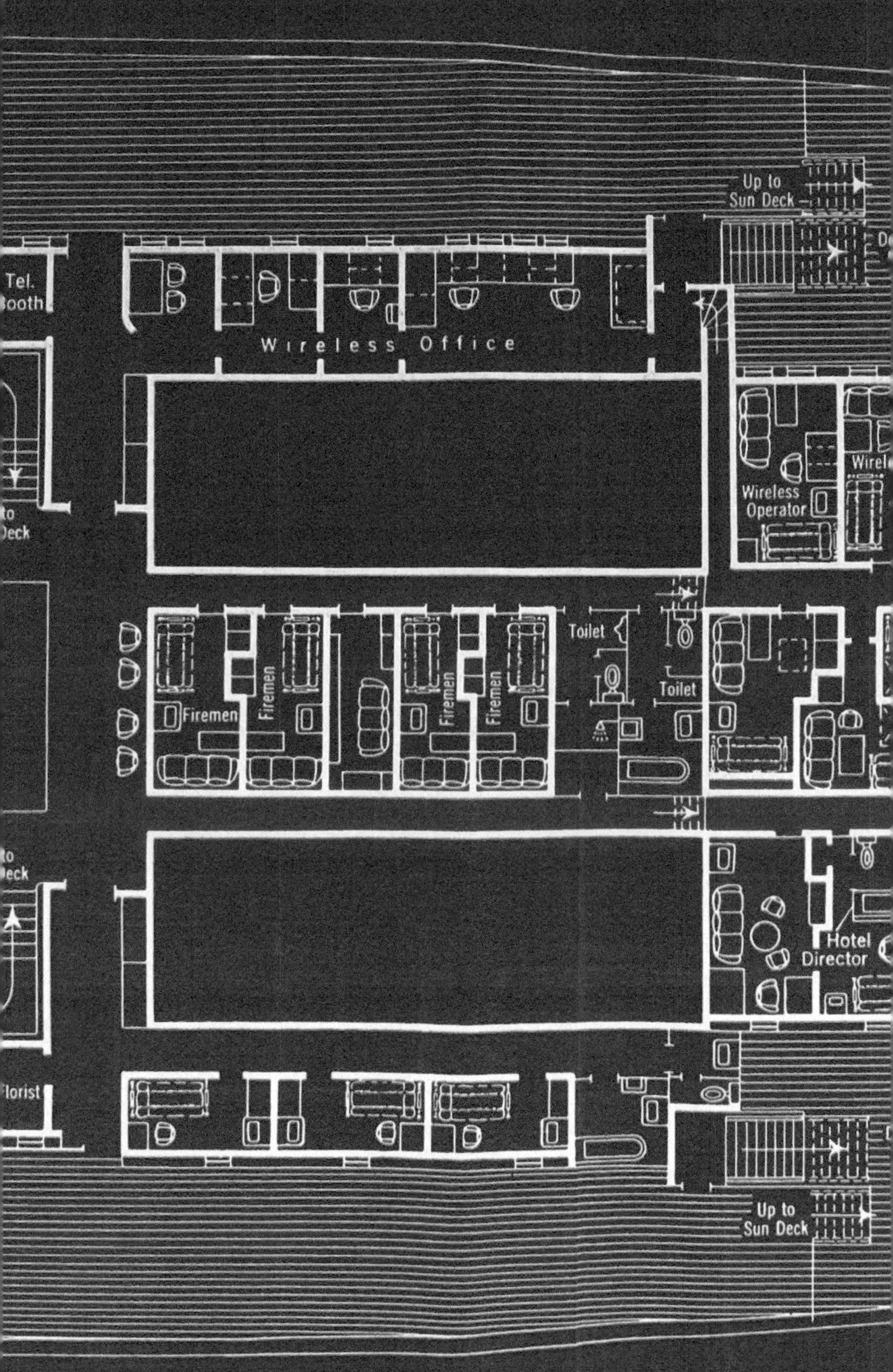
Up to
Sun Deck
Tel.
Booth
Wireless Office
Wireless
Operator
Firemen
Firemen
Firemen
Firemen
Toilet
Toilet
Hotel
Director
Florist
Up to
Sun Deck

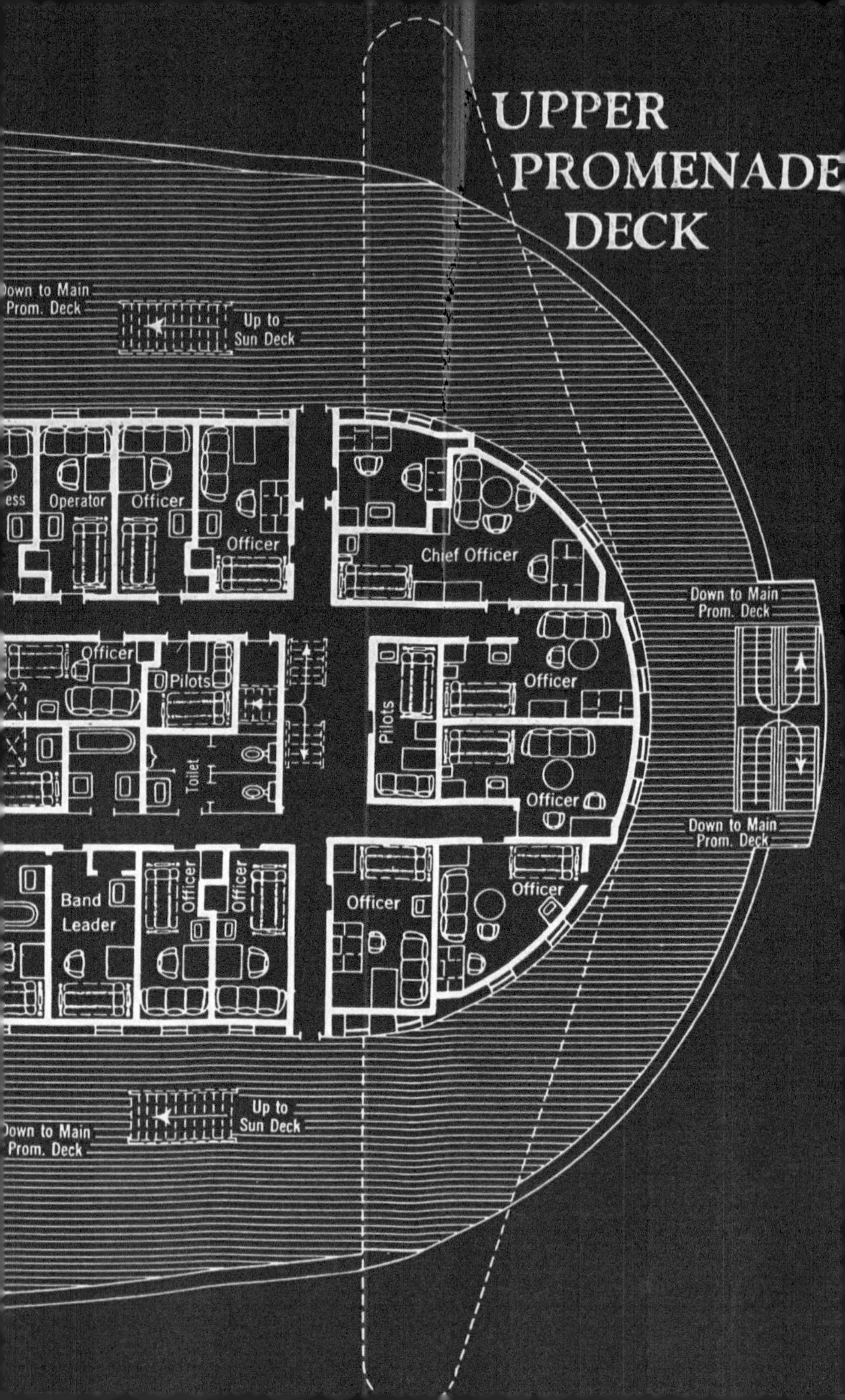
UPPER
PROMENADE
DECK
Down to Main
Prom. Deck
Up to
Sun Deck
Operator
Officer
Officer
Chief Officer
Down to Main
Prom. Deck
Officer
Pilots
Toilet
Pilots
Officer
Officer
Down to Main
Prom. Deck
Band
Leader
Officer
Officer
Officer
Officer
Up to
Sun Deck
Down to Main
Prom. Deck

Tensions between them were like sauerkraut bottoms catching on bachelors' stoves. In their stateroom, his gutful feed of seed and piss bubbled inside after a shaken run through the ship. O yes, the dynamic between him and Aurik was curdling in the aftermath of the *Library* revelation. Good for mystery-solving, the dumps inside him, but bad for brain fogs. Cumdumps blurred the vision, brought with offloadings up into him an itching distrust of the one man who should have been beyond any questioning. Not believing of the pumper into him, feeling himself starting to turn.

Keeping with the class of their *Smoking Room* meeting, Aurik had selected a second-class cabin for them, mid-ship on *C Deck*, away from aft and fore positions of crew on board. Any bitter brownshirts scouting for them would surely scour the first-class accommodations, while there was also a need to keep distance from the officers at the front and the lowly cabins of the turbine and boiler rooms. Where enginemen prowled to nut inside pretty boys like him.

This cabin was intended to be their happy medium. Cabin four hundred and eighty-six—what Aurik had chosen—would have suited a young professional making his way in the world. Perhaps a junior solicitor for a reputable Hamburg law firm, or a clerk in one of the Reich ministries. A promising future ahead. Comfortable. *This will do nicely*, such a man would have said aloud on entry for that trip, on business, to America. The walls were austere, as was *Bremen*'s style, but there was simple elegance and comfort in diamond-pattern carpet and striped couch. A single bed with mahogany bedheads, a basin beside it, a desk and, best of all, a porthole over the couch with a view of the sea to some new harbour as far as the eye could manage it.

O yes, this will do very nicely for he and Aurik, that is what he should have thought. He should have been able to picture some fuck meet-cute like follows . . . come bedtime, Aurik would insist on taking the couch, play at comrades who did not bum-bum. But as soon as the light was out, before even he'd a chance to wish his new *cum-rad* a good deep sleep, they'd be stacked in that single bed, finding space in each other in order to make the arrangement work. They'd had given each other the night off from grim solvings of a corpse fuck mystery. That was how it *could* have been, but that awful steward Kenneth had preserved a single bed before even nightfall.

They had carried their luggage with them from the *Smoking Room* and to their next place of sleep separate from any of the merry men, not letting on where they were to anyone. Those men were informers, sure, their intelligence was relied on, had to be. Though the merry men were needed, they were not to be trusted. All they had was each other, if only he could see that. Instead, he hovered at the boil of distrust.

'You mightn't like the fellow,' Aurik said heated as soon as the door of their stateroom was soft shut. 'I don't either. Clearly the queer sort. But he did impress me. And God, man, you need to trust me. I say we need him. I'm going after him. Do me this one thing: stay here until I come back. You said you see me now, as if that's supposed to make up for you ignoring me before. Well, prove it. Do what you're told. Trust me. See me. You drive me off the alps, you realise that, don't you? You're so beautiful. So important. Why didn't you *see* before? Why didn't you stop to think that maybe you shouldn't have jumped ship? That maybe this might be a trap. *Stay!* I mean it now.'

And like that, bags dropped, Aurik was out again in pursuit of the steward, cocktail napkin in back pocket.

He sat a moment. Simmering, dreaming of a third chance at a first fuck, but also feeling mad. No man had ever dared speak to him like that since the swing. Never one his own age, certainly. Any thoughts about listening. Staying put. Slipped through the holes in his mind. Though he did start diamond counting of the carpet—*around ten per row in the space between couch and bed, and another ten at least at right angles to that, so that comes to . . .*—just so he could tell himself he waited a little before going in pursuit. Just so he could pretend that he had changed. That he was not the arrogant sod who'd never tried shaking with the boys he flesh modelled for. At the *Junker-SS* schools for officer training, or the *Order Castles*, to instil in the hardest young military men the various ideologies of the Reich, if that's where Aurik had seen and sketched and touched him, or wherever-fuck else it might have been. *Adolf Hitler Schools*? One of the *Napolas*?

Were Aurik one of them handsome boxers?

He didn't recall ever hearing of *Lebensborn*. How was he to remember? He'd been moved and paraded about so much since being plucked from that swing. *No*, he told himself as he slipped from the stateroom into the passageway, *better I go along. Show this man, as grateful as I am for all he's done, who's in charge*. He was happy with that, though his blurry vision made convincing himself that he was seeing anything clearly anymore, without basis. The little sharp pains in the brain were a big bit scary.

Aurik had chosen their part of the ship well. Not a soul occupied the staterooms along their passageway.

He could have stayed put there all day without any bother . . . *but the decision has been had, can't turn back now*. He even peeped into a room or two, just to be sure. And yes, sure enough, they were empty. *Aurik is a good seed*, he thought, pausing at the first-class stairwell to the upper decks, settling the simmer. But not stopping long enough to let the thought dissuade him. Taking the steps two at a time to spirit his way.

That was one of the graces of this passage, he reflected as he reached the next landing. Being just crew with no passengers, there were many, many places to hide. The genius of Aurik's selection revealed itself more on the next deck up. Like layers of a tiered cake for a small party, he saw that the higher levels were at greater risk of a slice and eat. O yes, the situation changed as he rose. Even one deck up, on *B Deck*, he passed in the passageways men splattered in grey paint. It panicked him at first, before the power of his disguise kicked in.

Aurik had thought of everything.

Dressed as an officer. No *Bremen* officer was below deck, tending to the painting challenge. That left the men he encountered as the stewards and deckhands and the odd dish pig turned to a paint tin. They salute him as he passes in his crisp uniform. They avoid his eye. Maybe not recognising him, but daren't question him either. He liked that. Hovered with it. Being beyond question. That was what he was born to be. Hidden away. It folded a skip into his step as he ran the deck named on the napkin. This is the thing to be doing, he thought. He liked Aurik, but his seed-giver needed to learn.

Perhaps he was meant to lead, after all, for he had committed the cabin number of the tricky steward to memory in the most fleeting of seeing it slid before Aurik. Two hundred and thirty-one, *B Deck. Should you need it. Nice and snug, sandwiched between the Purser's Office and the stairwell*, he remembered. Why was such a location chosen? He hadn't time to think it through, also hadn't really the head for long thought anyway. No time, for his count of the diamonds wasn't all that long after all and because like Kenneth, the room was not without its tricks. Not in the *Vestibule* as the description would imply, but located along a passageway accessed next to the first class *B Deck* lift. Arriving, it seemed, not long after Aurik, who was knocking on the door of room two hundred and thirty-one.

He was exposed in the passage.

Dove into one of the corridors, to peak round the bend, with a full vantage of Aurik's back and the door to the cabin at an acute angle.

'I knew you'd come,' the steward said, sly in the doorway, wearing only a robe. 'Even sooner than I thought. Hungry boy.'

'I'm not here to play games,' Aurik said firm. 'Are you going to move aside to allow me in? We can't be seen together.'

'I have a better place. A place built for the private releases of men,' Kenneth said pulling the door closed. 'Come, handsome suitor.'

Taking Aurik's hand, the steward pulled his pumper down the corridor toward him, but around the bend to port, leading to the *Vestibule*. Careful not to follow too close behind, he would give the two a head start by checking out the steward's door. He turned the knob. Unlocked. It was one of those decision points in the adventure books he'd devoured as a child, probably because the stories were short. Would he stay and gather clues to the steward's intentions, or follow the pair to find out where they were headed, and maybe learn these intentions firsthand? He chose the path of the action man. Leaving the cabin door unopened.

Like with the diamond carpet in their stateroom, it took him no time at all to catch the pair up, three decks up on *Upper Promenade Deck*. In fact, he had come up a bit too fast.

'*Halt!*' Kenneth shouted, hand raised above the shoulder like an overzealous Nazi salute.

He froze, exposed again, about halfway down a long, open portside passageway leading from the *Vestibule* toward the bow.

'We're being followed.'

He dove through the nearest door just as the steward spun round. Back against the door, adrenaline pumping his heart with such force he felt like he might be sick. What if they saw him? What would it matter? he wondered. He reclined his head to try and calm himself. It was all white and musky smelling in the compartment. He's landed himself inside a men's restroom. It mattered that he had followed, yes. It mattered because he wanted to spy, he realised, and that's why he didn't want to get caught. That was the pumping blood in his veins. That was mistrust. Certainly, he didn't want Aurik to know this. Unsure whether Kenneth had seen him in that moment, still with back pressed against the door he turned his head to one side so his ear was flat.

'Maybe I imagined it, but best we nip in here in case,' came Kenneth's voice.

The knob behind his back turned. With the same nimbleness, the same need not to get caught, he dove into the men's one cubicle of the *Toilet*.

'Best I check whether there's anyone else here,' Kenneth said in salacious intonation, accompanied by the sound of knees hitting the tiles.

He climbed onto the bowl so not to be seen.

A slap of a palm sounded on the tiles.

'All ours,' Kenneth murmured.

Then the top of Kenneth's robe came over the cubicle wall, like a hand towel flung over a toilet attendant's arm.

'*What the hell!*' Aurik said.

'Hell indeed,' Kenneth replied. 'You want what I've got to give? Well, Mr Braun, you've gotta breed me for it. That's an order.'

He was right not to trust the man, *that fucker!* he thought dangling from the cubicle wall, watching Aurik fuck a lily-arse steward in the urinal bowl.

Something about Kenneth's eyes, rolling in the sockets, the slutboy grinning like a certain cat in a psychedelic children's tale. Inviting everyone, however innocent, into a gaping warren. Aurik was unable to come. The man's little dick in Kenneth's gape like overcooked penne pasta. Incapable of breeding a loose slutboy as instructed.

Though Aurik gave it a good try. Tongue out the corner of the mouth with the exertion, like a boy's first attempt at a Meccano kit. Speckles of white powder at the corners of Aurik's mouth made his cheating lover appear like a stage performer putting on a show.

Instead of making him feel better, that Aurik was not able to breed the slut despite best efforts, it prolonged the pain for him. As he couldn't look away, fingers white, gripping the cubicle wall to keep a look of Aurik. He certainly couldn't flee, not without being caught in his spy game. When Aurik started getting so soft the little cock receded inside, a sort of panic seemed to rise in Aurik.

That hurt him especially, seeing the man he had gone through much with, a man he'd shown something hidden of himself to, trying this hard to breed another.

'New order,' Kenneth said, a gleeful, squdgy thing getting spaghetti-fucked in the piss bowl. 'You're going to use me as a human toilet.'

That was an easy task for Aurik, already soft. To piss in the steward like the lily man's gape was a urinal cake used as target practice. From a distance.

Some went in. Most went out.

Kenneth started singing as this went on.

'Piss is social,' Kenneth said between song. 'But let's get personal now. Give me a log.'

Aurik swayed like a drunkard. Like a reanimated corpse.

The porcelain urinal cracked from its simple cantilever. It was no latrine. Not grounded. Not ever designed, nor pray imagined, to be used in this way. To be sat on with already a man in it. To cradle a man so that that man may be used by another to be shat in to.

It gave him all sorts of ideas.

At last, he had the cover needed to escape.

4 September

Bookseller
Up to Upper Prom. Deck
Florist Shop
Up to Upper Prom. Deck
Kindergarten
Childrens Toilet

MAIN PROMENADE DECK

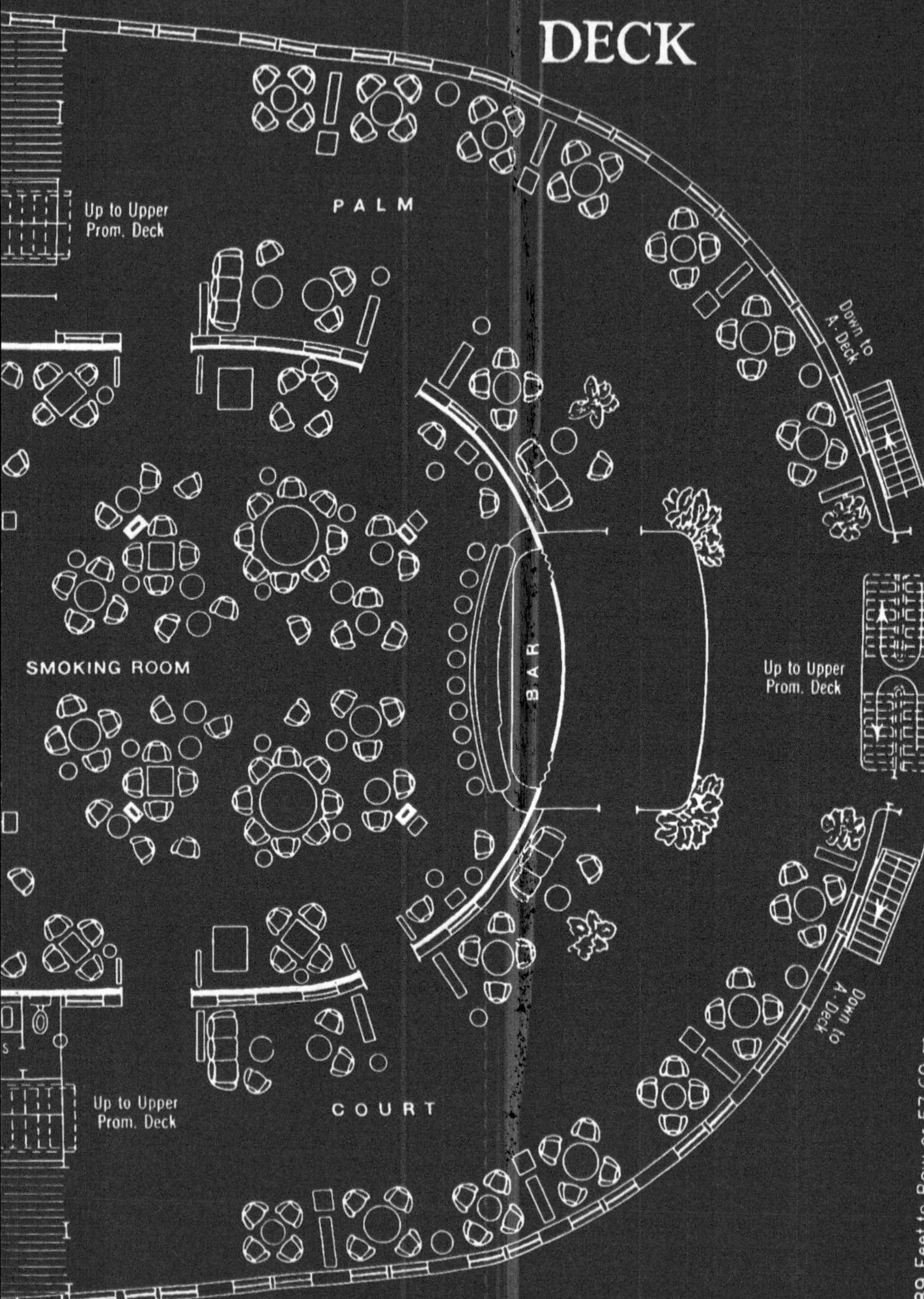

He fled through the ship as quick as flames to discarded paint cans in a troopship conversion. Not sure how he was feeling, what direction he should be headed, knowing only that the situation would become worse from here. And fast . . . now that he was alone again against a ship of men. Angry, was he? Betrayed? Either way he wanted to get on a dick quick, and the rougher and greasier the better. There was only one man for it. His engineman. How suddenly situations could turn at sea, how men could turn toward dirty acts in an instant. But he couldn't go in search of the greasy-rod bearer in an officer disguise. It was fine with the stewards in the accommodation corridors, they bent over on instinct at first flash of a shoulder stripe—like any man in ranking uniform were gold they'd panned their whole slut life for. Men tending to the turbines, however, real men, didn't bow down to such suit trinkets. If turned at all, it was generally by the soft puffs of the baker boys, or so he'd heard whispered among the men. Without any baked goods of his own, he'd need to turn on home baking.

He arrived panting back in their stateroom, the diamonds on the carpet coming at him like an autostereogram. He fell to the soft sole in a heap, but soon gathered himself when it occurred to him that Aurik might find him there soon. That was the last outcome he wanted right now. Then the pile of soiled and snatched German Labour Front clothes in the corner of his cabin gave him the mission. They'd been transported with his things from the *Smoking Room* and were now here.

Stinking and sticky like crusty knee-highs in the tent corner of Hitler Youth summer camp. He pulled them on. Instantly the scallywag gear transformed him into the stowaway from the locked-library mystery. Back in the slutboys' adventure tale; gave him a perfect distraction. The arse stitch stained from engineman seed, ship machinery grease slicks around the nipples and dick pouch, too. Back in disguise, he saw the *Library* through different eyes. Fosco had got *Bremen* out. For him. There must be some grand meaning to the murder. Then he remembered one piece of evidence he'd snatched from underneath Fosco's cold sweaty back. A page torn from a book. An English book, in a German library.

A bang on his porthole tore him from his thoughts, diving to the floor. Men on ropes outside, painting the ship a sea grey. A face peered in. Tilted head at his spread on the carpet. He crawled from the stateroom with his and Aurik's bag in hand. Of course, he had imagined the rope men. It was the middle of the night. There were no men on ropes. No faces looking in. Definitely not as cured as he thought. He was getting worse. *What fleshy hell is this? What monsters in the fog?* The hallucinations had started. He slapped his head with his palm, but it was too late, the face in the porthole was burned there. To haunt him forever.

He tried to focus. He would need to find a new place to sleep. He couldn't risk a note, Aurik would need to sleuth it out, and he quite liked not having to see Aurik for some time, anyway. Funny how his hurt at seeing Aurik fuck then piss into another man was fading a little already. Not the shitting, though. That was burned into him, too. But the other bits were fading. Was it because he did not care as much for Aurik as he thought, or because he did care, but something in him said there must be a reason for it all? Either way, he took Aurik's things with him. Of course, they would be together again. He was still plenty mad, mind. And would use that to find a man who'd raped him, to invite another crack.

Their bags stuffed temporarily in a turbine hatch nearby. He made his way down to the *Engine Room* and inside—seeing Aurik shitting into that steward, like hessian sacks into a cornhole sideshow game at a rodeo, keeping him hot and reckless. It was cleaner than he thought it would be, where the sweaty men worked in their grease coveralls. All shiny brass and smelling of oil and armpits and fresh coffee.

'I'm looking for one of your mates, a Mr Winter.'

'O yeah,' the nearest overalled greaser said, looking him up.

'I'm his boy,' he improvised. 'Told me to come look for him here. Just been to his cabin, not his crew cabin, but where he's been holing up. Cabin nine hundred and fifty-two, *D Deck*. He ain't there.'

Knowing and dropping Winter's fuck pad for all the pretty boys the man managed to snatch was a good touch, he thought. The flashes of Aurik piss and other things better than any all-night brew house to him now. Keeping him frisky and daring. No more wasting time.

'Been acting funny, came down this morning looking for monkeys of all things,' the greaser said.

'Monkeys?'

'You heard me. His boy, ay? What the hell, you might be able to straighten him out. Missed his shift.

Been hanging around the kid's playrooms, of all places. Fucked in the brain, if you ask me. I'd stay clear, if I were you, mate. But, hell, if you think you can get him clean. Go for it. But you tell him from me, from Carl, that I'm not covering for him no more.'

He turned to leave, not sure that this was any testimony he could trust.

'Boy,' the greaser called after him, 'try the first class *Kindergarten*, there's monkeys on its walls.'

His eyes narrowed in a distrustful fashion.

'Don't look at me like that, boy. I've kiddies. They like that crap. I keep an eye out for it. I might have pinched a toy or two to bring home. Damn kids always expect something when I get back, you know what I mean. And this boat won't be taking first-class brats anytime soon.'

Dawn was still several hours away, and the ship was in complete blackout. The high seas and high speed continued to tilt the walls at angles no passenger would have put up with. It smelled of the *Engine Room* in this dark place on *Main Promenade Deck*. He struck a match on the wall. It was like an Africa safari viewed through a camera obscura. Exotic painted animals all across the walls of the first-class *Kindergarten* could be seen through the flickering light, pressed flat against the walls to rise and fall with the ship's waves. Riding swells like some frantic scene from the Christian ark. There were three-dimensional animals too, these were more traditional. More of the woods and stables, with curved sleigh feet, of both wood and stuffed felt. A greyhound was mid-sprint, a dog waited with its tongue out for a treat and there were a few horses, too. All waiting for a ride. Stuffed toys sat on them at present, not getting up the momentum needed. Though the ship's throw did rock them a little. The animals creaking as they rocked to *Bremen*'s throw.

Creak, creak, creak

Glass eyes in the *Kindergarten* pulled the light from his match. Eyes like dead fish at the sea walls of a poisoned harbour. He wanted to run. It was like every Victorian ghost story. Everything moved in the single flame, even the walls came to life.

No, he thought.

No more running.

He turned round the room in search of the man who carried the smell of the engines and had put some of that inside him. Yes, he could smell the man. In the corner of the room was a winged back, for story time. The engineman wasn't in it. Another corner had a Punch and Judy show. He looked inside, but it was an empty stage. No engineman. No Punch nor Judy either. Judy showed herself in the next corner. Back broken, legs and arms dangling at an unhuman angle, on the rim of a children's slide. This was the darkest corner, with the strongest engineman smell.

His eyes strained to adjust. He reached over the slide to better see what was in front of him. A monkey on the wall with a fiendish grin, running up the slide.

In the dark his fogged mind played tricks. More hallucinations. Surely.

What was the shit-flinging smelly creature fleeing from? he wondered.

The desire to flee himself was strongest here, especially when, his gaze continuing down the incline of the slide, his light went out in a moment of intense pain.

'*Ah! fuck you's*,' he cried, sucking his singed index and thumb like a baby with no teether.

What had he seen just as the light went out? he thought as his eyes came over in the dots of a struggle to adjust to total darkness. Some frightful orgy of man and beast.

He fumbled with his matches, dropping them like useless tiny flares from an aimless airship. They rolled down the slide to stop partway down on some obstruction. One after the other, he struck and fumbled, until at last his shaking fingers could hold a match long enough for the flame to take.

He found Mr Punch.

Or what was left of the wooden thing. Gobbled up, its non-matching red and blue leather shoes sticking out like a midget wrong-way stuffed in a cannon. Except the mouth that ate the puppet was no iron chamber, it was the gob of his missing engineman, lips blue against the bull red sateen of woodman's trousers. His fallen tiny flares turning the skin black under their smouldering tips. The little illumination his sticks gave showing a dusting of white powder on the skin around the lips, like the engineman had rubbed cheeks with a mime. The eyes caught him most, though, glassier than any of the felt and wooden rocking animals in the playroom. Beady, like life had left long before the swallowing of Mr Punch had begun.

The engineman had the chin raised in the manner of a python swallowing some too-large prey, Mr Punch's beak protruding from the throat like the world's biggest Adam's apple. There were other beasts at play with the engineman on the kinder amusement; much bigger than Mr Punch and from which any monkey, however cheeky, however craving of mischief, would surely run. A felt rocking bear, head buried up the engineman's rump. Probably to scale of an infant grizzly, the girth of the bear's neck spread each buttock of the engineman so that the rounded sides were wider than the man's shoulders. And this had been a broad-shouldered brute.

Tight-arseholed too, if the brute's previous manhandling of his own arsehole was anything to judge the man by. This was a man who, in life, he reckoned, kept tight-lipped and unshaven the hole between the buttocks.

Into death, this bear had ripped the engineman a new one. And as with Fosco, there was no sign of preparedness to take anything inside.

All this assessment had taken place in the space of just a few seconds, only the length of the burn down of a single match. He had to touch Mr Winter to be sure the man was really there, but even in the feel of cold, dead flesh, he couldn't bring himself to believe the scene.

Just then, from a corner of the *Kindergarten* he was sure he'd already examined, a figure made like the monkey on the wall. Hightailing it out of there.

He was knocked to the floor with the mad dash. So too disturbed were many of the rocking animals, bucking their factory-made Steiff teddies from their harnesses as the room went dark again. The sound of galloping, glass-eyed things gyrating around him with all the intensity of the turbines' vibrations. As in he and Aurik's former stateroom, the floor—the ship's "sole"—paralysed him, until the figure was out of the playroom. But unlike the face caught sight of in that porthole window, this figure was no figment of an on-edge imagination.

In the moment before his tiny flame went out, he saw the engineman's hands and the horrid story they held. Arms above the gag on Mr Punch. At right angles, like a surrendering soldier at the front. Fingers spread and frozen in arthritic grip, fingernails torn up like bascules awaiting tall boats. Tremendous force up then down the slide could only have caused this. It reminded him of the resolve he'd seen from that same man now stuffed from both ends, when with two palms on the glass, a sash window into the *Library* had been opened. That determination to *see* death had come again, with tremendous force. The engineman, he realised, had invited the bear in. Backed on and off of it with a force that tore up the man's fingernails, ripped arsehole lip from arsehole lip to swallow the beast.

And then *he remembered!* that light dusting of white around Aurik's mouth, too. On Fosco, as well.

He had to get out. He had to *move!*

On all fours at first, clumsily, slipping on the red slick from where the bear had been allowed to rip open the man's cave. A helpless ferret of a thing, he was, trying to get out.

His slippery escape knocked the bear.

This made it worse, sent the engineman sliding again. The sound of flesh on the rubbing children's slip, like a butcher marinating; a sound sure to haunt him any time he again found himself with only dead things in the dark.

No! he shouted inside his mind, the *Kindergarten* behind him, but him still running. Not away from the situation. To it. The chase was on for the figure content to wait in the dark with an engineman arse-mounted on a grizzly. The sound of footsteps ahead told him which corridor to take, which stairwell, which door out to which promenade deck. Outside it was still not raining, but overcast, making everything black and all the surfaces damp with sea spray and the night. He closed his eyes. Could see better that way, it was so dark. The Atlantic spray laced him like the sideways rain in a hurricane. His mind stirring just as rapidly. *The footsteps have stopped.* Had he lost the stranger from the hellish playroom? He daren't let up the pace. Quickened it in fact, sprinting along the same promenade where the engineman had asked him had he wanted to see a dead body. The rough lad smeared in turbine oil, who seeded him so thoroughly, though he did not even know the man's name at the time of getting a gutful.

There was something wrong there. *What else don't I know?* he thought as he ran along the slippery promenade. What very basic detail was he missing? He'd passed the *Library* and that turbine hatch used earlier, the *Ball Room* he passed too, well aft now. He thought he'd best slow down——

Just as he tripped.

Face hot with the sensation of being made airborne, he took on the long strides of a sprinter just crossed the finish line. Trying to slow himself but being unable. Right foot one, left foot two, right foot three then collision. But rather than with the railing, for a tumble over and into the sea, he hit a figure that had been stood silently there—back to its playroom tricks. The figure was as rigid as a plank and like a pivot window on a horizontal axis, his crash into it sent the figure forward and over the edge from the waist, legs coming up to kick him back toward the superstructure like the basket of a Ferris wheel.

Laying on his back, the vibrations of the ship coming up through him; *please have gone in clean*, he thought. Though he feared, like with Fosco, that the figure might have struck one of the *A Deck* promenades. And unlike the throwing power of the engineman, that a body may have been snagged there this time.

He peered over the edge.

He couldn't see.

But he could hear.

'*Help me!*' came a shrill call through the crash of the waves. '*Please!* I don't want to die.'

He reached down the outer rungs of the railing. One. Two. Three. *There.* A hand four rungs down. Only slightly warmer than the iron. He could throw the hand off and into the sea. It would be a quick death.

No, he thought. He'd gone in pursuit for a reason.

One hand on the railing as an anchor, he grabbed hold and yanked with the other. Though an awkward angle, the figure was remarkably light and came up and back over with ease. Then flung arms round his neck, like a sloth a trunk. The boy from the dark room was a twiggy thing, brittle, like dried out tree tips. He scooped the boy up from under the knees and walked back toward the *Library*. Feeling his way.

Part of him searched the black for the tip of an engineman's cigarette. But there was none. That light was long gone. When he reached the familiar large sash windows of the *Library*, it was palm flat on the glass as he had learned. To open the room back up again with ease, to climb in with his catch in arms. Pulling out a match, he struck it on the wood panelling, let down the curtains and set the boy down in the winged back in the corner, next to the windows, the same he'd bounced on giddy in Aurik's lap. He did not wish to risk the electric light, for blackout enforcers would be sweeping the decks all night, and so from one of the cupboards he found a supply of candles and set about lighting a small number that he put in a circle around where Fosco's body had been found. Like the scene of some pagan devil summons.

The boy sprung to standing.

He was on it. Over to the boy, hand raised and brought down across the boy's face with such force that not only was the boy back in the armchair, by the armchair was on hind legs against the wall.

'Let me go,' the boy blabbered. 'Please don't kill me.'

No, this boy was no threat. No murderer.

His back hand had split lip and the boy cried now from the reared-up chair, looking as pathetic as a lamb in the jaws of a crocodile.

He felt no pity.

If what he had been told were true. If he was indeed to be the model for all men. The weak ones included. He needed to be firmer. Make the weaklings strong.

He let the boy cry and looked about the *Library*. It was as he and Aurik had a left it. *Yes*, he thought after trying the knobs, the doors are still locked and with no keys. And though reading material would probably have been most welcome for many on board during this dash into an unknown future, the books were of course undisturbed. No, none had thought to try the window to get in. Why would they? And the stains on the carpet—all black now, from blood and the knees of the engineman. These were not so consequential as to draw the eye of any who might have glanced in on passing along the promenade.

Satisfied with his survey, he pulled the boy out of the mouth of the chair.

'Stand,' he said, the boy's legs like undercooked pork belly. 'And stop crying.'

The boy wiped tears away, as he tore the shirt and trousers and little undies from the weakling with a kind of rage for the boy *not* being the murderer.

'Time-waster,' he said.

The boy was all bones, wiry black hairs on the arms and legs and crotch, out of which a pisser peaked, like a trembling fish among seaweed in the path of a white pointer.

He flicked the boy's dick.

'Pathetic worm,' he said.

Not because the boy had a tiny prick. Aurik's dick was perfectly petite.

Is perfectly petite, he told himself, hating the

time-waster more.

Nein, he loved a little fella in the pants. This boy was pathetic because all stood before him was puny.

'Pipsqueak,' he added, then spat. It landed as a bubbled wad across the boy's split lip.

The boy stood schtum, lips with blood and his spit and trembling.

'Well, lick it up, loser,' he said. 'You know you want to, yes.'

The boy did.

'Now you's bend over and *spread 'em, see*.'

The boy turned and opened for him. Wiry hair thick round the boy's button. And as hard as he could, he booted the boy in the shit box, sending the worm back into the chair.

'Make it quick,' the boy pleaded into the foliaged fabric, cheeks still spread. 'Don't feed me a bear.'

Now he was the one wasting time with all this getting a skinny arse spread. *Get to the point, yes. Find out what he knows.*

'What's your name?'

'Werner Weiner.'

It suited the weakling.

'What you doing in the *Kindergarten*, Weiner?' he said, pressing the grate of his boot above the arse, into the boy's tailbone.

'Please don't kill me.'

'Answer the question, yes.'

'I was looking for Curt.'

Curt.

So that was the engineman's first name. Certainly, this boy seemed to know the man better than he did.

'He fuck you on that slide?'

The boy started fingering where he'd booted.

'No, sir. But he did fuck me just about everywhere else on this ship. You could fuck me, too, if you like.'

He brought down the boot onto Werner's hand, eliciting a whimper from the boy, like the squeak of a dog toy in the mouth of a German Shepard.

'I don't put my dick in losers,' he said. 'Why was this Curt there if not to fuck a bitch like you?'

'Sir, *I don't know*, you have to believe me. He'd been acting queerly the last couple days. He took to playing with childish things. I didn't want him to fuck me no more.'

'Why were you looking for him then?'

'I wanted my Leica back. My camera.'

'You lend it to him?'

'Boys like me don't *lend* anything,' Werner said, another finger slipped in under his boot, a knowing look back at him from the contorted clamp into the armchair. 'When men want things from boys like me, they take them. And while I can talk about getting fucked in the arse with men, having photographs out there of it happening is another thing.'

Werner trembled under his boot, the fingering, it seemed, some kind of pacifier for the weakling. Like a self-cuddle after a night terror. Maybe he was starting to pity the sod a little.

'Have you searched Curt's cabin.'

'I don't know where it is.'

'I do,' he said. 'I'll get you your camera.'

His mind was a wee way agile again—adrenaline had worked like a watered-down Aurik remedy. He could see the pieces better now, his visit to the *Library* helped them fall. The shape of things clearer. He knew it was fleeting though, like a plaster over a killer snake bite.

'You followed Curt to that *Kindergarten*, yes. Then what?' he called to Werner, pulling the boy along.

Werner's bony arse and pinprick nipples were on show from where he'd torn at the boy's clothes. Werner held the long tears of deckhand uniform together like a dying man clutching a gun wound. The hour was wee enough into the next day that it was unlikely they'd be spotted in these corridors, the watchmen and blackout policers kept busy on the promenades.

Werner's clutching said to him the skinny boy was conscious of a distasteful physique.

'Speak, pipsqueak,' he pressed.

'I waited outside.'

'Didn't have it out with him?'

'No.'

'Why?'

'He had company.'

'Who?'

'One of the bakers,' Werner called short of breath. 'He'd taken up seeing this lad instead of me.'

He stopped a second, not to let Werner ease the chest, but wanting to watch the eyes for the next question.

'This baker. He as ugly as you are?'

Werner shrugged, then looked to the boy's shoes, the only covering left that concealed some of the bones. 'Is any man?'

There was a slight hesitation before the answer had come. This told him this baker was not good-looking.

'This baker a fatty? Round red cheeks only ma would pinch, yes?'

'I guess.'

He nodded and pulled Werner along again.

Taking shape, he thought. The white powder around that Curt's lips. That Aurik had too. It's come from the ship's *Bakery*.

A firming shape of things made him quicken his pull of the pipsqueak through the corridors and to Mr Winter's fuck room. He remembered Robert's comment over dinner on leaving New York harbour

. . . how long ago that felt now. Robert had spoken of bakers getting chummy with men of the engine rooms through bread. *Flour from bread rolls.* An arrangement between machine oiler and bread maker.

Werner was oily too, of the skin. Skinny and pimpled. But had a tight hole to fuck—he'd got the lad to show it to him. He could see an engine oiler being up for dumping some tension in. Especially knowing the kid would keep schtum about it. Taking the poor sod's camera to be sure. But the fat fuck from the second-class *Smoking Room*? Mr Winkler. He couldn't see Winter dumping one there. Why would the engineman bother with an ugly fatty like that?

But if he'd been drugged.

The guy could be persuaded with that.

Especially if it was the same stuff that had one hundred Nazi loyalists eating Italian mama's meatballs out of his anus. And had him thinking it was an inspired idea to serve these anal balls up for so many men . . . based just on one suggestion, nay insistence, by Robert.

You have to make men want to serve you. They need to hunger for you. Come to see you as their provider of food. That's an order, son.

Aurik! he thought in a rush, and he was a fool not to think of it sooner, remembering the glazed look in the eyes of the man, whiling away with piss then shit into that steward. Drugged eyes of a man who had only ever been loyal to him. Until that white powder came to blemish the chin and corner of mouth . . . to be followed by that Kenneth-given order.

Sorry I didn't see.

Hoping he was not too late, or that Kenneth was not cleverer than him in all things—*please still be there*, he thought.

He changed course.

The camera could wait, it was to the steward's cabin instead.

The pipsqueak went along, he gave the boy no choice, and when they reached the cabin door, came up that same corridor that he had kept himself out of Aurik's sight in during his jealous follow . . . he tried the handle. Yes, it was open still.

Ain't a good sign, he thought.

And inside he found another dead body.

He'd taken the wrong path when last stood at this door. The body this time being of a fat baker, a death so sinisterly simple—Mr Winkler, a dagger in the back. With the dagger-plunged baker before him, hope he held for finding Aurik alive plunged too, like the chance of him ever enjoying a bun made from flour.

He took the key from the inside of Kenneth's cabin door, to *lock, lock, locking* boy in with fat baker, pinned by backstabber. The kid was probably alright but he couldn't take any chances now . . . Hands shaking, that kind of tired where his vision started to jolt, not only blur. Like one of those lifts in the Edwardian liners, with the brass gates that pulled across in a great rattle and bang. **Bang, bang, bang** Was that only in his head, or the sound of Werner Weiner, crying and banging on steward door to be let out? Like a game of hide and go seek no one wanted to play anymore. He ran back to where he'd moved his and Aurik's kit, to climb under the covers. The bed had been unused. All their mattresses had escaped a drag up on deck so far. Under the quilt smelt of nothing except artificial fragrances of chemical cleaners. He hunted through Aurik's kit for some comfort. Like a small dog curled up on its master's fresh-off-the-foot socks, he wrapped his face in Aurik's woollen feet soils like one might dress a head wound. And then he prayed for sleep.

'*Right!*' he said, throwing back the sheets. 'None more of that,' stuffing Aurik's socks into his jock. It made him look frightfully big in front, like *Bremen* did beneath the waterline. The itchy scratch of the wool a pleasant sort of reminder that he still had at least a whiff of Aurik to one day sleep a night to. The sleep left him refreshed, like only men of his age could be given the stress of the last couple days. He felt brave again, too. Like he had when he'd set out along the raised highway in front of *Luxury Liner Row*, determined to find a man to help him set *Bremen* free. Well, he'd done that, he needed remind himself. And while the browns of this boat had it in for him, there was still a chance of success. It was late afternoon now. That served him well. Sleeping the daylight hours away was a good thing, he thought as he rubbed the creases from his ship-officer disguise. Washing sleep from the eyes with the cabin's basin, careful not to wet his nostrils or lips, the place reserved for Aurik's feet scent. His stiffener for whatever was to come.

He kept his head down up to *Upper Promenade Deck* via the first-class *Vestibule*. Sweeping back into the small toilet immediately fore of the firemen's cabins, imagining them fapping away behind him, waiting for a fire to spray on. The *Toilet*, with its cubicle for locking from sight the solids, and a urinal for letting loose liquid in full social view. Someone should really have taught Kenneth that, he thought. Although, and pondered, dropping to his knees in the place that only hours ago Aurik had last stood—sacred ground now, place of the last sighting—Kenneth must have known a thing about locking human waste away. For there was no mess. The porcelain gleamed. Not with any chemical sheen of a recent attendant's cleaning. No, a light matte film around the dips in the elegant sweeps in the urinal's design.

It truly was sculptural, he noted without having that word come to his muddying again mind. He knew nothing of Duchamp, of course. He was too young to, his parents too peasant to have ever told him the story of Dadaism, and he too arrogant to apply himself to learn, to read, afterwards. Of anti-art reactions to the Great War. While his countrymen were getting blown to bits in the trenches, a urinal was mounted in a New York art exhibition. One big "fuck you" to a world that had, by all appearances, no appreciation for aesthetics and masculine beauty and the truth of man in an artistic sense. How could it? Well, where some saw absurdity, Kenneth had shown in a grand kind of statement of performance art that beauty comes from all parts of a man. With men's best beauty coming from inside.

He lent in close. Aurik's base scent still in his nostrils. He ran along the lip of the urinal like a metal detector along the slacks of a perfect criminal, in search of any other traces. But they'd all been licked up. Damn the man, he thought, Kenneth clearly determined to keep taking Aurik from him. But as much as he hated the lily boy, what he'd seen stirred vividly inside him in a churning sort of way a kind of fascination for what he'd witnessed that kept his dick hard. Like the Adam to the apple. He could not unsee that. And what he hated most about Kenneth is that the fellow had taken a deep, fragrant part of the man he loved that he'd never had. *I love you, yes.*

It made him see the gent's inner bodily ablutions differently. Collectively. As manly sculptures. Not only to be washed away. The urinal before him, cracked at the point of cantilever from taking the kind of loads that its designer had never dreamt of factoring in. Shortsighted, a non-visionary, factory kind of sculptor. Not an artist or philosopher. As he felt himself now, with the urinal mounted before him, evidence of its use in a different function. Like a cricketer's groin cup, remade to take all of men's intimates, liquid or solid. It was perfect. The impulse to strip himself and "assume the position," to wait for one of the men of this sector of the ship, a wireless operator, or officer, or better yet, one of them burly firemen or five, to come by and perhaps, seeing him there as an extension of the receptacle, use him the why Aurik had used Kenneth. It filled him, this impulse. To be fit for purpose for all men's releases.

Piss is social, shit to be locked away, right? Tell that to the boys of the front. Shitting alongside in a man-dug hole, as intimate and bonding a moment as any nude swim with the horses between shell bombardment. Tell it to the boarding schoolboys, too, or the military cadets, shitting together in an ostensibly endless line of porcelain or metal receptacles with no barrier between them. At the time of first glimpse, white-knuckled over the rim of the room's one cubicle, he'd watched the scene like the newsreels of the *Hindenburg* burning. Never able to be unseen. Charred log, dark as peat and textured as wooden coal in a hearth. So sulphurous—that the nose is so attuned to. *Why?* Out of Aurik's brilliant white arse like the end of a baseball bat into the glove suck of Kenneth's spread. Ruining him forever.

O *the humanity!*

He burst out of the *Toilet* to continue fore along the corridor, up a small flight of stairs and into the sleeping den of the ship's officers. A risky move, but a handy location to have men happen upon him. Yes, he courted whatever might come of it. He was desperate now. Without any restraint. Try as he may to stuff down the will to be filled by all manner of masculine offspring . . . he could not. Feeling himself approaching a kind of keenness to be that beautiful porcelain thing, but better engineered, to take to a different purpose. Not to crack under cantilevered tension. He felt akin to when full with mama's meatballs. Back in the meatpacking district.

He ran the corridor of the officers' cabins, door after door flying past him without regard for the noise he made. His returned, muddy-minded recklessness frightened him, in an exhilarating kind of way. The memory of Aurik's log . . . so healthy and firm and richly dark brown, like trunks of trees in the Rominte Heath of his boyhood. He wanted nothing more than to fell these logs, to fill himself with them. It consu——

Thud

He'd knocked a man to the floor in his run from—or to?—the urge to consume what Aurik made.

Colliding at the intersection of the officers' quarters, landing as a limb entwinement on the stairs up to the captain's bed.

The bang did him good. Steadied him some, like the slap across the face of a hysterical mistress.

'Ease up, mate,' the man said, in all the trimmings of a senior deck officer, pulling him by wrist into a cabin at the extreme end of the corridor.

Two windows in the curved fore of the cabin gave a view of the ship's path, and of promenades for the bookends of the ship's four classes. A desk under one view, a seating area under the other. Not that he could see much of what lay ahead. It was getting dark outside, the skies overcast still, stopping any kind of light from above. The senior officer's grip of his wrist was firm as a knot well tied, it guided him to the couch with no view.

'Chief Officer Richard Horn,' the man said, hand outstretched. 'But you can call me Chief Officer *Dick* Horn.'

He took it.

'We meet at last, Mr Bauer,' Horn making coffee and serving it out. 'I've seen your pictures.'

Horn was Robert's age. Somewhere in the forties, but with an athleticism that made him sure the man could compete with any twenty-something. Made more handsome than boys his age by the little crinkles of experience he'd come to fancy, each side of dark eyes. Slightly gaunt features, from a disciplined diet and hearty cardio exercise—wilderness hikes mostly, he imagined, made do when at sea with vigorous runs around the promenades while passengers lay sleeping. A bony nose, with black hair that flopped with every movement and lightly peppered around the temples. Horn could have been Robert's darker brother, he thought. Here's another man's photonegative.

By *pictures*, he wondered whether this Chief Officer Dick referred to his propaganda films or the nude centrefolds in *SS-Leitheft*. Was this senior officer someone who had seen his dick in a statuesque pose? He was, it should be said, no Marlene Dietrich.

'You're trembling,' Horn said after several minutes without him giving a reply.

The coffee probably wasn't helping, he thought. It strong and bitter.

'You know me,' he said curt. 'Why I'm here.'

'Of course,' Horn said. 'Who do you think sent for you?'

As he and Horn drank coffee, no milk offered, the chief set out concerns about a captain's lackadaisical regard for Berlin orders. It made sense now, even if fatigue was back with its fog that made him slow to track Horn's story through. *Bremen*, the pride of Germany, had in its first decade two captains. The first who had taken early retirement after the Nazis' rise to power, bowing out in a struggle with conscience. The second, more the party man, or so it had been thought; the man who had demonstrated a willingness to serve the Reich, in the sheltering of spies on the liner, for instance, but who recently, in *Bremen*'s greatest hour of need, had, well, wavered. Horn had been there from the start. Been a key figure feeding back information from the inside. Biding time, it seemed, until the man could rise himself to *Bremen*'s call.

'I wanted to meet you immediately,' Horn said. 'That's why I set up that table for us on the roof of *Sun Deck*. But the captain called a meeting in the *Ball Room*, and you have eluded me ever since.'

'I stay with the stern,' he said. Too foggy to think about that table *up there*, seeming so long ago with Robert.

'Yes, I suspected as much. My duties keep me fore, I'm afraid. Our bump to-day is fateful, Mr Bauer. I assume command at night, while the captain sleeps.'

As do I, he thought.

'Once the sun sets. I can take you up on the *Bridge*. After dark, if you like.'

'Another time maybe,' he said.

It was probably Aurik in his thoughts that made him decline. Though an ally was needed now more than ever.

'Don't wait too long,' Horn said. 'Time is running out.'

'If we met on that first night, you'd have said what?'

The sun had sunk now, but he thought he saw Horn smile at the question, just as the man turned on a small lamp with a shirt draped over, then closed the curtains. Shutting the sea away like the end of a stage play.

'What I've told you already, about me putting out the call for you and my concerns about our captain. Along with some friendly advice and the offer to use me.'

He titled his head.

'I oversee all the officers, you know. I daresay your task would have been much smoother had you known you could lean on me.'

'You know about my . . . troubles, yes.'

'With the brownshirts, *yes*. Difficult to control that bunch at the best of times. Did you know that the captain had to actually ban them from strutting about the ship? Imagine that. Peacocking through the decks, stopping at every mirror to admire themselves. Playing soldiers has gone to their heads, that's for sure. Not as disciplined as your lot. The men in black. The browns are just thugs, if you ask me. And they have funny ideas. Some of the things I've been hearing.'

Horn's dark eyes looked at him like a dormitory master might at a schoolboy caught pleasuring in the baths. He remembered Robert's advice.

'I made a mistake, yes,' he confessed. 'Lost respect of the men.'

Horn cleared the coffee away. Fetching a bottle of Jägermeister and pouring two glasses.

'Respect is a funny thing,' Horn said. 'It can be both earned and commanded. From what I've heard, your attempts failed because you tried only the latter.'

'No time to earn respect,' he said. 'None here know who I am and why I'm here, including the cap.'

'That's where I can help.'

'Maybe later, yes,' he said, downing the drink and standing to leave.

'You know where to find me.'

'On the *Bridge*.'

'Yes. You sure there's nothing I can do for you now?'

He thought to his last time with Aurik.

'Does *Bremen* have a poop deck?'

Horn smiled, narrowing the eyes in a sign of being intrigued. 'Now of all the questions you could have asked.'

He shrugged. 'Was talking with a . . . *friend*, he said the *Titanic* was the last ship to have a poop deck. I wondered if it was true.'

Horn got up too, but to go to the bookshelf in the cabin.

'These sailors, seriously. Not one of the officers, I hope.' Horn shot up a hand. 'Best not you say who, otherwise it'd be straight back to Mürwik for him. Or,' Horn's eyes narrowed even more, in the manner of a poker player studying an opponent, 'Greenwich, maybe? And I don't need the headache of being any more men down.

'*Poop*,' Horn said running a finger along the spines of the books, mostly in German, but with a single shelf in English, 'from the French *la poupe*, for stern, with its root in the Latin *puppis*. But I know you have this fondness for the English, Mr Bauer.' Horn pulled a hardback from the English shelf—so navy it looked black—and brought it into the dim lamplight. 'In that case, we shall consult the British Admiralty on the matter.'

Horn opened the book to the back. Before the book flopped open in the fold of the chief's lap he had read *Manual of Seamanship Vol. I. 1937*, embossed in gold. Horn then read to him in the manner of a clean-cut missionary reading from the *Book of Psalms*. 'Chapter Fourteen, under "Principal parts of a ship and terms relating to them." we find "*Poop*.—A short deck above the upper deck right aft in the stern." Right, that answer your question?'

He nodded, even though really it hadn't.

'Come, Mr Bauer. You can be honest.'

He shook his head then.

'Yes, the British can be a bit dense.'

Horn then pulled from the draw of the desk a plan of the *Bremen*, unfolding it on *B Deck* in the man's lap. Horn then took his hand and pressed it into the centre of the plan. The plan was of such a size that instead of moving his hand along it, Horn pulled the plan under his pressed finger, like a record under a needle.

'An upper deck forms the main part of the ship, anything above it being the superstructure. *B Deck* is our upper deck. So, should we find a deck "above" *B Deck* "right aft in the stern," that means at the very, very back. Where, for example, you might dangle your legs with this friend of yours. You following me so far, Mr Bauer?'

He nodded, swallowing hard.

'Good. If we do find such a stern deck, then we have located the *Poop*. And look here, ending the pull of the plans across Dick's lap on the open deck of the tourist *Promenade*, right at the stern, on *A Deck*. We've found *our Poop Deck*. Does that put you at ease? Give you confidence to speak with your friend? To meet a man, maybe?'

He neither nodded nor shook his head, meanwhile Horn continued to rub the so-called *Poop* on the plans in the man's lap. It got him thinking . . . His understanding of ships was of such a rudimentary nature that he could only take this man's word on it. For instance, did it not make more sense that *A Deck* would be the upper deck in the scenario being described? He did not question the chief, though. How could he? It left him only more confused and stood to confirm that, for his purposes, he would stick with Aurik. Though, clearly, not the *Poop* as defined by the source from a country that has named it as such. But in his world, for this voyage, Aurik and his *Poop Deck* was the aft edge of the first-class *Promenade* on *Sun Deck*. At the shed, where games are played. A secret he'd keep.

'Of course, I could just be pulling you with all this. You wouldn't know either way, would you, son?' Horn said, like he was one of those electric deck plans found on each of *Bremen*'s levels. Exposed for all of this officer to see.

He had no come back for that.

Horn put a hand on his inner thigh. 'Let's look at another nautical term concerning the stern, son,' Horn said, flipping pages in the admiralty handbook from principal parts of the ship to miscellaneous sea terms, all the way to "P." Then, one finger scratching the page of the admiralty handbook; fingers of the other hand, the seam of his inside trouser leg; Horn did another reading. '*Pooped.*—A ship or boat is said to be pooped when a heavy sea comes inboard over the stern or when a ship is in any way damaged or rendered unmanageable through the action of such a sea over the stern.'

Horn let the words sink as the scratching reddened between his legs. He was not so simple of mind to miss their meaning.

'You look pooped to me, son.'

'I have to go now,' he said, standing up.

Dizzy, perhaps he'd stood a little too quick. Steadying himself a moment on Horn's English shelf.

It reminded him of something.

But what?

'A reader, Mr Bauer?' Horn asked, up behind him.

What was it with handsome men and reading?

'No,' he replied.

'Pity. Books are powerful in our world. More than they have ever been. Take this title, for instance,' Horn said pulling from the German shelves, *In the West, Nothing New*. 'I could get in deep *poop* for having this in my private library,' Horn said holding the book published in English as *All Quiet on the Western Front*. 'In '33, a Gestapo thug took it from one of my sailor rests in Bremerhaven. I took it from him. The book was banned and burned that same year, you know. Perhaps you may permit me a question now, before you run off.'

He did not answer, still turned away from the man, facing the door.

'Last evening, there was quite the commotion on the *Bridge*. Not long after I had taken command, a distress call came in, an S.O.S. from a stricken liner.'

Athenia, he thought.

'Believed to be a German ship and not far from our present position. It pulled all my officers to arms, kept men well away from these quarters here, for some hours, around a time when normally there would be plenty of souls about. I was forced to double the watch on the topside decks, and to pull in the captain, too. Quite the commotion. But, you see, turns out my wireless operator made an error in interpreting the distress signal. Copied down the incorrect longitude. Caused enough panic to keep me at my post for hours.'

He could feel Horn's breath on his nape as the man closed in on him. Distracted, thinking on what it was about the man's bookshelf that was so familiar.

'And when the chief's kept on the *Bridge*, he can't play as he'd like. You wouldn't know anything about that mix-up would you, son? Some kind of cover for some devilment about the decks? It was a clever move, if you were behind it. Reminds me of the tale of the Turkish cruiser in Messina in the Great War. Have you heard that one?'

He shook his head.

'Turkey was our ally then,' Horn said retrieving their glasses and topping them up, manoeuvres to hold him there. 'We'd transferred her one of our cruisers, and under the Turks this cruiser had entered the Sicilian port after being pursued by two

British warships. It looked like game over. But there was a heavy fog, and the captain came up with a genius ruse to slip away. It involved the ship's band playing topside, then being dripped into a lifeboat in the harbour one by one, playing in the lifeboat as the cruiser slipped out to sea. Genius. And it's got be wondering whether you, in your current state of mind, would be capable of such a plot. To distract me and the officers, to get things done, you know. But if not . . . well, it's got me questioning loyalties, you see. It would mean that someone else was playing the decoy. I need to know, son.'

Hands landed on his shoulders just as the cabin door swung open. Horn stuffed hands in blazer jacket.

'What's the meaning of this, Mr Weber?'

'Sorry, sir,' the wireless operator from Aurik's merry men said, furtive glances in his direction.

Was it Mr Weber who copied down the wrong position, he wondered.

'The captain needs you on the *Bridge*,' Weber said. 'Urgently.'

'I'll be there shortly, now leave us.'

'No,' Weber said.

'What did you say?'

'Sorry, sir. I mean, it cannot wait.'

'What? Speak, boy.'

'An iceberg warning. Dead ahead.'

Horn rocked a second, as if teetering on a decision that should have been most straightforward.

'You sure you got it right this time, Mr Weber?'

He is the one then, yes.

'Yes, sir. Quite sure. Sorry again, sir.'

Horn rocked a second longer.

'We'll pick this up later, Mr Bauer,' Horn said. 'What cabin are you staying in?'

'Four hundred and eighty-six, on *C Deck*,' he told Horn, the number of he and Aurik's second-class stateroom. 'Were on *A Deck*, eighty-one to seventy-nine, but had to move.'

It was clever of him, he thought, to give the man cabins he had actually stayed in. Of course, having moved on yet again. He was back of *C Deck* now, six hundred and sixty-six, with a nice escape path to *B Deck* and above.

'Gentlemen, after you,' Horn said after one more rock, not clear whether the man believed him, but duty bound to have no choice but to leave.

While Horn was staring down Mr Weber, he managed to fold up and stuff *Bremen*'s deck plans through his crack. Like he had with *Library* clues, he would study them later. Horn and Weber then ascended to the *Bridge*, leaving him back in the corridor again. It was his turn to teeter now. The encounter with Chief Officer Horn had left him conflicted. The prospect of a high-up ally in the cause should have made him happy, but could he trust the man? Could he trust anyone now?

At least before, steaming at twenty-seven point five knots, he could have told himself as a new day approached that the prospect of a safe harbour was a little more than a distant hope. But now with the iceberg revelation followed by what happened next. Just some couple minutes later. It was like something out of the dreams of dead soldiers in the deep trenches in the woods of the Argonne . . .

All engines stopped

It was that kind of event to bring perspective. Show him that even with a body count mounting, their situation could always get worse. It was an eerie feeling. Like what he imagined a paratrooper in the Luftwaffe might experience at the moment the cord was pulled. Quiet and peaceful away from the roar of mighty engines and adrenaline of an unnatural speed. Floating. Even the swells had diminished some; a relative calm at sea, but with a profound feeling of foreboding to go with the silence. Knowing you were heading into mortal danger. Knowing quiet was rarely good. Missing the noise, having gotten so used to it that you hadn't heard silence in days.

You can always feel more alone in the world, that all-engines-stop order on the fourth of September showed him. That same day, reports from Paris that *Bremen* had been captured by the British and interned at Portsmouth caused glee among the crew. False reports of course, phoney news drummed up out of the shame that all the King's men of the British navy, including its "Humber Force," consisting of cruises *Glasgow* and *Southampton* with eight destroyers searching the Atlantic just for *Bremen*, was failing. It caused delight. Even the provisioning of lifeboats that day was done with shanties.

But he was away from all that. Divorced of all-male group glee and arse-flick shenanigans. Curling up now in the urinal of the *Toilet* behind the firemen cabins. All quiet on the piss porcelain of firemen and officers. Feeling like his own mind was plotting against him. Not caring whether he'd be caught and committed to some human-test-tube asylum. Wanting for it, maybe.

He was snagged in a harbour fog without any band of men. But at least he had *art* to curl up in.

Only here did sleep came for him again.

In a crib of the piss of men.

Thumb in his mouth.

C-DECK

5 September

Beds

✠ Upper Pullman Berth

* Removable Upper Pullman Berth

Child's Berth

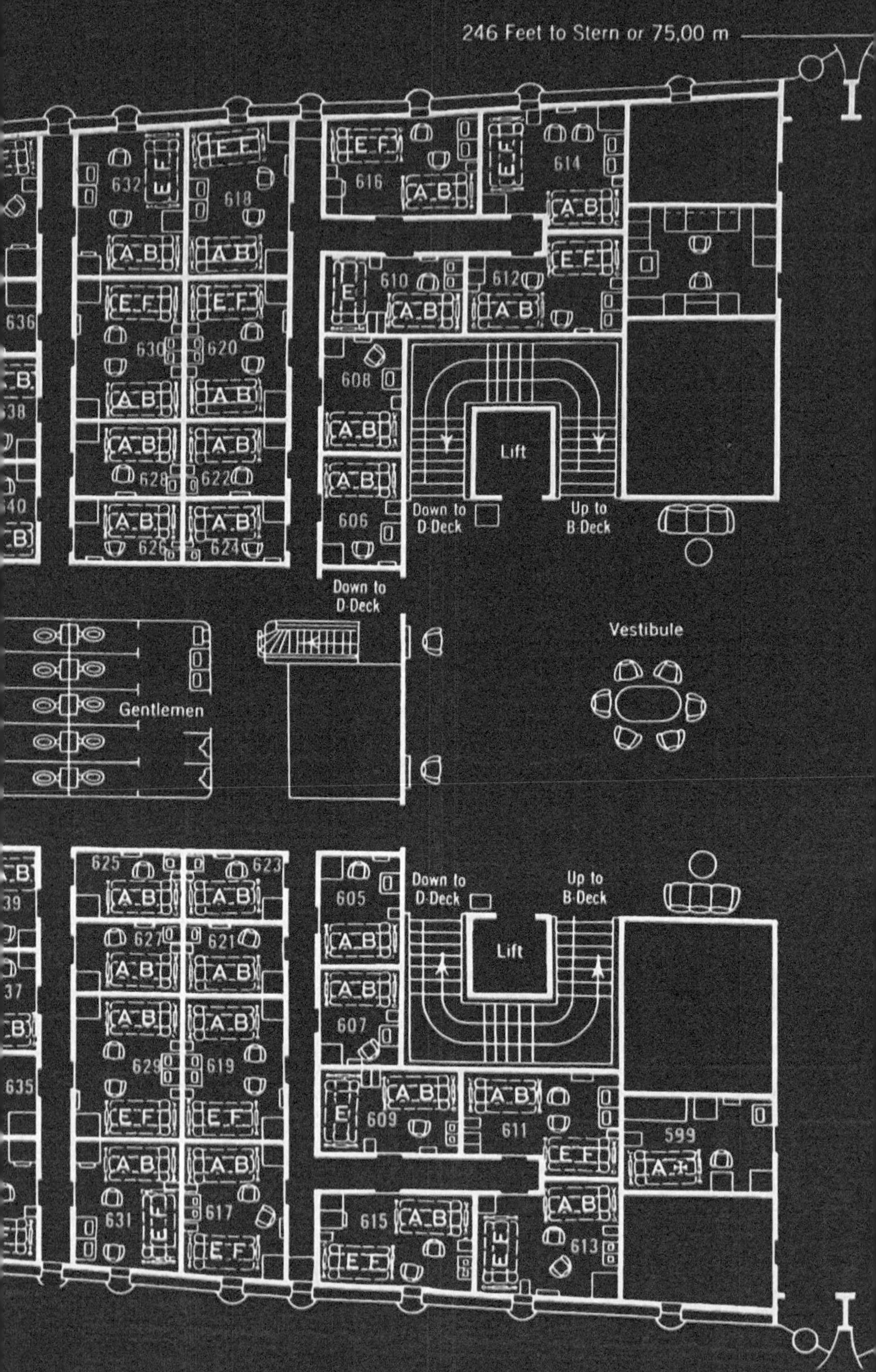
246 Feet to Stern or 75,00 m
632
618
616
614
610
612
636
630
620
608
638
Lift
628
622
Down to
D-Deck
Up to
B-Deck
606
640
626
624
Down to
D-Deck
Vestibule
Gentlemen
625
623
Down to
D-Deck
Up to
B-Deck
605
639
627
621
Lift
637
607
629
619
635
609
611
599
631
617
615
613

The fifth of September, '39. A day that would go down in the *Bremen* log as the most uneventful of her entire dash to a benevolent port. Well, a playing-at-friends port anyway. To a Soviet harbour, iceless year-round. He had no access to the captain's log, but had he, he imagined the entry for that day would simply state that no other ship had been sighted since a ghost ship of the previous morning. That's right, a ship was sighted on the horizon after the phantom-iceberg warning. They would never find out who that ship was or for that matter whether the iceberg warning was genuine.

Aurik was his ghost ship for the fifth. Haunting him round every bend, like the *Bremen* had already sunk but he did not know. And all that were left were ghost men. Every fine cut of a man he pursued, in elaborate costume. *Men's Showers* in all their forms were his favourite hideaways of the day. His forgetting places. Buried under a trolley load of smelly briefs that kept piling on and on and on with the rotation of watchmen shifts.

He stayed in his cabin at first. Six hundred and sixty-six on *C Deck*. With its same diamond carpet but two beds this time. For just one single bed with couch would be too much of a reminder of the room Aurik had picked out for them. Aurik would have been pleased with what he'd found. Far aft in second class, stairwells to *B* or *D Deck* were in easy reach, as were hatches out and into the sea, should it come to that. Werner Weiner brought him flowers from the *Florist Shop* on *Main Promenade Deck*, located as kind of part of the *Vestibule* and near the *Kindergarten*. The flowers brought to him were wilting. The petals soggy and stinking like the banks of a drained lake in the sun. There was not much left in the *Florist Shop* worth sniffing, the reprovisioning of the ship in New York had not, naturally, extended to the restock of flora from the port of call. Why would it?

What was left, Weiner fetched for him, so much that the dead flowers burst from his cabin and out into the corridor like moss through bark in a wet wood. Like some poor bastard's forgotten open casket, none interested in that chance to say goodbye. When asked why Weiner felt the need to bring him these dead petals, the sad thing said returning to the *Kindergarten* was a reminder of meeting him. Of *the best thing*. What a loser. But really, who was he to judge? '*Shoo!*' he'd say each time Weiner brought him dead flowers. But then he would head out naked into the corridor. Tempting a run-in with an *SS* man to body guard.

At the corridor end was a little table under a porthole. Onto the table he arranged a bouquet, but the dead flowers drooped like the necks of thirsty camels. He was keen shit at this. Rather than a splash of colour and an invite to a lover somewhere in the ship. Unlike rose petals in a bath . . . it was a morbid clump he'd put there, an ill-conceived potpourri. He waited for Aurik, still. The fog made him feel like he had no other option.

Aurik never came.

Each time he looked to the sea, to the circle view behind the dead flowers, he would catch a glimpse of another of those demon bosun boys, smiling through the glass in at him. He slapped the temple with one hand and plucked soggy petals with the other, showing arse to the ghost in the glass and stuffing the flower flesh into himself like a primitive, rose-water pestle and mortar. He spent hours in the corridors like this. Until Weiner, fresh out of dead flowers, came to him with another idea.

Go to where more than one shower could be found side by side, the Weiner had said, feeling like a ghost by this point now too. *Go to where the stink of man-musky bits will weigh you down like silt in a concrete canal.* That last bit was in his mind. Some kind of poetic statement on his loss that these places became on the fifth. These showering places for the sweaty *Bremen* men. And these were, cruel fate ensured it, most enticing in the rooms of the *Swimming Pool*. The first-class *Gymnasium* and *Medicinal and Electric Baths* on *G Deck* held showering promise too. He had to stay hidden, of course. Both because he was a wanted man and because gawking at the wash-up of another man was not, in his experience, yet naturalised. Sneak peeps were perfectly acceptable, but not himself naked and stroking, mounted on the vaulting horse from the *Gymnasium*, moved into the shower space like some Trojan sin.

The ideas he had these last few days . . .

But such thoughts *were* a comfort, if consuming. It got him pondering, these showers, as he peered through a hole worn in an engineer's briefs. It was a rare thing, only one man in the shower rooms. Watching the man who'd gifted these briefs to him take the opportunity in the shower to rub hard and then to completion with the steady flow of the steamy water. Just given them away, he thought, breathing deep. The scent, different in different parts. He took his time, like the fine wine. Starting with where the helmet of the engineer's dick slit had been. It smelt of urine, a little stale, bitter, pungent—from where the dick had squirted out a quick piss off one of the decks, or failing that, onto one of the turbines, for who would smell it among all the sweat and oil and coffee that characterised the engine rooms?

Just the slightest wiggle of his head, like a puppy getting comfortable on the scent of its master's woollen jumper, it was on to sweeter notes of the testicle sack. He rolled his head in full, one-eighty-degree sweeps, like a good boy checking both ways before crossing even a quiet Straße. The smell of sweat from the balls of a man hard stroking in the shower before his soiled-jocks' hiding spot. The balls spot was still warm and spread up his own cheeks. This was where the cock had nestled between the padding of widespread balls, like the cushion that carried a king's crown.

Then it was through the taint, *the gooch, the chad*, that stretch of so much erogenous potential and yet, for so many men, that was a lifetime's no man's land. The man working dick shaft in the shower was one of those lads never to go there, he could tell by peeping through the gaps in a ship's worth of men's dirty pants. That's why this was such a treat. Such a rare flavour. Like the wildlife biologist, up a tree with a telephoto lens. He was sniffing something right now no man had ever sniffed before. Well, he made the most of it, dragged his nose across it now. A no man's land? Not to be crossed. Fuck no; never, bro. Well, he crossed it now. Deep. All the way to the skids, where rich logs had been farmed. The most pungent part of a man. Man's inner beauty.

All he could think of was Aurik when he arrived there. Shitting into that steward. All he could think . . . *that should have been me*. Yes, everything reminded him of Aurik. But, too, this laundry basket was his escape from the world. It was his log cabin. His place on the lake to fly fish, to wade on in and forget Aurik, too. Just for a little while. Just with an anonymous, other man's soaped-up helping hand. And a chance to think on *what's next*, too. As the end of this passage approached. It cheered him up some, with the prospects. To remind him that this was temporary, should they get through now, which it looked like they might, and then somehow make it back to Germany. Then he would have a role to play in the war. And right here, buried with his men's trench bits, that was where he would lead. That is, if he wasn't already a dead man.

He decided then that *Bremen* would not be any convoy raider. No troopship either. No, he would use his influence to ensure *Bremen* would stay in a German port as a symbol to be filled upon filled with only the finest fighting men. He could even do their laundry. He could picture it. He'd get stuck in. Werner Weiner could help him, as the lad did that day. Standing in the corridor outside the showers, to come in on occasion, bury head in with the streaky briefs like a flamingo in the muddy flats, searching for a morsel from him, a word on whether or not he was ready to be wheeled on to some other location around the ship to get the whiff of the men.

'Not yet,' he said sharply on the latest Weiner drift in, the engineer turned to the wall to hide the soapy cock rub. 'Let the man finish. Come back in ten.'

Werner had proven to be a worthy, if wholly ugly, merry man. Breaking out of that baker's stab cabin to go in search of him. That was where the laundry trolley came in. And Werner got inventive. Sealing off the *Toilet* and getting out the tools of a man more appetising, Werner had taken nut after nut off the urinal mounting, until he tumbled into a bed of smelly jocks and coveralls, urinal cradle and all.

Yes, Werner was a good wheeler of the laundry trolley, the keeper and lookout of his position. Making sure his foxhole was not found. The men treated the poor lad poorly, called names, spat, rubbed shitty briefs in the sod's nose. Werner took it all with a calm dignity. Better than having to get fucked in the arse, he knew now. Werner would never need get fucked again, he resolved. That would be his reward to the ugly boy for a lifetime of service.

Perhaps feeling the pressure to offload, the engineer had needed only five minutes from the window of ten he'd given. Eyes rolled back as the engineer's pump of the soapy shaft reached an intensity on par with the *Bremen*'s in-flight turbines. He raised his head out of the pile like a camouflaged marine in jungle waters, to get a clean view of the end. When it approached, he needed duck under again, for the engineer came to the trolley. Had he been seen? he wondered. Either way the man pumped white on top of a hundred men's briefs, then fled. The goo of the man dripped down to his hiding place. He scooped it up to add to that same man's underwear, now his bandana face covering, completing the flavour profile. Licking up some as Werner wheeled him out. That was another resolution for the future. He would get a whole sense of the men who would fight in this great struggle.

There were a few wash stations across the ship. He visited them all in a similar fashion. His trolley also able to take on new armour to suit other spaces as well. Shitty jocks could be swapped for napkins in the dining rooms, which could be swapped again for towels in the sauna. All places he went gladly, save the *Swimming Pool*. He sent Werner in solo to see that one. That was too painful, and as restorative as his sensory immersion in all the rubbing bits of the ship's men was, his longing for Aurik was wheeled with him everywhere. A dull feeling that, while escaped from for moments . . . Wunderbar occasions of getting to know his countrymen more intimately than even their wives or girlfriends ever would . . . That dull feeling, yes, it was always waiting for him in the corridors after sampling all his countrymen's flavours.

Peering through the stitched seam of the trolley bag, he thought he caught sight of his closest comrade all over the ship. And boy did he follow up those leads. Giving instructions to Werner like the man were his first mate. More a devoted deckhand than of any officer class, but obedient and capable. He imagined Werner a little like the trusty, wire-haired terrier that might accompany an old sea dog on a Caribbean adventure. A comfort to him in a ship that, otherwise and though flavoursome, would be a reverberating chamber of loss always. A vast mausoleum. That was the fifth. A day of searching, full of fruits, but not fruitful in its sole purpose.

Now he stood facing the bow of the ship on *Main Promenade Deck* at the day's end. Taking his window to leave his trolley. While the rest of the men relaxed in the first-class *Smoking Room* at their backs, he was with Werner in *Palm Court*, the great red horizon stretched out before them through one of the windows like the cinematographer's dream of an ocean-liner epic. They were one sleep from Murmansk and there was a real feeling of "made it" among the men. It was in the air. Wounds were beginning to heal, he dared feel.

A few of the *SA* fellas coming out to strut the first-class promenade with champagne in hand even turned a blind eye to his place in *Palm Court*. They would recognise him, surely, from his meatballs. But also, now swelling with German pride, from all his pictures. A proud Germanic thing, such *a pretty thing*. The captain had previously banned such peacocking of Nazi party men on *Bremen* for fear of how such vehement nationalism might upset the paying guests. Well . . . there were no guests now, and even had there been, he knew without ever meeting the man that the captain would not have minded. When, at last, it looked like you may well have done it, against all odds, you let the men prance.

The sun was setting. The clouds still gave *Bremen* their hiding blessing. It would only have flattened the bubbles were it a clear night, but the reds of an end of day over the sea could be seen through the grey. It was every North German Lloyd brochure in *Palm Court*. But all nothing without Aurik to share it with.

'You can take out your disappointment on my arsehole if it helps,' Werner said at his side.

He'd forgotten he wasn't alone.

'Men have said I'm not as ugly inside as I am out.'

On the surface of it, this sounded like self-pity. A pathetic ploy to call out of him an opinion to the contrary. But the eyes of Werner Weiner told him the offer was genuine, as was the belief that the arsehole on offer to his missing of a much finer man was maybe comforting; a man sock not rotten as the skin of the face of the one offering it.

'I can see that, yes,' he said with a small smile. Like he imagined Aurik might have given him had things worked out different. Aurik would have said something like that to him after him saying, *Things'll be better now*, or something like that, he dreamed in the fading red of day. Aurik giving a small smile and nod, after they'd triumphed together. Once they'd beaten all who stood in their way. That baker and steward bound somewhere in one of the ship's hidden holds, instead of one stabbed and the other having stolen Aurik away.

'I have a hood I can wear,' Werner added.

He turned on the boy, the pox of the face not as putrid in the evening light. 'That what you want? For me to seed you.' He was willing to do it if that was the case.

Werner shrugged. 'I want what you want.'

'I want someone in my life to tell me the truth.'

'I don't like being fucked. Ever. Never ever,' Werner said to the dying sun. 'But when you look like I do. You don't have the luxury of choosing. Not when you want to be in the company of men. I always wanted a brother.'

He took back his willingness to seed Werner Weiner. In a good way. *Never ever*. It was getting cold suddenly, with the slip away of the sun, like the plunge of the nose of a stricken ship to a forever waterbed. He pulled Werner into him. Just with the one arm, like footballers in a scrum.

'You have a brother, yes,' he said, kissing the crown of Werner. Rather than repulsing him, it smelt sweet.

He longed for Aurik with every part of him. A platonic cuddle probably made this worse. But he pushed that down. Is this what leadership is about? he wondered. Platonic pleasures. Perhaps he'd learn to lust for that.

'Come little brother,' he said, no point staying there now the sun too had left him.

'Where?'

'You know how to shoot?'

Werner shook in his armpit. He didn't even recoil at the grease of the lad's face.

'Well, to the *Shooting Gallery* then, yes?'

Bowling-Alley

6 4 2

UPPER PROMENADE DECK

Inv.

Down to A-Deck

BALL ROOM

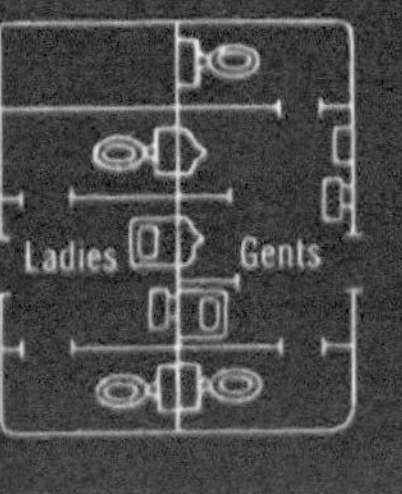

Inv.

Down to A-Deck

5 3 1

Shooting-Gallery

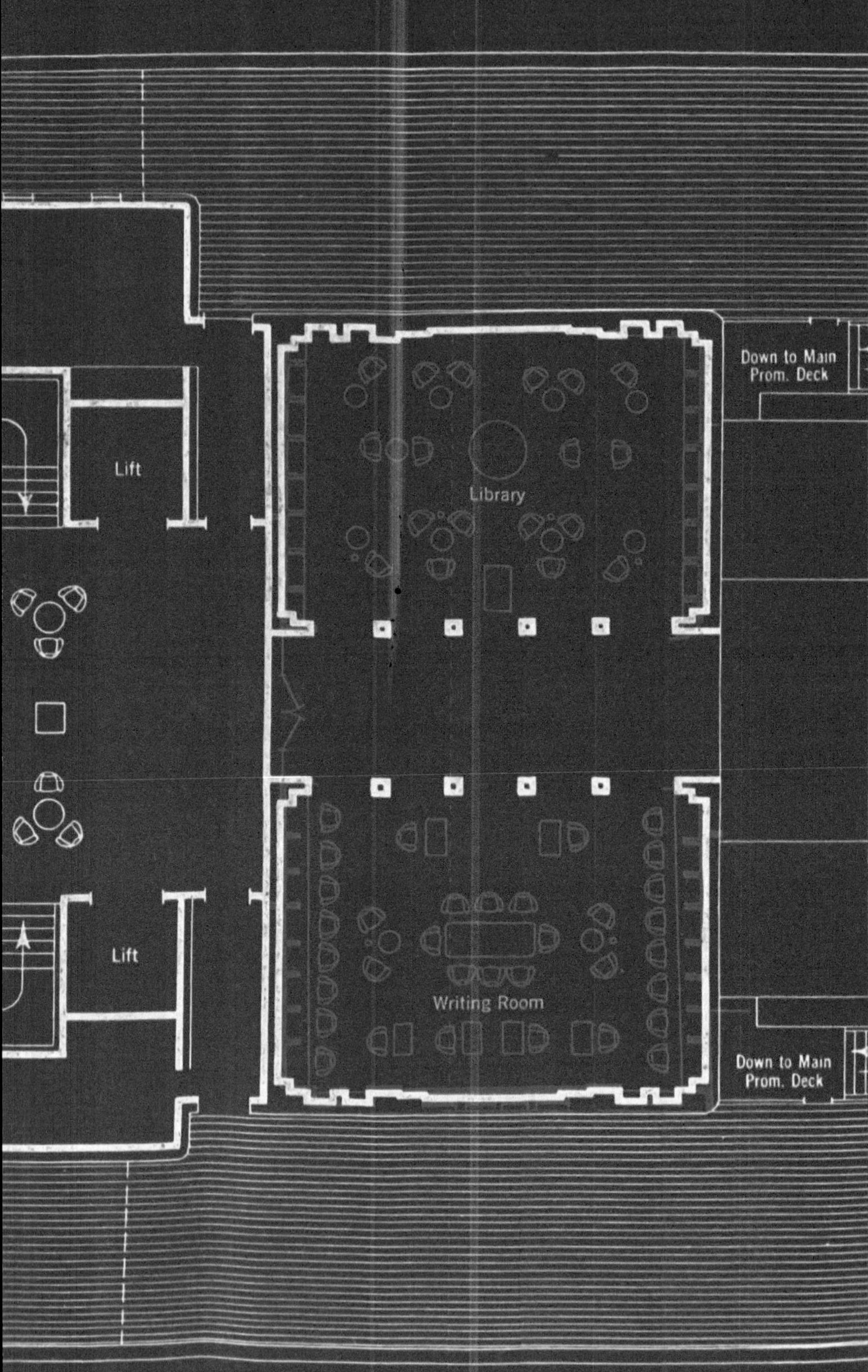
Down to Main
Prom. Deck
Lift
Library
Lift
Writing Room
Down to Main
Prom. Deck

Bremen's *Shooting Gallery* was one of the ship's finest entertainment offerings. *Popular Science Monthly* made much of its "ingenuous" motion-picture system in the October '29 edition. With sliding mounted-paper rolls and the interplay of light to show and then cover hits to projected birds, shooting at sea certainly had its thrills. They couldn't get all those bells to work, going old school with the gallery's gun pellets, drawing up on the paper, targets of their own. The *Normandie* was his personal favourite, no ill intent, just a bit of transatlantic rabble-rousing to imagined boys left in New York. Like one of *the Y* ballgames, now probably behind them. He was glad of the night coming. Ever since he'd woken up under the English cream of Robert on *Aquitania*, nighttime had shown itself to be his wingman. The most possibilities in the realm of men came then. When the wives and the children were sleeping.

Based on their current speed and position this was likely the last night at sea. And so, in the dead dark hours, while most of the men were busy below in the deep back alleys of their own bondings, he went topside to *Main Promenade Deck*. There he poked his head into the first-class *Smoking Room—yes, it's empty now*—and in he led Werner to the *Bar* built into the curve toward the bow. The alcohol was normally locked away from the crew, but his lessons from Aurik and Robert on building a company of men of varied walks of life, men on whom he could rely, meant he had with him a new steward with a key to the alcohol. Some random plucked from one of the *F Deck* crew bunks. As ugly and willing for brotherhood as Werner was.

'What's this?' Werner asked.

'It's the Hemingway, I had it the other day.'

The steward nodding approvingly. A little scrunch of the nose.

'You make a good one. Nice and strong. Better known though as "Death in the Afternoon," after one of Hemingway's books, you know.'

It had the ringing of a clue about it.

'*He* didn't mention that bit,' he took a long sip. 'I wonder . . .'

They all took a sip as he pondered.

'Walk and talk, yes,' he said, a little light-headed; but he would push through it—a bottle of iced champagne under the arm of he and Werner and a bottle of absinthe carried by the steward.

It was made easy for him being on *Main Promenade Deck*, just a quick pinball mosey along the promenade to the *Library* sash, drink in hand. Then, one by one, they were in. He dropped the curtains and switched on the lamps this time; the curtains were good enough blackouts this stage in his fog—he certain-as-fuck wasn't to be contending with candles. Yes, he would risk censor by the light sweepers if the good lighting could give him the chance of progressing in the case.

'It's about bullfighting, Hemingway's *Death in the Afternoon*,' the steward said once they were all in a cosy wingback each.

'About seeing red, yes?' he riffed, another long sip, as the steward mixed up their second batch.

'Sip slower,' the steward ordered. 'Hemingway's original instructions were clear, drink three to five of these *slowly*.'

The steward was more skilful than he at the stirring up of toxic substances. He fell to his knees on the spot where Fosco had once been arsehole and dick fucked. The drink was strong, but sometimes strong was good. The room was getting fuzzy; but, too, he felt like he might be able to make some things clear.

'A bullfighter puts up a red flag to tease the bull, yes,' he said, face rubbing the carpet, running his nose along the lines of turbine grease in the hand-woven floorcovering like they were the shit streaks in the cotton of the jocks he'd deep sniffed all that day in the laundry trolley—*time well spent, yes*. 'For the sport of it, yes, that's the bullfighter's flag. But that's not it here, is it? Fosco was found on a flag, our Nazi flag, now the national flag, after the *Bremen* stunt in '35.'

'The same year that Hemingway's recipe was first published,' the steward said, dropping to knees and crawling to him to join noses along the grease streak. Inhaling deeply. 'I smell, I smell, I sme——'

'Fosco was seeded. You smell the custard of a killer.'

But he couldn't ignore the similarities.

'First published, yes,' he said to the steward, noses together like two snouts in a trough.

'As *So Red the Nose*,' the steward rubbing his nose in a flirtatious fashion, 'or "Breath in the Afternoon."'

He slapped the steward, hard. Hard as Fosco might have done. He was *in character*.

The steward scurried to hide behind one of the wingbacks.

Werner Weiner smiled. The wily fellow knew better than to try it on.

'It's the time of death,' he said, pleased to have the floor to himself, to solve the mystery. 'In the afternoon. When *Bremen* was in port. That seems right. But tell me what you think of *this*,' he said, sliding the torn page over to Werner. The one he'd snatched from beneath Fosco.

Werner tapped on the *Rex* on the list.

'I thought *Rex* too.'

'What's Kenneth's role in it all?' Werner spoke up.

He raised hand in the manner of a slap down.

'Sorry,' Werner said.

'You're alright. But quiet now, yes. Papa needs to concentrate.'

He paced round the room.

It was all too familiar. He needed to try and see it in another light. So, he fetched the steward—no name volunteered nor asked—from the sod's hiding spot behind the chair that'd experienced so much. Then he stripped the lad.

'Now,' he said, 'assume the position, yes.'

Before the naked steward could ask what position he desired he came at the lad from behind with a kick to the heels, like one might a football toward a goal. Steward flipped like an egg with the squeal of a pig getting its curly tail tugged, ending up face planted on the semen and turbine stains, arse up and knees grazed.

'Good, yes,' he said, dropping to his knees and bringing his open palm down on the pink arse of the squealer before him with such force that tiny red specks spread into the crack and down the thigh in seconds.

'I don't want to play anymore,' the steward said.

He didn't reply to the squealer, turning to Werner instead.

'Sick of being rooted, yes,' he said, 'pull out that cock and breed a bitch steward for a change.'

Werner needed no further invitation. Though did require his knees on the steward's back and the spreading of the arse cheeks, as it took all of Werner Weiner's wherewithal to get a shaking little prick inside the squirmer.

But the trolley wheeler managed it, taking out a little of all the fucking endured over the years on the hole he spread for his sidekick, until the bum of a slut steward resembled a pastry cream with its lid ripped off.

All in service to the method.

It worked, too.

He realised some further things, Werner back in the wingback, the steward rolling on back doing angel wings—chipper now, with a custard filling running out over the carpet.

'Listen up, yes, whore steward and Werner Weiner,' he said. 'It went something like this.'

He paused at this point for dramatic effect. But it was lost on the fucker and the fuckee, caught up in their own cummy afterglow. One of the reasons he let Werner take to creaming was *that there*. He needed to hold on to the tension inside him. Use it. Same reason pro footballers were denied spending the night before a game with wives, mistresses and girlfriends. That nut tension could be useful on the field. Little did their coaches realise that many of these men found a way to release it earlier, in and onto each other in the hotel rooms booked by team financiers.

He went on, 'Just a handful could have done it, yes. Count 'em for me, Weiner. Senior First Officer

Bell of Cunard, none off the hook, yes. Can't be. Then the same level, Chief Officer Horn, one of our own. Then lowly crewmen, but who just as much might have done it.

'The engineman who fucked men then got himself a bear, Mr Winter—O *no!* death be no escape from my could-have-done-it list; a baker, *even more sus*, who also got himself dead, Mr Winkler; a wireless operator, Mr Weber, who just maybe saved me from a tight spot with Horn, but I can pay no favours; a signalman whose place in it all worry me from the start, Mr Wolf—why did he hang with the slutboys?

'Then there were two more. Almost there. A slut steward; no, no worry, not *you*,' he said to the squirmer cream puff, 'get on with your pigging. This steward I mean is one worth a name. But an ugly name, Kenneth. And I have to, how do them English say . . . "*chucks in*" my favourite, the best of all men, Aurik Braun, the last man standing from my personal guard, and now,' he rubbed his eye, 'missing along with Kenneth. How many's that, Weiner?'

'Nine, sir,' Werner said.

Neun, neun, neun, he thought with a chuckle. O yes, a good number for a mystery.

Just then, he exited the *Library* through the sash, ran another the promenade and indoors to the room across the corridor, into the first-class *Writing Room*, where he fetched paper and pen and then returned. If the two lads feared he'd abandoned them, they did not show it. Though did have a curious expression. Well, Werner anyway—the steward was deep in the wallow. Was Werner's expression because his run across the hallway might have seemed like more dramatic posturing? Well, it wasn't. Not in this instance. No. His laying out of what happened had begun.

'Take notes, Weiner, start with that list of sus men, yes?'

He allowed Werner to jot down the nine names, looked it over with a nod.

'Going in order, starting with Bell, the only outsider, and one I'm *fucking* keen to strike off. Yes, starting with him. Robert would have come on board long before offing. But he only joined me for dinner when we were well away from the pier. And when he did get to me, he was out of breath. Looked like he'd seen a ghost. What *were* he doing?

'Think it through. There be two rooms for pilots near the bow in cabins of *Upper Promenade Deck*. How I know this? Well, while our dark-eyed Horn were wondering whether to drop me to duty . . . and risk letting me slip his grab again, more on that to come . . . while this were going on, I were stuffing deck plans down my brown pudding crack. Folded easy enough, they did, and I've had time to look at them. So, yes, this were how I know.

'As a senior officer, Bell would have been offered one of these cabins. I know he was, as he said pretty much that to me. I'd bet he was given the bigger of the two cabins, though any put him within two doors of our own first mate of the ship, Horn. Horn teased about my love for the English, showed that he was jealous with some reading from a British Admiralty book. Embarrassed himself.

'I saw that Horn had a few of these books, showed me that he might have spent some time in British navy beds. Maybe he trained there. Do they let you do that in Greenwich? Or was it just a visit? Whatever the way, Horn and Bell knew each other. There is some history there, some hurt. And on seeing Horn, Bell changed his plans. Seeing Horn spooked him. That's why he came to dinner with me with his kit bag. And also why he turned down drinks with the captain. He thought of coming with me, running away, but it ended up being too close to home. I see it now.

'Bell had come on *Bremen* intending on staying. Maybe he had ideas of us being castaways together. Leaving boring life behind for an exciting adventure.

A storybook sort of life. Robert was talking *Treasure Island* at dinner. But poor Robert runs at the first sign of trouble. He's weak like that. Horn's bookshelf made me think of Robert and *Treasure Island*. It may sound silly but when you start to get to know Robert, it makes sense. He's the dreamer. Maybe he was trying to tell me something with that book. Push me to a secret hiding place that was tucked away but everyone could see. Like the pages of a book in a library.'

He walked to the wall nearest the sash window that had been left unlocked for a greasy engineman to slip on in. To the one shelf with books stacked tight, all others at a slight angle.

'I picked up on this me very first time in the *Library*. But I ignored the slanted books of all the other shelves because, maybe, they were from books being in the cabins of some of the crew. But no. Not before setting sail. Not when the ship was being searched and the captain was drumming into everyone the need for everything to be *just so*. Everything in its proper place. After the offing, maybe. But the *Library* would be locked then. Plus, the murderer was careful. The stage was well set. Until Robert came along.'

Aha! Yes.

He pulled a book from the stuffed shelf. A copy of *Treasure Island*, and in it a letter, by Robert, written on

Bremen stationery, the same that he'd just fetched from the *Writing Room*. He'd read the letter later, though a quick skim did reveal a warming about a certain chief officer. He nodded.

'Robert had gotten the idea on the way to meet me, that he would leave a note. Maybe I'd find it, maybe I wouldn't. The note is just addressed to "G" and signed "R," and the warning about Horn doesn't name the man. Robert is like that, likes to leave certain things to fate. Needs someone to grab and tow him along kicking to a happier life. Like our little piggy here,' he said, rubbing the belly of the steward with his boot. 'I should have forced Robert to stay. I wonder if he'll meet a lad like meself with the balls to do something like that. Give Robert his own treasure-island shipwreck. Ruin the fella in the best way.'

But he would heed Robert's warning. Still unclear about Horn's place in it all—he'd work up to that—the *Library* was a foolish place to stay. He'd got his little treasure, but, like the *Bremen* herself, it was best in this stage of the affair to keep moving. He couldn't afford to stay still for too long. Men like that become sitting ducks.

'Who's next there on our could-have-done list, Weiner.'

'Horn, sir.'

'He's too big to tackle right now. We'll come back to him. Next.'

'Mr Winter.'

'Ah, our second victim.'

And he realised some further things, Werner back in the wingback, the steward rolling on back doing angel wings still, even more chipper now, that custard filling a hardening lake on the carpet.

'Perfect,' he said with the glee of a puzzle coming together. 'But to the order of names, then. And I think I owe you a trip to Winter's cabin. To get a camera. Let's do that now.'

When Werner went to fetch the clothes of the pig he put up a hand.

'Don't bother dressing the pig. If we get seen, it's all over. So, he might as well stay ready for your dick again. That's right, that means you can bring along your new toy, yes.'

It had the now-familiar feeling of returning to the scene of a crime, heading to the cabin where you could hear what sounded like anchor chains. All but abandoned, on captain's decree; the sound of the bow pushing its way through the ocean, and having the ocean push right on back. The sound of grinding iron, which he'd heard while getting seeded for the first time. He expected he'd hear that noise forever.

'Hmm,' he said, pressing his hand to the mattress where the engineman had raped him. 'Same as when I were last here. See *here*, where I shit that dick out of me and all else as well that he'd put in me. It's all still here. And he went missing soon later, I figure.'

He found himself speaking poor boy in this cabin with the anchor chain bangs, before the cabin as well. Like he were back in those rags of a wheat fields boy. The camera was there, too, quickly found in the wardrobe. It were a stroke of luck. In it, still, the film.

'When were,' he steadied, rubbed the bum hole, 'when *was* this camera taken from you, Mr Weiner?'

'Wednesday.'

'The day we leave New York.'

'Yes.'

'And what time was this?'

'Around ten o'clock that night.'

His eyes rolled back as he did the math on that. Simple arithmetic was hard now. His brain was not what it once were.

He got there. At 2000 hours, the camera was taken. Robert had left him with the pilot just after 1800 hours, he'd having met the engineman just into the next day. Ten o'clock in the evening, the camera pinch. Smack bang in the middle of his bowling alley feeding. What did his greasy-hole invader want with a camera?

'What you do for this shipping line?'

'I'm a photographer's assistant, working for the *Abwehr* collection directorate. That's the Reich's military intelligence agency.'

'Your job for them?'

'Photographing harbours, mostly. *Abwehr* demanded current photo coverage in key installations in locations of interest, in the United States, Britain and France. What better guise for getting these images than a passenger photographer on Germany's premier ocean liner? When last in Southampton, while we were at anchor for two hours shuttling passengers,

I was shooting the latest positions of the harbour's antisubmarine nets.'

'In this trip? What shots were you getting?'

'Fort Hamilton, Governor's Island's installations and the old coastal artillery batteries in the Narrows, on Fort Wadsworth. All on arrival.'

'Hmm. We need to see the photos, I reckon. How soon can you make them?'

'To develop the film? I would need an hour or two.'

'Good, guard that film with your life, Mr Weiner. It may be very important. I think, yes.'

Werner removed the film from the camera. It was in a handy-sized roll, then inserted it into a metal cylinder, and between the man's arse crack.

He nodded in approval. His commitment to the ugly-but-pretty-bodied Mr Weiner, his promise that the man's arsehole would never need be buggered again, it was a promise he took seriously. It was a good place to store the film.

'But who to blame? Mr Winter did not kill our wiseguy. No murderer would flirt with getting caught like that. The killer, remember, fucked my Italian friend *after*. First I thought Mr Winter might have been the one to do this. You know, after discovering the body. But our little experience back in the *Library*,' he said turning on the pig, 'you know the one, piggy, where Mr Weiner here showed you the way.'

Piggy nodded.

'That's called psychology. I hated Mr Winter for fucking me with force. Deep hate for that. But I wanted it too. Even though all the world tell us men that we should not crave a bit of nut custard up the bum. I did. I have. And Mr Winter took that virgin experience from me. *But!*' he said, sweeping with a satisfied grin, delighted with his own cleverness. 'Do you know what I've realised? It was a first for Mr Winter, *too!* And that's why the man hatefully fucked me.'

'I don't follow,' Mr Weiner said.

'But it's so easy. Watching you trip over yourself to custard fill our little piggy over here proved it. You have been bent over and custard filled many times, you told me so. But never have you had the opportunity to custard fill another. I gave you that opportunity, my friend. A little reward to you for the loyalty you have shown. The service you have provided. And how was it for you?'

Lip service to the most recent fuck in the *Library* had the piggy licking fingers and getting stuck into a tasting of creamy centre Mr Weiner had given. But with a kind of sad look on the face.

'Don't worry,' Werner said to the pig, a tickle of the tummy. 'Eat as much as you like. I'll top you up later.' Mr Werner then turned to him and said, 'I think you know, sir.'

'Know what?'

'What it meant, to get some stuffing in my piggy. It changed my opinion on the matter of fucking. It was wonderful.'

'Thank you, yes. Had to hear it,' he gleamed. 'And right you are. But you would never have wondered had you not been fucked so many times before. Neither, maybe, come to think that the experience, from the other side, with a virgin bum, might be something nice. Something tasty. That's what happened with the engineman. I teased him in the *Library* in my hunt for clues that might solve the case of Fosco's death and fucking. But the engineman was not the killer, nor the fucker of the dead man. Had he been, he would not have been so disappointed back in this cabin to realise that the fuck he thought would be my first, wasn't.

'I was stretched out after carrying mama's meatballs, *remember!* and having all those men nibble them out of me. The grease slick of my bum-pudding pipe made the engineman think I were a seasoned cock bouncer. Kind of like the one that had bounced on Fosco's dick before the man died. The size of the load the engineman pumped into me, so soon after Fosco had been creamed, along with the anger the man had toward me—in the man's eyes, and all based on deductions—for not being the virgin pipe that was craved, tells us that another man fucked Fosco.'

'No cream now, cream later,' Werner whispered to the pig on the floor, pulling the cylinder from the crack and plugging the pig's cream hole with it. 'Made it nice and warm for you,' Werner said. Then nodded to him, 'I'm striking Mr Winter off the suspect list, and will get this film developed at the first opportunity. Where to now? I assume we can't sit in any one place for long?'

'You're a quick one, my friend. We head on, yes. And about the film. How soon can we manage it?'

'Depends on when the ship's photographer retires.'

'And when's that?'

'Around 2200 hours, in my experience.'

He checked his watch. It was a few minutes to ten o'clock now.

'Best be on the safe side and do one more stop before the *Dark Room*, yes. And what better nod to our friendship, and better send-off for our Mr Winter, than a return to the place where we met and Mr Winter came arse to head with a bear. That's right, to the *Kindergarten!*'

‘Permission to wait with my pet outside,’ Werner said as they approached the *Kindergarten*. ‘There’s some things not even a beast should see.’

‘We don’t want to break piggy. Good thinking, yes,’ he nodded. ‘Here,’ opening a small *Store Room* directly opposite the *Kindergarten* entrance, filled with stuffed toys and picture books and other kiddie things, ‘take five in here as I check on Mr Winter.’

It was a strange sort of anxiety, revisiting the site of a grizzly attack inflicted on the self. The kind of experience that made him prepared to risk a quick switch on then off of the electric light, rather than the matchstick stumble of the first encounter. In the flash of light he saw that the body was gone, and the room completely restored. The smell of sawdust and varnish thick, confirming that Mr Winter’s killer was someone with the means to not only kill in a most flamboyant and self-inflicted manner, but to cover it up with a complete sand and repolish of the wooden slide on which the engineman had invited the bear in.

'You saw the bear, too, right?' he said frantic, back in the *Store Room* where Werner was on the second page of a jungle-themed picture book, the pig on lap, pointing giddy at drawn monkeys swinging from vines.

Werner nodded, but with index finger on lips that said, *not in front of piggy*.

He nodded. Thankful he had another witness to the scene, to know it was not something imagined in a drugged mind . . . like that bosun boy at the porthole in a stateroom Aurik had picked out.

'We have to leave now. Get those shots done. We can't afford to waste any more time not seeing what's on that camera roll.'

'Who's next on our list, Mr Weiner?' he said once the film was developing and Werner had got the pig settled, sleeping in a cot set up in the *Dark Room*, with a stuffed animal in the arms. A monkey of all things, snatched from the *Store Room*. How quickly the boy regressed to slut pig after seeding, he thought, piggy snoring softly. He envied the thing. Thought of Aurik, who he had similarly regressed under rather quickly. Aurik. Someone who he would not have minded being a pig for. Pig masculinities. That was something he could get on board with. A little sigh now at the responsibility on his shoulders, inescapable in *Dark Room*, with its enlargers, processing equipment and its own drying compartment. A little sigh and a wonder whether he would ever be in the position to give it all up to pig out like that one there in the cot with blankie and monkey.

'Mr Winkler, the baker,' Werner said.

'Yes. We'd head on to Kenneth's cabin usually, where Winkler was stabbed. But the *Kindergarten* has told us that the scene will have been wiped clean. Much easier, I think, to clean up a little stab in the back than an arsehole ripped open by a bear.'

He paused on that last bit.

'Something in that, I'd say. Joint that down, Mr Weiner?'

'Yes, sir.'

He nodded. 'I was where?'

'A visit to Kenneth's cabin.'

'That's very dangerous, yes. And not necessary. Luckily, you had time to see the scene when I locked you in there. Sorry about that, friend.'

Werner smiled and tickled the pig's nose. It wiggled like the belly. 'You've more than made up for it. Can I keep him?'

He had not intended it, the devotion forming between Werner and the pig. The fuck was in service of his method, but he was pleased Werner was happy with the new pet. And it pleased him also to know he had at least one person on whom he could count.

'You can, yes. Sure, my friend.'

Werner beamed. 'Thank you, sir. I'll feed him every day.'

'You will, yes. Now, tell me what you found there.'

'Nothing, sir.'

'Nothing?'

'Nothing out of the ordinary.'

'Hmm, ordinary for a baker, maybe. Anything like that? Any baking stuff in there? Any pastries?'

'No, sir.'

He frowned.

'Well——'

'Yes?'

'There was an empty box. You know, the long rectangular ones that are used to store buns and such?'

'It was empty, yes?'

'Yes.'

'Any powder?'

'Yes, now that you mention it. All over the floor.'

'Yes,' he said, satisfied. 'The baker was in on it, alright. That's how the poison got around. To me between the stacks before dinner, then to the brownshirts for the feeding of mama's meatballs. And also to Fosco—I noticed powder around the mouth—and then to my dear Aurik. That's why he did what he did. That's why he shitted in a slut steward with me watching.'

'Does that make it alright, the betrayal?' Werner asked.

He raised his hand ready to put the cheeky bugger back in place, but then he remembered that they were friends now.

'He was not of good mind,' he said, calming himself, watching piggy. 'He was acting on the ideas of another, and something in those buns made him give in to it. That much is clear. That's why Fosco let a lily arse ride the dick. But, hmm, Fosco also had a pinprick on the neck. I wonder about that. Was it a top-up of poison, or did Fosco need an extra dose to go through with the arse fuck?'

He nodded to himself. Something in that, he thought.

'Yes, the baker was in on it. But not our murderer. Who else is there?'

'Mr Weber and Mr Wolf, and your own Braun.'

'Aurik is just for me, yes. I'll think on him meself. But for the other two, a wireless operator and a signalman. Two men Aurik *got* for me. But one who had found me already . . . Mr Wolf is in on it, yes. I never would have found Fosco without his idea of that place, where I also saw that Mr White of the Cunard Line. Not our killer, though. But not one of my merry men, no way.'

'And the other one?'

'Aurik has rotten luck. But was bound to happen on at least one good mate. Mr Weber is sound. He saved me from Horn, put himself in danger doing it. That is where I shall head next, I must.'

Werner knelt down to rouse the pig.

He stopped his friend with a hand.

'You stay here.'

'I'm not leaving you.'

'You may need to save me. And you need to get those shots done, yes. There's something good on it, I'm sure of it. No, I need to go on alone for this final solving of the mystery.'

Werner needed no further persuasion, a look of warmth in the eyes at the pig.

Before he left, he asked: 'Does it not worry you, how quickly your new pet has come to need you?'

Werner just smiled with a kind of knowingness that could only have come from years on years of experience of getting custard.

'He has no choice, does he?' Werner said. 'Poor pet.'

'What do you mean,' his eyes narrowing. 'You drugged him?'

'No. I didn't need to. All it took was one taste, and now he's done for life. It's not spoken about, but sex is more addictive than any drug. More ruinous.'

He thought of the urinal in his quarters, like a pacifier, his own cot in a dark room . . . now his only means of sleep. Seeing what Aurik did in that *Toilet*, it ruined him, too.

'It's different for every man,' Werner went on, still smiling. 'I've had my taste now, too. Now I know why I hated getting fucked so much. Because it reminded me of what I really wanted to be doing. Lucky for me and pet here, we found each other. My piggy found his bone and my prick's found his kennel.'

He left thinking on that. How did it apply to his own experience? To his desires from that moment he received his instructions from Berlin. He'd courted something of the fucks of men. He'd let that New York capo eat out of his arsehole like a bowl. Gone along with that sweaty, smelly engineman into the *Library* where he'd willingly defiled Fosco as a piece of ripe meat. Then put up nothing of a fight when that Mr Winter had planted some grafter butter deep in his gut.

Then there was Aurik. Everything he valued dear. Would anything with his Aryan photonegative have been possible without the grooming of an Italian then greaser? Was their wrecking of his house just a clearing of him out for the real delight?

That is what Aurik had been. A delight. One he would like to believe . . . *No!* he *had* to believe . . . not only that he would have chosen, but that he would have waded through flooded bulkheads to get to. O yes, it was a matter of freewill. And this was the lesson Werner Weiner had given, by virtue of the the man's wretchedness. Freewill and what it meant in a world of mansex, that's what he thought on as Werner pulled out a putrid little dick. Having to look away as the ugly fucker started stroking it, presumably to give the pig in a blanket a late-evening feed.

Piggies feed from a trough.

Men piss into one.

Shit is locked away.

But maybe . . . maybe men feed from shit troughs too, sometimes.

That image of Aurik and the most intimate part of the man, almost never seen. Except in war, perhaps. Side by side, brothers in arms, shitting together. And except on *Bremen*. It takes all sorts, he supposed, shaking the image of piggy feeding from the putridity of Werner Weiner and running back to the officer quarters, a bit wobbly on the feet.

'Thanks, Mr Weber,' he said in the *Telegraph Booth* just opposite the *Wireless Office*. He'd been lucky to find the man loitering in the corridor, to pull his spectacled insider in just after Weber had spoken with one of the deck officers. *How's that room change treating you?* the officer had asked the boy. *Very well,* Weber had replied. *Thank you for indulging me. It suits me well and my dicky colon. Nice and close to the latrine.* The officer had waved Weber away. *Please, I don't need all the details.*

'You trust me now, then?' buggy Weber said in the booth, smug after giving an officer more information than was desired.

'I've been thinking on all angles, yes.'

Weber grinned. 'Good. I can't be away from my desk for long, but you can come to my quarters now. Quickly.'

The path to Weber's cabin took them through the *Vestibule* past the firemen cabins and the *Toilet* that backed onto them. The *Toilet* where Werner had come true and carried him, urinal and all, to safety. His path then took him into the first room on the left after the small flight of stairs on the same corridor leading to Chief Officer Horn's bed. It was a risky move. But given the late hour, he took his chances with the follow, knowing that Horn would most likely be on the *Bridge*.

Weber pulled him into a small cabin.

'Mr Weber.'

'Łukasz, please,' the wireless operator said, dropping to knees and reaching for his crotch.

'Look, Łukasz,' he said having swatted the boy's hands away. 'It's not going to happen.'

'No, you look, *mister*.' Łukasz was shaking violently now. 'You have got to give me something. I've risked it all for you. Why don't I ever get a go, *damn it!*'

Łukasz's voice rose to increasingly unsafe decibels with every sentence, like the sound of a sub's propeller nearing a surface fleet. Risk of exposure was high.

Immediate action required. This was normally the point where he'd slap a man. But a Slavic man gagging for it warranted a more peasant touch, he reasoned. Opting to crepitate—fingers gripping the hair as hard as a slipped cliff walker the grass at the end, yanking the head back in a short, sharp crack that could well have paralysed the poor sod.

The wireless operator went as limp as a dummy between ventriloquist sittings.

'Łukasz?' he said to the torn-back head of the boy, who hands had dropped by the side. 'Still with me?'

Łukasz gave a gargling sound that told him the boy was, and this sound led to his next idea.

To hock hard and spit across the face.

The wad of his bile landed gelatinous on the half-inch thick spectacles of the Pole. Like some contagion on a microscope slide. Łukasz squinted through the spit on round glasses like a timid first-time submariner searching for sea monsters through portholes.

Thoughts of his urinal cot—on his mind since passing the *Toilet* that served the hoses of firemen—gave him the idea that followed.

'You are a lucky boy,' he said, releasing his dick from his pants. 'A crack, some spit and now, lucky you, I need to piss, yes.'

'Over the basin, over the basin,' Łukasz said, dazed, like a sore athlete after a full-body realignment.

'*Shut it!*' he said, starting pissing.

The sod's shower came in split streams at first for a few seconds that soaked the bed and hung uniforms in the cabin's little wardrobe.

Weber let out a murmured '*no, no*,' eyes darting to the piss points each side of the sod's eyes, the head still held there with the grasp of one hand. 'How am I going to explain this?' Łukasz whimpered. Perfect timing, too, as his stream focused to get the Pole square in the back of the throat like one of those painted heads with balloons attached that were end zones in a water gun carnival game.

Łukasz choked on his piss. 'Can't breathe, can't breathe.'

He titled the head toward the wardrobe of uniforms to allow the piss to pour out and the Pole to cough some up and clear the pipe. He wasn't a monster. And besides. The boy had asked for it. Granted, this was probably not what the lad had wished for. But it was what he was dishing out. And if he had learnt anything on this virgin voyage of his, it was that what a man trying mansex for the first time really wants is quite often not what might be asked for. Certainly not out loud.

There was pleasure in the dishing out, too. He was glad now that Łukasz had asked for this, he thought as the boy's bloodshot eyes teared up and his piss made a spit-up-then-swallow passage down the lad's throat. Like a blocked basin straight after some hard plunger pumps.

He had an image of Horn conducting inspections of the accommodations. *How would this be explained?* Not easily. The thought of it made him hard.

When the tank was dry he throttled the boy a bit. The spectacles pivoted off then on the boy's nose with his choke, sending droplets of piss and spit from the lenses. It was comical to watch. The boy letting out a grunt at each crest of the throttle.

But he mustn't get indulgent, he told himself as Łukasz's eyes rolled brown to white. Like in the *Library* with Werner Weiner and the steward cum pig, he was testing a theory here. This was a science in see-saw action. A feeling for limits in the will and wants of men. A wondering about freedom.

He let the boy go.

Łukasz hunched forward, hands on folded knees, fingers spread wide and whiter than the rest of the limbs on account of a hard squeeze. Then there were three quick arches of the back, like back in the *Bowling Alley* in night one—a cat exercising the spine—followed by a spewing. Łukasz's eyes waterlogged and leaking, mouth a perfect circle, the contents of the wireless operator's stomach gushed like the breech in a dam wall.

'Now look what you've done,' he said in his best disapproving tone, though his dick did the goosestep to the upchuck of his own piss and bits of cabbage and bratwurst from the man's mess dinner.

As Łukasz fought for air, he lowered the boy to his soiled boot using the other one. 'Lick it clean, yes.'

'I can't,' Łukasz said retching as he rubbed sick along the Pole's lips.

Łukasz started crawling toward the couch at the far end of the cabin. '*O God! the carpet, the carpet!*' Łukasz cried, a trail of drool marking the path.

'Cigarettes, Łukasz,' he said. 'And get back here.'

He couldn't help feeling a bit like the grizzly in the *Kindergarten*, he thought as he smoked and Łukasz sat holding stomach on the couch in the corner, under the window. He the grizzly, the one drooling and moaning about ruined carpet having made the grave misjudgement of inviting him in. Like the Devil into doubt cracks in a devote man's soul.

What was happening to him?

He hated cigarettes.

He squeezed the boy's cheeks, the tongue sliding out like a garden slug from a stood-on stone.

And he used that tongue as ashtray.

The skin turned black like a lamb's tender rump to a branding iron. The boy screamed. Wailed. Wept like women at the crucifixion.

He held the cigarette there, the Pole clamped in

place with the other hand.

'Now swallow it, yes,' he said when the cigarette was crumpled and now lodged in the bloody burn at the centre of Łukasz's tongue. He leaned in close to Weber's ear, 'do it, yes,' he said, then clamping a bunch of hair from the boy's head in his teeth and tearing the bunch from its roots.

Łukasz did as instructed. Silent now, but trembling. The broad Slavic brow of the boy laced with sweat, the hairline boxy, like one half of a square. He licked the sweat from the brow. It was salty. He licked the tears, too. He was getting a taste for the sweat and crying of submitting boys.

'Now I trust you, yes,' he said. A gentle kiss on the boy's matted crown.

Łukasz's crying got chesty.

'What would you like? Now you can ask, yes,' he said.

The boy shook head, 'nothing, I want nothing from you,' turning away to face the cabin panelling.

His cock still free and hard from all the "science," he spat on it as he had done Łukasz's glasses, rapid stroking his cock until the head started to pulse.

'Stick out your tongue,' he said.

Łukasz shook head.

He did the same as before.

A squeeze of the cheeks.

But it took no real force this time to coax the slug out.

Just in time to give cream to the burn, eventually. His custard landing in the small bit of torn-out hair first, then on the piss-smudged glasses, to arrive in more steady pumps right onto the ashen black and red circle of the tongue. To soothe it. The abuse having made the reward that much sweeter.

'My mother's Polish,' Łukasz said, throwing arms around his waist, playful licks of his oozing cock, then sucks of each of his balls in the sack. Then back to the cock. Cock, ball, ball, cock, ball, ball, cock. In the manner of a genuflect. 'Protect me.'

Łukasz's Slavic look would not go over well back in the Reich. Even though he had inflicted the pain, his soothing of the wound came as an absolution.

'Clean yourself up and get back out there, boy. Keep proving your worth, yes.'

But he said it with a tenderness.

'You did good, yes,' he added as he left.

The boy welling up again as he'd gently taken the arms from his waist and packed his cock away from the lick, suck, suck, of the wireless operator caught in a loop of cock, ball, ball devotion.

He headed down the corridor and into the

dirt.

Bremen's ten years in service, 1929 to '39, saw the rear end of prohibition in the States. The repression of want for a tipple that at last got its quench in '33, when beer flowed free again in time for Christmas—as Hitler got ready to toast one-year's anniversary as Chancellor. But the burn of repressed urges ran much longer and more hidden besides. For all the ten years of *Bremen*'s run. In the hallowed halls of her American port of call, where medicine men were thinking about and sniffing and treating men who were tasting *dirt*. On 30 December '30, an A.A. Brill stood in front of men of the American Psychoanalytic Association at the *New York Academy of Medicine* and, nose in the air, invited a deep sniff. He wasn't there, of course, and were he, he would not be able to recall such an action now that his brain was in the mud. But the nose-in-the-air gesture seemed likely in line with a conference paper title that was playfully lyrical. Imagine it . . . the reading aloud to colleagues over finger food that such a paper must have been.

Its title: 'The Sense of Smell in the Neuroses and Psychoses.' And its contents . . . well, it's all about 1930s men and the repressed place of smell among them. The 'very small part in the life of civilized man' that has the nose. About the deep displeasure of the civilised man for any manly odours, any smells coming from within. A 'coprophilic smell-desire' running contrary to civility. Case histories were presented, naturally, that included the 'definitely established' case of a man that when 'masturbated while smearing in the toilet, it may be assumed that the smell of faeces acted as a direct sexual stimulant.'

Brill was not alone in putting the civilised nose off finger food. In '37 and also in New York, a Lawrence S. Kubie read from 'The Fantasy of Dirt' to set out 'the complex system of fantasies which lurk behind the reality of dirt,' including that 'lurking curiosity' of he 'who swallows faeces.' What to do with such men? Unthinkable fetish tastes, seeing food from the bum. Lobotomise, maybe?

The body is a *dirt factory*. That was the takeaway over canapes of Kubie's thesis. *Fuck rearmament!* each second as a man is the production of *dirt*. In every man of every Nazi factory. A place and a thing. Lick it up, sweaty, manly dirtiness. That last bit was *the fog* talking. But turn to the expert . . . 'The body itself creates dirt,' Kubie said with a nibble and a dainty sip—or so he imagined; he wasn't there, wasn't really here anymore, either, he's in a crazed kind of dirty place of his own making. No mind for memory, no possibility remembering any sip or nibble anyway. But the words, they are recorded—so there's that. The body creates dirt, yes Kubie, tell it, 'and is in fact a kind of animated, mobile dirt factory, exuding filth at every aperture.' O yeah, fuck amen to that. The purity of Adam was buggered out of him near-two-thousand year ago. We're in the age of the machine now. The masses. Mass production and disseminat-ion. Of being human in a dirt-manufacturing plant, on an epic, masculine, disgusting scale.

It is a scale, the dirt in men's factory. Think about it. Not all humanly dirt is ranked equal. That's right, there's a hierarchy in the dirt products men excrete. So Kubie reckons, anyways. Want examples? Okay. What about tears? They're pure apparently, basically drinking water. We bottle them up. That's romantic, right? And men never cry, so how's that for a rare commodity. Rarer than you might think. Man and beast, that's biblical. And tears separate them. Men don't cry, beasts can't. So lick up those manly tears without guilt, they're the truffles of the dirt world. But try sniffing them out.

Pigs find truffles. And pig men have snouts for dirt delicacies far more pungent. But we'll get to that. Let's move down the scale. Semen could not be placed on this scale by Kubie, for there was too much ambivalence towards it . . . try telling that to a fella such as himself who'd had a dirty engineman plant rape seed in his gut. Then again, he'd also licked clean Aurik's incy cock after a seeding, the saltiness of it had made him smile into the bitter spray of the sea on their imagined *Poop Deck*. So, yes, maybe there was something to the ambivalence thesis.

Texture also has impacts on how we fantasise dirt, according to Kubie. Softness, wetness, sliminess and hairiness are always dirtier than hardness, dryness and no hair. As wrinkles are always filthier than smooth skin. Enter the scrotum of Fosco; soft, sweaty, slimy with the leak of seed slicking it up, and wrinkly. How his mouth had fallen open to take the sweat of a wog's balls sack in. He was the piggy.

Kubie was playing in the realm of fantasy. *The ego* for the canape classes. But the thrust of the man's talk being that this fantasy of dirt is a subconscious thing. And while we are all ourselves dirt factories, we must shun all that resembles our own products, in man or beast. Take the beast first, Kubie says that man does not use as food animal apertures associated with dirt. But it is simply not true. In the fashionable restaurants of Berlin, these parts are the delicacies. The tripe, the intestines, the testicles even.

But the real shunning takes place with other men. So brings on the grand masquerade, or concealment of dirt products from oneself to another, and the not wanting to see or smell or touch or *God forgive us* taste and eat and take into ourselves the factory floor products of another. O fuck no. That's why in the real world we have the cubicle walls for the ablutions, a polite way of shitting. Walls that don't hold in war, mind. When shitting side by side with a mate is often the only reprieve you'll get. Funny that. Wonder what Kubie'd think of it.

Other "products" of the dirt factory include: ear wax, desquamated cells between the toes, nose pickings, hair, dandruff, face and body sweat, spit, sick, pus, phlegm, nail cuttings, cuts of locks. But in this hierarchy it was, you guessed it, piss and shit that scrape the bottom of the clean-to-dirty scale. What was happening that he wanted to sample something of the grim barrel's bottom of other men. No, not just any men. Of Aurik, should he ever find the beautiful-filthy lover. Talk dirty to me? The time for talking had passed.

He'd blacked out. Lost time. But was back now in his *Toilet* behind sleeping firemen. In the shower this time, to wash away the dirt. It was one thing to be rough with a fellow. But to burn the boy's tongue. And get hard to that. He *was* the bear . . . He left the door open during showering. Scrubbed the skin, but it was clean. The bum hole too. The dirt was inside the mind, he realised in horror as some scratchings near there drew red rather than brown. Not a soul passed the corridor throughout all this washing and lancing of the dirt temples. But afterwards, as dressing, he heard the sound of feet on wet ground, like a walker's gumboots when that walker had waded in just a little too far. He dove into the corridor in time to see a figure dart into Łukasz's cabin. Bit hunched, bit sickly of silhouette, this figure. He went after it. Welcomed the chase like an addict clinging to larceny as distraction from lunacy. Łukasz's cabin was the first on the left, but only reached after two cabins on the right. *Odd that*, he thought, bursting through the door.

'What is you doing?' he said to Łukasz in a hot rush.

The boy was on all fours, licking at the carpet like a cat lapping up its own sick.

'Just cleaning up,' Łukasz said, tongue stuck to the carpet, an expression saying the boy knew this was not normal, but apparently not able to help it.

Something was very wrong, he thought as he ran through the ship, back the way he'd come. His seed had made a boy strange.

Turks and bands in lifeboats on the brain.

He slapped his face as he ran to keep away another tumble into black.

Need to see those camera shots.

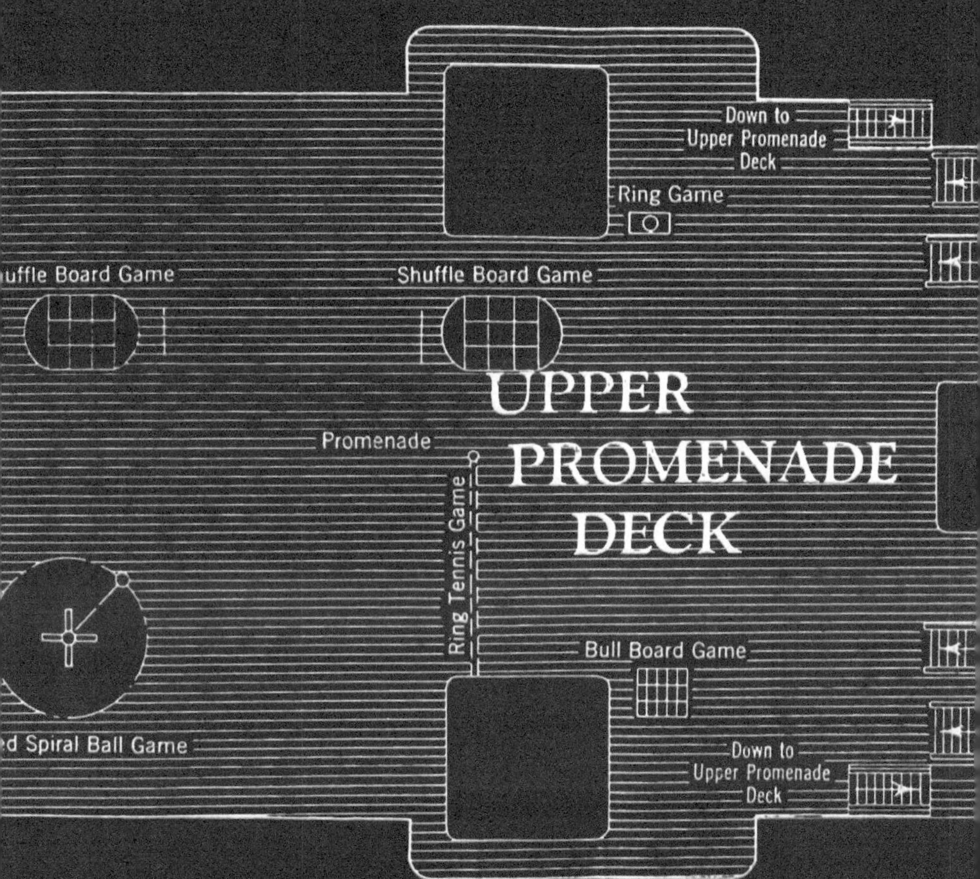

Down to
Upper Promenade
Deck
Ring Game
uffle Board Game
Shuffle Board Game
UPPER
PROMENADE
DECK
Promenade
Ring Tennis Game
Bull Board Game
d Spiral Ball Game
Down to
Upper Promenade
Deck

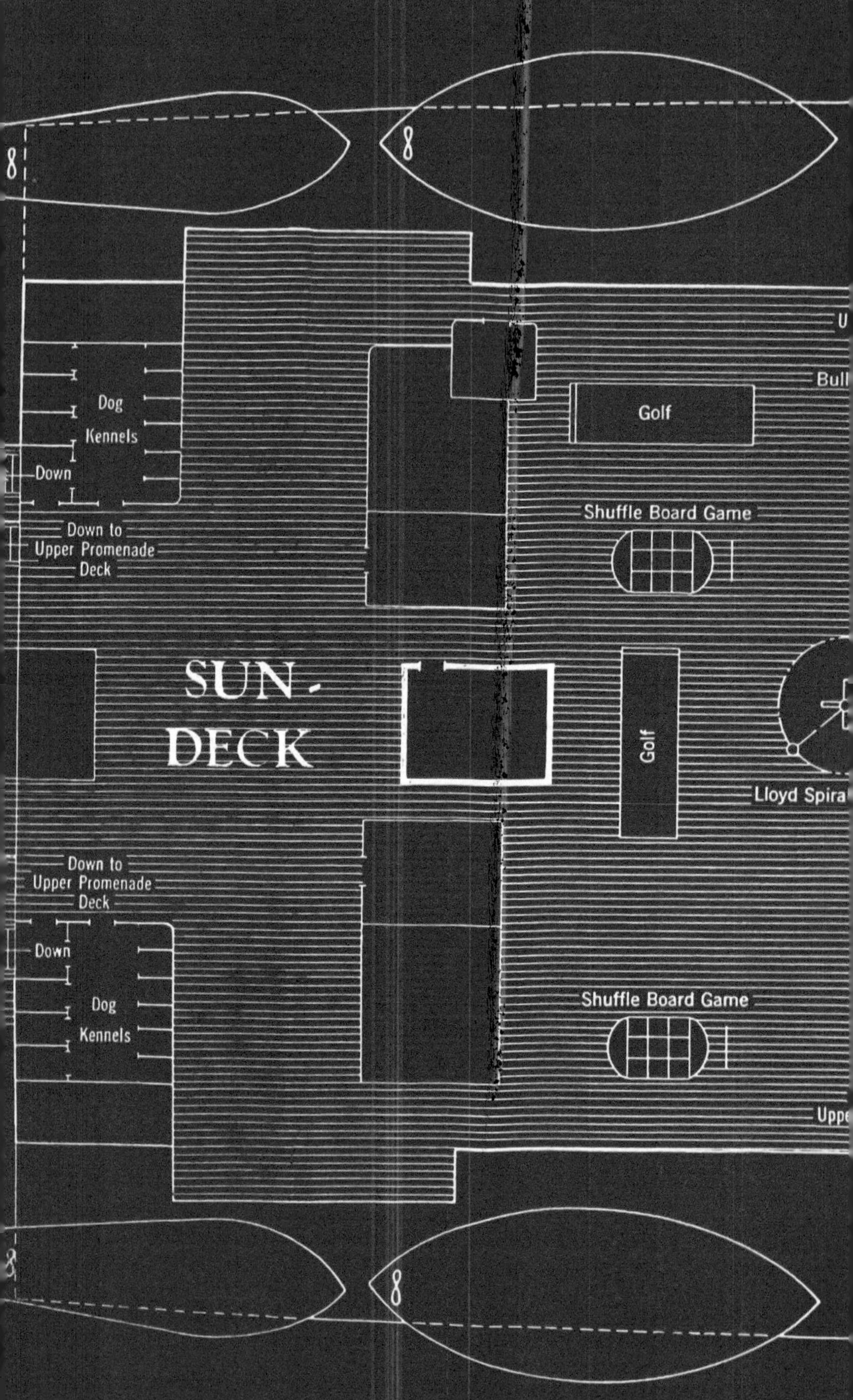

SUN-
DECK
Dog
Kennels
Down
Down to
Upper Promenade
Deck
Golf
Shuffle Board Game
Golf
Lloyd Spira
Bull
U
Down to
Upper Promenade
Deck
Down
Dog
Kennels
Shuffle Board Game
Uppe

He paced on his and Aurik's made-up *Poop Deck*, clutching one of the photographs in his hand . . . in shock. Before this, Werner Weiner had been eagerly waiting his return. The piggy tightly wrapped, ready to be transported to that someplace hidden. *You won't like this*, his friend had said when he came into a scene of hanging evidence, Werner pulling one of the photographs from its pegs and putting it behind the back. *I can't be sure, but I think it involves Aurik. Let me destroy it, the negative, too. You don't need to see it. You need to think of your mind now, of what you can and cannot cope with.* Red had risen in his cheeks at the possibilities of what it could be. Aurik's corpse? As grizzly an end as the greasy engineman? *Show it to me*, he'd said. *I need to see it, yes.* Somehow it was worse than all that he could have imagined, walking now toward the aft edge of the first-class *Promenade* on *Sun Deck*.

In a sinister turn of events, deck games had been set up, but not in any kind of gameplay-ready way. Scattered in a mid-game jumble on each of the painted-on boards. Cues, rope rings, and flat lead swallowed by leather, for shuffle, ring and bull board. Games underway for a full complement of players, but not a soul in sight. The pieces of the games sliding over the painted parts of the deck by the sway of the ship at speed. Like their players had simply vanished. Just like Aurik.

Past the games, that felt like a sort of gauntlet in the dark. Like tripping hazards that promised to send him slipping on the thin ice coating the deck and off into the sea. Past these he went by a little storeroom, door open, where the games' bits had come from—he presumed—and to that point on the deck's edge that Aurik had pointed to days before. Small buildings either side. And there he looked at the photograph again.

'*Aurik!*' he shouted into the night. 'I'm here.'

The sky was clearing and the moon was full and frigid, lighting up the games of the deck like little tombstones in an ancient graveyard, no rhyme nor reason to the living. He felt *all* mad there, on that stage under the moon, his mind playing tricks again. Hearing things this time.

Howling. I can hear howling, like wolves at the moon, yes. And footsteps.

'He told you, then,' came a voice over his shoulder.

A shadow stretched out over the games by the light of the moon. As chilling as the scene was, he did not run. Did not turn to face the figure, either. He just went on looking at that photograph.

Two bodies in the *Library*. Taken by a push of the lens through the meeting in two halves of sash curtains, the frilly sides of the frame told him. Aurik looking directly at the camera, dressed in *SS* uniform. Gut deep in a dead man.

'No, Mr Wolf,' he said. 'He didn't tell me nothing. That's why I'm here, yes.'

Wolf walked round to meet him. The signalman who'd been there from the start of his time with *Bremen*. More than *there*, who'd set him on his Atlantic highway to dead men.

'Do you like games, sir?'

'No.'

'Dogs like games.'

He heard howling again, the desire to run rising as Wolf walked toward one of the buildings on the cliff of the deck. His legs felt like bull-board pieces, like lead swallowed in leather, but he was too desperate to understand Aurik's role in it all not to follow.

Mr Wolf took him to a room full of beasts, a lantern just inside the door licking light over the howling mounds inside. It was a kennel. And smelt of one. But he well knew, the *Bremen* had no dogs. Inside the cages were beasts still recognisable as once standing on two legs. Though the clothes of men had been ripped into rags, and hands, what once were hands, had now become bloodied fist stumps. The knuckles like the bone pads of paws. The hind legs were worse. Knees now feet, all skin worn away just to bone. What was once the part of the leg from kneecap to feet had all the flesh and muscle torn away. Some of the beasts had even managed to get into the marrow. Those into the centre of bones were gnawing even now, too keen on feeding to pay him any heed. Those not feeding were licking their cocks. Bloody, too. Layers and layers of skin removed from the attention, like a lollipop sucked down to the stick. All lips eaten away, leaving just teeth and gums.

'Recognise them?' Wolf said, running fingers

along the cages, getting the dogs all riled up.

'My men,' he said under his breath.

'Nine cages for nine *SS* men. All given a special treatment and a single instruction, every day. Yes, one drug and the command, "act like a dog and do what your master says." They have received no food, only water. But dogs are hungry.'

Wolf put a finger into one of the cages, pulling it away just as the beast inside went for it, tearing a human tooth from the mouth in the process.

'Why?' he said, eyes wide.

'For science, for fun, for devilment,' Mr Wolf shrugged. 'Other men will decide that. But practically, to get them away from *you.* A sedative helps sleeping dogs lie during the day, and this part of the ship is off-limits, anyway. By order of the chief officer. It was easy for me as night lookout to do it. And I've enjoyed the company. They are man's best friend.'

He threw up on the floor and thought of Łukasz—definitely more devil than fun in all that, now that he was the one with the puffy eyes, his vomit running into one of the cages. One of his former guards made short work of cleaning it up, tongue reaching under the cage gate to get it all into the gut.

'Was Aurik in on this?' he said, more vomit coming.

'I want to say "*fuck yes!* the worst of the lot,"' Wolf said, pausing with a smile, 'want to say that just to cause mischief. But I think you know the answer already.'

He didn't.

'Aurik was drugged, too, of course. But got a different command. Marvellous drug this. Does something to the mind, changes its chemistry, makes a person think what they're being told is their own idea. Not only their idea, but that it's the only idea in the whole world. To do it, more important than breathing. As much as I've come to love my dogs, Aurik was a bit too pretty for this little kennel experiment. We had another job in mind for him.'

'To fuck that Italian, yes,' he said. 'But why?'

'To set the scene. To stir the pot with the New York City mafia. It wasn't enough to kidnap the man. He needed to come on board willingly, and with a backstory. A paper trail of having pulled strings along the docks to get *Bremen* out. Then, when *Bremen* is captured and searched by the British, and that mob capo is found fucked from both ends in the *Library*, on a Nazi flag, on a liner famous for making that flag the national symbol of the Reich. The Italian was like *Rex!* Imagine the headlines. *Why?* you ask, well to make money with one hand, from the British for

Bremen, a perfect troopship, then with the other hand get a handsome sum from the Americans, for getting the help of the New York mafia who had complete control of the docks. Roosevelt is nervous, sir, and Italy is an ally of Germany. Who would the mob side with when America inevitably enters the war? Better to make them choose a side now. Especially while there are other ships in New York ports for the pickings.'

It was elaborate, but what good espionage wasn't, he reasoned. And remembered how *Bremen* had gripped the world while in New York. '*Bremen* in New York' and 'London's ultimatum to Hitler.' That was the only news. There'd be big money in it, he reckoned, big gains to be had. And given the planning needed, getting a pay out from parties on both sides of the Atlantic was a smart return on investment of manpower.

'Why me?'

'We tried getting one of our own team in at first. You met the fellow, a British steward.'

He thought of Mr White in the *Meatpacking District*.

'But he was not *fit* for purpose. Too old. Getting that Italian interested required a particular kind of bait. You were the guy's type, lucky for us. Plus, you're a particular kind of symbol yourself. Having you part of it would help the headlines. And all you needed was a gentle nudge in the right direction. You were just *dying* for a little adventure, weren't you, pretty boy?'

'A nudge by you, yes,' he said.

Mr Wolf smiled, fingering of the cage gates getting the dogs riled.

'What did Aurik do in it all?' he said, showing the photograph, but pocketing it before Mr Wolf could snatch it away. Something in the Wolf's eyes telling him it was a surprise.

'Aurik has proved to be a slippery fellow. I don't need to tell you that. We gave him a dose of the medicine, so that he could see that seeding a nice Italian boy was the sort of thing he should be doing, a pulse notwithstanding. But then he got wise on us. Slipped away and tucked you away with him. Fought against the drug. Sobered up. We all make mistakes.'

'You made a mistake, yes?'

'Well, no, I'm being unkind to myself. A misjudgement, perhaps. We were juggling a lot. We're a small team, sir. Have some understanding of that. I got . . . I'll admit it . . . distracted. Drugging one Italian and ten division-one Waffen-*SS* men was one thing, but one-hundred-fifty odd brownshirts, too. It's easy to see how Mr Braun was able to slip away into the ship. And worse than that, tuck you away, too. But we got him back, didn't we? The *Athenia* sinking proved the perfect distraction for that.

'A simple switching of the co-ordinates in the *Wireless Room* by Kenneth delivering tea to poor, tired Mr Weber. He beat himself up over that, poor lad. But it proved the perfect opportunity to get Horn and the officers out of the way. *Athenia*'s why the Brits—what is this they say . . . *push coming shove?*—passed on *Bremen*, you know. That sinking will change everything. Like *Lusitania* in 1915. That was achieved in a similar way, you know. A little sailor in the ear of a wet U-boat commander, encouraging the strike. Effective operatives, those loose-tongued sailors.'

It was a lot to take in. And his brain was fast becoming not up to any of it. But he tried to focus. He remembered Aurik's paranoia around keeping out of sight and moving rooms in the ship, out of the more obvious first-class accommodations. The deep clean administered, to flush out anything that might be lurking inside him. The hesitation Aurik felt to seed him, after he'd copped that rape seed from the engineman and got his flushing. What is it Aurik had said when first inside him? *No!* Aurik had said to him, spitting. *We can't.* Though even memories as core to him as that were now fading.

'When a person is drugged, yes,' he asked, 'is it . . . catching?'

Wolf's grin got wider with this question.

It was like, as with the dogs, the skin was coming away from the skull.

'O, yes. Highly. That's why it'll be such an effective weapon in the war. Yummy, that *catching* bit. I've come to think of it as a kind of bug. Like a worm inside an apple. When administered, on the surface, all looks okay, but under the skin, in the core, something is being eaten away. And it's only a matter of time before those worms show through, and multiply. Getting passed on to other apples to feed on.'

His face went all tingly. He touched it, feeling the bulging of veins, wiggling under the skin like feeding worms.

'Why are you telling me this?' he shouted, his arsehole starting to spasm, where he had taken load upon load of Aurik's wormy cream.

'To drive you mad, of course. It will happen. Even just one dose is enough to do it, in some cases. Kenneth was fond of the drug. I called him *the worm chaser*. That's why the man had such a fondness for your friend. Mr Braun was riddled with worms. Kenneth was the one to give you your first dose in a bread roll on day one. But *I know* you've had it from multiple sources since.'

He thought on Mr Wolf's little smile on the stern after his deep flushing out. When all the inside of him had been scrubbed clean . . . only for him to be pumped full of Aurik's poisoned swimmers, again and again. Had Aurik done that to him on purpose, he thought in horror. Scratched away any natural sealant that might keep seed from seeping through to the rest of him. Picturing his insides like billions of open sores after the flushing out, mouths hungry as bottom feeders, open to all the brain-eating pathogens passed onto him from a dick of a man meant to be protecting him.

He gripped his hair and started to pull, like he had done with poor Mr Weber, imagining little spiders this time crawling under his scalp. Then looking at his shaking hands. *Not* imagining. He could see the spiders, yes.

'What's happening to me,' he said brushing the bugs away, his knees starting to wobble.

Wolf steadied him with a gloved leather hand, keeping him well away.

'You're going into shock. A heightened state of anxiety is never a good thing for a man with a damaged brain. You must calm yourself. A little game, perhaps?'

'Nomore games,' he said in a slur.

'Lucky for you then, as I suspect your game is coming to an end. But I must think of my mutts. Do you like the games I've set up?' Wolf said, coming in close to his ear. 'You're just in time. My dogs get their exercise at night. And like the *Bremen* with the body in the *Library* and the capture of the war's first sea prize, perhaps for once we can achieve a dual objective.'

Before he could fathom what fresh hell might be coming for him, the sound of metal scratching on metal, of the cage gates getting unbolted, had him on his knees and crawling towards the bow and among the strewn chew toys of the deck—the imprints of human molars like bullet holes in the moonlight, markings of nothing good.

The sound of raw bone grinding on the iron of the games deck shivered down his spine as he turned to see the dogs of his former guard close in on him around the central post of the Lloyd Spiral Ball Game.

'Before I give the order,' Wolf called above the rushing wind of the ship's full tilt, 'I'll give you a chance. Tell me the whereabouts of Mr Braun and Kenneth,' pulling a pistol, 'to die quickly with a single shot to the head. Or suffer an anguishing death, getting your arsehole torn open by a pack of dogs like your engine fellow did by the head of a bear.'

He didn't understand the question. His own search for Aurik is what had drawn him there. He tried to focus his worm-ridden mind, pulling his feet in as the dogs started nipping at them with their lipless jaws.

'I don't know where they are,' he shouted back, wrapping a hand around the rope of the game to pull him up the pole. But it would never get him high enough to be away from the hunger of the dogs.

'That's a pity,' Mr Wolf said. 'Hope you don't mind if I don't watch. I don't have the stomach for messy things. Like with the engine fellow, I'll give the order then leave you to it. Boys, if yo——'

The order! he thought, breathing deep to summon all the strength he had left.

'*No!*' he commanded in a sweeping spiral. 'I'm your master. You listen to me.'

Wolf looked amused a moment. 'It won't work,' the man said. Smiling, even, until one command wiped all that away.

'*Sit!*'

And the dogs did.

At some subconscious level, in some uneaten part of the damned-creatures' brains, there was a recognition of him as the one in charge. The only one to give them orders. And maybe, a more primal want to serve their original master.

Wolf turned and ran. And he even gave the man a head start. For the sport of it. Before giving the order, in the same deep-chested, authoritative tone:

'*Sic* 'em.'

It was a fuck feeding of total animalistic abandon. The dogs took it in turn, as a pack, a unit, to rip clothes with flesh from the body, to fuck the mouth and the anus and to eat the meat. There was no sating it, and the lust to feed and the lust to fuck seemed of equal importance in the dog minds of former men. Wolf squealed at the pitch of a boatswain's call, as the pipes between legs, one extending out, the other in, were put into tag team use. The mouth, too. Wolf putting up a fight, but all futile. Biting off one cock that entered his mouth was replaced with another, after Wolf's teeth had been torn from the head. Bitten-off cock not wasted. But fought over by two of the other dogs. As it happened, as Wolf was torn open by the feeding will of the nine, a slow crawl was made toward the gun. He didn't go after the gun himself. That gun was no longer intended for him. That gun was for the Wolf's self. But when near it, the gun was knocked into the sea. Wolf was in after it, screaming. 'Go fetch,' his final order to the nine, who leapt in gleefully.

Did it make him the monster to be left numb by the whole thing? To be glad that no clean-up was needed, the dogs having licked up all that trailed from Mr Wolf on the crawl to the railing and on in. No evidence of the signalman left, like all traces of unset *Butterplätzchen* dough licked off the groin after being mussed there by a pent-up family man. Was that the damage to his brain, taking away his empathy for his fellow man. He had to push it from his mind, impossible as it was, like the *Bremen*'s attempt to push the sea away with her bulbous bow. It was only an illusion that something so big could possibly be moved. Only something to tell oneself to have any chance of making it through. But the illusion was helped by a mission. New information at hand, and something to check on. Another body in another room of the ship that he, stupidly, felt content enough to leave unchecked in his solving of things. The third murder, after Fosco then Mr Winter, the one unlike the other two. The dagger in the back of a fat baker.

He kicked in the door of Weber's cabin. The boy was still playing clean-up; on to now the licking out of sick from the wardrobe. Any compassion he had for the boy he'd given brain worms to was gone with his stop off at Kenneth's cabin, the one that before he hadn't felt worth the risk. An unnecessary risk, he had reasoned. How things had changed. Mr Wolf, wherever the man was . . . on the surface of the ocean, he imagined, being thrown in Arctic waves as high as the ship's masts, frantic paddling from the dogs after more fucks and bites out of, as the great silhouette of the *Bremen* got smaller and smaller on the moonlit horizon. The vigour of the swim keeping death from easing the terror with a frozen slip under, the salt flooding into the man's torn-out arse, like a boat with no bottom . . . yes, it would have been risky, maybe it had been watched, that cabin. But as he knew now, it probably wasn't. For had he braved it before, he would have seen that the baker was still there, dagger in the back. And realised that the death was different.

He slapped the sod, sending a spray of sick back onto the hung uniforms.

'You like to watch, yes?' he said. 'You watched me before, in the *Toilet*. You watched Aurik and me on the stern, and you watched us in the *Library*, yes. When you told us about Kenneth. When you found out the man could not be trusted. And you've watched other times, haven't you? You like to watch men fuck, don't you? you dirty Pole. You knew the steward were a slut, and you had the man's cabin number. You'd seen it as we all had. Maybe you watched Aurik go to see Kenneth, then followed as I did. And when I left them to it, maybe you watched a little more and then decided you'd keep the two of them to watch a little more in the future, yes?'

Łukasz didn't deny it. He'd given the boy everything that was now dear in the whole world. Seed from inside him, and Mr Weber, maybe, would have told him. That would have been handy, squeezing such information out of the sod, had he not already worked it out for himself. The *Dog Kennels* had got him thinking . . . Of hiding places. Cages that on paper appeared to be in plain sight, but in the operational scheme of things, the policing of certain parts of the ship as strictly off-limits, came to be the perfect place to stash something away.

Go on! check those plans of the officers' quarters. *Spot it! if you can*, he'd thought. Maybe there was hope for him yet, for through the burrowed-out passages in his brain he still managed to spot a peculiarity on the deck plans. A room that shouldn't be there. Or rather. One that should have a door. A secret room next to where Łukasz's cabin now is. A cabin that, as he had earlier overheard, Łukasz had swapped a man for. One where, looking up at the small vent in the ceiling, a dirty little Pole with a voyeuristic streak could play out every fantasy. To watch and watch and watch.

Peeking in on two bodies who, on account of a murdered baker, might reasonably have been thought to be in hiding. Or, as luck would have it for the peeping Łukasz, two feuding parties would safely assume the man from the other side responsible for a disappearance of the other. *Tell me the whereabouts of Mr Braun and Kenneth*, one of Mr Wolf's coherent last uses for a mouth had said. That now, surely, had been ripped to the size of the man's whole face.

He punched Łukasz in the throat. The boy vomited some more, into the cabin basin this time. Where, while hunched over, he bound the boy using some rope found in the wardrobe. Łukasz didn't resist. He then removed the boy's boots and socks, soaked through in piss and sick, and stuffed them in the mouth, tying a scarf round the bottom half of the face to keep the boy schtum. Then, climbing through the small vent by way of a pull up off the cabin desk, it was a short belly crawl to the cabin just aft. But the smell of unwashed bodies made it an anxious one. What would he find when he looked down through the ventilation grate?

The secret cabin was larger than Łukasz's, but with a similar configuration. He took it in from the top vantage, where it resembled that spread from the plans he'd taken from Chief Officer Horn, save for the addition of a frontier element. Like a salon in a godforsaken outpost of the Wild West. Furniture overturned. The walls red with the blood of a brawl. Bodies bound like captives of a lawless sheriff. Gagged. Unmoving. *He's dead*, he thought. Hard to breathe, the metal of the ship's ventilation seemed to crush him like an automobile in a metal press. *I'm too late.*

But just as he started shimmering a retreat, the sight of Aurik, so long searched for, seen from above like the outline of a body in a country house mystery book, made him stay. He had to at least check, and when that decision was made, as if as some sign that maybe it would not all be heartbreak and saloon-door gunfights—eyes opened. Aurik squinting at the grate that he looked through, just as what held him gave in. He landed on Kenneth. The man was the source of the blood in the cabin, from where Aurik had kept the steward at bay with kicks. Aurik's boots and trouser legs and the walls around his lover splashed with blood in the same splatter that a bounce through mud puddles would create. He couldn't tell whether Kenneth was breathing, didn't care. Aurik was. He pulled the gag away and kissed the man. Aurik's mouth tasting stale and dry, like one's own after a long sleep, his handsome protector stinking of piss, and yet, was an oasis. He kissed it up.

'I'm sorry I left you,' he said. 'I'm sorry I didn't *see* that wasn't you. That you needed my help. Please forgive me. I do see you. I promise.'

Aurik didn't move, didn't kiss him back. Closed the eyes again, like the sign to him in the vent had been his lover's last breath.

'I'm going to get you out of here,' he said, pulling Aurik into his chest. Breathing deep the putrid-perfect odours of the man. Arms under the pits, to lift. But Aurik was a dead weight. 'I'll get you out, yes.'

But how? He searched the room for a door. Ran his hands over the joins in the panelling, pulling on them, wishing for a way out. There had to be one, surely. He pulled out the couch, the mattress, the desk. Nothing. Starting to panic again, having swept the room twice to land on his knees back by Aurik's side. A failure. Well, if there was a door, he couldn't find it. Then it dawned on him. *Of course!* Like in the *Library*, out through the window. This cabin had two. How diseased his mind had become that he could not even see a door in a window.

He hoisted Aurik up, arms under the pits, told his lover the plan for escape. It fluttered Aurik's eyelids but did nothing more. His man was too heavy for him to carry. Too bigger of a brother. With both of them running, it would be a risky gambit to get to Werner and the piggy deep in *Bremen*'s belly, but as a dead weight. To be dragged through the ship. No chance. He hadn't the strength.

'Come on, darling,' he said into Aurik's mouth, like his words were an amateur's desperate attempt at resuscitation. 'You can't give up. Not now. I need you to be strong.'

But it was no good. And to make matters worse, through the vent or the walls, he didn't know which, he heard the same voice as before, that officer who had swapped rooms in the name of the sod's dicky colon, banging on Łukasz's cabin door, calling the man's name. Creating a commotion that would soon draw a crowd and discovery, of Łukasz and the open vent into him.

Aurik's lips trembled.

He pushed his ear right into them.

'Leave,' Aurik said, so weakly, hearing it was almost lip reading. 'Leave me.'

He paced. The bangs on the door of the cabin next to them like the final ticks of a time bomb. He pulled back the curtain to outside. It was dark, of course, but the deck appeared to be clear. He closed the curtain again, to keep their light from being seen. The bangs on Łukasz's cabin door became less frequent. But terrifyingly more intense. Fists bashing turned over to shoulder slams and the sound of splitting wood, as grating as the cracking of bones by the dogs consuming the signalman.

'Please,' Aurik said, a little stronger now, like his lover was wringing out the last reserves of energy stored up. 'I beg you.'

'*No!*' he shouted. Probably loud enough to be heard, but too paralysed to care.

He caught sight of himself in the mirror. Gaunt and sunken around the eyes. How quickly he had outdone all the work of those special diets, given to him like veterinarians to a sick mutt. This was why he was never allowed to be anything more than a flesh sculpture. The officer-class workers of the Reich were permitted to rub him rough, sure; that was lip service to the origins of the Nazi party, weren't it? The

German *Workers'* Party, the "National" part added for a more broad-stroke appeal. Aurik looked the same. As ruinous. His photonegative, discoloured like film in a fire. He was in no position to help his lover. He could barely help himself. He was no Arno Breker muse anymore. He was a test subject of some awful biological weapon. His sculptural aspects had come in contact with the angry chippings of a marble vandal.

'I'm sorry,' he said, wondering whether the reason why Aurik kept eyes closed and was eager for him to leave was because he reminded his lover of an addict. Like the man's father.

He lifted Aurik up by the underarms, sweaty and stale, and into his lap. He could barely lift his lover. There was no way that he would be able to get Aurik out by a carry. He had not the strength. He was too far gone by whatever ailed him.

'I need to confess,' Aurik whispered with cracked lips, in his lap, like Christ after being pulled from the cross. 'I followed you on here. I took the place of one of the *SS* men, none of whom were loyal to you. But I did it because I was obsessed with you. *I am.* Have been since I first saw you, since you came by one of our inductions in Berlin. And then on every page, every fold of every magazine I could get you in after. I bent every opportunity that came to get close to you, then when you lept from that ship and into this one, I came too. I love you.'

Somehow, as peasant stupid as he was, he'd worked this all out. He'd seen Aurik, known that this one here was a sycophant. But he'd never minded, given it was Aurik. He'd seen this man all along. Then he realised . . .

'You need *a hit!*' he exclaimed.

Aurik was not responsive, which made him only more certain of what he needed to do. Setting free and stroking his cock with all the speed of the *Bremen*'s turbines pushing for thirty knots, the commotion next door made it difficult to stay hard, so he set free Aurik's prick too and planted his face on it. *How a thing this tiny can stink so much!* But then, it had gone days without showering, following a limp fuck of a sissy steward then successive pisses in the pants while bound. He *liked it!* Flaky and white, he scratched Aurik's smelly cheddar from under the foreskin, his teeth like a butter knife scooping up aged crumbling cheese. Aurik's smegma made him gag, in the best way possible, and brought a load rushing up his rod like an in-the-groove coal stoker.

'*Here it comes!*' he shuddered, as the banging turned into voices and fingertips at the rim of the vent next door.

His load came out slow and thick like paste, fat on the drug inside him and direct into Aurik's mouth. Could he see the worms in it? He cradled his lover for the feeding, like water given from a flask to the cracked lips of a desert survivor, whose head and mouth needed to be angled to take the lifegiving serum. The effect was as quick as a syringe into the vein. Colour coming back into Aurik's cheeks, a sucking of his dick head to get the very last ooze of his cream.

'Good boy,' he said, kissing Aurik's lips, getting a hit of himself there, 'let's get you out, yes?'

It was to the window and out. There was a drop down to the deck that kept promenade eyes from prying in to where officers laid head. Aurik needed some support under the arms to move, but that was manageable. Them out and onto the deck just as the expansion of metal from bodies crawling through a vent rung from the cabin next door. If Kenneth was dead, then as Robert had done, he and Aurik had undone a locked-room mystery with a single crescent swipe of a sash latch, and a three-legged run down the nearby stairs to *Main Promenade Deck* then down and down and down again, all the way to the *Swimming Pool* on *G Deck*. Strutters, they were, down the decks in pompous strides like the brownshirts used to. Their dicks out swinging for every goosestep.

He waited for Chief Officer Dick Horn on that man's take on the *Poop Deck*, watching the churn of the *Bremen*'s wake with a suicidal fascination, its white wash turned blue by the moon. He'd put out his invitation to the ship's nighttime commander after tucking Aurik away safe, with sausages and blankets and Werner Weiner as nurse. He wouldn't risk his lover for this final act. He'd save his sycophant whatever it took. The invitation to Horn he'd delivered in person. But from the shadows, having run up to the *Bridge*, where he'd shouted to the men there, *a meeting's needed on Poop Deck!* He knew it'd draw the top officer out. As he stood waiting, he had a pulling feeling toward the wake, like a lure had been cast from the stern and was tied to his waist. His own casting for Horn, unwise of him . . . likely to get the lure line tangled in the propellor and pull him in at any moment. Should he have tucked himself away with Aurik? Maybe, but also, no. For he needed answers, and the throb in his head told him he may not have long left to get them.

'You summoned me,' Horn said from behind, voice heavy and shadowy like a stage-left villain.

He turned to face the officer, the same feelings of unease coming from staring at the man in front of him as had come from the ship's wake. Handsome in black North German Lloyd uniform, four yellow bands on blazer sleeve, three broad one thin, like some golden warning in morse code.

'I need answers.'

'And you believe I have these.'

'Yes.'

'And that I will give them to you.'

'Yes.'

'Why?'

'Because of Robert Bell.'

Horn gave him a small smile, like they were in on a joke. Coming to join him at the aftmost point of *Bremen*'s decks that had sky overhead. Shoulder to shoulder, but facing different directions, like that split second when two ships passing in the night are at their exact midpoints.

'I wondered if he'd warn you about me. Robert and I met through introduction with a Cunard steward, a man by the name of Mr White. We were just boys then. We became friends, meeting up in New York when our ships were both in, before all the problems of party politics. Until relations between Germany and England turned sour again, and when that steward, a chief steward by then, tried to recruit me.

'I played along, learnt a little. You don't get to where I am without learning to play the field. I made the mistake of trying to warn Robert about the ways of his wife and the intentions of his father, two things I had learned. Co-conspirators, they are. I didn't mention Mr White in it all, didn't get the chance. Wholesome, naive Robbie didn't much like any of what I said. He didn't want to hear uncomfortable truths.'

'I do.'

'Ah, but you are different. Robert is safe. Sheltered. He has the luxury of choosing to go through life without getting hurt. He can pick and choose his own adventures. While you, Mr Bauer, are assigned things to do, have been since a boy. Mostly your assignments are just standing there, looking pretty; still, that makes you a target. And,' looking into him with the same expression as he'd looked at himself in that hidden cabin of the officers' quarters, 'by the looks of you now, you've been hit hard, and are going down.'

'You're in on it then, yes?'

'I am a villain, yes, if it helps you to think in such terms.'

'You poisoned me, yes?'

'Not personally, but I was aware it was happening.'

'You didn't try and stop it.'

'No. In fact, I gave them the idea. Bread rolls from the *Bakery*. Light and portable and innocuous. I'd gotten the idea just as we were about to enter New York. The stewards and the engineers had come to blows after the former caught the latter stealing pastries from the *Bakery* on *F Deck*. Three of the engineers were hauled before me. They denied it, of course, though the custard and whipped-cream stains mixed into the black oil of their coveralls, like chocolate stirred into a white mousse,' Horn seemed pleased with that piece of imagery, 'well, was all pretty damning. All very silly and perfect. A bit like you and your whole shtick.'

'Why do you hate me?'

Horn tapped palm to the flagpole, like a batter tempting a pitcher's spin.

'Tell me,' Horn said, spinning to stare him down, 'is Günther your birth name?'

'Yes,' he said. 'Why you ask me this?'

'Quite the co-incidence, isn't it? Given Hans Günther. I assume you know his work.'

He shrugged. 'Of course, but yes, it is my name. It is a common German name.'

'*It is!* but you're not common are you, Günther? Hans Günther, whose works are founding principles for this Reich's prejudice, concedes that only ten percent of Germans are Nordic Aryans. Interestingly, we, Germany, rank behind the United Kingdom and France—all behind the Scandinavian states, naturally. But this regime, in its hate pamphlets to children—children, Günther—ignore this fact. Riling against the French for inclusion of Blacks in the military.

'I hate *the idea of you*, boy,' Horn said flustered. 'But do we really have time to be getting into existential questions like that? I don't think so. You don't have the head for it anymore. Anyway, back to the bread rolls . . . The engineers and the topside sailors were always getting into squabbles like that. The softer sailors rarely daring venture into the black holds of the greasers; not proper sailors, the stewards. That's something men like me, having worked both sides, learn. Stewards, bakers and waiters on liners like these are soft, polite. Not real sailors. Not the ones to be found in the roughest wet holes in any port. Only the engineers and the deckhands are like regular sailors on ships like this. Tough.

'But also, on ships like this these real sailors, the men in oil especially, can scrub-up well, and there were often, shall we say *special favours* that were struck between these men when venturing topside, to reach agreeable terms with the galley crew and stewards. A quid pro quo arrangement. Sometimes the galley cooks might need auxiliary steam for their kettles, or uninterrupted power for their baking ovens. And these men rewarded in kind with certain baked delicacies. So, yes. With a baker *in on it*, the plan worked well.'

'Why do you hate me?'

Horn smiled, like that joke they were once in on was now all on him. 'You asked me that already. Getting a bit confused, are we?'

Have I?

He was.

'Perfectly understandable. I will give you some answers, Mr Bauer, but like you, my time is limited. I cannot be long away from the *Bridge*. I suggest you confine your questions to your own peril.'

He wobbled, gripped the railing but then pulled his hand away, taking a layer of skin with. The whole deck had a skin itself, now with part of him. The ship with ice and the waters *that* cold, little bits on the surface were solid. Like the chunks that form on the top of stale milk. His mind felt like that too. Lumpy. Stale. It was not easy for him to stay on point, to not be general. His mind felt as cotton in crashing waves.

'It true you sent for me, yes.'

'I was behind that letter you received from Berlin, yes. I may be a villain in your eyes, Mr Bauer, but like most men, I have my loyalties. My allegiances. My idea of what is noble . . . It happened right here, you know. In '35, when that hateful flag was torn from this,' reaching up to tap on a higher length of the flagpole that reached over their heads and out over the churn below, 'that moment, that event, when six brave sailors made a stand. Handsome as any German boy, but in a different way. They were Jews.

'It backfired, of course, led to *Bremen* getting its first dose of poison. A change of captain then gradually, like the killing of a body in stages using tampered soup, destroyed this ship. Yes, I was happy for you to be poisoned, Mr Bauer. I was happy for *Bremen* to be captured, too, if it came to that. If it might have saved her from ruin at party hands, who would have only bent her to evil things. My loyalty lies with Germany, this ship and her crew. Not the thugs put into her, not with the Nazi party and certainly not with you as some kind of ideological puppet of a hateful future.'

Maybe he was the villain in this story, he thought.

'Where'd the poison come from? What's its purpose?'

Horn smiled. 'Now that is one part in your downfall that I can take special credit for. Picture this . . . Our captain, distrusted after not following orders to return to Germany, proves the perfect stage for my plea with Nazi figures in Berlin to send help. This then led to me, as the senior officer who the party thought could be trusted, being let in on a top-secret mission. A wonder weapon, to become part of *Bremen*'s cargo. One our Führer was desperate to get back to Germany. To pump into our soldiers and make them into a kind of super soldier.

'After the trenches, after *the gas*, Hitler was someone obsessed with the potential of biological warfare. And Himmler was smitten with the idea, too. As were all the other evil henchmen. Here was a tonic that ensured troops always followed orders, where the party could be certain that all men would be servants to the Nazi dogma, no matter how far the front flung from the centre of power. At home as well. Put into the water. Propaganda would never be needed again.

'I was entrusted with this cargo. I didn't know what it was, of course. Not at first. Just crates and crates of little viles that I was told needed to be kept secret at all costs. Returned to the Reich undisturbed. They needed to have me onside because the ship was getting searched thoroughly in New York. I had the perfect place for them in New York, nice and close to my quarters. I know this ship, her every hiding place. I stored the viles there, and then moved them once we were underway.'

'Where did you hide them?' he asked.

'I think you know that. Next door to the only man on this ship I have come to trust. Probably because he's the only man who hates the Nazis as much as I do. Getting to know him was one of the sweet surprises for me of this voyage. I believe you've met, his name's Łukasz. You passed on your sickness to him. That was not very nice, Mr Bauer. Not an action of a great leader, if you ask me. But I'm hoping he will be alright. I have plans for him. He's a Pole, and a pretty one.'

'How did you learn what the poison could do?'

'The old-fashioned way. I needed a chip to get in with the cronies working for Robert's wife and father. Like a virus, these people infect ships without you knowing it. But I recognised one of them, one of the stewards, a Kenneth Arnold. A little bitch boy of Mr White's. I told him about the cargo, and he gave it a little taste. He is that sort, you see. The kind to lick up a white powder off the rim of a toilet in a seedy bar. Just because. Or maybe hoping for a bump. And O boy, did he get one. We had to restrain him at first. The drug needs fine-tuning. The slut wanted to go and fuck every man on the ship.'

'A slut steward doesn't mean you are a bad seed,' he said, thinking of piggy.

Horn raised an eyebrow, as if to question whether he was as brain-fucked as the man thought. Or maybe his compassion for men naturally bent on arse-fuckery showed that he was further brain-damaged than he thought.

'Where did the poison come from?' he asked, riding what he hoped was doubt in Chief Officer Horn.

'From Germany. In on the *St Louis*, actually. The same ship you came in on. A ship of ill fate, that one. It had been stashed there in secret by a fleeing Jewish scientist. Taken from Germany under the belief that the Americans would grant the ship asylum, and therefore the weapon would be out of Nazi hands. But the Americans' lack of heart meant the ship was sent away. That scientist has since been captured, so I understand, but his family made it to Britain. One of the reasons the scientist gave up the position of the poison was to ensure his family's safety. And the man is back in the Reich waiting the return of the weapon to continue human testing. Under Himmler, word is.'

'How does it work, this poison?'

'From what I can reckon, and in discussion with the ship's surgeon—over some port, *all purely hypothetical*, I told the good doctor. But from what the doctor explained to me, based on the behaviours I observed in this Kenneth fellow and repeated to the doctor, it targets the frontal lobes of the brain. The parts controlling our inhibitions, our sexual drive, and it peels this wide open, taking all our filters away. It also opens the brain to suggestion.'

His head throbbed, a stabbing, like an ice pick up the nose. He reached for Horn to stabilise, but the man drew back, like his skin were a contagion. Letting him fall again into the dirt.

Maudsley in London. This hospital was an asylum once, just for military men. In '33 one of its doctors presented case histories of patients with damage to various locales of the brain, to localise and connect this damage with changes in character. An 'interesting case' included was of a schoolmaster 'who had always shown homosexual characteristics in his "make-up"' and 'always been preoccupied with his bowels' but whose homosexuality became more overt with decline, when he 'clamoured for homosexual relations' as the brain died. And the correlation? The specific locale connected with the man's spiral into homosexual obsession and then abandoned inhibition? The growth of a tumour in the left frontal lobe.

Horn slapped him awake.

'Stay with me, boy. The poison, eating away at the frontal lobes——'

He scratched at the skin, but the nibbling was out of reach. The stabbing continued like the pins of a leg at sleep.

'——gives the first person to speak with the poisoned the power to set an intention that is sacred above all else. Like mad men going on a murder spree after getting a word from the Devil. Makes you give in to things you normally never would, pulls away those filters. In the hands of the Nazis. Well. The road our Fatherland has gone down has shown the power of suggestion. We all play that game. I did with Berlin about the captain. That was my *in*. He was at Lakehurst, you know, when the *Hindenburg* burned.

'That airship was meant to be called *Adolf Hitler*. What if I said to you, maybe the captain had something to do with that, loitering down by the mooring ties . . . with that crew. And was now out to do the same to

Bremen. A little far-fetched on the face of it, but not with a bread roll. That conspiracy suddenly becomes gospel, and there was already mistrust there. That's an example of what this drug can do. This drug pushes you over the edge, out of reason. Into single-minded obsession. That's how it works. But clearly, it needs refinement. It's too close to the sex drive. O yes, and it's killing the brain now.

'Even so, my little cargo got me what I wanted. My playing chip. My *in* into the inner circle, to learn the plan hatched by Robbie's bitch wife and daddy. It was: deliver *Bremen* to the British as a war prize and orchestrate a scene that would turn the New York City mafia against Italy, an ally of Germany, for good.' Horn pulled out a piece of paper from back pocket, 'if I may read you this Presidential order dated the twenty-eighth, the same day *Bremen* arrived: *Immediately upon the President being satisfied that Germany is in armed conflict with another nation with or without formal declaration of war seize all German and Italian vessels in American territorial waters remove officers and crew therefrom and take all precautions against sabotage in engine rooms or otherwise.*

'Now you see why such great lengths were went to by the Port Authority to keep *Bremen* in New York. There was even talk of holding *Normandie* up for eight hours. Your beloved Robert's *Aquitania*, for six, all in service to the illusion of neutrality. The profiteers were right to nudge you into the arms of that Italian meathead. But you were the one to swing it. Yes, you did well to get *Bremen* out. You can die knowing that.'

'And Robert knows nothing of this, yes?'

'I've worked hard to keep it that way. That's why I made sure Robert saw me when he arrived with the pilot. He will never know this. And maybe would not thank me for it if he did, but I made sure he wouldn't take that leap of faith and stay on *Bremen*. I made sure he was safe.'

'You are no hero. You were part of the murder, and the plan failed, yes.'

'Murder of that Italian. Yes, I was the one to jab him with a dose.'

The pinprick on the neck, he'd have thought if his mind was still all there.

'It was a pleasure to do it. He was being cocky, refused my offer of dinner. Said he'd sent a packed meal of meatballs to feed on. He'd planned to stay, you know. Head to Germany and then on to Italy. O yes, I was happy to be rid of him, and I helped set the scene, too. The flag under the Italian was my idea. It was the exact one torn from this pole in '35. I'd fished it out of the Hudson myself and saved it for some kind of moment like that one. My little monument to that day. Kenneth, having been stripped of all decency, stole some pole dancing with the Italian.'

Kenneth's arsehole was the one Fosco fucked.

'Then I suggested we use one of your guards to drive a message home to the mafia. Show them they'd been well and truly fucked over by the Nazis. Who better than a Waffen-*SS* boy to do this?'

'The page from the book?' he asked, confused, catching the thought as if it were a fish snagged by chance when reeling in. Hooked by the tail rather than the mouth.

'From one of the books on Robert's bookshelf. I'd snuck onto *Aquitania* and retrieved it, under the guise of a meeting with Mr White. My little sign to Robert that there was something in my warning to him. I knew he would have followed the story closely after *Bremen* was in British hands. Taken an interest in all the clues of the scene. Recognised the description of that page. Run to his own intimate little *Library* and where that torn page was, to find a letter from me.'

They were like brothers, he thought, thinking on the letter from Robert in that copy of *Treasure Island* and a similar slip into the library of another ship. That letter he still had not read. And that now, as his vision would probably never be clear again and he needed to steady himself with two hands, and close his eyes just to keep track of his questions in his head——

Where was he . . . O yes, that letter, he supposed now he'd never get the chance to read it.

'I'll leave yo——'

'One thing I don't understand, yes,' he blurted out.

Horn slapped him on the back. '*One thing*,' the man said, almost encouragingly.

That made him feel better about his eroding brain. It was a twisty sequence of events.

'Just one, yes. Why did you let *Bremen* get through? Kenneth were talking with stewards on the British cruisers, yes. And our position could easily have been given away to Kenneth by you or from Łukasz, when we were off the coast of . . . of . . . Newfoundland.'

'Ah, well, yes. I wasn't going to bring that up, but if it helps you in your final moments, that *Bremen* is not now in British hands stands as evidence that you have not been a complete failure in your little task we set. In fact, you can die with the knowledge that *Bremen* now has a real chance of making it back to Germany, thanks to you and your grubby engineman dumping our Italian in the sea. I still don't know how you managed to get in. I'm sure I locked those windows.'

He thought of enlightening Horn about Robert, but then figured, if he was dead anyway, at least he'd go out with a little locked-room mystery of his own.

'O well,' Horn went on, shaking the loose end away. 'Your engine friend had climbed through the sash—however he managed it—and given the puttied hole a close look——'

The thumb print grease lines on each of Fosco's bum cheeks, he would have now remembered if it were not for the worms in the brain.

'——and, now to his great mistake, given that cream pudding a little lick. It was enough to send the man over the edge, to seek out a hole, a living one, with a beating pulse, for the man to putty himself. Enough to poison the fellow. Enter you, Mr Bauer, through the hatch onto *Main Promenade Deck*. Just one lick was enough. Under the tongue is an effective site of administering any poison, of rapid entering into the bloodstream . . . so I understand from discussion with the ship's physician. That's what made the bread rolls so effective.'

His thoughts again turned to Łukasz, and then himself, as he realised that Mr Winter had given him another dose with the worm custard up his arse. No wonder he was so far gone by the time Aurik came his way. To poison him further.

'But that is your own sordid tale of disease,' Horn said as if his thoughts were audible.

Had he spoken them in the confusion?

'From my perspective,' Horn went on, 'with the body of the Italian gone . . . Well. I understand, the Americans dropped out of the deal. And the British hadn't much of an appetite for drugging their troops, so the drug could not be sold to them. Plus, were not keen on paying any more for *Bremen* than had been agreed on. They were confident they'd be able to catch us themselves, or at least force us to scuttle. Another power did like the idea of a single-minded soldier, however. And, most conveniently, we were headed straight for them.'

'You mean——'

'That's right. The weapon has been sold *to the Reds!* They can't keep the ship, of course. They'll have to send it on back, we're playing friends at the moment, remember. But they can get some of the samples, without the Nazis ever knowing. We have used a fair amount of it already, after all. What's another couple hundred viles of the stuff gone missing? This suits me, too, as it means I can have a better chance of getting my men home. And who knows, *Bremen* may be mothballed, to survive the war.'

His mouth moved like a fish out of water, his brain struggling now even to turn thoughts into words, let alone formulate questions.

'Feel that chill? That's the bitter kiss of the Barents Sea. We're rounded North Cape and are on the home stretch. Operation Basis North has been a success. We will be in the beds of the Russians soon. But I suspect you won't be with us for any of that local hospitality,' Horn said, a hand into jacket to retrieve a pistol that the man then placed on the deck.

He looked to the sea. *Really* looked this time. How harsh it was, how uncaring for any man. Rising and falling, throwing even a vessel as vast as this one about like a tug in a boy's bath. He grasped the railing.

'You may share the name of my country's current hate-thinker. But if I might leave you with the words of another. Of Max von Gruber of Munich: *Among the noblest specimens of mankind I have encountered in my long life, very few have plainly exhibited the characteristics which are said to be those of the Nordic race; whereas a considerable proportion of the brutal egotists and careerists I have met were typical 'Nordics,'* Horn took a deep long breath, like a violinist mid orchestral solo. Practised and each note memorised. This was important to the man.

'*A careful medical examination,*' Horn resumed, '*and a study of the personal and family history by a medical expert, conducted without prejudice, will give far better criteria for estimating the social value of an individual, than will a detailed examination of the colour of the eyes, the tint of the skin, etc. Similarly, what a man or woman is and does are far more important than the homoscope.* And with that, I'll leave you to your fate, and will miss your pictures.'

Like a window in a locked-room horror, once Horn was gone and everything explained, he looked down the barrel. Darkness taking him again.

The gun, a possible way out for him.

GODHAVN

BAFFIN BAY

GREENLAND
DANISH COLONY

Denmark St.

Angmagsalik

Granted H…
by Denma…

REYKJAVIK

LAND

Port Burwell
C. Chidley

JULIANEHAAB

Hebron

LABRADOR

IRON

Hopedale

Hamilton Inlet

Belle Isle Strait

NEWFOUNDLAND

Colwood

First English Colony 1583

ANTICOSTI

ST. JOHN'S

MIQUELON

PLACENTIA BAY

Fredericton

SAINT JOHN

HALIFAX

Portland

Sable

BOSTON

NEW YORK

AZORES (Port.)

ATLANTIC

BERMUDA

MADEIRA (Port.)

TROPIC OF CANCER

MARIGUANA

DOMINICAN REPB.

PORTO RICO
Ceded by Spain to U.S.A. 1898

PRINCE

SAN JUAN

VIRGIN IS.
Purchased from Denmark 1916

ANTIGUA

SEA

MARTINIQUE

ST. LUCIA

CAPE VERDE IS. (Port.)

St. Louis

DAKAR

Port Etienne

BARENTS SEA
PETSAMO
MURMANSK
KOLA (Russian 1553)
Kandalaksha
Tromso
NARVIK
Kiruna
Mulenia
Gellivare
Bodo
Tornio
Vega
Lulea
Kem
WHITE
Oulu
GULF OF BOTHNIA
NAMSOS
Steinkjer
Umea
TRONDHEIM
Molde
Vasa
FINLAND
Population 4 m.
Sortavala
Viborg
Hamar
Gavle
ABO
BERGEN
Vasteras
HELSINKI
KRONSTADT
Tikhvin
LERWICK
OSLO
NORTH SEA
SCAPA FLOW
STOCKHOLM
TALLIN
STAVANGER
HORTEN
Norrkoping
OESEL
SCOTLAND
INVERNESS
GOTEBORG
Halmstad
KARLSKRONA
WINDAU
LIBAU
RIGA
Kalinin
Glasgow
ROSITH
EDINBURGH
Pop 4 m.
COPENHAGEN
BALTIC
MEMEL
KONIGSBERG
SYLT
BORNHOLM
BELFAST
KIEL
GDYNIA
KAUNAS
Smolensk
HELIGOLAND
CUXHAVEN
SWINEMUNDE
WILHELMSHAVEN
HAMBURG
STETTIN
Minsk
DUBLIN
ENGLAND
BREMEN
Bristol
Cork
ESSEN
THE RUHR
Grodno
THE HAGUE
BERLIN
WARSAW
MILFORD HAVEN
LONDON
DUNKIRK
GERMANY
Pop. 86 m.
PORTSMOUTH
BRUSSELS
PLYMOUTH
LE HAVRE
PRAGUE
English Chan
BREST
PARIS
LORIENT
Munich
VIENNA
HUNGARY
ST. NAZAIRE
BUDAPEST
VICHY
BERNE
LA ROCHELLE
ODESSA
BAY OF BISCAY
Bordeaux
Geneva
VENICE
TRIESTE
RUMANIA
Pop. 16 m.
SPEZIA
BUCHAREST
SEVASTO
MARSEILLE
TOULON
POLA
BELGRADE
CONSTANTA
Vigo
Bilbao
ITALY
VARNA
CORSICA
SPLIT
SOFIA
BULGARIA
BLACK SEA
Porto
BARCELONA
ROME
Adriatic
TIRANA
SALONIKA
Istanbul
ISMID
NAPLES
FOGGIA
TARANTO
Bursa
ANKARA
MADRID
LISBON
Valencia
Palma
MINORCA
Cagliari
SMYRNA
CARTAGENA
MEDIT
PALERMO
Sevilla
BIZERTE
SICILY
CATANIA
ATHENS
CADIZ
GIBRALTAR
CEUTA
ALGIERS
TUNIS
ALEXANDRETTA
MALTA
RHODES
TETUAN
PANTELLERIA
SEA
CYPRUS
Straits of Gibraltar
ALGERIA
Population 7 m.
(From Turkey 1830)
CRETE
BEIRUT
CASABLANCA
FEZ
HAIFA
DAMA
MOROCCO
Pop. 6 m.
(French 1912)
Gabes
TRIPOLI
BENGHAZI
TOBRUK
PORT SAID
JERUSAL
ALEXANDRIA
PALESTINE
El Agheila
CAIRO
CABO JUBI
SUEZ
Asyut
LIBYA
Pop. 1 m.
(Formerly part of Turkish Empire annexed by Italy 1911)
Desert
EGYPT
Pop. 15 m.
(Independence granted by Britain 1922)
(Spanish)
PROPOSED ROAD
Gat
Djanet
Taoden
Tummo
RED SEA
Dongola
Berber
FRENCH WEST AFRICA
Population 15 million
(Placed under French Protection 1894)
Senegal
Kayes
(French 1815)
Bamako
Zinder
Sokoto
(1888)
OVERLAND ROUTE
KHARTOUM
SUDAN
ARCTIC OCEAN

He came to in a place of light. This time it was *under* the *Swimming Pool*, between the iron sheets of *Bremen*'s double bottom. Robert may have chosen not to stow away for this particular adventure, probably wise; but even, each step along the way he had felt that the British father figure smelling of cream tea was with him. Guiding him. Certainly, it was Robert's question to him on *Sun Deck* that had led to the discovery of the little secrets *Bremen* herself kept. A looking for hidden places that had also led him to where Aurik had been stashed. Robert had given him the idea of the perfect hiding place for him and his intimate band of men to see out the rest of the journey to Murmansk. O yes, a root around the bar adjoining the pool had revealed a hatch into the cavity that the *Titanic*'s skid along ice had brought into fashion. A completely sealed chamber underneath the hull. A hull within a hull. Word around the docks had been right, the *Bremen* did house munitions under her swimming pool.

He was losing time . . .

Having blacked out to wake bloody temple against boxes of an arsenal great enough to take out Horn and every other godforsaken man on board this ship . . . *too late, too tired.* How'd he got there? Then he remembered . . .

Remembered stumbling back from the stern deck, through the *Vestibules* of the second classes, along the hallways and toward the bow, to get at the way down to the pool. It had been a bounce-off-partitions possession. Pistol in hand, just in case he decided to take the window Horn offered. He had come close when he met a horde of brownshirts in one of the corridors. Which one he wasn't sure, but they were there. It was bound to happen. They were there to catch up with him for what he'd done, and unlike his former guards turned dogs, no *sit!* order would do the trick.

He'd dropped to the floor, accepting the fate, if that's what was to be. Until, at the front of the horde he recognised one man. It was Frankie Fischer, the first of the brownshirts to leatherjacket his meatballs, and take a whole one besides—greedy boy.

Frankie had dropped to knees like he did.

'*Master!*' Frankie said, as insane for him as ever.

And before he could react, before he could even bring the pistol to temple to speed the horde onslaught of revenge for his perverse-minded arse feeding, Frankie was swinging one of those skull crackers the stroomtroopers are known for. Swinging it round and round like a let-go balloon.

'*Run, master!*' Frankie cried, a bona fide hysteric, as the man's own comrades turned to crack Frankie out.

Had Frankie continued to be poisoned after his feeding? Or was there something more in the man's allegiance to him? Either way, it got him there, into the double bottom of *Bremen*, under the *Swimming Pool*.

Aurik was there.

Between the fades in and out of consciousness.

That was enough . . . having Aurik back for the end. Better than any sweet oblivion a pistol on any Horn's *Poop Deck* or corridor of brownshirts could bring.

Aurik had concern in the eyes.

'*Our Poop Deck*,' Aurik said urgently, eyes untrusting of their company. Of Werner Weiner, the ugly boy who'd been the only help through his search for the man hovering over him.

'Hush, my love,' he said, finger on Aurik's lips, cracked and dry. 'I went there, I saw what they'd done to the others. Your comrades. They are out of their misery now, yes.'

Aurik reclined, let out a long breath, gave him a scratchy kiss under the ear.

'Thank you, I suppose it's our turn now,' Aurik said.

'What for?'

'To be put out of our misery.'

He rolled his head to one side to look over to where Werner Weiner and piggy were. They were clean, not an ounce of poison between them. Yet had found each other. Done things no healthy brain should have men doing. Maybe together those two would find a way to carry on, but it was over for him and Aurik now. *What are you going to do, chief?* Werner had asked him while he taught the lad to shoot. *You don't have the numbers.* He has Aurik, he had replied, *I just need to find him.* The only army he needed.

And the idea of his knights had grown from there. Herr Himmler fancied the idea, too. But his was a purer idea. More ancient than any twentieth-century, ugly old Nazi could make reality.

Now, Aurik found, he was back on the Lötzen lake rope swing. There's a Teutonic castle there and Himmler was talking of building bunkers there too. Temples in stone to see out the war to come. The expansion into the east. But he'd cared nothing for any of that. He'd cared nothing for anything much of anything since his plucking from that swing. It was his golden ticket, looking the way he did. Being a thing of perfect Aryan beauty. A model to everyone.

But there had been some rebellion in his spirit. He had kept his roots some in the sunken lakes of East Prussia. Some other poor wheat pickers, not as blessed as he in looks. But when you're a young East German lad lake-swinging after hard harvests, high cheekbones and top scores in anthropological colour charts did not go far with the boys on the lakes. He'd returned there, made friends. With one boy in particular who had a cabin near Rastenburg. That boy was his connection to his roots, and he'd returned on occasion with his team of guards. Made them wait outside as he visited, with treats from his travels, and they'd naked swing together. Take photos, too.

He hadn't told Aurik any of that. If he'd the chance, he'd take Aurik to meet this boy.

There was so much he hadn't told Aurik. But also, nothing. Take his voyage to New York on the *St Louis*. The ship that had that same year taken all the headlines for the plight of its Jewish refugees. He was not on *that* voyage. For his voyage there was nothing remarkable to note. No story worth telling. No epic fall into the dirt. He'd hidden himself away in one of the cabins of first class. His fingers tracing the graffiti that had been etched there by Jewish hands whose stories of rejection and bounce from refused port to refused port promised the kind of adventure that would be written down and told again and again in oral history. Like the walls of grand hotels turned hospitals and training barracks in the Great War. Those were the tales that made a life remarkable. And if nothing else, *Bremen* had given this.

'Are you miserable, my love?' he said, pulling Aurik into him.

His lover had lost weight. Lost body mass. They both had. All signs pointed to dying. A body wasting. A lust disease that could not be hidden.

He kissed Aurik's concave cheeks, the pronounced throat apple, each of the closed eyes, waiting a response.

Aurik's lids opened, seeing him.

He kissed both eyes again, the blackly brown balls of a better world view. Kissed the tears away direct from the source. They were free to do things like that now. Certain death had taken from them any taboo, and restraint. They were filmy and wet, the eyeballs of his lover. Like the flesh of a lychee. He went back in, licking this time. Salty and thick. A tropical soapberry he certainly would never have tasted were it not for death being a sure thing. The *other path* that's always there but almost never taken. The sun oil and warm-water charts *Bremen* had brought aboard as a diversion. They'd lived theirs. That great southern passage. They were in the Caribbean now. Pirates there.

Aurik grabbed him hard by the scruff and pulled their lips together.

'I wouldn't change a thing,' Aurik said into his mouth, then spitting. 'We come into this world alone. But you and me. We leave it together. I would crawl through fire for you. Every time.'

He pulled their clothes off with what strength he had left. Werner Weiner buddled up piggy and gave him a nod. A little farewell, before disappearing into one of the dark recesses of the ship's double bottom. Bowing out, like the ensemble after getting a clap following curtain fall. It was the final moments now.

They were alone. Together.

He'd called it a fog throughout. But time among seamen had taught him it was in fact a *yaw*. Back to the Admiralty handbooks of a chief officer . . . If a ship does not steer a course that is straight and steady, if her head moves from one side to the other, she is said to yaw about. And if her ship's head is swung by the scend in the sea, swung in a manner as to throw her off course, she yaws.

He yaws now.

The iron was cold and vibrated with the ship's pushing through frigid high waves. He should have been frightened. Weeping. Cursing his lot in life. He was so young. But he felt none of that. Aurik had jumped ship with him, he now realised. Had been there all along, ready to save him. On *St Louis*, he knew without needing to ask. Waiting until he needed a hero. Followed him into ruin.

'I want to eat from you,' he said, no embarrassment.

Aurik kissed him.

'You want me to shit in your mouth.'

'It's my last wish.'

It was disgusting. Worm-ridden. A biohazard. His brain should have told him. But it didn't. It gave him hope. He saw things differently in the yaw about. The worms opened him up. It was a tale of the heart*worm*.

Bullshit little girls fantasise about vampires drinking blood, as if that's so much better. Stenbock gives us a homo metaphor in vamp cravings. There's also hung zombies fetishing flesh, narrower but still in the canon. But a boy asking another boy he loves to make a meal for him, just for him, long and hard and deep from one tum-tum into another. It maybe wasn't as girly kiss-kiss as canines in the jugular, but it was real. It was raw. It was sating. He chased after the worms.

It was his way of taking what he'd witnessed in the *Toilet* behind sleeping firemen, with their sweaty burly chests; sure; he'd accept that. Aurik shitting into a steward had given him the idea, his blown brain had clocked on. In the cracks, in the tunnels made by bugs in his brain, obsession with the steward scene had grown like grass up through cobbles. *There is eating and drinking in that*, he had thought at the time. And now he would be the one to one-up it. A freed mind had got him there. What was wrong with that. What was more loving?

'I want to feed you,' Aurik said, the brown of the eyes a bark of the finest log, the pupils diluted to give him all the trunk he craved, both of them with the energy of a high. 'I wanted to ask. I love you for it.'

'I want your log inside me. I want to choke on it, *yes*. That's how I want to go.'

Aurik spring up to crouching over him.

His lips fell open, his teeth like a bear trap at the ready, the dugout on the front. The one bastion of normality in a world war torn. The latrine and wash basin and swimming lake for a weary soldier.

'"In this night the boy gave himself to him as never before,"' Aurik whispered to him between the hairy knees of a squat, '"not in a sensual frenzy, but rather under the clumsy words of bashful love."'

'It's beautiful,' he said, the arsehole over him dirty and unwashed. Ripe. He licked it clean. Like an appetiser. An acquired taste. Like a youngin getting oysters for the first time. Threw up in his mouth a bit. Swallowed it down. The dirt of Aurik. It was the great delicacy. The lover's caviar.

'That's from the book I reached into the fire for,' Aurik said. 'The doll-boy in the book, his name was Günther. You are the Reich's perfect doll-boy. More beautiful than I deserve. It's not too late to change your mind,' Aurik said looking at him between legs, knees wobbling.

'It is, my love, yes,' he replied. Waiting for it to come. 'No turning back now. I am your fag-Günther. Your boy-doll. You are my fag-master. Forever, yes.'

It was insane. Splatter and sewer smell splashing over him. Not rational. More retching. Stinging the eyes. The sign of a diseased mind. Yet still . . . he could not help but feel hope. Welcome the taste to come—would it be milder than the stink? It would be nothing solid, how could it be? Not a healthy movement from one tum-tum to another. However messy it might be, he longed for it. However soggy sloppy the lumber. The chance to have had now everything that Aurik has to give.

'This is sausage to me,' he said to the demon bosun boys—*look, there!*—bobbing at the depths of *Bremen*'s double bottom; scary flashes that screamed in and outside his mind like lunatics shouting into restraints. He steadied himself, *sausage to me*, sounds and smells of Aurik's arse opening over him grew.

His tummy growled.

He checked his watch as the sight of a feed came, Aurik's feed pipe stuffed and dilating. Food deep and rich as his lover's eyes. It was one minute to midnight. To-morrow the *Bremen* would reach Murmansk, but he'd die choking Aurik's logs down first.

Or maybe. Just maybe.

He would eat shit and live.

www.ingramcontent.com/pod-product-compliance
Lightning Source LLC
Chambersburg PA
CBHW020931310726
48980CB00007B/716/J

* 9 7 8 0 6 4 5 5 5 5 3 9 4 *